I0771238

LONG ROAD TO LONDON

Lawrence Mensah Akwetey

WORKBOOK PRESS LLC
187 E Warm Springs Rd
Suite B285 Las Vegas NV 89119 USA

Website: https://workbookpress.com/
Hotline: 1-888-818-4856
Email: admin@workbookpress.com

Ordering Information:
Quantity sales. Special discounts are available on quantity purchases by corporations, associations, and others. For details, contact the publisher at the address above.

ISBN-13:   978-1-965732-02-1 Paperback Version

PUB. DATE: 23/01/2025

Dr. Lawrence Mensah Akwetey was born in the seaside town of Keta in the Volta Region of Ghana. He trained as a teacher at the Accra Training College, Ghana. He continued his further education at the University of Ghana, Legon, The London School of Accountancy UK and Pace University, New York (USA). He received his MBA and PhD degrees at the Middlesex University Business School, London (UK). Dr Akwetey is also a graduate of the Ghana Military Academy and Training School, Teshie where he was commissioned as a Sub- Lieutenant into the Ghana Navy.

Dr Akwetey is currently a Senior Lecturer and Researcher at the Global Banking School-University of Suffolk-London Greenford campus. He lives in London with his two children, Yvonne, and Michael.

He is the author of *Business Administration for Students and Managers* and *Investment Attraction and Trade Promotion in Economic Development: A Study of Ghana within the Economic Community of West African States* (ECOWAS) published by Trafford Publishing USA and Canada respectively. He is also the author of the novel Tears of Rose.

This book is dedicated to Almighty God for his bountiful care and to my parents, Sowah Davor Akwetey and Mary Adjoa Akwetey (all, of Blessed Memory), for the great love and care they sowed into my education and upbringing many years ago.

"Thy bountiful care
What tongue can recite?
It breathes in the air
It shines in the light
It streams from the hills
It descends to the plain
And sweetly distils
In the dew and the Rain."

Yvonne Akwetey and Michael Akwetey for their inspiration
and support in putting together this novel.

Contents

Chapter 1
Escape to Monrovia

My name is Yolandi Kolandi. I was only five years old when war broke out in the Republic of Liberia on the West African Coast of the Gulf of Guinea, by the vast Atlantic Ocean. The war started on Christmas Eve, 24 December 1989. The First Liberian Civil War of its kind was an internal conflict in Liberia from 1989 until 1997. The conflict killed about 250,000 people and eventually led to the involvement of the Economic Community of West African States (ECOWAS) regional body, the United Nations (UN), who fought quite tirelessly to bring the conflict to a resolution.

We were a family of six and lived in a little village called Bopolu in the region of Gbarpolu in the Republic of Liberia. The war was ragging fiercely and there were loads of unsubstantiated rumours that the rebels were shooting people on sight; they did not discriminate, they asked no questions. They just shot at anything that moved.

There were horrifying pictures beamed on local television all across the country. It was a huge pandemonium that had gripped the whole nation of Liberia.

Word had just reached us that the rebels were advancing towards Bopolu, my beloved village where I was born and had begun to grow up into a young man. On hearing this, the whole of the village was on the move. Families started evacuating their loved homes in the direction of the city of Monrovia where, at the time, there was relative peace and non-violence. We needed to leave too and we had to act quickly. We needed to leave Bopolu and also set out towards Monrovia.

Bopolu was approximately 100.5 kilometres to Monrovia. There were no convenient means of transport at the time to Monrovia mainly because of the war. There were no aeroplanes, no trains, no buses and coaches or even taxis working due to the war.

Just as the sun peeped out from behind the clouds on an early Sunday morning, all of us, the family of six, set-off on the 100.5-kilometre journey from Bopolu towards Monrovia on foot. Daddy, Mummy, Ameley, Zutor, Fogar and I; we started the journey on foot. Ameley, my elder sister, and the only female offspring of my parents, was 12 years old. My brother, Zutor, was 15 years old. Fogar, another brother of mine, was 13 years old, and I, Kolandi, was just 5 years old. We walked through the bush with no one in sight.

We walked through thick and thin forests on a day that was hot and sweaty. I struggled to keep up with the pace after about an hour's walk. My dad carried me on his shoulders as I could not match the pace of my other siblings.

I sat on my dad's shoulders and held on firmly to his head. Soon we were on the verge of reaching Tubmanberg. We had just 2.5 kilometres more to walk to reach Tubmanberg.

I told my parents I was tired, and that we needed to rest. But then we heard very loud sounds of rapid gun fire not far away from our location, although we had no idea where the gunfire was coming from. The rebels were either lurking around or were marching very close to our position.

"Let's, go, let's go," said Dad. "Hurry, hurry, they are near; if they get us, they may not spare us," he urged us on. My siblings and my mum picked up their pace to get away from them. We knew how close we were to Tubmanberg, and we hoped we could find some kind of refuge if we reached there. We stopped after another kilometre's walk when we could not hear the gunfire anymore.

We rested for about half-an-hour and continued our journey. My father held unto my left hand and held on to a medium sized bag in his left hand.

Not so long after, we could hear noises and the heavy footsteps of people. We guessed they were the rebel soldiers we so much dreaded and had desperately tried to avoid. They appeared to be just behind us. Would they see us? Would they catch us? We did not panic. We remained calm.

"Quick, quick," said my dad. He spotted an uncompleted building not far away. The building had no doors nor windows. The walls of the rooms were, however, high. They were high enough to conceal all six of us from the view of any passer-by. We hid in a deep corner inside the house. We all remained silent. Ameley literally clung to Mum. Mum wrapped both hands around her and rested her chin on her neck.

We peeped through some of the broken holes in the wall and saw about thirty rebel soldiers dressed in military camouflage uniforms. They were all wielding AK47 and G3 rifles. They were fully laden with long bandoliers wrapped around their torsos.

They had two magazines placed opposite to each other and held together by a wide band of cello tape. This way, one magazine was firmly loaded onto their rifles, and when that was emptied, they turned it around and fixed the other one. They chanted war songs as they staggered and marched their ways. It was clear as crystal that most of them might have drunk lots of liquor; cane juice as it was locally called.

We all heaved heavy and audible sighs of relief when they disappeared into the horizon. They did not see us. Thank God! We took the opportunity to have our breakfast. Mother had cooked some rice with potato green and cassava leaf stew. We enjoyed the food so much as we were all famished after going through this terrible time of stress and fear.

We continued our journey and soon reached Tubmanburg. The whole city was deserted and appeared empty. It was virtually a ghost town. We hurried quickly through the town centre and did not see even a bird on the road. We then took to the bush again in our pursuit to reach Monrovia.

Dad was not sure of what route to take: whether to go through Klay in Bomi County or to go through Bong Town in Margibi County. Both routes would take us through Carreysburg on our way towards Monrovia. Dad suddenly realised that, not only was the Klay in Bomi County route shorter in kilometres than the Bong Town in Margibi County route, but it passed through Brewersville in Montserrado County.

More so, the journey ran parallel to the Atlantic Ocean by this route. And so, we set off through the bush in the direction of Klay in Bomi County.

As the sun made its way to bed, we had not reached any village, nor did we locate any uncompleted building where we could pass the night. We decided to continue walking until the sun fully set behind the horizon; and wherever we reached at the time, we would lay our clothes down on the bare ground as beds and pass the night there. Fogar raised the fear of wild animals attacking us, but Dad dismissed that fear by assuring us that the only animals in the bush were antelopes, rabbits. and hedgehogs. These were not wild animals.

We sat down under an oak tree with very bushy leaves, the foliage of which formed a comfortable canopy over us. It felt like we were under a real roof. The idea of a serpent falling from the tree on us came to my mind. I voiced it out in a rather frightened-childlike manner. Again, Dad reminded me that snakes did not bite, unless they felt threatened. Mum served the remaining rice and stew for dinner. We all ate, laid our clothes on the bare grass, and lay down side by side. Ameley was close to Dad and I was close to Mum.

Lying close to Mum made me feel secure and protected. Ameley, our only sister, lay nearer to Dad, who appeared to have created a protective cordon around her. I slept deeply and soundly as if I were in my own bed at home, due to the fatigue from the long walk. And so, did most of the family. Dad, however, was most of the time awake, and on the lookout for both any rebel activity and animals which try to trespass our temporary bedroom.

We woke up in the morning and used some of the little water we carried with us to wash our faces and brush our teeth. We did not have breakfast because there was none. Mum, however, had some biscuits in her bag. Thank God for mothers! She shared them among us, and we nibbled at them, as we journeyed on.

We could not reach Brewersville before dusk set in. We had had no lunch and I was hungry. I complained several times to my dad, but he kept encouraging me that we would soon reach a village before Brewersville where we could buy all the food we wanted to eat before night set in. We walked, walked and walked, but no village appeared in sight, nor did Brewersville.

I kept whimpering that I was hungry. I began to impede our progress; but my siblings showed me support by encouraging me to press on. And that we would see a village or town soon. Were we going to make a bedroom in the middle of the bush for the second night? I began to wonder. My main concern, however, was the fact that there would be no dinner for us.

After another hour or so of walking, we spotted what looked like light in the not-too-far distance. A huge sense of relief suddenly dawned, not only on me, but the whole family. But then what type of light was it? Was it a streetlight? A light in a house? Light from an ocean-going vessel on the

Atlantic Ocean? We were not sure.

Getting closer, we noticed it was an isolated house built entirely of red bricks. It had not too high a fence wall around it. The fence wall was painted a bright red colour. It looked beautiful with security lights on each of the concrete pillars holding the cement blocks together in the wall.

How could we go in? Who did it belong to? What if there were rebel soldiers in there? Ameley was a young girl in her prime. She could be vulnerable. Dad summoned courage and pressed the bell at the gate of the house. For about fifteen minutes, no one came out of the house. Was it abandoned?

Just as we started to lose hope, the scarlet-red doors opened and there stood a huge and heavily built over six-footer male in front of us. He wore a bushy moustache that covered his entire upper lip and rose to cover the front of his nostrils. His eyes were reddish and they rolled like rollers in a Russian roulette. He looked serious and studied us from head to toe.

Surprisingly, without saying a word to us, he beckoned us to come into the house. He took us to his *piasa* (living room) and gave us water to drink. This was an African traditional welcome in the true sense.

"Who are you and what brings you here?" He said in a very polite Americo- Liberian slang.

Dad took up the responsibility and narrated our ordeal which started from Bopolu. He listened to us well. He then said we should be hungry. I nearly answered yes but held back in full respect to my parents and older siblings.

"Patience," he shouted. There came the response from a beautiful young lady, about 21 years old with beautiful skin and hair.

"Yes, Daddy," she answered. She sounded like a soprano; her voice was beautiful.

"Please prepare some food for our visitors, then prepare the guest rooms for them and show them the bathhouses," he instructed the young lady. She did as she was instructed. We each had a bed to ourselves and Mum and Dad shared the other double room.

Who said there is no God? There is God and He watches over His own and all that believe in Him and give their lives to Him. I said these words silently in my mind as I thanked God for this intervention.

I woke up to see Dad chatting with our host in the sitting room. I later got to know his name as Major General Joseph Gbanda (Retired). He was a medical doctor attached to the Liberian Military. He used to work at the Todi Military Hospital for many years and retired just before the war broke out. He was highly respected in many quarters of the Liberian society. He never discussed politics and never dabbled in it. He was as free as a bird and had no problems with anyone.

His wife joined us later at the breakfast table. We had good food; I mean real good food. I had not eaten like this for a long time. We retired to the piasa and were watching television. Mum, Dad, the General and his wife stayed at the breakfast table for quite some time chatting. We spent another night with this family, after which we exchanged, not only numbers but pleasantries, thanked them profusely and bid them goodbye.

"Fare you well," they said as they saw us off to the gate of their mansion.

And so, we continued our journey towards Monrovia. Brewersville appeared not to be too far away now. I held on to my little bag in my left hand while Dad held on to my right hand as we walked along. I was full and never felt hungry. I was full of energy and kept the pace. The bag contained just a couple of my trousers, one pair of shorts, two shirts and a couple of T-shirts.

Mum carried on her head the food flask given to us by the kind family, filled with food and drinks.

Just after about an hour's walk through the bush, Ameley shouted, "Lion, lion." We all turned in the direction she was pointing and saw the animal racing towards us. Dad quickly recognised it and calmed us down that it was not a lion, it was a stag. Lions do not live in this part of Africa, he told us, they live in the bushes of East Africa. He reminded us that we were in West Africa.

We walked almost the whole day and soon the sun started to nosedive towards the horizon once again. The setting sun provided a kaleidoscope of beautiful scenes of mingling colours in the distance on the western plateau where the sun was going down.

"How long do we have to go on again before we reach Monrovia?" I asked my dad.

"We will reach Monrovia soon," came his polite and encouraging reply. We saw the sign showing Brewersville: 5 kilometres; Monrovia 13.9 kilometres. Another half-an-hours' continuous walking brought Brewersville in sight. We sat on the bushy outskirts of Brewersville to have our dinner. Mum opened the food flask and we all had dinner. It was rice, cassava leaf stew with bananas and mangoes.

Just as we finished dinner, we heard noises in the not-too-distant background, the rebel forces again. But this time they were not moving in our direction, although we could clearly hear the noises they were making.

"Are the rebels coming after us, Dad?" I asked nervously. Ameley calmed me down and assured me they were not coming in our direction. Then, 'Gbogom! Gbogom!', we could hear shells falling about a kilometre in the direction of the location we had settled at. Night was almost near. The birds, animals and other living creatures had started to settle in their dens and on their perches.

"Are they coming after us? Are they coming to kill us? Should we run away?" I kept asking nervously.

"Runaway where in this bush?" Fogar whispered to me. "Keep calm," he said in a voice that assured me that we were all safe.

Just then, we saw the silhouette of someone running towards us. At first, it looked like a horse that had either bolted from its keepers, or one that was in the wild. Coming closer, it appeared like a gorilla coming towards us. I was shaken to the core. Mum stayed silent and petrified. Ameley clung to Dad's left hand, while I clung to his right.

A bit closer it looked like a human being. A young man in his early twenties with bushy dark hair, a thin moustache and a goatee ran towards us. He stopped by us, panting heavily as he tried to catch his breath.

"Help me, help me," he murmured as he tried to catch his breath.

"Sit down young man," Dad said to him. The young man sat next to Zutor. Mum gave him some water to drink. Just as he started to introduce himself to us, Dad cut in. Without asking him whether he was hungry, Dad requested Mum to give him some food to eat. He wolfed the food down with such speed that we guessed he might not have eaten all day, or even for a couple of days.

He confirmed this later. He thanked Mum, and indeed all of us for the food and started to tell us his story.

"I am from Bendaja in the Grand Cape Mount County, not too far from the border with Sierra Leone. I was captured by some of the rebel forces who bound my hands and dragged me along with them. I was their prisoner for fourteen days as they journeyed towards the epicentre of the war in Gbanga."

"One night, as they were all intoxicated with cane juice, and slept heavily, I managed to untie my hands and feet and escaped from them. This was about two days ago. I have been walking and running continuously for the past two days without food or water. Providence has made me locate you here." "Please take me as one of you," he pleaded.

We all slept under the Odowa tree that night. We all slept deep and sound except Dad. He slept fitfully and kept his eyes on our new companion. We had breakfast in the morning and set off on the rest of our journey. Our new family member, whose name I later got to know as Akogovi, offered to carry me on his shoulders.

I had no objection and I enjoyed the rest of the journey sitting on his shoulders. He was very well built physically, with large eyes, a deep voice and a handsome round face nearly resembling that of a famous movie star.

We passed through of Brewersville and saw nobody. We had just about 12.5 kilometres to reach our target destination, Monrovia. A few miles to entering Monrovia, we began to see occasional scattered buildings: open houses, flats and other types of dwellings.

"Where are we going to stay in Monrovia?" Ameley asked our mum in a rather low voice.

"I really don't know yet, but I'm sure our Father in Heaven would put a roof over our head," she said in a motherly assuring manner. Dad could not answer the question of accommodation either. He looked pensive and appeared to be deep in thought as if something was bothering him. Zutor whispered to Fogar that it looked like Dad was worried about where we would stay in Monrovia.

We were just about 2 kilometres from the town centre of Monrovia and my confidence kept rising, but the issue of where to stay in Monrovia, was a bother to the whole family. All of a sudden, Akogovi, who appeared to have heard the conversation between Fogar and Zutor, asked the party to stop.

"What's the matter?" Dad asked.

Akogovi started with his story. "I have a family house just a few metres from where we are now. During the early days of the war, the rebels came into the house, demanded money and when they could not get it, they shot everyone in the house. My whole family was wiped out. I only survived because I hid under my bed in my bedroom with the door firmly locked," he paused.

And then, he recollected, "one day after the incident, when I ventured out to buy food, I was captured by a rebel group. And that was how they captured me. I escaped three times but three times I fell into other rebel soldiers' hands. I still have the keys to the house. Let us go there and there is room for every one of us," he said.

I noticed a huge relief on Dad's face. We went into the house; a beautiful house painted a pale magnolia colour. We entered and there were flowers along the fence wall; they were overgrown since no one attended to them. ,

There were two living rooms. Photos of Akogovi's parents and siblings adorned the walls of the living room. We all sat down in the living room and Akogovi said to us, "You are all welcome to your new home. From today onwards, you are my family. I am your family, and this house belongs to all of us." The sitting room chairs were made of soft brown leather and were comfortable to sit on.

The kitchen was very spacious and had large windows that looked onto a garden at the back of the house. In fact, there were two kitchens, this big one, and a kitchenette by the master bedroom; which Akogovi had offered to mum and dad. The rest of us, settled in our various rooms.

There were eight bedrooms, each with its own bath and toilet. The beddings were nice, but dusty. After shaking out the dust, they were as nice as those in the house we had left a couple of days earlier.

Chapter 2
Monrovia

We settled in Monrovia. The war activity in the capital city had considerably died down. No gunfire, mortar-fires or bombs could be heard in the city. Commercial activity was just beginning to get back to normal, albeit at a very slow pace. Most banks had reopened; and so, had restaurants, supermarkets. Commercial vehicles painted in all kinds of yellow hue had begun plying the ever-growing busy roads of downtown Monrovia.

Robertsville International Airport had also re-opened to flights and was quite busy. Aeroplanes taking off flew directly over our new house. I enjoyed watching them climb high into the skies until they either hid behind the snow-white clouds, or completely disappear. This gave me the lofty ambition of becoming a pilot one day.

My relationship with Akogovi became quite close. In fact, he virtually became our elder brother, since he was older than all of us. He was 21 years old and was in his second year at the University of Liberia; a beautiful university located by the Atlantic seacoast, not too far away from the President of Liberia's official residence and offices popularly known as the Executive Mansion.

As the official residence of the President of Liberia, many tourists flocked there for sightseeing and take photographs of the edifice. Akogovi was almost always studying. Emulating him, I also developed the habit of reading, and Akogovi became my teacher at home. I read most of the African Writers Series. I read Flora Nwapa, Chinua Achebe, Cyprian Ekwensi, James Ngugi, Elechi Amadi, Can Themba, and many more. Akogovi received a lot of visitors at the house; most of them were his mates from university. Most of these visitors came because they had not seen themselves for a couple of years due to the just ended civil war.

The University of Liberia re-opened and Akogovi had to go back to school. He stayed in a hall of residence on the university campus most of the time. We only saw him during the weekends, or when they were on semester holidays. He, however, kept in touch with the whole family via telephone and on social media.

Dad was a trained teacher and Mum was a registered nurse. Due to the recently ended war, there arose loads of vacancies in both of these professions in the capital. Mum applied for work at the local hospital and was successful. The hospital was about 1.5 kilometres away from our house. She sometimes walked to work or picked a local taxi. She also occasionally used the '*holei- holei*'—the local private minibuses that were cheaper to ride in than a taxi.

Mum was pleased with her job. She worked with both doctors and nurses who became family friends and visited us at home sometimes. Most of the patients who she looked after in hospital, on their discharge from hospital brought us gifts of food items such as vegetables, dry and fresh fish as well as other groceries such as milk, canned fish, and wheat. We never fell short of food in the house.

Mum used to prepare food, package it nicely in food flask, and take it to Akogovi on campus. I used to go with her. He was always grateful for this gesture from Mum.

Campus was a beautiful place with a sprawl of very beautiful buildings. On one of such visits, Akogovi showed me around the campus. I saw and visited the lecture rooms, students' dormitories, lecturers' residences, private shops and restaurants scattered all over the university campus. The girls' halls of residence, clearly labelled as such, were a bit of a distance away from the boys' halls. However, when we walked past the girls' halls, I saw so many boys lurking around these ladies' halls that I started wondering whether there were male residences too there. Akogovi however told me these were for females only. I was so intrigued by the whole campus atmosphere that I said to myself I would try and go to university when I grew up. Mum told me that would be good but I had to learn hard in secondary school and make good grades at the examinations.

Dad was a teacher at the local Roman Catholic school about 300 metres away from our house. This afforded me the opportunity to be enrolled in the school. I had then attained the age of 6. Ameley, Fogar and Zutor all got places in the same school.

They were in higher classes since they were older than me.

Later, Ameley asked Dad to send her to the girls' convent, where the students lived in residence with the Reverend Sisters who looked after them. It was called the Convent of Jesus and Mary.

I was so happy in my stage one class. Most of my classmates were of the same age, or nearly the same age as me. I made new friends and was always full of stories from school that I used to narrate to Mum when she came home. My teacher, Mrs. Larvie, was just like a mother to all of us. She taught us all subjects and always took her time to explain things to us.

Occasionally, she would tell us stories and fables—most of which were fictional yet but carried lots of wisdom and lessons of life. She also spoke of the big wars that were fought around the world many years ago. Any time she spoke of wars, she almost always made passing references to the just ended Liberian civil war. I listened to her with great interest and attention, but never divulged to her that my family and I were victims of this war.

We lost our house in Bopolu, our friends, our livelihood; but I kept all to myself as I really did not grasp the intricacies of war at the age of 6. Ameley was in Year 9. She had just three more years to enter university. Fogar was in Year 8 and Zutor was in Lower 6th Form. Apart from Ameley who was in boarding house at the convent, all of us were day students. We commuted to school daily. It was the Christmas five years after we had settled in Monrovia. I was 11 years old and was in Year 7. I had just entered secondary school. Most of my classmates that I started primary one with were still with me in the same class. Some had left the country with their parents for other African countries.

Maame Yaa was one of them. She had left with her family back to Ghana where they originally came from. They came to Liberia when her dad was appointed Ghana's ambassador to the Republic of Liberia. She was my friend. I knew her parents and she knew my parents. I was not able to take her contact number in Ghana before she left, so, I lost contact with her.

Akogovi had finished university. He did a Bachelor of Science degree in electrical engineering. After working at the country's National Electricity Corporation for his National Service to the nation, he got a really good job at Perrysburg, about 22 kilometres from central Monrovia. That was where the Voice of America (VOA) (Liberia Plant's) power plant was located. He was employed as an engineer officer at the VOA power plant. He commuted daily with the US Embassy shuttle buses that picked their staff from home to work and brought them back after their shifts.

A few years passed, and all my siblings had completed their university degrees. Zutor graduated with a BSc (Hons) Degree in Business Administration with a Marketing major. He worked for a company called Lintas, which was at the time, a hugely successful advertising company, not only in Liberia but across the whole of the West African sub region. The company's head office was located in Accra, Ghana. Ghana was about an hour and thirty minutes' flying time from Robertsville International Airport in Monrovia.

Ameley, our princess, had a flair for science subjects. She graduated with an MD Degree from the University of Liberia Medical School. She did her housemanship at the local hospital in Monrovia. Fogar, like my sister, Ameley, was a good science student. He graduated with a BSc in Pharmacy and was attached to the country's biggest pharmaceutical company where he completed his National Service after a year.

What this meant was that, at university where I was an undergraduate studying for a BSc degree in the Biological Sciences, I had able siblings who, together with Mum and Dad, were all very well employed and equipped with the requisite resources to look after me. I got whatever I asked for. Most of the times, my siblings would provide me with what I wanted before my parents got hint of it.

Mum and Dad had a few more years in their jobs before retiring. They worked hard and built a beautiful house on the outskirts of Monrovia. We did not move into the new house immediately as Akogovi wanted us to rent the new house out and still live with him. Mum and Dad initially agreed with him. However, after discussions with my other two brothers and Ameley, who all lived at home at the time, we agreed to politely turn Akogovi's suggestion down and told him we wanted to move into the new house.

Mum and Dad assured Akogovi that he always had a room allocated to him in our new house, and that he could come over and stay with us, in which case he could rent his family house. We moved to our new house and Akogovi moved in with us. We were the only siblings he knew and had. He then rented out his family home, that had given us so much shelter and comfort in our biggest moment of need, to tenants and earned some income from that.

A few years passed. I was now 22 years of age and had just graduated with a First-Class Honours from the University of Liberia with a BSc Degree in the Biological Sciences. I did not follow the medical degree course that I had initially dreamt of after all. I had wanted to follow the footsteps of my elder sister, Ameley, and become a medical doctor, but that did not materialise. I did my National Service with the Food and Drug Authority (FDA) , mainly in the science laboratory conducting tests and helping in research into food and drugs for certification.

Akogovi got married. It was a big ceremony, which . attracted more than 150 guests. Friends from far and near were all invited, and they honoured their invitations. They included former secondary school and university mates, colleagues from his workplace at the American Embassy (VOA Power Plant) where he still worked, family friends and many guests invited by the bride and her family.

Akpene, Akogovi's bride and wife-to-be, was a stunningly beautiful young woman. Her bridal dress was an aesthetic thing to look at. She was about five feet eight inches in height and commanded a strikingly feminine body shape that slightly jerked from side to side and she walked. With her left hand in her daddy's right arm, she was walked majestically in tune with the bridal march towards the altar of the most beautiful cathedral in the city.

She smiled gracefully as she walked past the huge number of guests who stood up to show respect for her as soon as the bridal march was struck. And as she smiled, captivating dimples appeared on both sides of her cheeks. 'Here comes the bride', the music continued to play, as she strode in all elegance, beauty and pageantry towards his soon-to-be husband who kept his focus on his bride from that distance. He looked back to catch a glimpse of her bride walking down the aisle.

Soon father and daughter were at the altar. Her dad let go of her hand and walked back gently to take his seat in one of the seats placed in a semi-circle in front of the pews. Akogovi stole a glance at her and smiled.

I was Akogovi's best man. I carried his wedding ring in the breast pocket of my jacket. I wore exactly the same outfit as Akogovi. It was a Kentucky styled suit. Blue-black trousers with a creamy-white tuxedo to go with it over a snowy white shirt. I also wore a large yellow bow tie which drew the eye even from the distance. My siblings were very well dressed too.

Ameley, attended the wedding with her boyfriend, and wore a beautiful flowing white dress embroidered with stylised petals of flowers on the front of the skirt of the dress. Fogar and Zutor wore blue velvet suits over blue shirts and blue flying ties. They also came with their girlfriends who were beautifully apparelled.

The ceremony was conducted by the Rev Father Joseph Campbell, the vicar in charge of the cathedral. These were the officiating clergyman's opening remarks. "Dearly beloved, we are gathered here today to witness the solemnisation of Holy Matrimony between this young man and this young woman," he said. He continued and emphasised the significance of the vows they were about to exchange. He also reminded the couple of their duties and roles in marriage.

He concluded with the philosophical words, "Marriage is a beautiful thing." He also quoted from the scriptures when he said, "...he who finds a wife finds a good thing."

There was then the giving away of the bride. This was the opportunity for Akpene to honour her parents. It is traditionally a father-moment but the couple chose to include Akpene's mother, so she rose and stood with him in response when the officiating clergy asked, "Who gives this woman to be married to this man?"

"I do," answered Akpene's dad in a deep bass voice which belied his broad smile. Akpene's mum grinned wistfully and nodded appreciatingly. And then came the exchange of vows. The officiating minister reminded them that their vows were promises to each other, but in front of God. Then he asked them to repeat after him the familiar words of 'to have and to hold, for better for worse' vows.

This was followed by the exchange of rings. During the exchange of the rings, they said to each other facing and looking into each other's face, "With this ring, I thee wed."

Then there was the pronouncement of marriage. The officiating minister looked into the smiling faces of the bride and bridegroom and said, "I now pronounce you husband and wife."

This was met by a thunderous applause from the congregation

that seemed to go on and on and never stop. There were shouts of congratulations echoing from all corners of the cathedral auditorium. And then people started to chant "kiss, kiss, kiss". It seemed the moment everyone had been waiting for: the first kiss as a married couple. Akogovi appeared shy but was determined. He held both hands of Akpene and kissed her on the lips. It lasted for about fifty-five seconds, accompanied by wild cheering from the crowd..

Rev Father Pious van-Vere, assisting Rev Father Joseph Campbell, wrapped up things up with a few last words of wisdom to the couple; and, as is traditional and usual for a religious wedding, the couple knelt to be blessed. Then there was the recession. The Recessional walk was the reverse of the processional walk, where the couple exited the ceremony together as newlyweds.

Theirs was laced with music and dancing to one of the local artiste's music entitled *My Lovely Elizabeth*. The ceremony had ended and the bridal party and all invited guests made their ways to the wedding reception. And so, for the first time ever, the new couple was introduced to the world of marriage and as man and wife, a real couple.

I worked in my job as a biological scientist for four years. I was now 24 years of age. I enjoyed working with the food and drug company. I had a girlfriend but was not married. Maame Yaa should have occupied that position if she and the family were still in Monrovia; they had gone to Ghana with the family on completion of her father's diplomatic duties in Liberia, and I could not trace her.

All my siblings had now left home. Akogovi, Zutor and Fogah had all bought their own houses and moved in with their spouses. Ameley had also gotten married and they were living in the beautiful house they had bought together. I was the only child still living at home with my parents. I, however, occasionally visited all my siblings at their places of abode.

They frequently came for family dinners and other occasions in my parents' house. I was quite happy at home. My girlfriend, Clarissa, was almost always with me at home.

After dinner one day, I informed my parents that I wanted to travel abroad to pursue further studies. My Mum assumed I wanted to go to the United States of America. Freed slaves from the United States of America arrived in Liberia in the year 1822. This was fifty years before the abolition of slavery in America, and Liberia became independent in the year 1847.

On arrival, the freed slaves declared, "The Love of Liberty Brought Us Here." This has remained the country's national motto till today, boldly embossed on the country's Coat of Arms. This relationship had made thousands of young Liberians who wanted to travel abroad, either to pursue further studies or to seek greener pastures abroad, almost always choose the United States of America as their destination.

However, I wanted to go to London, England, and told my mother so. Mum asked rather absentmindedly where London was. I remined her that London was the capital city of Great Britain, or the United Kingdom and Northern Ireland. "Oh yes, I remember. One of our doctors' son is studying in London. That is fine then, but what arrangements have you put in place?" She quizzed.

"I'm still planning it; when I am done, I will let you and Dad know," I said convincingly to my mum.

One month passed. I sat down with Mum and Dad at the dining table. I told them I wanted to go to London to further my studies. After a series of questions, which I believed I answered quite convincingly, they agreed in principle. I told them that I would want to go to London via Accra in Ghana. "Why Ghana?" Mum asked.

"Because Ghana was a former colony of the United Kingdom, it is comparatively easier to fly out from Ghana to London," I tried to convince them.

Mum and Dad tried to reason that through with me. "But who do you know in Ghana?" Dad asked.

"A Ghanaian friend who I attended the University of Liberia with," I answered. Again, Mum asked whether that was Maame Yaa and her brothers? Mum knew Maame, but I told her no, and reminded her that Maame was in the primary school with me. "My friend is called Kofi; Kofi Asare," I said to Mum.

"Do you have enough money to travel with? Your flight to Ghana; accommodation in Ghana; food and other essentials while you are in Ghana?" Mum asked.

"Yes; I have made some savings towards the project. I believe I can make it," I tried to convince her.

That evening, Clarissa passed the night at our family home. We discussed my proposed journey to London. "Why London?" Clarissa asked.

"Oh, I just like London. I actually prefer London to New York, Los Angeles, Washington or Chicago," I said to Clarissa. I tried to convince Clarissa that there was less gun violence in London as compared to most of the American cities. I told her that for example, London Police did not carry weapons. Clarissa and I discussed so many other issues concerning my trip.

I promised her, when I got to London, and was ready to marry, I would come down to Liberia and marry her. She said immediately she would be happier being married in London.

She then asked me why I would not want to marry her before leaving for London. I immediately reminded her that we both were not yet ready for that then.

"Will you keep your promise and wait for me no matter how long it takes?" I asked Clarissa.

Clarissa asked, "How long would it take you to get there, complete your course and come back for me?" I told her I was not too sure. I assured her that time would tell. I kissed Clarissa goodnight and we both fell asleep.

The next morning, Dad called me to the breakfast table. After breakfast, he told me I had all his and mum's blessings for my proposed travel. He said he wished me well. He, however, said he had a word of caution for me. I waited eagerly to hear these words of caution. He went up to his bookshelf and brought me an A4 sheet of paper with a few words boldly written on it.

"Take your time and read it, Son," he said, and he sat and watched me read the message. It read:

10 December 1914: Massive explosion in West Orange, New Jersey in the USA. Ten buildings owned by the legendary investor Thomas Edison were engulfed by flames. Fire brigades from six to eight different stations rushed to the scene to put off the fire but could not curb the chemical fuel inferno. After having tried all that, he could, Thomas Edison calmly stood there watching the fire destroy his entire life's hard work.

His 24-year-old son came over and stood next to him. In a childlike voice, Edison said to his son, "Charlie go and get your mother and her friends; they will never be able to see a spectacular fire like this in their entire lives."

Astonished and shocked by his father's response, Charles said to Thomas Edison, "Our entire factory is being burnt to ashes, Dad."

Thomas Edison replied in complete composure, "Yes, our factory is being burnt down to ashes, but all the mistakes we have made so far in the factory have also been burnt down to ashes. We would start all over again tomorrow."

That evening, Thomas Edison told a New York Times reporter, "Although, I am 67 years old, and I am completely exhausted from running around and trying to control the fire; tomorrow I will start afresh all over again." And so did he. The next day was a fresh beginning for Thomas Edison and his son, Charles, in trying to rebuild what had been destroyed by the fire.

He continued to say, "Often this is what life does unto us (render you broken). Our dreams are shattered. Our hopes broken. Efforts baffled. Great people, they do not cry, they try to rebuild their dreams. Great people do not give up, they meet the challenges that life throws at them head-on."

"Great people do not go through, they grow through the difficulties that come their way. They start all over again with great hope, with great determination, with grit, and that is why they reach the highest peaks of success that most people can only aspire for. That is why I say, 'No Challenges No Success'."

I looked up at my dad and thanked him for these great words of encouragement and wisdom.

Chapter 3
Accra

I arrived at Roberts International Airport in Monrovia on a bright Wednesday morning to take my flight from Monrovia to Accra-Ghana. Clarissa, my parents, and all my siblings with their spouses came to the airport to see me off. I was about to commence my journey to London.

"God, grant you journey mercies; safe journey and have a nice flight," Clarissa whispered into my ears. I thanked her. She also blew me a kiss from the distance as I waved at all of them from the tarmac walking towards the aircraft. The aircraft was an Airbus 350 manufactured in Toulouse, France. Air Liberia had purchased the aircraft just over a couple of years before. It looked huge, and I was particularly excited as that was the first time I was to travel by air.

The aircraft took off at exactly 1100 hrs. Greenwich Mean Time. It was on time. After the pilot greeted us on the aircraft's internal address system, he informed us that the flight was going to take one and a half hours. The leader of the cabin crew team asked us to fasten our seatbelts and get our seats in an upright position. With that, the aircraft taxied and zoomed off with tremendous speed into the early morning clouds. I said goodbye to Monrovia; but just for now I hoped.

We touched down at Accra's Kotoka International Airport exactly at half- past midday. A beautiful airport just like what I saw at Roberts International Airport. We went through immigration. I had nothing to declare at customs. I was carrying just a simple suitcase bought for me on my last birthday by Clarissa. I spent about half an hour by the carousels on which the passengers' luggage kept going a merry-go-round until the owners picked them one after the other.

I picked up my luggage, walked through customs and stood outside the arrival hall in the fresh Ghanaian air albeit in the burning mid-afternoon sun. A young woman approached me and asked me whether I knew where Hotel Continental was in Accra. I told her I did not know as that was my first time of coming to the city. She looked disappointed with my answer but thanked me anyway.

Lots of people were waiting outside the arrival hall looking out for families and other travellers that they had come to meet. A taxi driver approached me and enquired whether I needed a taxi. I replied politely in the negative.

Just then, I felt a tap on my shoulder. I reacted sharply by turning around, and falling into the waiting arms of Kofi, who embraced me with a very broad and welcome smile. "Welcome, my brother," he said.

"Thank you," I replied with an equally broad and excited smile.

Kofi picked up my suitcase and we walked about a hundred metres from the main Kotoka International Airport building in Accra. He signalled for a taxi. Together we took the taxi to the Continental Hotel, just about 5 kilometres away from the airport. Continental Hotel was a beautiful and imposing edifice. Walking into the reception area of the hotel, I remembered the woman who had asked me for directions to the Continental Hotel.

As fate would have it, as we checked in at the reception desk, the same woman joined the queue waiting to check into the same hotel. I greeted her took the opportunity to explain to her what I had told her earlier and pointed to Kofi as my host. She smiled in understanding. Coincidentally, we met again at dinner that evening.

The woman, whose name I later found out to be Akosua, was an interesting conversationalist and we chatted for about two hours before retiring to our rooms. Akos, as she preferred to be called, worked for the United Nations in Geneva, Switzerland. She looked 32 and had a strikingly beautiful physique and stood about five feet eleven inches tall.

She had studied for a BA (Hons) International Relations degree at the University of Ghana before travelling to the London School of Economics in London, where she completed her Master's degree in the same discipline. She spoke impeccable English. She was instantly an inspiration to me; particularly as she studied at the same institution, in the same city and country where I had set out to do my further studies: London, England in the United Kingdom. We exchanged business cards and promised each other to keep in touch.

We checked out of the hotel the following morning and drove for an hour to Kasoa, a suburb of Accra, where Kofi lived. Kofi had rented a two-bedroom flat. He showed me into one of the bedrooms. This was going to be my residence until I left Accra for London.

Kofi taught science in the neighbouring Kasoa High School. I followed him to the school sometimes and watched him teach and interact with the students. Soon, I became friendly with many of the teachers in the school, including the headmaster.

I frequently got in touch with my family in Monrovia. I called and talked to Mum and Dad. Then Zutor, Ameley, Fogar and of course, my darling Clarissa. I spoke to Akogovi too. We would talk and talk and talk in excitement during these phone calls. Clarissa would always tell me she missed me. And I would tell her I missed her too. We took any opportunity we got to send each other text messages, and sometimes links to music that we both enjoyed. Mum and Dad always encouraged me to remain focused on my objective of getting to London to continue my studies.

It was my plan to stay in Accra for a month (4 weeks) before departing Accra for London. But just during the second week of my stay in Accra, Kofi informed me that he was leaving Kasoa and was relocating to Kumasi, about 248 kilometres away from Accra. He explained to me the reasons behind the decision to relocate, and I understood him perfectly. He had not only got a job with a high school in Kumasi, but also had to go to get engaged to his future wife, who lived and worked in Kumasi.

He gave me the choice of staying in the two-bed flat until I left at the end of my fourth week or moving into a one bed flat. For economic reasons, I opted to move into a one-bed flat. I had no special reason else for this decision, but I felt I must move.

Kofi left for Kumasi. He arranged for and settled me comfortably in my one- bed flat which was not too far from where we lived. I would be staying there for only two weeks. Then I would get ready and fly out to London. I had my air ticket money with me. I also had enough money to see me through the cost of living for at least six months in London.

I would get a part time job for the twenty working hours allowed students in the United Kingdom.

In my third week at Kasoa, something traumatic happened to me. The front window of my living room of my flat was taken down during the early hours of the day. It was about half-past two at dawn. I then heard footsteps in the living room of my flat. Was it a domestic animal that had strayed into my room?

Before I could finish thinking this over, my bedroom door opened. I got out of bed and rushed to put on the light in the living room but was pushed back by a very heavy hand. I nearly froze but summoned courage to shout, "Who are you?" Suddenly, I heard gunfire at my front door. I knew it was a gun because of the onomatopoeic sound made by the machine.

"Shhhhh, keep quiet," two of the intruders said in deep male voices to me. Before I could say anything, another gunfire sounded at the same spot around the entrance of my flat. I was not only petrified, but I was also momentarily confused. I lay still in my bed. I said nothing. The intruders ransacked my room and took away the only suitcase I had with me. It contained all the money I brought with me from Monrovia.

They ran off without hurting me for which I was grateful to God. I could not sleep for the rest of the morning. I rushed to make a report at the Kasoa police station.

The Kasoa police came to my house where the robbery took place. They took my statement, fingerprints on my front door and told me they would investigate. Three to four weeks passed. I went to enquire from the crime officer the progress made with the investigations.

"How far?" I said to the crime officer at the Kasoa police station.

"We are on it, no lead to the criminals yet," he would say to me casually but emphatically.

The robbery happened the week before the last that I was to leave Accra for London. My ticket money and all other monies meant for my expenses in London had been stolen. I had to pay rent for the next four weeks if I wanted to stay at the same flat but did not have a cent to my name. I still did not plan to stay in Accra for more than the four weeks that I had originally planned.

Should I inform my family back in Monrovia? I did not want my parents to get a shock at this unfortunate news and fall ill. Should I tell my siblings? If so, which one of them should I confide in? The eldest or the only sister I had. They all had their families to look after. I would not disturb them. Should I let Clarissa know? All these questions and ideas kept revving through my mind, yet I did not panic. I kept both my cool and focus.

In the interim, I decided to tell Kofi what happened. Kofi too had just relocated. He was in the process of settling down. I discussed the issue with him, nevertheless. He sympathised with me. He asked me how much was stolen. I told him the amount: USD 10,000. He advised me to try and pay the rent for the next four weeks, try and get a job, work, and get enough money and then travel.

I reminded him that I had just exhausted the rent I paid for the last three weeks, and I did not have enough money to pay for the next four weeks. Kofi paid the next four weeks' rent for me. I decided to stay for another four weeks. 'A friend in need is a friend indeed', I soliloquised.

I still had not explained to my family in Monrovia why I had not flown to London after my initial four weeks. I gave all sorts of excuses. I told them I had got a teaching job in Accra and would want to teach for a couple of months before leaving. Universities in London would resume with fresh students in September of the year and it was just after Easter. It was April and I had a few more months ahead of me.

Four weeks had passed and it dawned on me that I needed to pay rent at the end of the coming week; week five. I was not working, although I had sent an application for a teaching job at Kofi's former school. I wanted to teach any subject in the Sciences. I could specifically teach mathematics, biology, chemistry, or physics. I had been a biological scientist for quite some time and I was quite sure of this.

It was a Sunday evening. I knew the landlord was going to come on Monday for his rent. The landlord was a tall, retired sergeant major in the Ghana Armed Forces. His name was Salifu Muniru. He stood over six-foot-tall and wore a bushy salt and pepper moustache. His voice was unsurprisingly deep, and he spoke with an appreciable level of authority and command.

"What am I going to tell him?" I asked myself audibly. Should I tell him about how my money was stolen? After a long deliberation on this, I decided to tell him when he came for his rent. This could be a genuine excuse for non- payment which I believe he could empathise with.

Sergeant Major Salifu Muniru (Retired) came on Monday evening. He sat in my living room. He asked whether I had his rent ready for him in a surprisingly polite manner. I replied in the negative. I cleared my throat and wanted to start my story. Before I could say a word, he informed me that he had heard of the robbery.

And that he spoke to the local police and was told that they were confident of making a breakthrough soon. After a rather short conversation, he gave me the option of paying it anytime that I had money or choose to go to a refugee camp nearby called Buduburam. Buduburam was a camp set up by UNICEF in Ghana that hosted Liberian refugees who had fled the civil war in their country. He knew I was from Liberia.

However, what he did not appear to know was that I was not a refugee. That week, in the midst of adversity, I had some good news. Kofi's former school, the Kasoa Senior High School (SHS), responded to my application positively, and invited me for an interview. I attended the interview on Tuesday and started work the following Monday.

The week was turning out to be a good week for me; promising rays of light were beginning shine across my path. The police called me and invited me to the Kasoa police station charge office. I attended to their invitation after work that Friday. There were about ten cellmates all siting and peeping through the iron bars from behind where they were being kept.

The officer in charge of the case, Detective Inspector Thomas Bukari, invited me to his office. He closed the door behind me and offered me a seat. I sat down. He started narrating to me the brilliant investigative job they had done on my case. They had a lead. Two young men kept changing US Dollars for the Ghanaian Cedi at a foreign exchange bureau in a small town called Agona- Swedru. Agona Swedru was about forty kilometres away from Kasoa.

The frequency of their visits to the foreign exchange bureau to change the Dollars was consistent, virtually every day. This aroused the suspicion of the owner of the bureau, because these young men—who neither looked like tourists nor 'boggers'—seemed to have an inexhaustible supply of dollar notes.

The shop owner clandestinely informed the Agona Swedru police, who had earlier on received a wireless message about the robbery in Kasoa and the amount of money stolen. By a special collaboration with the foreign exchange bureau, the police laid in wait for their next visit at the bureau. The arrangement went according to plan. The two young men came into the shop to change USD 500 into the local currency, the Cedi. In the middle of the transactions, the police swooped in and detained the two suspects. They were cautioned that anything they said would be used in evidence against them in the future in a competent court of jurisdiction. The police questioned the two young men about the origins of their US dollar notes. Though they looked stunned and shocked at their arrest, they refused to speak.

The Police then switched to plan B. They separated them from each other and sat them in two separate police vans parked outside the bureau. There they were quizzed individually. They gave different answers during the interviews. One said the US dollars were sent to them by his brother in the USA. The other said an expatriate whom he had worked for, who had left Ghana back to the USA gave the US dollars to them before leaving.

Bingo! That was what the police wanted. On talking to each other on radio and hearing the two different conflicting statements made by the two suspects, they were quickly manacled and whisked to the Agona Swedru Police Station.

At the station, the forensic tests revealed that the fingerprints taken on the door handles of my flat matched their fingerprints. The police had told them that they would be dealt with leniently if they told the truth, and they complied; they admitted to the robbery. That evening, two police vans travelled the short distance from Agona Swedru and brought the suspects to Kasoa police station.

The police conducted a search at their home addresses and retrieved some of the money. Out of the USD 10,000 stolen, they were able to retrieve USD 3,600. This included the USD 500 they had wanted to change at the bureau.

I was asked whether I could identify them. I replied in the negative because I could not see their faces that night. They were brought in handcuffs to the officer in charge of the investigation's office and I took a good look at them.

They were subsequently charged with the offence and prepared for court, prosecuted, and sentenced to seven years each in prison. The USD 3,600 was given back to me. This was not enough to see me through my London journey. Although, I could buy a ticket of Accra-London-Accra from it, it was not enough to pay for my university fees. I, therefore, used some of it to pay for my rent for the next three weeks in addition to the one week rent I owed. My landlord was happy when I narrated the outcome of the police investigations to him.

Six months passed and I was not able to put aside enough money to reach the USD 10,000 equivalent that I set off on my London journey with. I was receiving salary from my teaching job. But then I had to pay rent, provide food for myself, buy clothes, and entertain myself. Soon, it was November, and university admissions at the London School of Economics had closed. Thus, it meant I could not enrol on the course for that year.

How would I explain all these to my parents, siblings and Clarissa? Clarissa could not understand what was going on. She asked whether I had gotten a new girlfriend in Ghana who was pinning me down in the country. I always asked her to be patient, and that at the right time I would explain what was happening, to her. She was still impatient and suspected foul play.

There was not much pressure from my parents or siblings, although they found it difficult to understand the different versions of excuses that I kept giving them. But there was relentless pressure from Clarissa. She was on the brink on a breakdown. I might have been influenced by a new girlfriend I met in Ghana, was the thought that was taking root in her mind, and I was unable to reassure her by not telling her my story. Finally, when the pressure became unbearable and threatened the very foundation of our relationship, I decided to tell her what had happened; tell her the truth and nothing but the truth.

Clarissa was taken aback when I narrated my ordeal to her. She empathised with me, and encouraged me to work hard, get some money, and try again to find my way to London. I told her I was grateful for her understanding and that I was going to do just that. Although, I could ask my parents and siblings for the money for my travel to London, I decided not to do so. I was determined to be independent and not burden anyone. I would bite the bullet and get to London by whatever means.

I reapplied to do my Master's degree course at the London School of Economics in the September of the following year. I was given an unconditional admission. I had worked hard to get the university fees, my living expenses and set aside a little towards my air ticket. Although I had not saved enough money as I would have wanted, yet I decided to leave my job by the end of November that year, to focus more on my travel plans.

November came and I still had not been able to get the money I needed for my airfare. How would I get to London? I thought to myself, "why not by road?' "I would go to London by road," I said to myself without having a definite plan. As if in an answer to my internal turmoil, that week's papers carried several stories of many young Africans travelling to Europe by road.

In the second week of December that year, I decided to set off on my journey to London by road, since I still did not have enough money on me to go by air. I was a little apprehensive, but also relished the challenge. So, on the16th December, I boarded a bus from Kasoa to Accra, in what would be a grand adventure.

I checked in to a cheap guesthouse on my arrival in Accra. Early the following morning, I checked out of the guesthouse, took a taxi and headed to the Kotoka International Airport.

My journey to London was entering its second phase. The journey had started in earnest.

Chapter 4
Ouagadougou

We boarded an Air Burkina aircraft heading to Ouagadougou, the capital city of Burkina Faso. The aircraft took off on time; exactly at 1000 hrs. GMT. We landed after just about one-and-a-half-hour's flight. The Thomas Sankara International Airport, named after the assassinated former President of Burkina Faso, was clean and well-kept, but modest. We were driven by long buses when we descended the gangway on the tarmac to the arrival hall.

There were both military and police personnel stationed all around the arrivals hall. I presented my Liberian passport to the immigration officer. She looked at my name and picture in the passport, asked me to confirm my name; I did. She asked me what my mission in Ouagadougou was and for how long I was going to stay. I nearly thought of telling her that I was on my way to London by road.

I hesitated for a split second. I then decided to tell her the truth. "I am passing through your country on my way to London by road." She looked at me over the top of her spectacles with visible scepticism on her face as she returned my passport to me. She stamped my passport, looked again into my face as though she was going to wish me good luck, and handed the stamped passport back to me. I thanked her and took a slow walk away from her desk.

I picked up my luggage on the conveyor belt and passed through immigration and customs easily without any problem. As I walked towards the entrance of the airport into the public area, it suddenly dawned on me that I had not got a house to go to. I had not booked any hotel accommodation ahead of my arrival in Ouagadougou.

"Do you want a taxi?" One of the many taxi drivers waiting around the front of the arrivals hall asked.

"No, thank you," I answered. The fact of the matter was that I had indeed wanted a taxi, but where to, I was not sure. My negative answer to the taxi driver was actually said absentmindedly, and rightly so because I did not know where I was going.

I looked at a brochure containing a list of hotels, guesthouses, and Airbnb's. I started to think hard as to which of these three categories of accommodations I should choose. I was not sure how long I would have to stay in Ouagadougou. How much money did I have? Perhaps the hotel would be too expensive. Should I just get a simple guesthouse? How much would it cost? And for how long would I be staying in Ouagadougou? And if I stayed in an Airbnb, that would mean I would be staying with a family or even families. Would my privacy be compromised if I stayed in an Airbnb?

I had to make a decision; and that decision had to be made quickly as the evening sun was on its way towards the horizon. It was nearly four o'clock in the evening, and I needed to get a place to lodge fast.

I rested at a café about a kilometre away from the airport. I bought club sandwiches and some soft drink to quench the hunger that was beginning to rear its head at my stomach. I kept looking at the list of hotels, guesthouses, and Airbnb's as I munch my sandwiches. I had decided. I would go to a hotel; at least in the first instance.

I took a cab to one of the hotels on my list. In fact, I chose the one showing a moderate charge of 55,000 CFA per night: *Hotel Afrique*. A quick calculation on my mobile phone indicated a charge of USD 91 per night. I could afford that for at least a week, I assured myself. The good thing was that it included breakfast, but not lunch or dinner. The taxi took nearly thirty minutes to reach my hotel. I paid the driver 5,000 CFA and thanked him.

I checked into *Hotel Afrique* and was shown to my room. I called Clarissa, I called Mum, I called Dad, I called Ameley and I called all my other siblings. I had conversations with all of them. The average time for each of them was about thirty minutes, except Clarissa. I spoke with Clarissa for about two hours. She was the last I called. She told me how she missed me and how she prayed for me each day. I missed her too.

My telephone chat with Clarissa soon changed into a WhatsApp video call. This went on till late; well after ten o'clock. She lay in bed in her white nightclothes and looked as innocent as a baby.

Clarissa looked at me and I looked at her admiringly. As we chatted, she would smile at something I had said, and when she did, her dimples on her cheeks became prominent. Was I confused or was I just missing her? We chatted, phone-cuddled, and kissed each other goodnight, several times.

The next morning was a Sunday. I asked directions to the nearest church, although I would have preferred asking for a Catholic church, at that moment, any would do. I was lucky. The nearest church was a Catholic one. A brochure on the church at the hotel indicated to me that mass would start at ten o'clock. I attended the morning mass at the *Cathédrale Centrale de Ouagadougou* that morning.

The mass was sung in French. Even though I had forgotten quite a lot of the language I was taught in high school in Liberia, I sat through and used my limited French to follow parts of the service. I was also able to follow most of what was said in the sermon. I realised then how beneficial it was for me to have studied the language. I was one of the few who had taken the language seriously, while my mates played pranks on the French teacher, and laughed at his nasal tone.

I had now stayed at the hotel for nearly a week. I had paid nearly CFA 275,000 for the five days that I had been there and knew that at that rate I would soon run out of money. I had to find another accommodation before the weekend. I was now torn between checking in to either a guesthouse or an Airbnb. I realised how economical this would be in preserving money for the rest of my journey.

I decided to lodge at a guesthouse this time. I chose a simple one, *Le Palais Bleu*. It was a beautiful building painted in pure shimmering white. The windows were deep-sea blue in colour. Its architecture was Roman, with arches and curves adorning its walkways, verandas, and windows. It looked good and was going for only CFA 20,000 per night.

I said to myself I could afford this for another fortnight. I, however, needed to be sure of the exact date I would leave Ouagadougou for the next city or town northwards towards the next country, Niger. But I had not made that decision yet.

I moved out of the guesthouse and checked in into an Airbnb after a two- week stay. I had calculated my finances and that was the best option I had in the circumstances. Soon I noticed my cash level was getting low.

Should I leave now for the next city on my way upward towards Niger, or wait, work, and get some more money to replenish my cache before I set off?

The family I stayed with at the Airbnb were very kind people. They charged me just CFA 10,000 per week and provided me with breakfast and dinner as well. I felt at home. The landlords and their children, two boys and a girl, became my family in Ouagadougou. I was, however, aware of the fact that Ouagadougou was not my final destination, and I should not get too comfortable. I was travelling to London. That was my reality, and it pricked my mind from time to time.

I took the decision to work for some time in Ouagadougou to earn and save some more money before I set off on the next stage of my journey. With my little French, I got a job as a teacher at one of the high schools in Ouagadougou. The school was located at about a half-an hour's walk from my house. It was called *Lycée de Ouagadougou*. A beautiful school with about 300 students. Some were in the boarding house, and others were day students who commuted between school and home.

I taught English Language. My high school French Language became very useful all of a sudden. I started teaching five different classes. I taught English Language and English Literature. I did Geoffrey Chaucer's *Canterbury Tales*, Chinua Achebe's *Things Fall Apart* and George Orwell's *Animal Farm*, among others, with my students, for English Literature lessons.

Soon, I started earning some good money. I was aware I was in transit and used my money sparingly. I saved some good money.

I became very fond of one of my fellow teachers at the school. She spoke no English, not even a little. She was called Angelique. Not only was she stunningly beautiful, but very intelligent as well. She held a Bachelor's degree in biology. She told me she had aspired to enter a medical school and become a medical doctor but could not fulfil her ambition.

I was aware I had to reach London in time to go to my university in September. We were in January, and I always reminded myself I had some months to complete the journey. At the latest, I had to be in London by July. The worst-case scenario would be August. University would re-open in September. I would not miss it this time.

Angelique visited me at home frequently. In fact, she was there almost every day. We became really close pals. But I always had Clarissa's picture at the back of my mind. I loved Clarissa so much and would not want to lose her. I always found time to talk to her as often as I could. I have to be honest to say Angelique's presence sometimes frustrated that effort. I could not speak to Clarissa anytime Angelique was around me.

I had to be the tongue in this situation where I am located between two sets of teeth. I had to be careful not the be cut.

My landlord and his family kept feeding me for almost nothing. What I paid for rent would not even cover the food they gave me. I was most grateful to my new mum and dad in Ouagadougou. Not too long, I began to realise that Elise, one of the landlord's daughters, was making advances towards me. She became pensive anytime Angelique visited. After such visits, Elise would be cold towards me for a day or two. I tried to tolerate this for some time. One morning, my landlord called me and asked me whether I knew anything about a robbery that had happened in their house a couple of days before. The robbery took place in the front shop the family used to sell groceries such as sugar, bread, sardines, soap, other household items. I said no. I did not have any idea about the robbery.

Dad told me Angelique and I were the last persons to come home just at the time the robbery had occurred. It was his cold tone at that moment that made me realise the robbery had nothing to do with us. He was fighting his daughter's battle. If Elise could not have me, they would disgrace me, and embarrass Angelique.

They threatened to call the police and they did. The police searched my room and found nothing. They put Angelique and I in a police van and took us to Angelique's house. Angelique lived in the same house with her mum and dad.

Angelique's dad enquired from the police what the matter was. The police told them that they had a search warrant to search Angelique's premises. They spent about half-an-hour in Angelique's room and found a soap, the type that my landlord sold in their shop. They asked where Angelique got that soap from. She told them she had bought it from the nearest supermarket called SGGG. The police then took us to the local police station to interrogate us further.

After taking a statement of caution from us on oath, we were asked to go home without charge, and no further action would be taken against us. I was seriously embarrassed with the whole issue. A totally innocent person like me being interrogated by the police on suspicion of robbery. What if my parents and siblings heard of this. What would Clarissa say should she hear about this?

It had become crystal-clear to me after the robbery incident, that I continued to live with the family at my peril. I had overstayed my welcome and all the courtesies I enjoyed from my landlord and his family. I refused. In fact, I told them I would look after my own food arrangements.

Elise's mum appeared to be unhappy. I, however, suspected that it was a mere pretence. In truth, she did could hardly stand me, and I am sure she would prefer if I found myself new accommodation. I decided to leave the house. Indeed, the whole affair was a strong prompt that it was time for me to move on. Schools were about to start their mid-summer break. I made up my mind to go on to the next lap of my journey.

But what would Angelique say? What would be her reaction? Surprisingly, she was understanding. And we agreed to keep in touch, or she could even come to London when I settled. But what of Clarissa? Things were getting complicated.

I moved out of the Airbnb. I had stayed there for a month and a half. I could not go to stay with Angelique. I had to lodge at a hotel for one week. I had now made the decision to leave Ouagadougou. I was torn between going West, in which case I would be moving upwards towards my destination of London through the West African country of Mali. If I went East, I would be going through the West African country of Niger; but I could turn West towards Mauritania after reaching Niamey. I took out my map of Africa and studied it carefully. I then realised that I would still go through Timbuctoo in Mali to get me closer to the northwest, towards Mauritania.

The Mediterranean Sea was the only buffer between Europe and the North African countries of Morocco, Libya, Algeria and Egypt. Of these, it was Morocco that was closest to the continent of Europe. It had a very narrow portion of the Mediterranean Sea crossing into Spain. I needed to aim at reaching Casablanca in Morocco.

Going through Niger would enable me to move northwards much closer to these North African countries that bordered the Mediterranean Sea. A second look at the map confirmed to me that going through

Niamey in Niger would be taking my journey eastwards, and then turn northwest towards Mauritania, via Timbuctoo in Mali and then further North towards Casablanca in Morocco. Going eastwards further would be taking me in the direction of Tripoli in Libya via the vast Sahara Desert.

I needed to avoid Libya. I did not want to go via that route. I had heard so many unsavoury stories about how they treated migrants. I decided to travel to Niamey in Niger anyway, and instead of continuing via Agadez in Niger which would be leading me eastwards towards Libya, I would travel from Niamey towards Timbuctoo in Mali.

The other issue was should I travel from Ouagadougou to Niamey by road or by air. Travelling by train was completely out of the question. That part of Africa had no intercity or international railway links. The roads were poor. Most of them were not even tarred.

Angelique was still looking morose knowing that I was going to travel and leave her behind. I assured her I would be in touch when I reached Niamey; and also, ultimately when I arrived in London. I kissed her goodnight in my hotel room and we both slept off.

The distance between Ouagadougou and Niamey was 536.7 kilometres. The journey by road would take a minimum of eight hours thirty-three minutes Angelique saw me off to the coach station. The coaches were in different categories. There were the VIP coaches that had air conditioning in them. There were the Red Coaches which were comfortable to travel by as the seats could easily convert into mini beds for passengers to relax on during the journey.

There were also the 23-seater and 33-seater Mercedes Benz buses which plied the same route. They were the cheapest and had no air conditioning in them. I decided to take the VIP coach. The fare was CFA 60,000. That was just about USD 100. I could easily afford that. We took our seats. The coach was full; 56 passengers in all.

The station master blew his whistle, quite akin to what is done at the railway stations in Europe, and the coach slowly exited the station and sped off.

We were on our way to Niamey in Niger. I was on the next leg of my journey to London. We set off at about 10 o'clock in the morning. I got a comfortable seat at the rear of the coach. I pulled out my map again and looked at the route the coach would take to our destination. We had to travel through about six major cities: Ziniaré, Kaya, cross a river at Bouroum, Dori and then the border town of Seytanga.

The VIP coach lived up to its standard. It was indeed a VIP coach quite comfortable with a washroom situated at the middle position of the coach. For about 45 minutes, we travelled on black tarred road. After that, the road was all red earth. Billows of red earth filled the air anytime another vehicle sped past us.

I sat in the last row at the back of the coach with four other passengers seated to my right. I spoke some French and was, therefore, able to engage in or respond to conversations my fellow passengers invited me to join in. Seated next to me was a beautiful lady about 25 years old. She spoke to me in exquisite French. I responded with my high school French. We understood each other though.

She asked me where I was from and where I was going to. I told her I was going to Niamey. She then asked whether I was a Niger national. I answered in the negative and told her I came from the Republic of Liberia. She continued to ask me what I was going to do in Niamey. I told her I was on my way to London in the United Kingdom by road. She looked at me and was quiet for about 60 seconds. Then she spoke again.

"How is that possible?" She asked. "And why did you not go by air?" She concluded. I told her that was the plan originally but circumstances beyond my control and original plans made me take this route. I explained to her how I intended to go through Morocco into Spain; and from there find my way towards London. She nodded at me in an absentminded manner.

Soon the VIP coach reached Ziniaré, where we had our first stop. We all got down from the coach into a sort of shopping area full of restaurants and cafes. The time was past midday. A good time to have lunch since I had my breakfast at the hotel in Ouagadougou.

I sat down with Fatima, as I later got to know her name was. I bought lunch and we ate. She told me she was a medical student training to become a medical doctor. Her university was in Ouagadougou, although she was a national of the Republic of Niger. She spoke some good English too.

We set off on the next leg of our journey. Two kilometres away from Ziniaré, the coach started to move slowly. It was moving at about 15 kilometres per hour instead of the 70 kilometres per hour. Soon, the vehicle came to a dead halt. The driver spoke to us on the internal public address system:

"There is a problem with the engine of this vehicle," he said in French. "The coach would not move until engineers came from Ziniaré to repair it," he concluded. We all got down from the coach very disappointed. Most of the passengers were annoyed and did nothing to hide that fact.

There was no shopping mall around where the coach had broken down. It was thick bush on both sides of the road, and there was no shelter. We could also not walk back to Ziniaré as it was quite a distance and would take some time. We had no choice but to hang around in the bush until the coach was repaired.

I found a little clearing in the bush where we stopped. Fatima and I sat down on the green grass and continued our conversation from where we left it at the restaurant where we had lunch. Fatima told me about her whole family and what they did. Her father was a medical doctor in Niamey, having trained in Lyon in France. Her mother was a midwife who also trained in Paris, France.

She had four other siblings. They were five in all; two boys three girls and she was the last born. I also told her the story of my life; from Bopolu to Monrovia, then to Kasoa in Accra-Ghana, Ouagadougou and now on the journey to Niamey. She listened to me with great interest as she stared straight into my eyes as I spoke. She occasionally smiled, and when she did, beautiful dimples prominently appeared on both sides of her cheeks. She reminded me so much of my lovely Clarissa back in Monrovia. But I had no business telling her about Clarissa.

It was now approaching three o'clock in the afternoon and no engineers had arrived. At four o'clock, the driver of the coach informed us that a replacement coach would be coming for us. We remained there till eight o'clock and still there was no coach to take us on the remainder of the journey. We were told we had to spend the night at a hotel in Ziniaré as no coach would be available until the following day.

Most of the passengers were not amused. Some complained of missing meetings scheduled for the next day. The coach company apologised profusely. Three 33-seater Mercedes Buses belonging to a hotel in Ziniaré came to pick us. The coaches had *Hotel Serafina* written on them. And that was also the name of the hotel. We were checked into our hotel rooms, all 56 of us. My room was on the second floor and Fatima was on the third floor. We had dinner together and went back to our rooms.

We waited all day the next day for the coach replacement, but no coach came for us. We had to stay at the hotel for another full day. Fatima and I took the opportunity to explore the town of Ziniaré. We went to the local cinema after dinner. Earlier during the day, we went for sightseeing by the shores of the *Nokonbe* river that ran through the city.

We saw fishermen casting their nets in the river. When they pulled in their nets, we could see they were full of big fishes. Some tried to escape back into the river and were smacked with the paddles the fishermen used to propel their boats. By the river bank there were a series of stalls fitted out with gas stoves and burners where fish caught could be grilled. Fatima paid for a good-sized doctor-fish. The cook knew her art. The fish was cooked firm on the outside, but soft and tender inside. We wolfed it down with pepper sauce and couscous for lunch.

Just as we were finishing lunch my phone rang. It was Angelique calling from Ouagadougou. "Have you reached Niamey?" I answered in the negative. I narrated the full story to her and she sympathised with me. No sooner had I finished speaking with her than the phone rang again. This time it was Clarissa. I had not spoken to her for a whole week. I excused myself and spoke with Clarissa. We spoke for about thirty minutes.

Fatima did not ask me who I was speaking with. She was so gentle and a well-behaved lady. We chatted for a few more minutes at the lunch table and then proceeded to where the other passengers were gathered waiting for the replacement coach.

The replacement coach had arrived. We embarked on the coach and continued our journey towards Niamey. Fatima was just blissful to talk to. Our conversation never stopped until we reached the next rest stop which was in a town called Kaya. Kaya looked like a predominantly industrial town. There were several factories built around what looked like an open space within a grassland. Billows of thick black smoke billowed from the some of the factories' chimneys.

Due to the time wasted during the breakdown of our first coach, our stay in Kaya was not long. We stayed in Kaya for only fifteen minutes.

We stretched our legs and arms, had some fresh water to drink, and got back on the coach. Still trying to make up for the time wasted, the driver decided to skip our next rest-stop which was Bouroum. We only looked at Bouroum town from the distance from the windows of our coach.

Three more hours of driving non-stop brought us to the town of Dori, from where we descended towards the border town of Seytanga. We all alighted from the coach and showed our passports to the *Garde-Frontiéres* who were guarding the border between Burkina-Faso and Niger. As we walked across the border into Niamey, we passed the *Douanes* (customs) and the Douaniers (customs officers) who sat idly and watched us walk pass. We were now in the republic of Niger territory.

We were in a little border town called Téra. Téra looked like a commercial hub. There were brisk businesses with motor bikes ferrying passengers across the border in both directions. There were also the *Goro Boys* who had no job doing at the border other than harassing passengers crossing the border with offers of taking them across safely for modest fees.

Their main targets were people crossing the border without valid travel documents like passports, identity cards or a *laissez-passes*. All the passengers on my coach had valid travel documents. And so, we crossed the border into Niger without any incident.

We boarded the coach again, after customs and immigration, and left Téra heading towards Niamey, the capital city of Niger. The road network from Téra towards Niger had black asphalted coating for just about 15 kilometres. After this point, it was red earth till about an hour and half drive, till we hit another black asphalted portion that led to the ferry where the river *Sirba* flowed into the huge Niger River. The ferry was late. It was now about ten o'clock in the night. We joined a convoy of about a dozen other coaches which were all lined up waiting for the arrival of the ferry. We waited for an hour and still no ferry appeared. Suddenly, there was an announcement on the public address system that the ferry s e r v i c e for the evening had been cancelled. Fatima was sitting next to me. I looked her in the face and she did the same. I said nothing and neither did she. We shook our heads and gave wry smiles.

The mosquitoes at the waiting area were ferocious. Fatima had a piece of cloth that we shared to keep the mosquitoes at bay. It was not big enough so we had to sit really close. We slept sitting on the bench, trying to stay within the small piece of cloth, and swatting away the smart mosquitoes who moved their attack to our faces and the back of our necks.

Finally, we gave up on any attempt at sleep. The weather was humid and I decided to take a shower in the facility provided at the waiting area. I came out refreshed and convinced Fatima to do the same. An hour later, at six o'clock, the ferry finally arrived. We boarded the ferry on foot as our coach and the other ones drove slowly to take their positions on the ferry.

All twelve coaches and some smaller vehicles also came on the ferry. Soon the ferry set sail, and after an hour's sailing on the huge *Niger River*, we disembarked, bordered our coaches back and headed towards Niamey in Niger. We reached Niamey at about ten o'clock that same morning. Thus, the journey that ought to have taken eight hours and a few minutes, ended up taking twelve hours.

Chapter 5
Niamey

I retrieved my suitcase from the belly of the coach and waited for Fatima to do same. We walked a few metres away from the coach station and found a café. I ordered coffee and sandwiches and Fatima opted for oats porridge. When her oats came, it looked so appetising and I changed my mind and had porridge too. It came with toast and scrambled eggs. It was a good breakfast.

"Where are you going to stay in Niamey and for how long would you stay?" Fatima asked me. I told her I was not going to spend more than a week in Niamey. She said, in that case, she could accommodate me in her family house.

"What would your parents say when they see me with you in your house?" I asked. She replied that her parents were cool, and that there was no problem. In fact, Fatima had already rung the mother and briefed her on the stranger she had met onboard the coach, and who was on his journey to London by road. Fatima's mum had also briefed her husband and both were aware of my impending presence.

I was not sure myself though, as to whether I should accept Fatima's offer. The idea of going to either a hotel, guesthouse or an Airbnb passed through my mind. I also thought of how much money that would cost me and how much money I would save if I accepted Fatima's proposal. I was aware of the expenses ahead of me on the next leg of my journey.

She was emphatic on that point. I felt a little uneasy at her huge eagerness to stay close to me. It made me think of Clarissa with guilt. And I also thought of Angelique.

However, thoughts about my fees at the London School of Economics was enough to change my mind. The fees were not cheap. This was the university that very many former African leaders had attended, and their children and grandchildren too. I wanted to march with these people and their ilk. After a few minutes of deliberating on this issue, I accepted to go in with Fatima. At least I was not going to share a room with her.

Fatima's family residence was imposing. It was a magnificent building that stood on a hill a few kilometres from the Niamey Airport. It was built with red bricks, in the style of houses in the United Kingdom. It was a storey building with five bedrooms at the top, and a guest room, complete with toilet facilities, on the ground floor of the building. It had two outhouses (boys' quarters), and a security post at the gates.

When we entered the gate, Fatima's parents and her other two siblings, a girl, and a boy—came out of the house to meet us. All of them embraced Fatima and gave her *bisous* on both of her cheeks. I was not used to *bisous* back home in Liberia, but having spent some time in Ouagadougou, I had learnt the style and managed to do credit to myself.

We sat in the *piasa*, a huge sitting room, cooled by the air conditioners. We exchanged greetings and Fatima introduced me. Both Fatima's mum and dad asked me why I decided to travel to London by road, when I could have done it in six and a half hours by air. I told them about my love for adventure. I also told them of the story of an individual who had accomplished this feat in the 1970s and then lived in France.

From their facial expressions, they were still sceptical, but for the gentleman and lady that they were, they did not press me for more details and nodded their heads rather absentmindedly without further questioning.

The houseboy ushered me into the room I had been offered. My room for at least the next week or two. It was the guest room complete with air conditioning and toilet and shower. Fatima had finished her semester exams and would not be going back to university until September that year. From the many plans she tried to include me in, it was plain to deduce she would like me to stay in Niamey with her till it was time for her to return to school.

However, by the same September, I had to be in London to start my Master's degree programme at the London School of Economics. We had dinner that evening. The food was delicious; succulent veal on a platter of braised rice, with Niçoise Salad as a side dish. I ate to my satisfaction as apart from the grilled fish at the riverside, we had hardly had a decent meal since we left Ouagadougou. Fatima stayed and chatted with me for a while in the living room and then we bade each other goodnight.

She climbed the stairs to her room upstairs and I walked lazily to my room on the ground floor. It was now about eleven o'clock local time. I had a shower, put on my pyjamas, said my nightly prayers and lay down on my bed. But then I thought of the next leg on my journey. I took out my map and studied it. I realised that from Ouagadougou to Niamey, I had travelled eastwards. But Morocco, which was my penultimate African country before I entered mainland Europe, lay to the West.

Thus, from my map, it was clear to me I had to travel in the direction of north-west if I was going to go in the direction towards Morocco. What that meant was that the next major city of my journey would be Timbuctoo in Mali via Gao. I was aware of this. The distance between Niamey and Gao was 440.7 kilometres and was to take six hours and forty-one minutes to reach by road. The distance between Gao and Timbuctoo was 612.3 kilometres and that journey would take nine hours forty-seven minutes to complete. I put away the map and went to bed.

I slept like I had carried building bricks for an entire day. The tiredness from the journey from Ouagadougou to Niamey contributed greatly to this. I did not stir in my sleep.

I joined Fatima and the rest of the family at the breakfast table at about half-past-eight in the morning. There was a variety of breakfast choices on the table. Among them were scrambled eggs, porridge, French baguette (bread) butter, cheese, marmalade, coffee, and tea.

I had a little of every food item on the table. The two of us were left at the dining table. Fatima suggested we go see downtown Niamey. I agreed, but before we could make a move, Fatima's mum and dad stopped us in the hall. It seems they were still curious about me and wanted to ask me some more questions.

It was not hard to talk about myself, and their quiet attention spurred me on. I told them about the war in Liberia, which they said they had followed on the international news media. I told them about how me, my parents and siblings walked from Bopolu in Northern Liberia to Monrovia in the south after we were chased out of our village in by rebel soldiers.

I told them about how we met a young man in the bush who had also ran from the rebel soldiers. I told them about how the family of that young man were killed and he alone survived and was subsequently caught and kept captive. I told them about how this young man became our de-facto family member and hosted me and my family for a long time in Monrovia. I told them about my university degree, my profession ,and my work experience in Monrovia. I did not tell them about Clarissa; it was not necessary.

I then changed to my journey from Monrovia to Kasoa, Accra Ghana, Ouagadougou and then Niamey on my way to London. I finished my narrative by telling them the next leg of my journey would be to Timbuctoo in Mali, from there I would journey up towards the north-west until I reached Casablanca in Morocco, and thence Tangiers, which would be my last African city before I crossed the Mediterranean Sea, into southern Spain.

They then asked me what my mission in London was. I told them I had gained admission into a university-London School of Economics-where I was to pursue a Master's degree in business administration. They nodded their heads almost simultaneously in an apparent approval of my mission. They, however, appeared not to be so much in *d'accord* with my *modus operandi* of travel to London. Notwithstanding, they both wished me the best of luck with my plans and retired upstairs to the balcony.

Fatima had waited patiently and listened with rapt attention as I explained myself to her parents. Just when she took my hand to head out of the house, my phone rang. It was Clarissa. I did not answer the call. I sent her a text message that I would call her in the evening. I asked her to expect my call at about ten o'clock Monrovia local time.

As we stepped into the front yard, my phone rang again. This time it was Angelique. I followed the same procedure and texted her to expect my call in the evening.

We set out to Niamey City Centre. We took a taxi that drove past the Diori Hamani International Airport which stood about 300 metres in the far distance. Soon we reached the city centre. The city was rather small. It was not as big as Accra, Lagos, or Abuja. Most of the ground was red earth that rose into a fine dust into the atmosphere anytime the wind blew or a vehicle passed.

As we got off the taxi at the city centre, we were surrounded almost immediately, by children and middle-aged women begging for alms. I had a CFA 1,000 note in my hand. I gave it to one of the children. Suddenly, another child standing by started wrestling the CFA 1,000 currency note from the one I handed the money to. I separated them and found another CFA 1,000 for the other child. Niamey lies on, on the eastern bank of the Niger River. It had a population of 978,029 in the most recent census. The Niamey Capital District covered about 670 km² and had about 1,026,848 people. Noticeable in the city's centre were groups of poor, young, or handicapped beggars. It was, however, a modern city and served as the administrative, cultural, and economic centre of the country.

A major attraction in the city of Niamey was the Niger National Museum, which incorporated a zoo, a museum of vernacular/traditional architecture, a craft centre, and exhibits including dinosaur skeletons and the Tree of *Ténéré*. The *Ténéré* Tree (French: *L'Arbre du Ténéré*) was a solitary acacia, of either *Acacia raddiana* or *Acacia tortilis*, that was once considered the most isolated tree on earth—the only one for over 400 kilometres (250 miles). It was a landmark on caravan routes through the *Ténéré* region of the Sahara Desert in northeastern Niger.

Other places of interest included the American, French and Nigerien cultural centres, seven major market centres (including the large Niamey Grand Market), a traditional wrestling arena and a horse racing track. Most of the colourful pottery sold in Niamey was hand made in the nearby village of *Boubon*.

We visited the local zoo, the national museum and walked about one kilometre to the Tree of *Ténéré*. There was the belief that just a simple touch of the Tree of *Ténéré* brought good omen to people who touched it. So, I approached the tree and touched the trunk as well as the leaves.

That reminded me of the story I had heard of the same experience tourists have at Harvard University in Boston, Massachusetts in the USA, when they touched the shoes of John Harvard. There too it was believed that the act of touching the feet (shoes) of the statue of John Harvard brought good luck and prosperity.

We went for lunch in a small but impressive looking restaurant. The starter was *Soupe àl'oignon*. This was a traditional French soup made of onions and beef stock, usually served with croutons and melted cheese. Our main course was *Boeuf Bourguignon*. This was essentially a stew made from beef braised in red wine, beef broth and seasoned vegetables including pearl onions and mushrooms.

It was my first time of eating such food, but it was delicious and I enjoyed every bit of it. Fatima, on the other hand, had eaten it several times and it was her favourite anytime they went out for dinner as a family. We had chocolate *soufflé* for dessert.

We left the restaurant about half-past-two in the afternoon. Fatima wanted to go and watch a movie. I agreed, although I was not really a movie person. She had been an excellent host so far, so I had to make concessions. The movie started around half-past-three. It was a Chinese film like the Kung Fu films we used to watch in Monrovia.

Apparently, Fatima liked such Kung Fu films. Surprisingly, I enjoyed the film. I did not get bored as I used to get whenever I went to the movies in Monrovia.

We arrived home just before sunset. It was about half-past-five in the evening. Dinner was already waiting for us. We had dinner together with the family. The food was the complete opposite of the French cuisine we had at the restaurant. It was predominantly African food with a Nigerien bias.

There was *Shinkafa*; dense balls of pounded rice served with meat and vegetable stew and *Tattabara*; flamed-grilled flattened whole pigeon. There was also *Deguidegui*; Tomato stew served with a mix of spaghetti and macaroni commonly known as *Maka,* and *Brochettes*, chunks of beef and mutton on a skewer cooked over an open fire.

I enjoyed the last two better than the first two. It was cultural cuisine at its best.

Fatima and I remained at the dining table and chatted for a while before retiring to our respective bedrooms. No sooner had I reached my bedroom than the phone rang. It was not Clarissa, and it was not Angelique; surprisingly it was Fatima. She told me she was going to have a shower and would call me in an hour. I said to her I would be expecting her call.

It was about half-past-eight in the evening. I was aware Angelique would be calling at about nine o'clock and Clarissa at about ten o'clock.

Fatima called exactly at thirty-five minutes after eight. I had taken my bath and was in my pyjamas and lying in bed. She asked whether I enjoyed our day out. I replied in the affirmative. I told her how I had enjoyed the various tourist centres we visited. I also told her about how I enjoyed the film. She also confirmed to me how she enjoyed my company on the day trip.

Fatima sked whether she could come to my room that night and spend about an hour with me. As if I had not heard her clearly, I politely asked her to repeat what she said because I did not hear her clearly. She repeated the same request. I reminded her of the presence of her parents and siblings in the house. It would not be appropriate if they saw her in my room at that time of the night, I told her. Fatima dispelled any fear or embarrassment and encouraged me to prepare to receive her. She said there would be no objection from her parents or siblings, even if they saw us. What if she was wrong and I was thrown out of the house?

It then dawned on me that Fatima was a pampered girl and could not do any wrong in the eyes of her family. I had wanted to give her the go-ahead to come into my room. But then my instincts kept telling me that was a wrong move. I was also expecting calls from Clarissa and Angelique that night. At the same time, I did not want to embarrass my host, who to all intents and purposes, had been marvellously kind to me.

Eventually, I convinced Fatima to come the next day instead of that day. She agreed and went to bed. Clarissa called and we spoke for about an hour. I also talked with Angelique for about half-an-hour. Both calls went well. I did not give any details of where I was lodging to either Clarissa or Angelique.

Fatima came into my bedroom at about half-past eight the following night as agreed. She sat on my bed as we chatted. She told me how she was fond of me and would want me to stay with her in Niamey for some time. I was cognisant of the fact that she would go back to university in September, and I would also do same the same month.

But as she would go to Ouagadougou as a continuing student, I had a long way to travel to London to start university as a freshman. She laid by my side on bed as we continued with the chatting. She held my hand and kept rubbing at them as she continued chatting with me. I was not only excited at that stage but was confused with fear. Suddenly, she pushed against my lips and kissed me passionately. I returned the compliments and kissed her passionately too.

We cuddled each other in bed for a considerable length of time. She enjoyed every bit of the cuddling and kissing, and so did I. She left my room for her bedroom just before the grandfather-clock in the living room chimed midnight. These nocturnal visits continued for some time.

It was three weeks since I had arrived in Niamey. I needed to start thinking of the long journey ahead of me. I informed Fatima of my intention to get going. She asked me when I wanted to leave. I told her I had already spent three weeks in Niamey, and that I should already have been my way.

Fatima asked me where my next leg of the journey would take me to. I told her I had to head towards Timbuctoo, enroute Gao. Both cities were in the Republic of Mali. She asked me to spend one more week with her in Niamey. I agreed.

A week before my departure from Niamey, Fatima and I went to town, as we were wont to. We went to the shopping mall. For lunch, we decided on a restaurant that served locale cuisine, and not on the one where we had French food previously. In fact, my three weeks spent in Niamey had made me accustomed to some of the lovely local Nigerien cuisine.

No sooner had we stepped out of the restaurant after the lunch than we were stopped by the Nigerian *Gendarmerie*. They spoke to us in fluent French. They asked us for our names. I told them my name and so did Fatima. To our horror, they told us of a robbery in a local bank, and the description given for one of the robbers fitted my looks.

"Good Lord," I cried out in English. My speaking in English exacerbated their suspicion of me being a suspect. Why was that? According to them, people and so-called eyewitnesses had told them one of the robbers spoke in English. Fatima defended me vigorously. She told the *Gendarmes* we had just finished having lunch at the restaurant behind us, and that she had been with me all the time. The *Gendarmes* were adamant.

They invited us to go with them to the local police station. Fatima called her parents immediately and told them of the horrible misfortune that was brewing against her and her visitor. Fatima asked the *Gendarmes* to wait for her father to come. The *Gendarmes* asked her to tell the father to meet us at the local police station. We followed them.

We arrived at the main premises of the *Police Nationalé*. I was thrown into a cell without even being asked one question. Fatima's father had just arrived. He requested to speak with the commander of the station. He did. He explained to them that I was their guest and was a friend of his daughter. He told the commander of the station that we had only come to town for lunch and sight- seeing. And that there was no way I could have been involved in a bank robbery. The commander, who recognised Fatima's father as one of the medical doctors at the main hospital in Niamey, sounded empathetic to my plight. He told Fatima's dad that he should not worry. He explained to him that he would make sure his officers expedited action on this case, and that it would be resolved soon. We had now spent nearly five hours at the police station.

I could see Fatima and the father through the bars of the cell where I was kept. There were other inmates in the cell with me. We were about twelve people in there; most uncomfortable experience!

All sorts of ideas and thoughts raced through my mind when I was behind those cell bars. Did I make a mistake of staying with Fatima all this time? Was God punishing me for something? Should I have continued my journey without spending all this time in Niamey? I thought of my parents and siblings in Monrovia. Did I make a mistake of not flying directly to London from Accra? I kept on praying to God as these thoughts raced through my mind. It was now getting to seven o'clock in the evening. Just then, the second-in-command (2IC) to the commander came down to the charge office and asked me to be brought out from the cells. Was I on my way home? Would I be released? Just as I was deliberating over all these possibilities, I was told there was going to be an identity parade.

I was confident, for I knew I was innocent. But when misfortunes strike, people could just push you into trouble of which you are completely innocent. Could this be the case here? I wondered. I kept reciting the first three verses of Psalm 27 in the Holy Scriptures in my head:

The Lord is my light and my salvation whom shall, I fear? The Lord is the stronghold of my life of whom shall I be afraid? When the wicked advance against me to devour me, it is my enemies and my foes who will stumble and fall. Though an army besiege me my heart will not fear; though war break out against me, even then I will be confident.

About eleven other young men of my age were brought in. They were going to be decoys whom I would line up with for an identification parade. We were lined up. But just as the process was about to start, the deputy commander's radio chattered into life. It was the commander himself. He asked his deputy to come to his office immediately. He obliged.

He came back with the news that there was not going to be any identification parade. All the eleven invited participants were asked to go home. I was still standing and waiting for what was going to happen next. Was I going to pass the night in these smelly and unhygienic cells? I knew my God would deliver me. I thought of Daniel; I thought of Shadrach, Meshach, and Abednego: all delivered from danger by God, according to the Holy Christian Bible.

I was confident, particularly as I knew that I was innocent. It could have been the case of a mistaken identity. I was thinking through these scenarios in my head. I quietly said to myself, "If God could deliver innocent Daniel from the lion's den; and deliver Jonah from the belly of the whale, why would He not deliver me an innocent person from this danger?"

Almost immediately, three thug-looking young men were frog-marched into the police station behind the counter. They were stripped of their main clothing and pushed into the adjoining cell to where I was kept for some time. Their faces were swollen which indicated that they were subjected to some severe beating. They looked perplexed and lost. Fatima, her father, and I were ushered into the office of the commander.

The deputy commander saluted briskly and was excused. The commander spoke to us in French. He apologised to me profusely for what he described as a gross mistake by the people around the bank as well as the *Gendarmerie*. The commander further informed us that the real robbers had been apprehended. They were three in number and all had been arrested and they were in the cells on the ground floor. He also told us that all the money stolen at the bank had been retrieved from them. More importantly, he said the three men confessed to the robbery and pleaded for leniency.

Fatima and I heaved huge sighs of relief almost simultaneously. At least I was not going to spend the night in a police cell for an offence I did not commit. I told the commander I had never ever been put in a police cell in my life. He again apologised and said that it was a routine process to put suspects into the cell on arrival at the charge office. He informed us of a compensation scheme for people who suffered mistaken identities and were found to be innocent.

He reached for a payment invoice for me to sign. I saw the sum of CFA 200,000 written on the invoice. Again, I used my high school French to read the narrative on the invoice: *Pour les inconvénients qui vous ont été causés à la suite d'une erreur d'identité pour un vol de banque*, which literally translated into English meant 'For the inconvenience caused you as a result of mistaken identity for a bank robbery'. The commander handed that cash over to me.

I accepted the apology and the offer and received the money. We all confirmed to the commander that his apology had been gracious. We thanked him, walked out his office downstairs and walked out of the station. At the door, were the two *Gendarmes* who arrested me at the shopping mall. Both walked to us, one took my right hand as if he wanted to give me something. Then they both said to me in not very fluent French, *"veuillez accepter nos sincères excuses."* I understood his statement as please accept our sincere apologies. I replied immediately back in French, *"Ne vous inquietez pas, ces choses arrivent."*

We arrived home at about half-past-eight that evening. Dinner was ready and waiting for us. I sat at the dinner table with the whole family We spent about just thirty minutes briefing Fatima's mum and her siblings on the unfortunate incident. They all agreed that it was an ill wind that blew me no good. They encouraged me to put the incident behind me and move on. I did.

Fatima stayed with me in my room that night. She did not go back to her room till about five o'clock in the morning. The pattern repeated itself intermittently till the day I was ready to leave Niamey. Fatima helped me to make a booking for a coach from Niamey to Timbuctoo enroute Gao. The distance between Niamey and Gao was 383 kilometres. I thought to myself that it was not as long as from Ouagadougou to Niamey.

I, however, realised that the road was desert land all the way. Red dust blew everywhere and the road was pot-holed. I changed my mind about the coach trip. A second look at the map showed that I could reach both Gao and Timbuctoo by a ferry on the river Niger. I told Fatima what I thought. She agreed with me and emphasised that would save me being drowned in clouds of thick-red dust if I went by road.

I cancelled my coach booking and booked the fast-speed boat to Gao by river on my way to Timbuctoo. Fatima saw me off at the quay side. Her eyes welled up with tears and she struggled to hold them back. I assured her that I would be in touch with her daily, and that when I settled in London, I would let her join me there, God willing. She kissed me a passionate goodbye. We embraced one last time and she turned and walked away from me. I walked briskly into my boat ready to sail on the huge River Niger to Gao. I said goodbye to Niamey.

Chapter 6
Gao

We set sail at about ten o'clock in the morning. Our boat, a powerful Catamaran passenger ferry, was a modern one which had an amazing speed. The passenger seats were comfortable and nicely laid out. The general ambience in the boat was something to write home about. There were restaurants, bars and even movie houses on board the boat. I felt comfortable.

I called my parents, Akogovi and the other siblings, and Clarissa and Angelique to inform them where I was on my long journey to London. I called Fatima last. This was because she enjoyed talking with me and would spend at least an hour or two on the phone with me. She was happy I was on my way to Timbuctoo. Reaching Timbuctoo would make me quite close to Morocco from where I intended leapfrogging the Mediterranean Sea into the south of Spain. I needed to continue going westward. But I needed to stop in Gao for a couple of days.

Looking out from my seat far into the horizon gave a wonderful montage of bushes and plenty of sand dunes that lined the banks of the river Niger. This picturesque view provided an apparent scene of the clouds touching the waters of the river in the horizon. Birds of different species and colours, some of which I was seeing for the first time, flitted over the river. The majority appeared to be seagulls who could rest fearlessly and comfortably on the surface of the water.

The river current tossed them upwards and downwards and they appeared as if they were in their own personal boats. The hue of their colours was distinct. Pure white, and sometimes laced with sea blue colours around their necks. They occasionally dived into the water for a short while as if they had located some fish they wanted to catch. We were told there were crocodiles also in the river, although I did not see any.

We arrived at the ferry port in Gao after a four-hour journey. The port also served as an international port of entry into the Republic of Mali. Bamako, the capital city, was well below us to the south-western part of the country. I was heading northwards and would not be passing through the capital city.

I showed my passport to the immigration officer and was let through without hindrance. I had not booked any accommodation for myself in Gao. I said that to Fatima when she called me in the boat. No sooner had I stepped out the river port than my phone rang; it was Fatima. She informed me that she had sent me a text message indicating a guesthouse that she had booked for me in Gao online.

I said thank you to Fatima several times over. I told her I had just come through immigration and would call her once I reached the guesthouse.

The guesthouse was called *La Maison Blanche*. I hired a taxi that took me directly to my guesthouse. It took about some thirty minutes' drive to get there from the ferry port. While checking in, the attendant asked how long I was going to stay at the guesthouse. Before I could say anything, she told me that Fatima had paid for a whole week for me. That's marvellous, I said to myself.

I signed for my room key and walked towards room number 057. The room was on the first floor of a 6-storey building. My room was spacious and clean. Clean modern toilets and showers and state-of-the art lighting. I was delighted. The day was far spent and I needed to eat dinner. It was about seven o'clock in the evening.

I called the concierge and asked the time the guesthouse restaurant closed. I was told dinner was served between five o'clock and half-past-ten. I still had time. I wondered whether I should have a shower first before going to have dinner. After a few minutes of thinking, I decided on the latter.

I went into the restaurant looking a bit scruffy and tired. My hair was unkempt and clothes dishevelled. As I approached the restaurant, one of the waiters met me at the door and ushered me to a table. There were few people at the restaurant at the time; Just two couples having a quiet dinner. I ordered *Tiguadege Na,* which is the national dish of Mali. The waiter told me it was good food and everyone who ate it liked it. It had two recipes. One was with meat and the other, which was vegetarian, was without meat. I opted for the one with meat. It was an okra bean soup which was also very typical of this region of Africa and was delicious. The food arrived in less than fifteen minutes.

I ate, and true to the recommendation of the waiter, it was delicious. I really dined my fill that evening. I went back to my room, had a shower and sat on the bed and watched a bit of television. As promised, I called Fatima. We spoke at length. She continued talking about how she had missed me. I assured her that it would not be too long before we saw each other again. To that she said a big Amen in English, with a thick French accent which got me laughing.

No sooner had she ended the call than my phone rang again. It was Ameley, my sister, calling from Monrovia. I discussed the latest leg of my journey with her. I, however, did not tell her, or indeed any of my family members back in Monrovia of my experiences in Niamcy. I did not tell Clarissa either. That night, I ended up talking to all of them, including Clarissa who I spoke to last.

I had a good night's sleep. The guesthouse had a policy by which guests were sent text messages informing them that breakfast was ready. I woke up, brushed my teeth, cleaned my face and torso with a warm wet towel, combed my hair, put a little talcum powder on my face and headed out of my room towards the restaurant. That morning, I had a millet-based cooked cereal, for breakfast. I also had scrambled egg and some bread with jam. I then had a cup of hot coffee. Back in my room, I had a shower, got ready and left for town. I had a tourist map with me. I was confident I could see my way around downtown Gao. There was no Fatima to show me around town; neither was there Angelique. Gao was a city in Mali and the capital of the Gao Region. The city was located on the river Niger, 320 km East-southeast of Timbuctoo on the left bank at the junction with the *Tilemsi* valley.

For much of its history, Gao was an important commercial centre involved in the trans-Saharan trade. I paid for and joined a group of other tourists to visit the great Askia Mosque. The Askia Mosque was a UNESCO World Heritage Site and worth a visit if you get to Gao. The late 15th century pyramidal tomb and mosque were built by Askia Mohamed for the emperors of the Songhai empire. The *Tomb of Askiu*, as it was also called, was strikingly beautiful to look at.

Our tour guide informed us that if we visited *Djenne, Mopti,* etc. and liked the mud mosques, we would appreciate the architecture here as well. Due to the remote location, the heat and perhaps questions over security, we found it was very quiet at the tomb—just us and the caretaker—though it was also a functioning mosque. Thus, whether the site was busy or not depended on the time of day it was visited. It was an impressive ancient building with a tranquil ambience.

Our next stop with the same tourist group was a visit to a large sand dune, *La Dune Rose,* on the west bank, opposite Gao. The view from the dune was terrific, the river was huge in the distance, and sailing in a boat on the river alongside the dune, the city of Gao looked like a toy model in the distance. We saw some small villages next to the dune as well as small settlements on islands dotted in the river. The endless plains of the desert with only sand and shrubs, seemed to stretch as far as one could see; this was more or less the southern border of the Sahara Desert.

In fact, it was confirmed to us that, that was the starting point of the great Sahara Desert. Later that afternoon, the dune appeared more beautiful; this was because of the shades brought about by the setting sun. *La Dune Rose* probably was the biggest dune in Mali, at least the most well-known and I would say also probably the most beautiful dune in this part of Africa. I got back to my room at the guesthouse totally exhausted.

This time around, I decided to have my shower before going to have my dinner. I had local Malian food this time—*couscous* and an *okro-* based soup. The couscous tasted like *gari* (dry roasted grated cassava) that I had the opportunity of eating when I was in *Kasoa* in Ghana. It was delicious.

My mobile phone rang. I answered the call. It was not Clarissa. It was not any of my family members in Monrovia. It was not even Fatima. It was a young man who was in my tourist group during the visits to the tourists' places in Gao earlier in the day. His name was Gameli. He told me he hailed from Keta in the Volta Region of Ghana. We spoke for only fifteen minutes.

He asked me how long I was going to stay in Gao. I told him I intended staying for only a week. He told me the Gao tourist centre operated daily boat-rides across the river by the sand banks to an island just about 300 metres from the shore. He asked whether I would be interested. I asked him to call me in the morning, when I would know whether I would want to go or not. He obliged and thanked me.

We met the following morning at the riverside. We arrived there at about ten o'clock and the boat set sail about an hour later. The boat was relatively small. It was nothing close to the Catamaran that I took from Niamey to Gao.

It sat only 15 people at a time. That part of the river was comparatively shallow. The average depth was not more than six feet for the 300 metres distance from the riverside to the island.

There were times also that the depth of all the 300 metres of the river from the shore to the island could be as shallow as two feet. And anytime that happened, most tourists preferred to wade through the river, all the 300 metres to the island and back. Anytime the depth of the river went so low, boat operations were halted. They only resumed operations when it was high tide again; and the river was about six feet deep.

We alighted from the boat at about a quarter past eleven that morning. There were a few tourist shops on the island. There were a variety of African arts and crafts in the shops. Good oil paintings spectacularly depicting the desert sand, the river Niger, and the Askia Mosque were among many of the paintings that were on sale. There were restaurants and snack bars scattered about the island. The island was about 2 kilometres in length and breath.

Gameli and I spent some good time on the island. We had lunch together. And it was during this lunch together that he told me that he was also on a journey to Europe. He told me about his journey from Accra. He talked about how he flew directly into Niamey from Accra, and then continued the same day from Niamey by air to Gao. He said he could not get a direct flight from Accra to Timbuctoo, and how there were no direct flights at the time from Niamey to Timbuctoo. The only available flights were from Niamey to Bamako, the Malian capital. I asked him the country he was going to. He said Italy. "Why Italy?" I curiously asked. He explained to me that he had some friends from high school who had been living there for a few years; and that they always pressured him to try and find his way there.

He said they assured him of better jobs, living, and indeed greener pastures over there. He, however, confessed to not having enough funds to purchase an air ticket to take him directly to Italy, and consequently, he had to go by road.

He asked what my target destination was. I said to him I was on my way to London. I continued and explained to him that I had the means of travelling by air to London; but for some unknown reason I decided to go by road. I told Gameli I had to reach there a month before the month of September to commence a Master's degree programme at a university in London. We started walking back to the main riverside where we alighted.

We noticed that so many of the tourists had left. Most of them waded back to the desert sand bank where we bordered the boat in the morning. Alarmingly, we noticed that the high tide had returned and the river was deep. But no boat had come. It was about half-past-four in the afternoon. We waited for another half an hour and spotted a boat on its way to the island. The boat arrived but we noticed that the boat was old.

It was not as new as the one that brought us in the morning. We were about 15 people exactly left on the island. We managed to board the boat and headed towards the other side. But just about ten minutes into our trip, the engines on the boat stopped working. This made the boat drift with the tide in the middle of the river. The waves of the river's waters tossed the boat rather violently. It was disconcerting and uncomfortable.

The coxswain tried the engine over and over again, but it would not start. We remained in the middle of the river and at the mercy of the tide which was very high now was dragging the boat in a very fast current downstream, without any sort of control. Soon we noticed the boat was taking in water. Everyone started panicking and moving away from the flooded side of the boat. The coxswain radioed to the shore requesting a replacement boat to come urgently. The boat now started listing and was jerking from side to side as if it was going to capsize.

Gameli and I held on tight to the woodwork by the side of the boat. Suddenly, one more passenger in the boat stood up and moved from port to the starboard side of the boat. The boat immediately lost its balance and turned over; it had completely capsized.

There was pandemonium everywhere. I managed to still cling to the side of the boat, holding on fast while the rest of my body was submerged in the water. I managed to hold my mobile phone above water, although a few splashes of the water had hit it. I shouted out to Gameli asking where he was. He was right behind me also clinging furiously to the woodwork at the side of the boat. The slightest mistake and we would be washed away by the current of the river, which kept getting stronger.

Some of the people in the boat started swimming towards the shore which was just over 100 metres away. I could swim but not in a river as big as this. This was not a swimming pool and I would not risk it. I looked around, and almost every one of the 15 of us were holding on to a lifebuoy. For some reason, and by providence, the capsized boat, to which Gameli and I were clinging to keeping our heads above water, started veering in the right direction, towards the shore. I said the right direction because it was miraculously drifting to the riverside port where we boarded it.

A replacement boat met us just about 75 more metres to the shore. The rescue team on board the replacement boat, 6 in number, managed to pick all the floating passengers clinging to lifebuoys. Gameli and I were the last to be picked. I heaved a huge sigh of relief when we got on board. At last, we were safe, even if we had not reached land.

The authorities did not allow us to go our individual ways immediately. They held a short meeting with us. They apologised to us. They offered a hospital check-up to anyone needing one. They apologised for our wet clothes and offered replacement clothing to those who wanted any. Finally, they refunded half of our ticket monies to us. We were grateful.

After we left the meeting, I walked down with Gameli to the taxi rank. We took different taxis since we lived at different parts of Gao. I headed East, and he headed towards the West of the city.

Back in my room at the guesthouse, I said to myself that I had seen enough of Gao on my journey by road to London. I needed to leave as soon as practicable towards Timbuctoo on the next leg of my journey. I took out my map and studied it in detail. How would I like to travel to Timbuctoo? Should I travel by road, or by the same river transport that brought me to Gao from Niamey?

Going to Timbuctoo by air from Gao was out of the question. I did not even think of it. I either had to go by road or by the river. Eventually, I decided to go by road. How long would I be staying in Timbuctoo? I was aware I had to reach London at least a month before universities opened in September. But then I had all these travels to do, mostly through the desert, before reaching my first European city.

After breakfast I took a taxi to the coach station at Gao. I was on my way to get a coach to Timbuctoo. The distance was 612.3 kilometres and it would take the coach nine hours and forty-five minutes to reach there. While buying my coach ticket, I felt a gentle tap on my right shoulder. Who could that be? I knew no one in Gao. I turned and looked and it was Gameli, my friend from Ghana. I asked him what he was doing there. He replied he was also on his way to Timbuctoo.

I got seat number 52 at the back of the coach. Gameli got seat number 54 also at the back of the coach. One fellow passenger sat between Gameli and I. The coach took off exactly at ten o'clock in the morning. What that meant was, if the coach kept to its official timing, we would arrive in Timbuctoo at about ten o'clock in the evening. The coach gathered momentum. It was cruising at about 60 kilometres per hour. The road was a fully asphalted and dual carriage way- but for 10 kilometres only.

The road ran through a very long heap of desert sand. As the coach kept moving, trails of dust could be seen billowing behind it. There were other road users. Most of the vehicles plying the road were huge trucks carrying agricultural produce between countries. There were not many private saloon cars on the road. I did not speak to the young woman sitting in between Gameli and me. I did not want to engender another Fatima of this trip. I kept speaking over her to Gameli. I realised that did not show good etiquette. Before I could apologise to her, she offered to change seats with me so that I could sit next to Gameli and so we could comfortably carry on with our conversation. I turned the offer down.

This was because I felt a certain comfort and a secret excitement anytime the bus jerked or swerved, and she was pushed against me. That feeling was good. And it was only because of that feeling that I wanted her to stay where she was. I even stopped talking across her to Gameli.

Seven of the almost ten hours of our journey had passed. We had just under 100 kilometres to reach Timbuctoo, when the coach developed an engine problem. We all alighted from the coach. Was this déjà vu? My mind immediately went to the experience Fatima and I had on our way to Niamey.

It was getting late too. If we waited for a replacement coach to come, that could be coming the following day. What could we do? It dawned on me, and not for the first time, that my journey to London was very eventful. And I had not even completed half of the journey.

Some passengers took their luggage and started walking through the desert sands towards Timbuctoo. Was that practicable? Yes, it was. About 17 people started walking. I conferred with Gameli and we joined them. After walking for about one and a half hours, all 17 of us stopped at an oasis. There were very few houses around. But there were some huts scattered about a central part of the settlement.

One of them was a shop that sold drinking water. We all had some water to drink and continued on foot towards Timbuctoo. I was lucky my travelling bag was not heavy. Gameli had only a computer bag that he strapped around his shoulders. Another thirty minutes of walking through the desert sands brought us to yet another oasis. This time there were about twenty-five camels that were for hire. We were told the camels could take us more quickly than going by foot. This was not free. We were also told that the camels would not take us to Timbuctoo proper, but to a small town just 5 kilometres away where we could catch a ferry to Timbuctoo.

Initially, I thought that was a good idea. But then, I asked myself why I did not go by boat from Gao to Timbuctoo in the first place. We mounted the camels. All 17 of us and headed in the direction of Timbuctoo. My camel moved at a steady pace; not a great speed, but I was happy I was not walking in the hot desert sand.

All of a sudden, I heard a thud behind me. As I turned to look, both my small bag and I fell off the camel to the ground, following my suitcase, which had made the noise when it fell. I landed awkwardly on my right hand. I thought I had sprained the hand. I remounted the camel gingerly, and the journey continued. We reached that riverboat town within an hour or so. We all dismounted from our camels and headed for the ferry port, where we took the boat on the remainder of our journey to Timbuctoo.

We all reached the ferry port in Timbuctoo close to midnight. The place was awash with little motels and commercial activity was brisk, even at that time. Gameli and I quickly booked ourselves into a motel for the night. We were now in Timbuctoo. The next day, we would decide what steps to take on the next leg of our journey with Casablanca in mind.

Chapter 7
Timbuctoo

We woke up the next the morning, had our showers, and breakfast, and headed towards the centre of town. My travel map reminded me of the next city and the next leg of my journey to London. I intended to spend just a week in Timbuctoo before setting off on the next leg of my journey. Gameli and I lodged into a guesthouse. We were now in downtown Timbuctoo. Gameli and I went for sightseeing after checking into our accommodation.

I found out that Timbuctoo was literally built on sand. It was located right in the middle of the Sahara Desert. Many tourists come to the city to visit the university. Also known as the Sankoré University, it was founded in the medieval period and is one of the earliest universities on the African continent. The city itself was founded in the 11th century by the Tuaregs. Timbuctoo became a major trading centre—primarily for gold and salt, and slaves and ivory.

With its distinctive mud mosques rising from the sand, the town was a centre of Islamic learning and scholarship by the 14th century. Apart from the *Sankoré Mosque University*, there were also the *Djinguereber* and *Sidi Yahya* mosques. Today, Timbuctoo was an impoverished town, although its reputation made it a tourist attraction, and it had an airport, which made it easy to visit. Timbuctoo has been a UNESCO World Heritage Site since 1988. In 1990, it was added to the list of world heritage sites in danger, due to the threat of desert sands.

We decided to visit the Sankoré University on the outskirts of the city. So, we took a local bus heading towards the university town. Founded in Timbuctoo, sometime between the 14th-15th century, Sankoré was the oldest university in the country. It was also the oldest university on the African continent. The university buildings were all mud-based. The walls were reinforced with thick mud walls. There were spikes planted inside a dome of the outside walls ostensibly to hold the mud walls together.

This made it look like the Askia Mosque built by Askia the Great in Gao. We took a guided tour of the University. Timbuctoo's literary output was enormous and included works covering the history of Africa and southern Europe, religion, mathematics, medicine, and law. There were manuscripts detailing the movement of the stars, possible cures for malaria and remedies for menstrual pain. This was as historical as it was exciting. This really proved to me that tertiary education really started from Africa. Our guide told us that, in ancient times, many scholars travelled from Europe to come and study at the Sankoré University in Timbuctoo.

Gameli and I had lunch at the university cafeteria. Most of the tourists visiting the university also had their lunch there. School was in session and we mixed freely with the Sankoré University students for lunch at the cafeteria. A young university student sat by me at the lunch table. She was very dark in complexion and had beautiful white eyes. She wore an African tie-and-dye clothing which very much matched the colour of her beautiful skin. She concentrated on her food and studiously avoided both Gameli and I.

Gameli's mobile phone rang. He excused himself and walked towards the open area of the cafeteria to answer the call. I took the opportunity to politely greet the young lady sitting by me. I asked her what her name was and the country she came from. She was initially taken aback that I spoke to her. Then she smiled. She told me her name was Ayeshetu and that she was from Conakry in the Republic of Guinea. She was doing her first degree in the biological sciences. She then asked me exactly the same questions I asked her. I told her my name and the country I came from. She asked if I was studying at the Sankoré University. I responded in the negative. I then told her the story of my journey, and my ultimate destination. Not surprisingly, she asked why I did not go to London by air and chose to go by road.

She expressed surprise that I chose to go to London by road from West Africa; and that my choice could not only be a very long one but also a very painful journey. I defended my situation by telling her that I wanted a little bit of adventure. She nodded her head absentmindedly as if she understood my explanation. I gave her my phone number and where I was staying at the guesthouse. She packed her books and excused herself and went out. She told me she had lectures that afternoon, and that she would be in touch.

Gameli returned and we stayed on at the cafeteria for another thirty minutes before taking the local bus back to town. It was getting to four o'clock in the evening. As before, Gameli took another bus to his guesthouse, and I decided to walk the short distance to my guesthouse. I had a quick shower when I reached my room, decided to have a short nap before going for dinner. Dinner was served between the hours of five o'clock and eight o'clock in the evening. I woke up at about a quarter-past-seven that evening. I brushed my teeth and went down for dinner at the guesthouse dining hall.

I came back to my room after dinner. Angelique called and we spoke for about fifteen minutes. She was concerned that I had not reached Morocco yet, and that I was delaying too much. I assured her I would be on my way soon and would soon be in Morocco by the Spanish border. As soon as I ended my call with Angelique, the phone rang again. It was Clarissa this time.

Coincidentally, she also expressed the same concern as Angelique. I repeated the assurance I gave Angelique to Clarissa. I was actually expecting my latest friend, Ayeshetu, to ring. Instead, when the phone rang next, the call was from my parents, then my siblings, and then Fatima. I finished talking to them all. It was now past eleven o'clock at night. I was still expecting a call from Ayeshetu. Her call never came.

I slipped into sleep, woke up at two o'clock at dawn to check my phone. Ayeshetu did not call. "Did I fire a friendship blank this time?" I asked myself. I went back to bed and slept off till the next morning.

Just as I was brushing my teeth, the guesthouse telephone rang. I picked it up and asked the person at the other end to hold on a minute. I washed my mouth, got back on the phone and asked who was calling. The call was from the concierge of the guesthouse.

"You have a visitor," they told me.

"Who is it?" I asked curiously. The name came back as Ayeshetu from the Sankoré University. I was torn between surprise and bewilderment. I told the receptionist to send her over to my room. She came. I sat her at the writing desk and asked her to excuse me for a few minutes. I went into the shower and had a good washdown. I came out from the bathroom well dressed for I took all what I was going to wear in there with me.

I exchanged greetings with Ayeshetu in French. She spoke very little English. I reminded her of how beautiful she looked. She responded by giving me a captivating smile. As if by design, the dimples appeared on Ayeshetu's cheeks as well. They looked pretty. It brought me good and vivid memories of some of my earlier friends.

We went for breakfast together. Back in my room, Ayeshetu told me she wanted to take me out for sightseeing. I asked her whether she had a particular place in mind. She talked of the *Djinguereber Mosque* and the movies. I agreed. Ayeshetu took me to the town centre where we got on the local bus on our way to the *Djinguereber Mosque*. It was a huge tourist attraction. There were many tourists there walking in and out of the mosque.

The *Djinguereber Mosque* located in western Timbuctoo was a famous learning centre of Mali. It was built in the year 1327 and cited as *Djingareyber* or *Djingarey Ber* in various languages. Its design was accredited to Abu Es Haq es Saheli who was paid 200 kg of gold by Musa I of Mali, emperor of the Mali Empire. According to Ibn Khaldun, one of the best-known historical sources for 14th century Mali, al-Sahili was given 12,000 *Mithkals* (a unit of weight usually 4.25 grams in the Islamic world) of gold dust for his designing and building of the *Djinguereber* in Timbuctoo. The *Djingareyber Mosque* was made entirely of earth plus organic materials such as fibre, straw and wood.

Ayeshetu was standing by my side when a tourist came close to us and spoke to me. He asked me whether I was from Nigeria. I replied in the negative. He asked me where I was from and I told him. I asked why he wanted to know where I came from and what my name was. He said he was from Nigeria and I resembled a very good friend he knew back in Lagos. I was aware of what happened to me in the Niamey shopping mall, and so I was careful who I spoke to. I could not afford to suffer another humiliating incident of mistaken identity.

We left the mosque and Ayeshetu suggested we went to the local zoo before going to have lunch and then to the movies. It looked to me that my newly found friend in Timbuctoo was well prepared to entertain me. However, would our friendship just stop at the *Djinguereber Mosque*, the local zoo, lunch and the movies? I wondered. Even as I was enjoying

Ayeshetu's company and the trip, my mind was on other things. The calls I had received earlier had me planning the next leg of my trip, in my mind; the next leg of my journey which would be from Timbuctoo westwards heading north towards Casablanca in Morocco.

I was honest with myself; in that I was finding it quite difficult on which route to use towards Casablanca. I could go westwards at an angle of about 15⁰ through Nouakchott in the Republic of Mauritania. Nouakchott, the capital city of Mauritania, had a seaport with seagoing vessels. When push came to shove, I could just jump unto one of the merchant ships and head towards Casablanca. Alternatively, I could go at right angles, 90⁰ north through Algeria. But this route looked very long and almost the whole journey would be through the Sahara Desert. Thoughts of those endless dunes, and reports about the Tuaregs, who sometimes converted themselves into criminal gangs and robbed travellers dissuaded me from using that route.

All these ideas kept racing through my mind. I was also conscious of the reopening date of the LSE in September, and I had to be in London at least one clear calendar month before the university reopened.

As suggested by Ayeshetu, we went to the local zoo. The zoo was not as big as I expected. There were the African elephants, lions, tigers, desert lizards and snakes. We wandered around the zoo looking at the animals. It was interesting to watch them looking at us with stern eyes from their cages. There was a small crowd of tourists gathered at the lions' den. There was an off-tour area where the lions could be seen close-up by visitors.

The cages were sizeable, had a concrete floor and were protected with heavy iron bars. They had log and a wooden platform, for the lions to climb for exercise. There was also a water bowl and a place for food in one corner of the den. They were arranged in such a way as to facilitate their bodies being hosed down with water, both to cool them down and also clean the cages. We stood close to some of the iron bars where a huge male lion was sitting. He had a magnificent mane that started from around his neck and went all the way to the middle part of his back.

His eyeballs, bloodshot, stared at us as if he was thinking of how to pounce on us and the other visitors. One could literally touch his body through the iron bars. I turned back to tell Ayeshetu how beautiful but dangerous the lions looked. Suddenly, there was a loud cry and uproar from behind me. The lion had grabbed hold of the forearm of one of the visitors who tried feeding it with fruits. The young man pulled backwards as hard as he could. But the harder he pulled back, the more the lion sank its claws into his forearm. We could clearly see blood oozing from his forearm.

Ayeshetu clung to me in a clear state of panic as if the lion would break out its cage at any moment. There was nothing any one of us could do to rescue the situation. We all looked on helplessly. There were hysterical screams from a few of the visitors when the lion tried to pull the victim closer to the cage either to smell or taste the blood on his arm. But the screams seemed to distract the lion and prevent it from pulling the victim closer.

I tried to surge forward to help pull the victim backwards, but Ayeshetu held me back. "The lion may break out and get you," she said. I convinced her that the bars were strong enough to keep the animals at bay. I went nearer and helped the victim to keep pulling away from the claws of the lion. There were streaks of blood still oozing from the forearm of the victim and splashing on the ground. I kept holding on to him and pulling him back.

A zookeeper came running to the scene. In fact, he was the keeper in charge of the lions. The lions knew him quite well. He fed them regularly. And any time the lions saw him coming, the lions instinctively knew he was bringing them food. They would, therefore, run in his direction. He made his guttural noises by which he gathered the lions into one place.

Unfortunately, the lion had chosen this day of all days to be stubborn. When he didn't let go of the young man's arm, a collectively groan went up from the crowd. But the keeper had a Plan B. He had been followed by two other keepers who had wheeled in large chunks of meat. The lion keeper started hurling some of these chunks of meat into the enclosure. At this, the lion let go of the man's arm and went to feed. That saved the young man's arm from further damage. He was immediately rushed to the zoo hospital for treatment.

We left the zoo soon after the incident. We had lunch in a restaurant close to the zoo. Ayeshetu hardly touched her meal; she was still shaken by the incident at the lion enclosure. We hurried through the meal and headed towards the movie house.

It was a Friday evening and so the movie house was packed. We bought some popcorn and took our seats. The title of the film was *Super Django*. The entire film was in French with English subtitles. It was full of action, daredevil antics, and incidents. No one would dose off watching such a film.

Just as we all started to enjoy the film, the fire alarm rang. It was a continuous deafening blast of very high-pitched noise. Almost everyone in the theatre stood up, but there was a quick and loud announcement on the public address system for people not to rush out in panic. We were told to stay where we were, and we would be guided out. I guess the authorities did not want a stampede which could prove dangerous when people are trodden on. But then thick smoke started billowing into the auditorium.

Almost spontaneously, there were shouts of '*kayi, kayi*' in the local Hausa language. No one wanted to stay in the theatre and get suffocated by smoke. People started forcing the fire and emergency doors open. Ayeshetu held tightly on to my left arm as I tried to wade through the pandemonium towards a fire exit. It was not easy. There were rows of people in front of us. I encouraged Ayeshetu to hold on tightly to me as I persevered with my push towards the exit.

The smoke was filling the auditorium and with choking intensity. We could hear people coughing and trying to catch their breaths behind us. "*Kayi, kayi, magana yazo,*" people continued to shout in the local Hausa language as they pushed towards the fire or emergency exits closest to them. Eventually, the sheer force of the people in the theatre forced all the exit and emergency doors open.

We all broke out of the auditorium as though we were fired through the barrel of a gun. We were able to breathe fresh air once again. Our clothes had blackened spots from the black soot from the black smoke. Obviously, we could not continue watching the film. I used a handkerchief to clean some of the soot on my clothing as well as that of Ayeshetu. We left the movie house. We did not wait for any compensation or apologies from the authorities. We took a taxi and went directly to my guesthouse.

Lying in bed that night, I mused "My day has been full of activity, drama and excitement but I am not tired." I took my energy from my companion for the day: beautiful Ayeshetu. She wore a loose boubou, which though voluminous, managed to be revealing as well. Throughout the day, I had caught myself stealing glances at her petite but exquisite physique. She wore her long dark hair loose. Her pixie small dark face was made even more attractive by the crimson red lipstick on her lips. Ayeshetu could not go back to campus because it was so late in the night. More so it was a Friday and she had no lectures the next day which happened to be a Saturday.

I began to think of how my journey to London by road appeared to be getting filled with unpredictable and rather unpalatable incidents. "Long painful road to London," I said to myself. It was my intension to leave Timbuctoo on Sunday on my way Nouakchott in Mauritania.

We woke up to a very bright and sunny morning on Saturday. The gentle north-east Trade Winds blew across the Sahara Desert. One could see skeins of sand caught in whirlwinds far away in the distance. The sandstorm developed into all sorts of clouds: cumulus, nimbus, cumuli-nimbus, etc. It reduced visibility considerably and all vehicles plying the road had to do so carefully, and with their headlights on that morning. Malian National Television kept repeating weather warnings and the national weather was presented every half-an-hour.

I went for breakfast with Ayeshetu. We had a millet-based cooked cereal with bread, cheese and butter. The orange juice we had was sweet. It was freshly squeezed that morning and was so refreshing. We chatted a bit at the breakfast table after the meal and then went back to my room. Ayeshetu asked whether we could go out for the day for yet more sightseeing.

But she herself was quick in pointing out that the whole of Timbuctoo was under a siege of sandstorms. Consequently, we decided to wait and watch the weather and see whether it would improve within the next few hours. We chatted more and more over a game of Ludo. Ayeshetu told me almost everything about herself; her family back in Conakry, the siblings and how she decided to attend university in Timbuctoo rather than in Conakry.

I did same; I told her everything about me except Angelique and Fatima. I did tell her about Clarissa though, to which she tried to hide subtle signs of jealousy and discomfort. She asked me if I would be marrying Clarissa when I completed my course in London and went back home. I told her I could not know there and then.

I asked her whether she would rather I married her after my course in London. She grinned mischievously with a pout and replied "*Si*" which she followed with some flirtatious French words which I did not fully understand. But she quickly added, the decision depended on me.

All too soon, it was past midday and time for lunch. The weather did not get any better, but looked like it was getting worse. Did that mean we would be spending the whole day indoors? Soon the dark grey clouds began to form more ominously in the sky. It was going to rain. I had never witnessed rain in the desert. If it did rain, that was going to be my first experience of such desert rain.

The clouds became heavier and darker, and soon the heavens opened. It started raining as if water was being poured down from a giant hose. Heavy, torrential rain. We walked along the corridor into the dining hall. The food smelt nice. Saliva started flowing in my mouth. I swallowed a couple of times.

We had *Riz au graz*, a dish of rice, meat, and vegetables. The meal was delicious and filling. We washed it down with *jinjinbere*, a ginger and lemon drink sweetened with sugar. The rain was still falling, as we left the dining room. By the time we arrived in my room, the rain had become even heavier.

"We are stuck in here," I said to Ayeshetu. She replied in a soft voice and lay down. She fell asleep almost immediately. As I sat watching the sleeping beauty, I took the map to look at, to bolster my resolve to leave. I had made up my mind; I would leave the following day for Nouakchott. After I had made my travel plans, I put my travel map away and lay by Ayeshetu. Soon, I fell deeply asleep.

When we woke up, I told Ayeshetu I wanted to leave the next morning at ten o'clock. She said she wanted to spend one more day with me before I set off to Nouakchott in Mauritania. She also reminded me that the day was a Sunday and we ought to go for Sunday mass in the local Catholic church. She said she was a regular worshipper at the cathedral located on the way to their university. I expressed surprise at that, because she had a Muslim name. She explained her parents gave her an Islamic name, but she was actually a Christian. Thinking back, I was not too surprised. There was a Mohammed who worshipped with us in the Roman Catholic Cathedral in Monrovia. So, there was a precedent.

We had dinner a little later that evening. In fact, Ayeshetu told me, because of the heavy lunch, she did not want to eat anything heavy. So, we had tea and bread with butter for dinner. We talked deep into the night until sleep caught up with us.

We attended the ten o'clock morning mass at the *Cathedral de Marie* which was about fifteen minutes' drive from the guesthouse towards the Sankoré University. I said a little prayer for protection on the long trip I had ahead of me. I asked God Almighty to take control of the remainder of my journey to London.

We decided to stay in town after the church service. We visited other places of interest. The weather was very good. Brilliant sunshine and very little wind. There were no sandstorms like the day before. Neither was there heavy rain. We had lunch in the city, and after, I suggested to Ayesha we go to the movies at another movie house. She rejected the idea initially citing our experience of what we suffered the day before.

I convinced her that we should go to another movie house and we would be safe. She agreed and we went to watch a Nigerian romantic film. The film had a good plot and the story was good advice. I learnt some of life's lessons from the film. Back at the guest house, we had dinner, showered and retired to bed. I was going to travel the next day, Monday.

Ayeshetu was not keen on my leaving, but I had no choice. I needed to reach London on time. I explained the situation to Ayeshetu. I promised her I would be in touch throughout the rest of my journey, and also when I reached London. She accepted my position with reluctance, and we embraced and left the guesthouse for the coach station.

The distance between Timbuctoo in Mali and Nouakchott in Mauritania was 1,384 kilometres and would take me twenty-one hours going by road. That would be almost two days. It would be just one hour and forty minutes by air. The idea of going by air ran through my mind. I quickly dispelled the idea and decided to go by road.

Ayeshetu saw me off to the coach station after breakfast. I got my travel ticket. As I waited for the roadmaster to call us to board the coach, Ayeshetu and I stood aside from the crowd, holding onto each other tenderly. . Soon we were called to board the bus. I embraced Ayeshetu passionately and kissed her passionately on the lips, oblivious to the other people milling around us. I noticed that her eyes had welled with tears which she did not want me to see. I pulled her towards me one more time, kissed her on her cheeks and said to her *au revoir* in French.

I boarded the coach. My seat number was 52. I could see Ayeshetu still standing t where I left her. The engine revved, the gears grated, and we were on our way. I waved to Ayeshetu, and she waved back till we could see each other no more.

Chapter 8
Nouakchott

We left the bus station exactly at ten o'clock in the morning. The road was asphalted but there were heaps of desert sand on both sides of the road; as if they wanted to reclaim territory that they had lost to the construction of the road. The asphalted black road, this time, continued for a longer distance than that from Niamey to Gao. Exactly an hour into the journey, the compass on the walls of the coach indicated that the coach was travelling towards south-southwest instead of the southwest that I had planned on my map. What that meant was that we were going south instead of the north-west that I had planned.

I pulled out my map and had a closer look at it. The coach was vindicated. The map clearly showed that there was no route either north-west or westwards towards Nouakchott. There was not a single road layout in the northwest or western direction. The map confirmed to me that from Timbuctoo, we had to descend to Goundam, then Nlafounke and then, having travelled for about two hours, resume traveling westwards towards the town of Amourj.

By going that route, Amourj was the first town in the Republic of Mauritania. We alighted from the coach at Amourj and formed a queue to pass through passport control at immigration. I had my passport and vaccination card for yellow fever ready. When it was my turn, I presented my passport to the immigration officer. She was a beautiful Fulani-looking lady. She had curly hair and looked like a Caucasian and African mix.

She asked me what my final destination was. I told her I was travelling to London in Europe. She frowned in a typical African fashion, looked at my face again, stamped my passport without uttering a single word. I said to her *Merci* in French. She nodded the head admiringly with a grin on her cheeks, but still with that surprised look on her face.

After passing through immigration, we resumed our seats on the coach. I pulled out my map again. It showed me a long list of towns and cities we had to pass through before reaching Nouakchott: Timbedra, Aloun el Atrouss, Kiffa, Aleg, Boutlimit and then Nouakchott. These cities had about 300 kilometres between them. I noticed that, after the coach had left the immigration post of Amourj, the coach started climbing towards the northwest, exactly the direction I had planned to travel, and I was pleased.

We started climbing further towards the north-west after passing Kiffa, The next city was Aleg. We alighted at Aleg and it was about one o'clock in the morning. The coach driver told us before we alighted from the coach that he was tired and wanted to have a rest. He said we would resume the journey at ten o'clock in the morning.

A few of the passengers appeared disappointed. They appeared not to be pleased with the driver's announcement. But then, the majority, including me, appreciated the driver's respect for our safety. What was worse, a tired driver driving us into a ditch where our lives would be in danger, or losing a little time and arriving at our destination late?

Aleg was a fairly large town. The coach parked at the city centre where there were lots of motels specially designed for travellers in transit. I walked into one of the motels to book a room for the night. I heard someone mention my name. Who could this be in a strange land as such? I turned and it was Gameli.

Apparently, he was on the same coach with me and I had not had the foggiest idea he was on board. I walked with him into the courtyard where the rooms were located. I got room number 007 and Gameli room number 025. Other passengers from the coach also booked rooms at the same motel. I had a goodnight's sleep.

In the morning, I had a warm and soothing shower. Rejuvenated, I changed into fresh clothes and went for breakfast. I met Gameli at the breakfast table. For a moment, I wondered why I kept meeting Gameli at almost all of my in- transit destinations. He almost always crossed my path. Had he been trailing me? No, I did not think so. In any case, I greeted him warmly and had breakfast with him. I walked with Gameli to the coach station.

Most of our fellow passengers also walked with us to the same station. We reached the coach station at half-past nine in the morning. We were thirty minutes early and had some time to wander around the place. Just as we wanted to find a seat and sit in the waiting area, the announcement came on the public address system that our coach was ready for boarding and that all passengers should start boarding. I had hardly sat down than the announcement came.

It took exactly thirty minutes for us to board the coach. The coach driver stood by the entry coach door and was directing passengers. He looked refreshed and alert. He appeared smarter and his hair well combed; an indication that he had had a bath or a shower and tidied himself up nicely. His clothes looked clean and well ironed too. In fact, he looked more than ready for the journey. It was a good thing that he took the decision to have a rest.

All passengers were now on board the coach. The coach driver made a roll call. Everyone was present, no one was missing. The coach driver took his seat. He spoke on the loud speaker inside the coach. He apologised for the decision he took the day before to stop and have a rest at Aleg. But he also explained to us why that was the best decision he took under the circumstances.

Most of the passengers, including me, applauded him with the clapping of hands. And I noticed that, even the passengers who showed disappointment of the driver's decision earlier that day also joined in the applause. This indicated to me that all the passengers had come around to the decision the driver took. The driver thanked us for the applause, turned on the ignition and reversed in order to turn properly onto the road out of the coach station. He manoeuvred the coach skilfully out of the station and soon we were on the highway, on our way to Nouakchott.

We drove for about two and a half hours without a stop. The coach glided smoothly on the macadamised road towards the next town of Boutlimit. That was the penultimate town before Nouakchott. Apart from the driver's skill, it appeared the coach must have been new and well-maintained. The road from Aleg to Boutlimit was not asphalted but macadamised; a coating of gravel chips mixed with bitumen, yet one hardly felt the difference.

Soon we were in Boutlimit. We were to go down and have a rest for a whole hour. It had just struck one in the afternoon. It was lunch time too. I appreciated the one-hour break. That gave me ample time to go and have lunch and stretch my legs. I joined Gameli. I told him I was hungry and he said he was too. He however disagreed with my suggestion to go and look for a restaurant and said we should just buy food from the vendors who plied their trade from wooden stalls around where the coach had parked. We entered one vendor's joint. There were a variety of food items on display. The vendor had covered all the food items on display with clean white linen cloth to avoid flies perching on them and contaminating them.

I ordered some rice with fish stew and salad. I had earlier requested cassava leaves and potato green stew, a favourite way back in Monrovia. The vendor was totally lost as to what food that was; she confirmed this with a polite, *"non, nous n'avons pas cette nourriture ici,"* to me. I understood her perfectly.

Gameli also ordered the same food like me. It was not a restaurant but the surroundings were clean, and the food nutritious and tasty like home-cooked food. For a moment, I felt it was my mother who prepared that lunch for me. I missed them and Monrovia very much; especially, my rice and cassava leaves or potato green stew. We got back on the coach on time and drove towards, Nouakchott.

We reached Nouakchott after another one and a half hours. Overall, the journey that was to take twenty-one hours ended up taking more than twenty-four hours. But the delay was for a good reason.

Nouakchott was a harbour city. The city was built on the Atlantic Ocean just as London was built on the river Thames, or Egypt on the river Nile. Nouakchott was the capital and largest city in Mauritania. It was one of the largest cities in the Sahel region of Africa. The city also served as the administrative and economic centre of Mauritania.

Nouakchott was a mid-size village of little importance until 1958, when it was chosen as the capital of the nascent nation of Mauritania. The name, Nouakchott, could be loosely interpreted to mean 'place of the winds.' It was also the largest and the most populous city in Mauritania.

The country of Mauritania was generally one of the safest countries in Africa, particularly the coastal region from Senegal to the south and to Morocco in the north. Like Mali, Mauritania was mainly a desert country spanning the Arab Maghreb of North Africa and the western Sub-Saharan Africa. The country had a population of 3.1 million, divided between the Arab-Berber population to the north and black Africans to the south.

We got down at the main coach station. I needed to look for either a hotel, guesthouse, or motel to lodge. Nouakchott was a fairly modern and big city and there were lots of hotels and guesthouses around. I made up my mind to go in for an Airbnb or a guesthouse. I got one. It was a guesthouse located very near to the beach. It was called *Maison d'hotes Jeloua.*

Not surprisingly, there was brisk marine life and other activities there. There were fisherfolks pulling dragnets out of the sea daily, a view of ocean- going vessels arriving and setting sail from the country's main seaport, *Port de l'Amitié.* There were fishing trawlers departing and arriving in large numbers along the coast. *Port de l'Amitié* in Nouakchott was advantageously located at the crossroads of the routes connecting Africa, Europe, and America and was one of the leading public commercial ports south of the Sahara for ships sailing from Europe.

I developed a habit of going to the seaside and watching the ships set sail with their three very loud blasts that signalled their departure from port. Similarly, the huge ocean-going vessels, some of which had queued for days outside the harbour due to congestion sounding their horns as they entered port, ably guided by the harbour master in a tow boat.

Back in my guesthouse, I lay down on my bed and started calculating the days left for travel and arrival in London. I looked at my map again and I was happy with myself for deciding on the right trajectory or route towards Casablanca. The route going north from Timbuctoo at 90^0 north would have taken me through over 3,000 kilometres of desert land with virtually no roads, but heaps upon heaps of desert sand. The only people I could have met on the road would have been Tuaregs on camel back or driving their overloaded lorries.

Travelling more than 3,000 kilometres on camel back or in an open overloaded truck across the huge Sahara Desert would have been an absolute nightmare. The route at 30^0 west was a better one, and I was glad I made that decision. It was the month of March, I left Accra in December. That meant I had spent four months on the road; or better still, I was in the fourth month of the journey. So, if I were to reach London by the month of August and get ready for the university to reopen in September as was my plan, I would be on target.

That meant I had April, May, June, July, and August ahead of me to complete my journey. Another quick look at my map also reminded me that I had at least more than five more cities to cover before reaching the Mediterranean Sea on the Moroccan coast. I had to travel through the border city of Nouadhibou in Mauritania, into the next country on the west coast: Western Sahara.

In western Sahara, I had to go through their bordertown of Guernguarat on the Western Sahara side, then through Barbas until I reached the next major city of Dakhla. The next major city for me would be Laâyoune still in Western Sahara. From there, I had to cross into the border town of Tarfaya in Morocco where the next two major cities left would be Casablanca and Rabat. I would then reach my last African city of Tangiers, located on the Mediterranean Coast. I was elated at the distance already covered; I felt I was in Tangiers already.

As soon as I put down my map my phone rang. I picked it up. It was Clarissa. I told her I would call her a little later in the evening as I was just going to have dinner. She agreed. Barely five minutes after, the phone rang again. It was Angelique. She started by expressing how worried she had been about me for she had not spoken or heard from me for nearly two weeks. I apologised and promised to call her back later in the evening.

As if it was pre-planned, just as I put on a shirt and was about to go out for dinner, the phone rang yet again. It was Fatima. I went through the same drill with her and promised to call her back later.

I went down to the dining hall. Guess who I met at the dining hall: Gameli! I had not the foggiest clue that he was staying at the same guesthouse with me in Nouakchott. He also expressed surprise at seeing me. We had dinner that night. It was my first time of eating a proper Mauritanian dish. We had *Thieboudienne*, a coastal Mauritanian dish of fish and rice, which is considered the national dish of Mauritania. It was served with a white and red sauce, made from tomatoes.

I enjoyed the meal so much, particularly since I had not had a fish meal in a very long time. I went back to my room and Gameli went to his. As promised, I spent the whole evening on the telephone talking to my friends; first was Angelique, then Fatima, then Ayeshetu and finally Clarissa. I told them all where exactly I was, and the trajectory of the remaining legs of my journey. Not surprisingly, they all said I was making good progress.

Fatima and Clarissa, however, reminded me that I would have been in London long ago, if I had travelled by air, and not by road. As much as I told them I understood their points of view, I also made it clear to them that travelling to London by road was my choice.

I had some time on my hand and so I decided to stay in Nouakchott for a whole month. One day, I went to the beach where the fishermen were dragging their nets ashore. Out of sheer instinct, I joined them and was helping pulling the net. I was not a registered employee with the fishing company, but so it was with pull-nets that anyone could join in to pull the dragnet ashore. I was young and energetic. So, I made a good display of my physical strength in pulling the net.

When the net reached ashore, it was a big catch. Local women came in with big aluminium pans to carry the fish to the sandy beaches a bit further from the seafront. As I stood back and watched, one of the fishermen came to me and asked for my name. I told him my name. He thanked me for the good job I did and gave me an appreciable quantity of fish. It was quite plentiful and I was initially confused as to what I was going to do with the fish.

He also told me I would be getting some money when the fish was sold and people were being paid. I took the fish to my guesthouse and sold it to the restaurant owners. I got some good money for it. I went again the next day, and thank God, this catch was even bigger than the first. I went through the same drill. And so, I started making some money in Nouakchott. Though I had planned well and had enough money to get to London, it was comforting to have a safety net.

On my fourth day at the beach, the same man called me and told me the whole fishing company liked and admired my attitude to work. They asked me whether I would like to join their fishing trawler that went to fish on the high seas. They said I would earn good money and also get fish from that job. I thought about it for a few minutes. I agreed to go fishing with the trawlers.

I was not altogether green with fishing. I used to do some fishing in the sea when I was in Monrovia. So, I was not completely a stranger to the job. I joined the fishermen on the trawler. The trawler, for some reason, was named in English: '*The Fisher King*'. I was not sure what that meant in the English language; I, however, thought that whoever couched that name tried converting French into English. If that was the case, it was not a bad idea.

We went to sea. That was my first time of fishing in a fishing trawler. I never felt seasick. I was quite used to the sea when I was in Monrovia. My university where I studied was literally built on the seashore. Thus, I was used to seeing and bathing in the sea water just as much as I wanted to. The sea was calm that evening. I kept wondering why most fishermen who fished with trawlers preferred going to sea during the night.

After some time, I came to the realisation that night fishing enabled the catching of more fishes than during the day. This was probably so because of the warm nature of the sea water during the night. During the day, the African sun very gradually warmed up the whole of the Atlantic Ocean. This reached its peak just as the sun began to go down the horizon. Then when the atmospheric temperature dropped during the night and the weather turned cold, the reversal of the same process happened.

The cold night began to cool the warm sea and the process reached its peak as the morning sun broke out. That was why we had cool seawaters during the day in the hot sun, and warm seawaters during the comparatively cooler atmospheric temperature of the night.

That night, we cast the net over and over for at least three times. Our catches were stored into a large ice hold located at the stern of the fishing trawler. My job was to separate the very different species of fish caught, putting like with like. Thus, I put all snappers together in one container, all the barracudas into another container, all the tunas in another container, and so on. I enjoyed doing that.

The captain of the trawler was so pleased with my work-attitude. The fishes were then boxed in cartons and clearly labelled, '*The Fisher King Company*'.

The job of labelling also fell to me. I labelled the various boxes containing cartons of fish and entered their various total figures into a ledger. Those were my main duties anytime we went to sea. I was paid weekly and very well too. I had earned a lot of money from both my weekly wages and fish that I brought home to sell. I had virtually become a fisherman.

I had quite a bit of money on me. Judging from what happened to my money in Kasoa in Ghana when robbers raided my home and stole a great deal of the money I was travelling with, I decided not to keep these monies with me at the guesthouse. I opened an account with an international bank in Nouakchott. It was the HSBC bank.

I had now spent three weeks in Nouakchott. My plan was to stay in Nouakchott for four weeks. So, I was left with just a week to go. But then, I was being carried away by this fishing job where I was earning quite good money. I was torn between leaving after the coming week when I would have made the four weeks I had planned to stay in Nouakchott or extended it for another month.

I was also cognisant of the fact that I had London to reach in time to be able to enter university in September. But then it was the month of March going into April. Could I leave in the third week of April? I kept pondering over this which left me in a total quandary. "I would make a decision by tomorrow," I encouraged myself.

I was lying in bed that evening when my phone rang. It was Ayeshetu. She greeted me nicely and I reciprocated the greetings. She told me she had missed me; I said the same thing to her; in fact, I said to her that I missed her more. I discussed the decision I was deliberating on with her. She first reminded me of the importance of reaching in time for the impending university registration and commencement of my studies.

But then, after I had explained to her the time I had on my hand, she advised me to stay in Nouakchott for another four weeks. She, however, sounded a caveat to me; she said to me if I stayed for a further four weeks, then my journey from Nouakchott to the next city should be by sea. This was because going by road would be longer and more unpredictable.

Unpredictable in the sense that, the journey by road from Nouakchott to Dakhla in Western Sahara via Nouadhibou, Barbas, on the N1 international road would be very long and tiring. Furthermore, as had been the case on at least two occasions during my travel, the coach could break down. I agreed with Ayeshetu. My mind was made up. I would stay for another four weeks. Ayeshetu expressed the desire to fly into Nouakchott and spend those four weeks with me. I was excited about the idea. I told her I was going to send her an air ticket. She turned down my offer and said to me she was able to procure an air ticket herself.

Her university was on their Easter break and so she was not going to miss any lectures.

Ayeshetu arrived at the Nouakchott-Oumtounsy International Airport at about four o'clock Saturday afternoon. I met her and brought her to my guesthouse by taxi. It was about an hour's drive from the airport. We reached home just as the sun was disappearing beyond the horizon with beautiful fire-tinged clouds. In fact, sunset in Nouakchott was a beauty.

We reached home at about half-past-six in the evening. We decided to go for dinner right away. We had dinner and went to my room. Ayeshetu appeared tired. She had a shower, said her prayers, and went to bed.

She reminded me that the following day was a Sunday and that we would be going to mass at the nearest Roman Catholic Church. I had been to mass more than once in the nearby *Cathédrale Saint-Pierre*. So that was not a problem.

We set out to church after breakfast the following day. The cathedral was full to capacity and there were other congregants sitting and standing outside the church auditorium watching the service on screens mounted around the church precincts. We were early and so we got a very good seat in the church auditorium itself. The mass was celebrated by the local Archbishop. It was during Lent, and so there were preparations being put in place for first, Good Friday and then Easter Sunday. The Archbishop preached with great passion and would punctuate the sermon with humming hymns whose lyrics supported the homily. The service was very inspiring.

On our way home from the church, we decided to visit the local aquarium. It was a huge building with huge amounts of water divided into different segments, each holding specific varieties of fishes. We went to where the sharks were. There were a few sharks in their tank swimming in circles to and around all corners of the tank. One of the sharks was bigger than me and seemed to have its beady eyes on me all the time. It was quite unnerving.

Next, we visited the whale tank. I had never seen a whale before. I was awed by the whales which were more than twice the size of the biggest shark at the aquarium. We were told these were small, and some whales were four times the size of the biggest shark. We also visited the sealions. They behaved just like trained dogs. They acted as though they understood the commands from visitors, and moved too close to the glass barriers and drew the attention of visitors, by barks, growls, and grunts, as if they wanted to be petted. We saw the stingray. It was so huge. In fact, I had never seen a stingray so huge and was floating beneath the water quite close to the bed of the fish tank. We visited where the penguins were kept. It was a cool environment, to mimic their natural environment in the arctic. I had never seen a live penguin before, and I was excited to see one. They would dive into their pools, exit and shake out their feathers. They waddled about as if their bottoms were much heavier than the rest of their bodies. One male penguin was obviously trying to get the attention of a female. If other males made an attempt to come close, it would bark aggressively and move menacingly towards them.

The aquarium had a restaurant. It served visitors to the aquarium and was quite popular and heavily patronised. We had lunch there. It was mainly seafood Both Ayeshetu and I enjoyed the freshness of the food. We left the aquarium, hired a taxi, and went back to the guesthouse.

I woke up early on Monday. I would be going to the seaside that day. My work would begin at five o'clock that afternoon when we would have left the harbour for the deep sea to fish. It was a whole night's job and we would return in the morning. Ayeshetu was aware of this. I had briefed her on my work patterns and she understood me perfectly.

But that morning, I wanted to show her where the fishing office was. So, we went to the beach together. I showed her the offices from a distance. I was not on duty that morning and did not want to be seen during my off hours. We walked around the beach looking at how the ocean-going steamers came into port and left port. The exciting part was when they were entering the breakwaters. That was when the harbour master would either guide them into port or lead them out of the port.

We returned to the guesthouse for lunch. I left for work at about four o'clock in the afternoon. I asked Ayeshetu to call me anytime if she wanted me, or if there was an emergency. She never called and I was satisfied that all was well with her. The night's catch was good. As usual, I brought some fish home. I took them to show Ayeshetu first before going down with them to the restaurateurs. Ayeshetu liked the fishes and said she would have cooked them herself had we been in our own house.

We were now in the third week of my added four weeks in Nouakchott. Both Ayeshetu and I had just one week more to leave Nouakchott. She, back to the university in Timbuctoo, and me on my journey to London via Dakhla.

It was the beginning of the week. A good and bright Monday morning. The sun retreated behind the clouds that started forming that morning. The clouds got darker and thicker and in no time, it began to rain heavily. That was after we had come back from having breakfast. Ayeshetu and I retired to bed. The rain had caused the temperature to fall considerably. It was cold; considerably cold. The rain came in with strong winds as well and continued for a long time.

It was four o'clock in the afternoon and I had to go to work. I kissed Ayeshetu goodbye and went to work. I was going to be back with her the next morning as was usual. We set sail to the deep sea to cast our nets that evening. The weather was rather dull as though the rain that fell in the morning was going to return during the night.

By the turn of the hour of reaching deep sea, we had cast and drawn the first net. We caught a sizeable quantity of fish, mainly mackerels. It appeared they were swimming together as a shoal when they hauled themselves into the net. This was about nine o'clock in the night. We would be casting the second net in an hour's time. Though the hour was up, we could not cast the net.

This was because the wind had picked up and the captain of the trawler and the coxswain were all waiting for the wind to die down a bit before the net was cast. Another one hour had passed. It was now eleven o'clock in the night and the wind had not died down. In fact, it looked like it was gathering momentum. Soon, it started to rain heavily and the wind had metamorphosed into a storm; a tropical storm. Indeed, we had a storm at sea and it was proving to be a severe one.

Our boat started swaying from side to side. First to port, and then to starboard. Normally, the trawler should be stable because it had stability and equilibrium devices fitted that were to stabilise the vessel. So, there was no reason for the vessel to start swaying, except for the force of the gale-force winds in which we were caught.

The captain announced from the bridge that all of us should keep calm. I was scared and so were the other members of the ship's crew although we did not express it. It could, however, be clearly seen on our faces. No sooner had the captain finished making his first announcement than the vessel began to heave rather heavily on the crests and throughs of waves. Soon, the vessel began to take on water.

The wind blew harder and whipped the waves into a frenzy. The situation was getting worse. The storm was still raging. Visibility was poor. Water in the boat made it to list more to the port side taking in yet more water. I stood nervously by one of the life boats nearest to me. Suddenly, the wind blew the vessel strongly from the starboard side making it to take in even more water. I was nervous but stable. I did not panic, although I felt like screaming the words, 'Master, the Tempest is raging…!'

So many thoughts raced through my mind. What if the vessel sank? We were about 5 nautical miles from shore. I could not swim that distance. I thought of my parents and siblings back in Monrovia. I thought of Clarissa. I thought of Angelique. I thought of Fatima. I thought of Ayeshetu waiting for me back at the guesthouse. But most important of all, I thought of my impending registration at the London School of Economics.

After taking on more water, the boat began to list heavily. The captain instructed all persons on board the vessel to put on their life jackets. There were more than enough on board and so everyone donned their life jackets within minutes. Suddenly, the lights on board the boat went off. Water had entered the engine room.

We all took out our flashlights and switched them on. This provided some amount of light—a considerable amount of light—on board the vessel. We tried to launch the life boats, but it was obvious they had never been used, and were stuck. Suddenly, a stronger gust of wind blew from the starboard side of the boat. It turned the vessel almost 90° on its portside. More water gushed into the boat, making it list heavily portside. It, however, was still floating.

We all got into the sea water but still held on tenaciously to the side of the boat. I pulled the string on my life jacket and air filled the jacket. This helped to increase my buoyancy. I looked to my left and right twice. I saw other members of the ship's company also clinging to their sides of the boat and treading water vigour, even though they were wearing life jackets. Surprisingly, the captain was still inside the almost-capsized vessel. I wondered why he had not left the vessel.

It later became clearer to me that, in maritime law, during a shipwreck the captain of the ship should be the last person to abandon ship. That made sense to me. The captain was cool. Maybe so many years of experience at sea had made him so. But what action was he going to take? Make a distress call? Abandon ship? There was no electric power for the ship to use to make a distress call or restart the ship's engine.

Luckily, there were flares on board. The captain fired a couple of flares into the sky to attract attention. The flares signalled to the rescue team ashore that either our boat was sinking or there was a serious emergency on board. It was now well past midnight. We were still hanging on to the wings of the boat with the greater part of our bodies still submerged in the sea water. I was getting tired. My arms were fatigued and beginning to ache.

If I let go, I would drift away from the boat and might be attacked by a shark or some other big fish. I tried to cling on. Another couple of hours had passed and it was getting near to daybreak. No help had come. I had almost given up because my hands had become numb and lost all feeling. Suddenly, a rescue helicopter appeared above us and was hovering over the capsized vessel.

The captain came out of the vessel and managed to stand on the starboard side of the ship and waved at the helicopter. And then there appeared a rescue ship coming towards us. It looked like they got the message of the vessel in distress. They might have seen our flares. In my attempt to look up at the helicopter, my hands finally slipped and I fell fully backward into the sea. I remained calm as I floated with the help of my life jacket.

Suddenly, I started drifting away from the vessel. Within a matter of minutes, I was about 50 metres away from the floating capsized vessel. I shouted and raised my right hand. My mobile phone was in my left hand. I had so far protected it from getting into the sea water. Soon, I was over 100 metres away from the capsized vessel. I could see from afar that the rescue boat had stopped alongside the capsized boat.

I tried to swim back nearer to the two vessels but the sea current was pushing me back. It was so strong. I was now quite tired. I had swallowed some sea water and was feeling weak. Would the sea currents take me away? Where was my captain? Where were my shipmates? Was it a matter of everyone for himself and God for us all? I asked myself.

I heard the noise of the helicopter getting closer to me. I looked up and the chopper was at right angles to my head and hovered. Then a winchman was lowered by the winch towards me. On reaching me, he asked me to stay calm and not panic. He strapped my body to his and soon I saw myself hoisted in mid- air going into the helicopter. It was a timely and most welcome rescue.

I was flown directly to the sickbay back at our offices on dry land. The medics tried to get me to throw out some of the seawater that I had swallowed. I vomited some of it. I was asked to relax. I stayed at the sick bay for another two hours and was allowed to go home. It had been an eventful night. This was making me realise that the path I chose to travel to London was indeed a rather painful one, if not a long one. But it was my choice and I was determined to make it succeed. When I got home, I was still shaken, was shaking from the experience. I told Ayeshetu about our misadventure. She sympathised with me, and put me to bed, and wrapped herself around me. I finally managed to fall asleep. I did not tell my parents or siblings or anyone else what had happened to me. I had dinner with Ayeshetu. The next morning, I went in the company of Ayeshetu to the offices of the fishing company. I was delighted to hear that the fishing vessel was re-floated and all my other colleagues on board the vessel that night were safely back ashore.

In fact, I saw the vessel berthed at the local drydocks for some repair works to be carried out on it. I had only a week more of my extended four weeks left to stay in Nouakchott. Having reviewed and discussed my plans extensively with Ayeshetu, I decided to quit the fishing job. I also decided to leave two days ahead of the week I had left.

Consequently, I informed my employers that I was quitting the job. I told them I had to continue with my travel and that my time to leave was due. They had no problem with my decision. It was a Monday and I was asked to come back two days later to collect my final pay. That would be Wednesday. I went to the office on Wednesday and was paid my last wages. It was a lot of money. It surpassed my expectation. I was very happy and so was Ayeshetu.

I still got nightmares from my experience on the high seas. It made me dread going near the sea, or indeed any kind of large body of water, like a river. I told Ayeshetu that I had changed my mind from going to Dakhla by sea, due to my recent experience. I told her I had developed a phobia for the sea. And for that reason, I would want to go to Dakhla by road. I told Ayeshetu that I had done my research, and found out the road from Nouakchott, through the smaller towns, all the way to Dakhla was part of the African Development Bank's Intercontinental Road project.

For that matter, it was likely to be a motorway all the way to Dakhla. It was called *Autoroute Nouadhibou* of the N2 motorway. We both looked at the map again and confirmed the quality of the road network. We agreed that I would leave on Saturday. Ayeshetu would also leave that same day. I tried to buy Ayeshetu a return air ticket but she had already got one. So, I decided to give her some money to take back to university. She initially was reluctant but I was able to convince her to accept the money.

The departure time for my coach was two o'clock in the afternoon on Saturday. Ayeshetu had a flight at ten o'clock in the morning. We had breakfast together. We packed our luggage, checked out of the guesthouse, thanked the concierge and restaurant staff, and left for the airport. After checking in, I waved goodbye to Ayeshetu. She waved back at me with a look of 'I will miss you' written all over her face. Soon, she disappeared behind the check-in desks.

I took a taxi to the coach station. I checked in and waited for boarding to commence. Someone tapped me from behind on my left shoulder. I had a premonition it would be Gameli, and it was. Our meetings were getting uncanny. It was like he was monitoring every move of mine on my travels. This was the second time we had met at the coach station and travelled on the same coach.

What surprised me most was how he happened to spend exactly the same number of days at the various stops, including now at Nouakchott. Surprisingly, we never run into each other during our long stay in Nouakchott.

We boarded the coach. It was a beautiful brand new one painted in bright vibrant colours. It was Yutong made in China. In fact, all the other coaches at the station were Yutong. The coach driver welcomed us on board. He started the ignition, and gently eased the bus onto the main thoroughfare. We were on our way to Dakhla.

Chapter 9
Dakhla

The distance between Nouakchott and Dakhla was 822.2 kilometres by road. It was scheduled to take nine hours and forty-nine mins. The road was very good. It was an asphalted road all the way. There was no presence of the huge sand dunes through which the untarred road meandered between Gao and Timbuctoo. I sat on seat number 52 right at the back of the coach.

We left Nouakchott at ten o'clock in the morning exactly. After two hours' drive, we had reached *Nouadhibou*, the last city of Mauritania before we entered into Western Sahara. Another half-an-hour's drive saw the coach arriving at the border post of *Guerguarat* in Mauritania. We were made to alight. We formed a single queue through immigration where our passports were checked.

The lady who checked my passport asked me where I was coming from and where I was going. I told her I was from the Republic of Liberia in West Africa and was on my way to London. She was clearly taken aback took a second look at me. Though she did not say anything, The incredulous look spoke volumes. She handed me back my stamped passport after rifling through it a second time.

As we were about to board the coach, one traveller was stopped. There appeared to be a problem with his travel documents. The border guards made him sit in a cordoned-off area, while they went through his documents meticulously. No one knew why he was singled out among us. Was he carrying contraband? We milled around the coach for nearly three hours while his documents were verified. Eventually, he was released with his travel documents and he re-joined us on the coach.

He was not told why he was detained for those hours. All his travel documents appeared to be up-to-date and in order. He had been calm the entire time and did not show any signs of exasperation.

We got back on board the coach and drove off towards the next city called *Barbas*, also known as *Bir Gandouz*, where we were made to take a thirty minute-break. I went with Gameli to grab some food at one of the numerous food stalls that were spread all over this town. It was a coastal town and so there were lots of fish dishes to sample.

I ate grilled snapper and was happy with it. Gameli had fried squid. The squid looked very appetising but I preferred my grilled snapper. It was now about half-past-six in the evening. We had been delayed for nearly three hours. It meant we were going to arrive in Dakhla around midnight. The journey from *Barbas* to Dakhla was uneventful, although it was more than double the time we took to reach *Barbas* from *Guerguarat* on the Western Sahara border with Mauritania.

The N1 Motorway was an excellent road. There were no potholes in the entirety of the road; It was quality asphalt road all the way to Dakhla. I relaxed at the back of our coach and enjoyed the journey. Although, I dozed off occasionally, I was quite alert. My hand luggage was firmly under my feet. I had a bit of money in there and so I watched it like a hawk guarding her chicks.

As anticipated, we arrived at Dakhla at a quarter-past midnight. The coach pulled into the coach station which was a large compound complete with seats, benches and makeshift beds for travellers stranded overnight who might want to sleep. I did not know the city of Dakhla well; neither did Gameli. Together we decided to take a seat at the sitting area and stay there till daybreak.

We sat down next to each other and saw many of our fellow passengers doing same. At about half-past-one at dawn, I told Gameli I was feeling sleepy. He suggested to me to go for one of the makeshift beds. I did. I laid down and used my hand luggage as a pillow upon which I comfortably rested my head. I slept comfortably because I knew with the hand luggage under my head, no one could pull it without me realising; and as such the money I had inside was safe. Gameli sat on the seat not too far away from where I felt asleep.

I woke up about five o'clock and had a shower at the public bathroom specially provided for travellers like us caught or stranded at the coach station. Gameli had a shower too. We both set off to town. I needed to look for a guesthouse where I could lodge for at least five days before continuing the next leg of my journey. I did not intend to stay long in Dakhla; in fact, I had no business doing in Dakhla.

Gameli told me he would be leaving the next day. I asked him where his next port of call was. He said Laâyoune. I took out my map and realised that was also my next port of call. I tried to convince Gameli to spend at least five days in Dakhla. I told him he needed to rest well. One of the reasons I gave him was that the journey to Laâyoune was about twice that of Nouakchott to Dakhla. He looked reluctant. He agreed with me eventually and decided to spend five days with me in Dakhla.

We lodged at *La Crique*, a hotel instead of the guesthouse at which we initially intended to lodge. Located in Dakhla, *La Crique* was on the beach front. The *Al Kassam Mosque* and *Garden of the Mosque* were local landmarks, and the area's natural beauty could be seen at the Dakhla Public Garden. At the hotel, we were handed a brochure with the heading, '*Soyez Politiquement Neutre*', which literally meant 'Be Politically Neutral'.

Further reading of the brochure made this much clearer: The city of Dakhla was located in a contentious part of the world known most widely as the Western Sahara. There was a long-standing disagreement as to whether it belonged to Morocco or whether it should be an independent country. I said to myself, my travel had a goal which was not political. I did not have a political agenda. My visit to Dakhla was just to be in transit in pursuit of my long journey to London; nothing else.

I recognised that there were people on both sides of this debate, and very hotly too. The brochure, and for that matter the hotel, kindly requested that we refrained from sharing our political opinions or comments in any shape or form. That sat very well with me. I was neither a Moroccan nor a Western Saharan/ Sahrawi. I would be leaving the country, no matter who it belonged to, in five days.

That evening, I spoke to my family back in Monrovia. I told my mum I was getting closer to London. She interjected with the remark that, had I travelled by air, I would have been in London by then. I told her I knew that but gave her the confidence that my choice of the mode of travel to London was making me learn a lot of things in life. I told her my experiences were making me a mature man. I did not, however, elucidate on any of the experiences I alluded to.

I spoke to my dad. He was upbeat to hear from me. He told me he was delighted to hear my voice. I summarised, without going into much detail, my journey so far from Ouagadougou to Dakhla. He was excited. He told me I was indeed gaining lots of knowledge which would help me in the future. I spoke with Ameley. She was delighted to speak with me. I assured her I was doing well and was on course to reach London well before the universities opened in September.

I told her I intended reaching London a clear month before the university reopened. She encouraged me to persevere and meet my target dates. I asked her about her husband. She said he was doing well. I asked her whether she was enjoying married life. To that question, she asked whether I was feeling jealous that someone had taken her away from the family. She reminded me that we were all one big family, and that her husband was part of the family, and so I should not feel jealous.

I told her, I was not jealous at all, and I loved her so much as a sister. I also said to her I missed her so much. My only sister. I spoke with Zutor. He asked me where I had reached in my long journey to London. I told him I was in Western Sahara, just about to enter Morocco. I pointed out to him that Morocco was the last African country after which I would cross the Mediterranean Sea into the European country of Spain.

He sounded enthusiastic and encouraging and gave me all his blessings. My conversation with Fogar was brief. Like Zutor before him, he asked me where I had reached on my long road to London. I repeated to him exactly what I said to Zutor. He wished me the best of everything on the remainder of my journey.

I also spoke with Akogovi, our adopted brother. He was so happy to have heard from me. We talked about some interesting parts of my journey. I told him I was determined to succeed and would reach London on time. He said a few words of encouragement to me and wished me well on the rest of my journey.

We arrived in Dakhla on a Sunday evening. Monday morning, Gameli and I had breakfast at the hotel dining room. It was a five-star hotel and so the ambience within the hotel and the quality of food, cutlery, and other amenities were miles better than those we had been used to in the guesthouses where I had stayed on the earlier parts of my journey. But quality went with cost, so the price of the room was about double what I paid in Nouakchott.

But since I decided to treat myself and be happy, I thought very little of the cost. Gameli and I went to town for sightseeing just as the sun had reached an angle of about 45 ° on its journey from the bright east towards the west. The sunshine was brilliant. Dakhla was a medium sized city of just over 100,000 people located 400 kilometres north of the Mauritanian border.

The city was built on a peninsula that ran down from the mainland creating a lagoon area that was popular for kite-surfing and wildlife. We went to the beach where many swimmers were surfing. My recent experience on the sea meant I could not join in any of the sports on water.

Gameli and I hired a kite each. We flew them as we used to when we were young, in our respective countries. I remembered we used to fly kites on the beaches of Monrovia when I was a little boy. Gameli also recounted how he and his mates used to fly kites on the sandy beaches of the seaside town of Keta in Ghana. We ran with the kites against the direction of the wind. Though it was fun, it was like a workout at the gymnasium. We ran forward, backwards, and to the sides, so that our kites could catch the breeze and soar into the skies.

We spent about an hour doing this and thoroughly enjoyed every bit of it. We then went into what was a mini zoo to look at the wildlife that was kept there. The were no lions and tigers. But there were African elephants, antelopes, crocodiles in ponds and different types of lizards. We stood by a short tree on which was an iguana. We got closer to it but it did not move. Its eyes were closed. When it opened them, the eyeballs rolled forwards and backwards the same way the chameleon rolled its eyes 360 °. A zookeeper asked whether I wanted to have the iguana on my shoulder. I hesitated at first. Although, I had not seen an iguana before, I read about it in school. I knew it was a genus of herbivorous lizards that were native to the tropical areas of Mexico, Central America, South America, and the Caribbean.

I also knew that iguanas were not dangerous or aggressive to humans, but they could dig lengthy tunnels, damaging pavements and building foundations. Iguanas do bite people but only in self-defence. Their sharp teeth are specifically for tearing plants apart but their bite could be really painful to humans. Fortunately, they give a warning before doing so. Unlike many reptiles, iguanas do not carry the salmonella bacteria on their skin and so are not dangerous to pets.

So, with some courage, I agreed for the iguana to be placed on my shoulder. It was a big iguana which weighed about 5 kilograms. It sat down quietly on my shoulder and opened its eyes widely. Although, I knew that iguanas did not bite, unless they felt threatened, I was cautious; extremely cautious. I did not cough, sneeze, or laugh. I stayed as still as a mummy so the lizard would not feel threatened in any way.

It rested on my shoulder for about five minutes during which other tourists visiting the wildlife centre took pictures. Its eyes rolled forwards and backwards. No movement of my body. I made Gameli take a few pictures on my cell phone for me.

We arrived back at our hotel just in time for dinner. That was going to be my first dinner in Dakhla. Breakfast was good, but I had no idea what dinner would be like, particularly at the hotel. Gameli and I had some snacks in town but did not have lunch, so I was a bit famished. There were a variety of food items on the menu.

The menu had, among other food items, the following: Couscous-meal paste, with meat and vegetables; *Tajín,* camel meat; *Madem* solely from dromedaries; grilled goat meat served with boiled potatoes; *Meifrisa,* a traditional dish of the region; and various types of roasts. I ordered for the grilled goat meat with potatoes. The grilled goat meat was not only tender and tasty but smelt appetisingly good as well. I ate as if I was eating both lunch and dinner together. In a sense, yes, I did. The food was so good.

I retired to my hotel room for the evening. For the first time in a very long while, I turned on the television. Most of the stations were in Arabic and I could not understand a word that was said in any of the programmes. I, however, managed to get a few English channels such as the BBC, CNN, CGTN and VOA. I tuned into the BBC particularly to listen to what was happening in the country to which I was headed.

I was tired from the day's activities, so soon afterwards, I switched off the television, said my evening prayers and went to bed. Surprisingly, no one called my telephone that evening. I thought of Angelique, Fatima, Ayeshetu and Clarissa. I wondered why Clarissa did not call. She called almost every other evening.

I thought of the situation for a while and decided to call her. She responded with excitement and said she was getting ready to call but had just dozed off. I believed her. She was a good girl. She loved me and I loved her so much.

It was a Wednesday. I had been in Dakhla for three days now. I would be leaving the city in two days' time. That would be Friday. Gameli and I decided to go to town and see other places that we had not visited, after breakfast.

We had just finished breakfast when one of the waiters led two gentlemen to where we were sitting. The waiter said to us the two gentlemen were looking for us. They were well dressed in trousers, shirts and ties that looked descent. We did not know anyone in Dakhla and neither were we expecting anyone. They sat opposite us at the dining table and greeted us politely in French.

We responded in English which made them realise that we spoke better English than French. They also spoke some English, but not fluently. Some of their English pronunciations nearly made me laugh; but clearly, it was not the time to laugh at anything. It was not a laughing matter. They asked of our names, where we came from, what we were doing in the country and for how long we were going to be in Dakhla.

I told them my name, and where I came from, and that I was on my way to London by road. Gameli also told them his name, where he came from, and said he was on his way to Rome. They requested to see our passports. Luckily, both of us carried our passports on us that morning as we were going to go to town without going back to our rooms. We gave them our passports.

I wanted to ask them what the issue was but did not know how they would react. Why were they interrogating us in this manner? I suspected they were special branch security or policemen.

They scanned our passports, held on to them and started talking to us. They told us they had reports that some guests at our hotel were discussing their country's political situations and were condemning why Morocco should lay claim to Western Sahara. They said Gameli and I fitted the description of the visitors reported to them.

I looked into Gameli's face with utter surprise. He looked into mine with fear written all over his face. I summoned courage and smiled. I told the two gentlemen that they had got the wrong people. I shifted to my limited but good French and told them that we had no business talking about the politics of the country. I made it clear to them that we did not know who even ruled Western Sahara.

It was just because our route to Europe passed through here and we decided to spend a few days there. The shorter of the two, who introduced himself as *Inspecteur de police* Gozzir, did not appear convinced by my explanation. The taller one was nodding his head all along as I spoke. Gozzir turned to his colleague, who was introduced as *Inspecteur de police* Kazzir and had a quick word with him.

I saw from the attitude of *Inspecteur de police* Kazzir that he wanted the matter to end there, but *Inspecteur de police* Gozzir disagreed with his colleague and insisted on taking the two of us to the nearest police station for more interrogation.

I asked myself what kind of ill wind was blowing that morning? Were the gods of our forefathers angry with me? Or was it Gameli that always brought the bad luck? I had never believed in any other god apart from Jehovah God who was my shield, defender, and protector. So, I prayed silently, and consoled myself that because we were innocent, and put our trust in the Lord, we would come out unscathed.

We joined them in a police van and went to the police station. They made us sit behind the counter. Immediately, I quickly recollected what happened to me in the company of Fatima in Niamey. I was put behind a police counter in the same way. It dawned on me that my long road to London had landed me, innocently, twice behind police counters. I said to myself I would put these incidents to experiences and tell my children one day in the future when I become a parent.

We sat there for about two hours without anyone speaking to us. Should we request for a lawyer before giving evidence? Or in fact, should we be saying anything to them at all? *Inspecteur de police* Gozzir approached us and signalled us to come to the counter. All of a sudden, the counter telephone rang. He picked it up and immediately came to attention. He did not say much, but rather listened to what was being said to him. It was his superior ;the commandant of the station himself He was called *Commandant de police* Sulleiz. He requested that we should be brought to his office. We climbed the stairs and entered his office. Realising, as we spoke, we came from Anglophone countries he spoke to us in English. His English was good. Good pronunciation with a little French accent. He asked *Inspecteur de police* Gozzir to leave the office. He spoke to us for only ten minutes. He apologised to us for all that we went through.

He said we were not the ones they were looking for. We did not even utter a word. He gave our passports back to us. He called on a junior officer and asked him to drive us back to our hotel using his, the commandant's, private saloon car. We thanked him and left the police station. We were not compensated this time as was the case in Niamey. We were just happy to leave.

The day's events made Gameli and I to decide to leave Dakhla the next day on the next stage of our journey. In fact, Gameli wanted us to leave that night. I persuaded him to stay and leave the following day. Leaving that night would have wrongly signalled either guilt or cowardice on our part. We did nothing wrong. We had been victims of circumstance once again.

We woke up the next day, had breakfast, checked out and headed towards the coach station. My next journey was going to be from Dakhla to Laâyoune. My map indicated to me it was over twice the distance from Nouakchott to Dakhla. But we had to go. The road was still the beautifully asphalted N1/N2 motorway. We got our tickets and waited for the station master to board us. The coach, just like the one that brought us from Nouakchott, was another Chinese-made Yutong. We took our seats and were soon off on our journey to Laâyoune.

Chapter 10
Laâyoune

The distance between Dakhla and Laâyoune was 533 kilometres by road. It was scheduled to take six hours and nineteen minutes. The road was very good. It was an asphalted road all the way. There was no presence of the huge sand dunes through which the untarred road ran between Gao and Timbuctoo. As usual, I positioned myself on seat number 52. Gameli preferred to sit in front of the coach, immediately behind the driver. I could barely see the back of his head from my distant backseat.

The coach moved faster than the one we used for the journey from Nouakchott to Dakhla. We drove past beautiful villas, intriguing villages, and collections of cottages built in the Moorish style. Most of the roadside stretches were, however, empty. Unlike many other African countries where one could see vendors displaying goods and vegetables for sale by highways, this one was different; no such vendors lined the roadsides.

There were, however, fuel filling stations strung along the highway and so were rest-stops where vehicles and travellers could pull into and have some refreshments. We were now about two hours into our journey towards Laâyoune.

The next official rest-stop for the coach, where we could have a thirty-minute break, was about another hour away. I wanted to attend nature's call. I could have gone to the facility on board the coach but I usually preferred going to the ones at the coach rest-stops. Those ones were usually cleaner, more spacious and had better toiletry facilities than those on the coach. Soon the hour had passed, and we were at the coach rest-stop.

It was our first one for this journey. Thank God, I had managed to hold myself for the past hour. On getting down from the coach, I virtually dashed to the washrooms. I was glad I waited for the hour to use the washroom here. I was not disappointed. The toilets were sparkling-clean and so were the showers for anyone who wanted to have a wash down.

I joined Gameli at one of the snack bars in the main waiting area. We had some snacks, mainly Walkers crisps and Coca Cola. Soon our thirty minutes were up and we had to go.

We continued through Echtoucan without stopping. The coach passed the N1/N2 motorway that was constructed to deliberately by-pass metropolis Echtoucan. We could only see the town centre from a distance to the east and to our right. To our left, we could see the huge Atlantic Ocean just about 100 metres away from the main highway.

The sea was turquoise in colour nearer to the beach and appeared a very deep blue further out to sea. It was clear that Echtoucan had some of the most gorgeous beaches in the world; perfect for that beach getaway that families craved. From the coach, we could see families and holiday makers swimming and plunging into the shallow waters of the Atlantic. To the right, and opposite the shallow waters to the left where people were splashing and swimming, were a long range of hotels built opposite each other like an army battle formation.

The thought of stopping and spending a few days in the city came to my mind. But I quickly asked myself whether I was a tourist or someone on a mission that was time-bound. The need to reach London hit me with a new urgency. I had to get to London and get registered at the London School of Economics, latest by the last day of August. That would accord me a full month's time in London to get myself prepared for my studies.

Thus, the idea of a stop in Echtoucan as I did in Niamey, Gao, Timbuctoo, and Nouakchott evaporated from my mind. I was focussed on reaching Laâyoune on time. The long seacoast of beaches continued for a few more kilometres. The coach then went through portions of the highway where the road passed some hilly areas. These parts of the road were not straight and plain. There were meandering, valleys, and steep hills that the coach had to negotiate.

The manoeuvres caused most of the passengers in the coach to shift from side to side, sometimes violently. Anytime that happened, the coach driver apologised. The meandering part of the road ended after about two kilometres and then we were back on the straighter part of the highway along the seacoast where we could see the Atlantic Ocean one more time.

Again, we began to see people scattered by the beaches to our left. To our right were the hotels, most of them painted a blazing white and juxtaposed to each other as I saw in Echtoucan. This indicated to me that we were nearing another big city.

And indeed, true to my reckoning, another half an hour's drive brought us to the seaside city of Boujdour. Unlike Echtoucan, it was one of the coach's rest- stops. And we had a whole one hour instead of the thirty minutes that we were used to, to refresh ourselves.

We took advantage of the hour to go to the beach. Even though I was a bit jittery, I followed Gameli's lead; we removed our shoes, folded our trousers legs knee-high and allowed the soothing cool sea water to rise up our legs. Later, we had a short walk along the seashore, wading through the shallows of the beach.

We got cleaned up and went looking a fast-food restaurant for a snack. We had quite a few to choose from. There was McDonalds, Kentucky Fried Chicken, Nando's, Sam's Chicken, and a few others. We decided to eat at McDonalds. I ordered for a Chicken Sandwich Meal, which came with a bottle of Coca Cola; and Gameli had a Big Mac Meal which also came with a Coca Cola. The meal tasted much better than we remembered, because it was the first time in a very long while, since we had such meal.

Someone would refer to it as junk food, but we loved and enjoyed it. At that moment, for us, it was a delicacy. We finished our meal and walked through the arcades with different games that fronted the beach. I was tempted to play some of the money games but restrained myself. Once again, I reminded myself that I was not on holiday; I had to reach a certain place at a certain time for a certain purpose.

And that purpose required money too. I did not play any of the games. Soon our time was up and we had to go back on the coach.

We set off on the last leg of this particular journey. We drove by the seacoast with a full view of the beautiful Atlantic Ocean. We had two towns more left to reach Laâyoune; first, we had to pass through Lemsid, and then Foum el Oued, both on the seacoast. The first was almost on the same latitude with Laâyoune while Foum el Oued sat on the main Atlantic Ocean seacoast. Laâyoune was about a couple of kilometres inland, but not too distant from the sea.

The coach sped gracefully through these two-seaside towns and soon we reached Laâyoune. It was our last city in Western Sahara before we crossed the frontier into the next country, Morocco. I told myself, bit by bit, I was getting nearer to London. I was quietly excited within. We alighted from the coach. It was about six o'clock in the afternoon.

The evening sun was just on its way to dip behind the horizon. Beautiful scenery as usual. A kaleidoscope of all the colours of the rainbow; red, orange, yellow, green, blue, indigo, and violet mixed together.

Gameli and I looked for a guesthouse. We got a guesthouse called *Hadrian's Wall*. We were not sure why the guesthouse was named in English as Sahrawis spoke mainly French. We checked in and settled. We were not going to go out that evening because we were tired. We, however, needed something to eat. We went to the guesthouse dining hall and had dinner. Laâyoune, also referred to as El Aaiún, was the largest city of the disputed territory of Western Sahara and was de facto administered by Morocco.

The modern city was thought to have been founded by the Spanish coloniser Antonio de Oro in 1938. In 1940, Spain designated it as the capital of the Spanish Sahara. The city, which was located at the north-western part of the Sahara, 13 kilometres inland from the Atlantic Ocean, was situated in the geographical region of Saguia el-Hamra. It was the capital of Western Sahara from 1940 to 1976 when Western Sahara was a north-west African overseas province of Spain known as the Spanish Sahara; since 1976, it has been the capital of the Laâyoune province of Morocco although it is not internationally recognised.

I intended staying at Laâyoune for a week. I was not sure how long Gameli wanted to stay. I did not ask him. After dinner that night, we went back to our rooms. I took out my tourist brochure on Laâyoune which I picked up at the coach station. I was curious to find interesting tourist attractions and places where we could visit. The city had so many tourist centres. The top attractions included the St Francis of Assisi Cathedral, Laâyoune Grand Mosque, Centre Artisanal, Laâyoune Off Road and the Sahar Western Trip bicycle tours.

While looking through the brochure I came across this advertisement:

"The White Dune, located on the eastern shore of the lagoon, about 50 km from the city centre is simply beautiful. For those who leave by their own means,

take a track on 10 km after driving 40 km on the asphalt road. The swimming in this area is fabulous but be careful because the guides do not give instructions while there are ditches not far from the edge."

I got interested in the challenge. I called Gameli on the guesthouse intercom and asked him to look at the advertisement in the brochure. He had also picked up a copy at the coach station. I called out the page number to him and he opened it up.

"That is 50 miles away. How do we get there?" He asked.

"We could go by local small buses or hire a car and drive," I replied.

He did not sound enthusiastic about the trip that night. I did not push him. Just before I could say my prayers and go to bed, Fatima called. She told me she had a surprise for me. I asked her what the surprise was. She explained to me that, since I informed her that the next stop on my journey was going to be Laâyoune, and I would be there for a week, she had bought a ticket to pay me a surprise visit. She said she missed me so much and wanted to come and stay with me for the one week that I was going to spend in Laâyoune.

I was both excited and taken aback. I responded in the affirmative to her request and told her I would meet her at the King Hasan 1 International Airport located in Laâyoune. Her estimated time of arrival was ten o'clock the next morning.

I had breakfast earlier that morning. I called Gameli and informed him about Fatima's visit and the changes in my movements and plan for that day. He was still in bed and spoke with a sleepy voice. He had not even been for breakfast that morning. I arrived at the King Hasan 1 International Airport in Laâyoune at half-past-nine in the morning. The arrivals display indicated that Niger Airways, which Fatima was scheduled to come to Laâyoune with, had arrived half an hour ahead of schedule. That indicated to me that she must be going through immigration and customs. I waited for another half an hour. I sat down on a bench located directly opposite where all arriving passengers exited into the open place at the arrivals hall. Another quarter of an hour and there came walking Fatima, my beautiful friend. I stood up, gave her a warm embrace and a bisous. I told her she looked even more beautiful than the last time I saw her.

She thanked me and reciprocated the compliments. She said I was looking stronger and more handsome. I received the compliments wholeheartedly. We rode in a taxi back to my guesthouse. Fatima told me she was famished because she could not have time for breakfast since she was in a hurry to get to the airport in Niamey. I told her it was time for lunch, anyway. I informed her the guesthouse served great food and asked her to join me at lunch. Without much ado, she placed her suitcase on top of the bed, opened it, picked up her wallet and off we went to the dining hall.

I did not know of the whereabouts of Gameli, and I was not really concerned. I now had a very important visitor and did not want to bother him . In fact, since he appeared not to be all that enthusiastic with my initial suggestion of visiting the lagoon, I had a good excuse.

Lunch was very good. I had fried rice and grilled goat meat and a hot pepper sauce. Fatima had fish soup with some boiled rice. We retired to my room. Fatima appeared tired. She went into the shower, had a wash, changed her clothes into something comfortable, and took a nap. She had woken up at about five o'clock in the morning that day to catch her flight at seven o'clock. Thus, she was not only tired but a bit sleepy too.

I had another good look at the tourists' brochure. In addition to The *White Dune*, there was also another attractive tourist attraction which we could go to. This was the *Sunrise with camel ride* at the Sahara pyramids desert. It also looked attractive.

Fatima woke up just about dinner time. She brushed her teeth, tidied up her hair, changed her clothes and we descended the stairs to the dining hall. We met Gameli there this time. I introduced Fatima to him and he welcomed her warmly. But Gameli had finished eating and was just on his way back to his room. Because we both had a heavy lunch, we decided to have something light for dinner. We had apple pie with custard and some French baguette with goat cheese. The French baguette was warm from the oven and tasted divine, particularly with the goat cheese. I enjoyed it very much and so did Fatima.

Back in the room, I showed Fatima both advertisements: first the *White Dune* and second the *Sunrise with Camel Ride* at the Sahara pyramids desert. I asked her which trip she was interested in. She jumped at both. She suggested we went to the *White Dune* that day, and the *Sunrise with*

Camel Ride the following day. I thought it was a brilliant idea. I agreed.

In bed that night before I dosed off, I reflected on the rest of my journey to London, my rent in London, my university fees at the London School of Economics and other ancillary issues. I asked myself whether I was on a tourist trip or an educational trip. I could not get a perfect answer to my own question. I asked myself whether I was using my money wisely. Again, I had no clear-cut answer to that question.

I was, however, convinced of the fact that if I needed to be happy, I had to make myself happy. No one else would sell me happiness. With regard to money, I had made all the calculations, both in my head and on paper and was convinced I was being prudent. I had money on me, and I had money deposited with the HSBC bank.

Unknown to me, the fishing company I worked for in Nouakchott compensated us handsomely for the shipwreck incident I had on my last fishing trip with them. They had paid the money for my compensation into my HSBC bank account. I never anticipated any such payment. All I needed to do was to have fun where I found it appropriate and remain focused on my long road to London at the same time.

These thoughts lulled me into sleep. We both slept well that night. We woke up early, had our toiletry, and went down for breakfast. We had cereals with camel milk, baguettes, and cheese. It looked like both Fatima and I had fallen in love with the French bread (baguette) Laâyoune style.

We left the guesthouse and joined a taxi to where the minibuses left for the *White Dune*. It was going to be about 50 kilometers' ride, but that was fine with us. It was going to take just about an hour. The taxi took about twenty minutes to reach the bus station. The vehicles plying this route were mainly 16-seater Toyota Hiace minibuses.

We set off with one other tourist towards the *White Dune.* The road ran along the beautiful coast of the Atlantic Ocean. Again, there was a phalanx of hotel buildings, juxtaposed to each other along the road when one looked to the right. They were all painted a brilliant white. After about a quarter of an hour's drive we lost sight of the hotels.

We started seeing clumps of date palm trees ranged alongside the road. The earth was sandy and looked brownish white in colour. So many were the date palm trees that one could not easily count them from our minibus.

Soon we arrived at the *White Dune*. It was a beautiful scene even from the coach. We walked closer to the resort and the closer we got the more beautiful it looked. We bought our tickets at the gates and entered the *White Dune* site. First, we went to *Tiznit* and entered the inside of the castle walls, then inside the typical houses along the palace and the city hall. They were beautiful with excellent medieval architectural designs on the walls, windows and doors.

We also caught a glimpse of Spanish colonial architecture. We then went to the incredible *Legzira* beach which is reputed to be one of the most beautiful beaches in the world. I had it in mind to swim so I took a pair of swimming trunks in my backpack. Fatima did not have a swimsuit, so we bought one there and then, in one of the many shops that were located around the site. *Legzira* beach was a beautiful place. The sea water was shallow for a very long distance.

Fatima was a good swimmer and so was I. Fatima swam far off into the sea. I decided to stay close to shore, swimming along the shoreline. I was very tempted to swim out to her, but recent events were still fresh in mind, and held me back. We enjoyed the soothing water for about an hour and a half and came back ashore. The swim accorded both of us good exercise. I had not had such good exercise in a while.

Across the road to the other side was the *Khenifiss* lagoon inside the *Khenifiss* National Park. It was an amazing place where one could go on a boat-ride around the lagoon. We went for the boat ride. Just Fatima and me. It was just wow! The boatman controlled the outboard motor with great skill, drawing figure eights at a good speed on the water. The experience was exhilarating.

We went to have lunch at the *Top Castle of Mirleft*. It was the restaurant of a posh hotel located on top of the hill with amazing views. We had *Arroz Frito Chino con Camarones,* prepared with shrimps caught fresh from the Atlantic Ocean and *Deliciosa Receta,* a pasta dish. It was a combination of Chinese and Italian dishes. Very tasty and succulent meal. Fatima and I enjoyed the food very much.

We decided to leave as the evening sun was once again descending towards the horizon to the west of the city. We returned to the minibus station. It took us an hour to drive back to Laâyoune city centre. Fatima wanted to go and watch a movie but I was tired and we came to a compromise to go the following day.

It was getting dark and I did not want to hang around town for too long. My experiences in Dakhla, a matter of clear mistaken identity, flashed through my mind. That was one of the reasons why I wanted us to reach our guesthouse as soon as possible. Also, my experiences in the company Ayeshetu at the movie house flashed through my mind.

I nearly told Fatima what happened as an excuse but caught hold of myself up just in time. What if is she asked me whether I went to the movie alone or with someone? Would I lie to her? I was not sure, but I was glad I did not divulge my experiences with Ayeshetu at the movie house to her.

We got back to the guesthouse in time for dinner. Actually, we were not feeling hungry because of the exotic but delicious lunch we had on our day out. We, however, walked down to the dining hall and shared an egg omelette with tea. We dawdled at the dinner table and talked about my time in Niamey, a wonderful experience, except for when I was mistaken for a bank robber. We recalled the highs and lows of that experience.

That prompted me to tell Fatima how Gameli and I again became victims of mistaken identity in Dakhla. How they thought we were discussing local politics. How they thought we were pointing accusing fingers at authorities who were ruling in Western Sahara at the time. And how it was virtually a taboo to discuss politics in either Western Sahara or Morocco. Fatima teased me and called me 'the mistaken identity young man'. She wondered why it was always me who was mistaken for someone who had committed an offence.

She asked, teasingly, why would they not mistake me for someone who had just won ten million dollars in the national lottery? Her latter remark made me laugh a lot. I told her jokingly that, with ten million dollars, we would both be on our way for more holidays in Hawaii in the United States of America.

We went back to our room. We had only two more days to stay in Laayoune: Thursday and Friday. I had to leave on the Saturday. And so would Gameli, to the best of my knowledge. Fatima was aware of this and had booked her return flight for the same Saturday. Her flight would leave at ten o'clock in the morning. My coach was scheduled to leave at four o'clock in the afternoon of the same day. That would give me ample time to go and see Fatima off at the airport.

We sat down on the bed and chatted at length. Fatima placed her head on my shoulders and was looking right into my pupil as we chatted. It tickled me a bit. I had an unusual feeling throughout my body. I reacted by throwing my arms around her as I spoke. As the atmosphere grew more romantic, I found it hard to concentrate on what I was saying in our conversation. I observed that Fatima too was taking in very little, if anything at all.

I tried to convey to her what I had planned for us to do the following day. Again, I could see that, although Fatima was looking directly into my face as I spoke, she was imbibing almost nothing. Her eyes turned slightly red in colour, and continued to roll from left to right, and right to left in their sockets. She stood, changed into her nighties, and lay on the bed. I also changed into my pyjamas and lay beside her.

We both woke up a bit late the next morning feeling pretty tired. Breakfast usually closed at eleven o'clock in the morning. We, however, managed to reach the dining hall by a quarter-to eleven that morning. There was plenty of food. We had cereals with camel milk, as well as French bread and goat cheese. Goat cheese was a local delicacy. As usual, we both enjoyed the breakfast.

As we ate, I kept stealing glances at Fatima. I was quietly admiring how beautiful she was. The colour of her eyes reverted to the normal snow white. The dimples were still there any time she smiled. She was just a beauty to look at. We decided to do the camel ride that day. Fatima did not get it in the previous night when I mentioned it. She was in a different mood when I told her. She jumped at the idea and we decided to go.

We left the guesthouse, took a taxi, and arrived at the same minibus station where we boarded the minibus to the *White Dune*. We were on our way to *The Sunrise With Camel Ride* at the Sahara pyramids desert. The distance to the venue was a bit longer than that of the *White Dune*, and therefore took half an hour more.

We arrived at *The Sunrise With Camel Ride* at the Sahara pyramids desert at about midday. It was a very beautiful tourist centre. There were the options of spending a day, two or three nights or even five days in hotels in and around the resort while you were on the camel ride tour. We decided to spend just a day and return later that same day.

As we entered the resort, we saw this sign boldly displayed at the venue: "*Support this operator: Times are tough for the travel community right now. To show your support, consider leaving a review or posting photos of tours and experiences you have taken. Your support will go a long way in helping tour operators worldwide get back on their feet down the road.*"

Fatima and I mounted the same camel and rode through the desert sand. Fatima sat behind me and held on to my midrib with both of her hands. I could feel her bosom pressing against my back. It was a pleasing sensation and I relished it quietly. Much as I enjoyed the contact, I had a job to do, and needed to concentrate. I had to control the camel. It was like riding a horse, yet quite different, because of the pitching movement of the camel. So, I was sort of a novice, and needed my wits about me. Our camel moved fairly fast, but not too fast. Other tourists riding their camels were spread across the wide desert. As we moved along, both of us clearly showed excitement at our new adventure. Occasionally, Fatima would lean forward and whisper into my ears, "I love you, Yolandi." Focused on the control of the camel, and with an apparent state of absentmindedness I would say, "I love you too, Fati." This seemed to excite her and she would hold me tighter, her bosom pressing harder on my back.

We had altogether about one and a half hours of camel riding. We rode back to where we took the camel and handed the animal back to the park keepers. It was late in the afternoon and we decided to have lunch at the Sahara Desert Cafeteria. We had lunch and a few drinks, relaxed in the desert sunshine for a while and decided to end our adventure and head home.

As we walked towards the exit of the park, we had to pass by about a dozen of the camels that had been tethered to the walls. I thought I recognised one of them as our camel. I asked Fatima to wait while I went to verify. It had a ribbon woven into its tail, so I walked behind it and took a good look at the tail. It was indeed she. I gave it a goodbye pat on the rump.

She gave me a strong back-kick. I felt a severe pain on my left knee. I knew horses and cows did this when they felt threatened. I never knew camels did the same. I cried out loudly and fell to the ground. The camel stood calm. For fear of the animal advancing on me on the ground, I dragged my body out of its way and cried out loudly for help. Fatima cried out in alarm and attracted the attention of some of the camel park attendants who stood about a hundred metres away from us.

I was still sitting on the ground when the attendants arrived. They looked at my knee which was already swollen. I was in a lot of pain. I never knew a camel's kick was so powerful and caused so much pain. It really hit me hard. I could hardly stand. The keepers radioed for an ambulance and I was taken to the local clinic located on the site.

Fatima rode in the ambulance with me on the very short journey. A doctor ordered an x-ray to be taken on my knee immediately. That was done. I went to see the doctor with the x-ray film. Thank God! No bones were broken. The doctor administered an injection on the knee to alleviate the pain. He bandaged the knee and gave me a couple of strips of paracetamol tablets to take home and take anytime I felt pains. He advised me to rest the knee.

I thanked God for His mercies; it could have been worse! We reached the guesthouse that evening just before dinner. Although, we had lunch at the Sahara Desert Cafeteria, it looked like events of the immediate past three hours or so had made both of us hungry. We had dinner, went for our evening showers, and got straight into bed.

I woke up the next day feeling a lot better. The swelling had subsided and the redness of the skin on the knee had started to disappear. We had two more days to spend in Laâyoune. It was a Thursday, and we had to leave Laâyoune on Saturday. Fatima suggested we went for yet another adventure on Friday before we left on Saturday. I asked her to suggest a place for us to go.

She said she would look through the tourist's guidebook for a suitable place. We went for breakfast after which we came back to our room. We decided to spend the entire day indoors together. We chatted, made phone calls, played games on my laptop, and took funny photos on our phones. We took a break and went for lunch. It was just about this time that I thought of Gameli. Perhaps I was feeling guilty for having abandoned him because Fatima had come. I had not seen him for a while and wondered if he had left without informing me.

We met him coming into the guesthouse dining hall as we were leaving. I had a short chat with him. He told me he had planned to leave on Saturday. Coincidentally that was the day I had also planned to leave.

We planned to take the ten o'clock evening coach which would leave Laâyoune for Casablanca. This was going to be in Morocco proper. It meant we would have left Western Sahara for Morocco. Gameli excused himself and walked into the dining room for his lunch.

We spent most of the afternoon playing the game of Monopoly. Fatima had brought the game along in her suitcase. She had brought it all the way from Niamey. I remembered playing this game with my siblings several times back in Monrovia. I also played it with my mates at the university. So, I had a fairly good knowledge of how the game was played. Fatima had too. She was good at buying the houses and the hotels at the most expensive sites and making good investments as well. Her two favourite sites were Park Lane and Mayfair, the two most expensive sites on the property board. I, on the other hand, liked to build my houses and the hotels on the cheaper sites. These included Old Kent Road, Whitechapel, Kings Cross Station, The Angel Islington, Euston Road, Pentonville Road, Pall Mall, and Whitechapel. Fatima also invested in houses and hotels on Coventry Street, Piccadilly Circus, and Trafalgar Square.

We both enjoyed the game very much. So much so we almost missed dinner We went for dinner, had our showers, said our evening prayers, and went to bed early. It was delightful to have spent the whole day in our room. It felt really good. I was totally relaxed, and so was Fatima. Fatima's visit had been worthwhile. After dinner, Fatima had looked through the tourists' guide and suggested we went on a hot air balloon ride. That sounded exciting. I had never before been in a hot air ballon. We had booked one for about eleven o'clock the next day.

Coincidentally, we woke up rather early Friday morning. Maybe the excitement of the ride was the reason we couldn't stay longer in bed, even though the scheduled time was at eleven o'clock for our hot air ballon ride. We had breakfast and made our way towards the hot air balloon station. We took our time and walked casually to the taxi rank. The taxi took about half an hour to reach the hot air balloon site. There was quite a crowd there already.

There were two of the air balloons with tourists already floating in the air in the distance. Another one had just taken off from the ground and was gaining altitude. We were about half an hour early for our flight. We settled down, relaxed, and waited our turn. As the time got closer, I began to get a bit nervous. I told Fatima, who laughed gaily at me and told me to be courageous and that all was going to be well. She looked so confident, as if she had done it several times before. I wondered how she could be so confident about the hot air balloon flight while I was trembling inside like a coward.

Fifteen minutes to our scheduled time, the flight organisers called out our names. "Yolandi Kolandi and Fatima Ghamsha," on the public address system. I responded and both of us walked towards the flight deck. They called the other seven tourists who were to be on the flight with us. They responded and joined us up at the deck. So, eight of us, all tourists, plus the pilot making nine of us got ready to on the ride.

We were given a fifteen-minute briefing on the dos and don'ts of the flight. We were to always keep calm and listen and obey the instructions of the pilot. The briefing was quick but detailed. Hot air balloons work on a relatively simple principle. By heating the air inside the balloon, it becomes lighter than the cooler air on the outside. This causes the balloon to lift off the ground upwards and float, as if it were on a cushion of air. Obviously, if the air in the balloon is allowed to cool, the balloon begins to descend gradually. The average hot air balloon-ride would last for forty-five minutes to an hour, but the whole experience can take up to four hours.

We were scheduled to be in the air for an hour. The wind that moved the hot air balloon apparently was not scary in the slightest. As a matter of fact, one could not even feel the wind, because we would be travelling with the wind. We were advised online to avoid skirts and dresses when on the flight, because they could be caught in the ropes that held the balloon to the riding basket. We were advised to bring sunglasses along with us on the flight. Most importantly we were told we could not go to the loo while in flight, so we had to be sure we visited the restroom before we went on board.

While the sights to be seen during a hot air balloon ride can be majestic, getting into the basket, taking off and landing would always be challenging. The smaller the balloon, the less lift capacity it will have and the hotter it must be inside the balloon for it to rise and fly. The maximum continuous operating temperature for most hot air balloons is 250° Fahrenheit or 121° Celsius. In the aviation world, hot air balloons are noted to be incredibly safe, and the safety has improved continually over time. Accidents are uncommon, and fatalities even rarer. Between the years of 2000 and the June of 2016, only 21 hot air ballooning fatalities were reported in the United States. Each company will have its own age restrictions, but it really boils down to whether one could handle being on one's feet for an hour or two because there is no getting off mid-flight.

"Get on board," shouted the pilot. We climbed into the *gondola* or basket, the chamber in which all the passengers and the pilot rode. This was connected to the *envelope*, the part of the aircraft that looked like a balloon; some pilots called it a *bag,* by means of stainless-steel suspension cables. The burner was turned on and a huge flame lit up and started blowing hot air into the envelope or balloon. Soon, the balloon started swelling up.

In a matter of minutes, the take-off had begun. Fatima held on to my hand firmly as we saw the buildings and also the date trees in the desert below us got smaller and smaller as we rose. Within ten minutes, we had risen to about 1,000 feet. I could see far into the distance and saw the massive amounts of sand in the dunes in the Sahara. Some of the other tourists brought out their cameras and started taking pictures.

For a moment, I wondered what they were either filming or taking pictures of. There were no significant buildings in sight. Neither was there a grassland land to be filmed. Just a very long and huge pile of sand dunes that stretched far into the horizon. Fatima too took out her camera and started taking pictures. Although, I was tempted to ask what she was taking pictures of, I hesitated and did not speak. I was glad I did not. I would have spoiled her joy and excitement if I had asked.

Our flight was scheduled for an hour. Midway through the flight, the pilot announced there was a problem with the burner. He repeated the announcement and there was dead silence on the ship. One could hear a pin fall. Fatima edged closer to me and held on to my midrib. We started losing height. The balloon was losing its buoyancy as there was a marked reduction of the hot air blowing into it. The pilot did not only look worried but totally disoriented. He radioed flight control on the ground. He was asked to carry on trying to re-ignite the burner. Try as he did, he was not successful. He had lost control of the navigation too and we were drifting slowly but steadily towards the sea to the north-west of Laâyoune, some 25 miles away from the desert.

Soon we could see the huge deep blue Atlantic Ocean beneath us. We were drifting aimlessly in the wind. We were at the mercy of the direction of the wind. The balloon was losing hot air fast, but the little left inside it was keeping it aloft for the time being. We had now spent almost two hours in the sky, and we continued losing height albeit at a slow pace. The airship was quite close to the waters of the sea now. I had it in mind that when push came to shove, I would jump into the water and swim or remain afloat. Fatima was, as usual, holding on to me. I told her not to be scared and that the situation would be under control.

Soon, we could see a couple of sea-rescue helicopters hovering in the sky not too far away from us. The hot air balloon was now just about 100 metres the surface of the sea. No one was talking. The pilot was still working hard on the burner. We started looking into the faces of each other without uttering a word. I saw a woman and her male companion in the corner to my left reaching out for their rosary. They started praying visibly, and audibly too.

A couple of other tourists joined in what had become an open prayer meeting. I had no choice but to join in, and so did Fatima. We called on God to intervene and rescue us. We said we did not want our hot air balloon to crash into the sea. We called on God to perform a miracle for us and repair our burner. Suddenly, we heard a loud "Whoosh", the noise of how fire erupts when a naked light is introduced to petrol.

We looked in the direction of the burner and lo and behold, the burner had ignited; the flame was burning bright and blue. . God had listened to our prayers. The balloon started gaining height again. The pilot was in full control now. We were moving towards where we started from. The prayer group, as we virtually became, just broke into singing songs of praise to the glory of God. We sang *Amazing Grace*. We sang *How Great Thou Art*. We also sang *Immortal, Invisible God Only Wise*.

There was joy mixed with relief on board the air ship. We had now been in the sky for nearly three and a half hours. Twenty minutes after re-igniting the burner, we arrived and landed safely at the air base. There was relief clearly written on the faces of each and every one on the air ship. We all congratulated the pilot on a very good job done. Fatima and

I picked a taxi and left for the guesthouse. We reached the guesthouse in time for dinner.

Our ordeal in the hot air balloon did not give us the chance to have lunch. We were famished and needed to eat. We wolfed down our last dinner in the guesthouse in silence, each pondering on what could have easily been a different story.

We had breakfast for the last time at the guesthouse Saturday morning. Fatima and I had packed our travelling suitcases ready the previous night. Fatima's flight was at one o'clock in the afternoon. My coach would depart Laâyoune for Casablanca at six o'clock in the evening. I saw Fatima off to the airport. She told me she had enjoyed my company and lamented she would be missing me a lot. I assured her we would meet again soon, and so she should not worry.

I kissed her on her lips and got a little bit of that red stuff on my own lips. I noticed that tears had welled up in her eyes. I pulled her to me one more time, kissed her on her cheeks and said to her, *"Au revoir, mon cheri."* I saw her walk through the departure gates. She tuned and blew me a kiss, followed by a long wave till she disappeared behind the walls of the airport security check on her way back to Niamey.

Back at the guest house, I took a taxi and went straight to the coach station. Gameli was already there. I greeted and chatted with him for a while. I told him about our experiences on the hot air balloon flight. He listened attentively to the story and exclaimed, "Praise God," after I had finished narrating the incident to him. Just then, the station master called us to board our coach. We formed a single line and went into the coach one after the other. I boarded the coach. My seat number was 52.

Chapter 11
Casablanca

The driver stood in his cockpit, welcomed every passenger on board, asked us to sit, relax and enjoy the ride, and resumed his seat. I could hear the ignition of the engine running under my seat. After everyone had taken their seat, the driver eased his coach into drive and soon we were on our way to Casablanca. The distance between Laâyoune and Casablanca was 1,418 kilometres by road. The journey was scheduled to take thirteen hours and ten minutes.

The road was very good; it looked like the more we approached mainland Morocco, the better the road network became; better than all the roads that we travelled on in Western Sahara. It was an asphalted road all the way. Happily, as was the case between Dakhla and Laâyoune, there was no presence of the huge sand dunes through which the untarred road went between Gao and Timbuctoo.

We left Laâyoune at six o'clock in the evening exactly. After a two-hour drive, we had reached Tarfaya, the border town of Western Sahara and mainland Morocco. For some reason, I kept thinking that because Western Sahara had a political link to Morocco there would be no borders between the two. I was wrong. To the contrary, we were made to alight at a crossing. Just like the earlier border towns, we formed a single queue through immigration where our passports were checked.

As fate would have it, on this trip too, as was the case earlier at the border town between Nouakchott and Dakhla, another person was detained. The lady who checked my passport asked me where I was coming from and where I was going. I told her I was from the Republic of Liberia and was on my way to London. She also looked into my face a second time as if she was going to wish me good luck. She stamped my passport and handed it back to me. I walked away happily.

We had to wait on the detained passenger for one hour. In fact, the driver had to go to the immigration office to enquire what the problem was. As soon as the driver reached the office, the young man's passport was stamped and released to him. We all boarded the coach, and before long, we were on our way.

As we took off, I could see Gameli sitting right behind the driver. I could not understand how it was that Gameli and I always met on the same coaches and travelled on the same days, although we had very little interaction when we decided to spend individual times in some of the cities on our way to Europe.

Soon we had left Tafaya behind. The coach driver announced on the public address system that our next stop was going to be Guelmim. We would stop at Guelmim and have dinner at the rest stop located there. It was getting to ten o'clock in the evening and I was feeling hungry. I had to eat something.

Fatima had made some sandwiches for me. They were in my hand luggage. I also had a can of Coca Cola in the bag. I munched on the sandwiches and drank the can of coke. It held the hunger at bay till I would have something more substantial to eat when we arrived at Guelmim.

We arrived at Guelmim at midnight. We still had a long way to go. We had to pass through the towns of Agadir, Mogador, and Safim before reaching Casablanca. We alighted from the coach. Gameli alighted before me but waited for me to get down and we walked towards a night café where food was still being served. We bought pilau rice and fish stew and had a late meal. The food was very satisfying as I had not eaten a proper meal before leaving Laâyoune. Gameli did not pass any comment on his food, however, the seriousness and focus that he placed on the plate of the pilau rice and stew sitting in front of him spoke volumes. One needed not hear any word from his mouth to guess how much he enjoyed the food. We left Guelmim at about one o'clock in the morning. The next town ahead of us was Agadir.

We, however, were not going to make a stop at Agadir. We had another 201.7 kilometres to go. I pulled out a novel from my bag and started to read. I found it hard to concentrate because I started feeling sleepy. What even exacerbated my lack of concentration was the fellow passenger who sat to my left. I was by the window seat and thus, there was no one sitting to my right-hand side.

She was a slim, curly haired young woman, who appeared tired. She had all the looks of a Fulani and the perfume she wore had a nice bouquet. She was sleepy too, and more than once, had leaned on my left shoulder as she dozed. I remembered how I met Fatima on my journey from Ouagadougou to Niamey. Was this going to be *déjà vu*?

I must be honest, her occasional sleep on my shoulder did not inconvenience me in anyway; I found it almost pleasant and comfortable to say the least. It was most comfortable when she occasionally leaned on me and her bosom touched me. I did not look in her direction. I continued looking into my book, but the fact of the matter was that my concentration was gone, and so was the sleep. Once in a while, she would start awake and briefly manage to stay awake for about five minutes.

And then she broke the ice! She asked me whether I was fine and whether she was inconveniencing me with her leaning on me during her sleep. I responded in the negative. I told her I was perfectly fine. The coach ploughed on and soon we passed Agadir.

My fellow passenger soon resumed her sleep and this time slept flat on my thighs. She was fast asleep. Soon, I had to place my hand across her shoulder and hold onto her so that she would not fall to the floor of the bus. Her bosom pressed against my forearms and that was very comforting to me. I realised that my left hand was firmly on one of her breasts. Once she did not complain, I did not remove my hand.

Soon I started dozing off myself, but my left hand was still at that position. It had not moved. We reached Mogador, our next stop on our way to Casablanca. It was officially our next stop. It was about six o'clock in the morning. We were to spend one hour at this rest stop. The stop had public lavatories and shower halls for travelling passengers. I took advantage of the facilities and went to have my morning toiletries.

Mariam, my new Fulani friend on the coach, also went to do same in the ladies' section. She joined me at breakfast in one of the coffee shops at the rest stop. The Mogador Rest Stop had so many restaurants. I did not catch sight of Gameli at the stop. I did not look out for him because I had a new friend who I was keeping company. My conscience was pricked that it seemed every time I made a new friend, I forgot him. That was not good on my part, I realised.

Marian and I had coffee, club sandwiches and French cheese. Mariam offered to pay for them but I beat her to it. I paid before she could get her purse out.

She told me she was grateful and also thanked me for not getting upset when she fell asleep and laid on my thighs. I told her that was fine; but if only she knew the comfort I had derived from the experience! We spent about an hour at Mogador. I felt rested and well-fed. We resumed our seats on the bus and soon were on our way to the next town, Safim.

Safim was just 135.5 km away from Mogador. From the speed of our coach, I reckoned we would reach the town in about an hour plus. The road from Mogador to Safin ran parallel to the Atlantic Ocean, which was clearly visible to our left, from the coach. To the right, were the many towns and clusters of hotels and guesthouses, all painted the usual bleached-white colour.

One could spot huge ocean-going vessels making their ways, either northwards into the Mediterranean Sea, possibly on their way to the continent of Europe, or towards the south, to the west and southwestern coasts of Africa.

I started chatting with Miriam. She asked me in more detail where I was coming from and where I was going. I told her I was coming all the way from Liberia on the West Coast of Africa and that I was on my way to London to enrol at a university there to study for my Master's degree. I asked her to, in turn, tell me a little about herself. She told me her parents lived in Casablanca.

She was a student studying in France. She had gone to Laâyoune for a holiday to visit an old school friend who lived there. She was on her way back to Casablanca to her parents. She would be returning to France in September to carry on with her studies. Curious, I asked her what degree she was studying for. She told me she was a medical student.

She also told me she had an interest in pharmacology; however, she still preferred to study medicine and then specialise after her completion of both her main studies and housemanship. She told me she would like to specialise in paediatric medicine. I congratulated her and told her that I was highly impressed. I told her since I was going to live in London and she would be studying in France, there was the great probability that we would see each other again in Europe when we all settled in.

We had now passed the township of Safim and were on our final leg to Casablanca. The coach did not pass through the city centre. Rather, it passed straight along the coast, parallel to the Atlantic Ocean. We had less than two hours to go. It was about a quarter-past ten in the morning. I estimated that we would be reaching Casablanca latest by eleven o'clock that morning.

Miriam asked me for my contact. I gave her one of my business cards that I used in Liberia. She realised I was a biological scientist. She then asked me the course I was going to pursue in London and the university I was going to enrol at. I told her I was going to purse a Master's degree in business administration; an executive MBA to be precise. And that I was going to be at the London School of Economics.

She then reminded me that most of the past African Heads of States and their families all went to study at the London School of Economics. She also confirmed that many of their children and grandchildren still studied there. I agreed with her and told her I had read that from an article published in one of the Liberian Newspapers. She wanted to know how long I was going to spend in Casablanca. I told her I was not sure. I would, however, like to stay for a week if I had good company.

She looked wistfully into my face and smiled. There was nothing not to like there. Pearly-white teeth, shy dimples on both cheeks, frizzy Fulani hair, topped with a very pleasant personality. She drew nearer to me and whispered into my ears, "I will be there to keep you good company." I pretended I had not heard what she said. I asked her to say that again.

She came closer and this time boldly repeated the same words into my ear. I looked at her with a smile, put my arms around her waist, pulled her close, and embraced her, as if to say thank you. She gave me her mobile number and, not surprisingly, the address of her house as well.

We had now arrived in Casablanca. The city was quite close to Rabat, the capital city of Morocco. Casablanca, however, was the commercial capital of Morocco. For me, it was the last-but-one city to my last port of call in Africa, Tangier, before I set foot on mainland Europe. After my seven days in Casablanca, I would have to leave and head directly towards Tangier. Tangier was located on the Mediterranean coast; it was the closest point in Africa closest to the European country of Spain.

Miriam had her siblings waiting for her at the coach station—two adolescent boys and a younger girl. They ran to embrace her and gave her *bisous* on her cheeks. And because I was standing with her, her teenage little sister accorded me four *bisous* as well. Although, I appreciated the gesture, I was a little taken aback. but accepted it as the French style of greeting.

Her brothers shook hands with me welcomed me to Casablanca. I responded warmly to their greetings. They entered their car; the younger brother was at the wheels. They sped off. Miriam waved at me and I waved back.

Now that my new company had gone, I was left alone. I had to look out for Gameli. He spotted me from the distance and shouted my name. I turned, waved and walked towards him. He wanted to know how long I was going to stay in Casablanca. I told him I intended staying for seven days. He said he was not sure but he was not under any pressure to leave sooner than seven days.

We went together to book into the *Dar Tahra* guesthouse, just a fifteen- minute-drive from the city centre. *Dar Tahra* offered a large garden with an outdoor swimming pool, seating areas, lounges looking onto the garden and pool, twenty-four-hour reception, and free unlimited Wi-Fi.

Decorated in the Moroccan style, the rooms and suites at *Dar Tahra* featured satellite TV, air-conditioning, and a private bathroom with a bathtub or shower. The suites had a view of the pool or garden. A continental breakfast was served daily, and Moroccan cuisine was available for lunch and dinner. *Dar Tahra* offered other services including a laundry room service, and a hammam (Turkish bath) at additional cost.

The guesthouse was 18.6 miles from Mohamed V International Airport and there was a tram stop just a walking distance from the guesthouse. Free private parking was also provided on site. I told Gameli this was one of the most sophisticated guesthouses that I had come across so far on my long road-travel to London. He agreed. It had all the facilities of a four or five-star hotel.

I advised we enjoy it while it lasted. I checked into my room on the first floor on the building. Gameli was given a room directly above me on the second floor.

I checked into my room. A clean bed, airy well-lit washrooms, and cool air conditioning blowing nicely around the whole room. I took off my clothes and entered the shower. I had a relaxing shower and was about to doze off for a bit of siesta when my phone rang. It was my lovely Clarissa. I shouted her name loudly in excitement and told her I had just reached Casablanca.

I told Clarissa I wanted to take a siesta. and would call her without fail after dinner in the evening. I blew her a kiss on the phone. She told me she missed me a lot. She also said she loved me, and I also told her I loved her. I went to bed. It was about two o'clock in the afternoon.

The phone rang again. I did not bother to pick it up. I really wanted to sleep and then wake up and answer calls in the evening. But then instinctively, I wanted to see who had called. So, I picked up the phone to view the missed call. It was Miriam. I immediately sent her a text message and assured her I was going to call her in the evening after dinner.

I woke up at about seven o'clock in the evening to a knock on my door. Instinctively, I remembered how the secret service came for Gameli and I in Dakhla. I wondered who would be knocking at my door just hours after my arrival at the guesthouse. I reached for the doorknob, hesitated for a minute, and then plucked up courage and opened the door. It was a big relief to see Gameli at the door.

I let him in and prepared to go with him to the dining hall. We went out together for dinner but could not locate the dining hall. We went to the ground floor and could not find it there. So, we enquired from the concierge. He directed us to the first floor. We found the dining hall located at the far end of the first floor on the western corridor of the building, opposite where my room was located.

The *Dar Tahra* had a magnificent dining hall. A large spacious double-volume room capable of holding and seating over 100 guests. As stated earlier, the guesthouse served continental breakfast daily and Moroccan cuisine was available for lunch and dinner. We ordered for roast chicken and pilau rice; a rice dish whose recipe usually involved cooking with oil, turmeric, cumin, cinnamon sticks, cardamom pods, curry leaves, fresh coriander, salt and pepper, and cooked in vegetable stock.

The food was very well prepared and delicious. We enjoyed it very much and washed it down with some freshly squeezed orange juice and made our ways back to our rooms. I bade Gameli good night and went to my room.

It was now about half-past-eight in the evening. I had a quick shower and reached to my phone. I called Miriam and spoke to her. I confirmed to her that I was comfortably settled in the guesthouse. She asked for the name and address of the guesthouse. I gave her the details. I asked about her family and how the parents and the siblings were doing. She told me the whole family was doing great. She asked whether I had had dinner. I responded in the affirmative and told her exactly the food I had.

She sounded so happy to have spoken to me. Miriam asked me when she could visit. I gave her the option to choose any day of the week that suited her. It was a Sunday. She said she wanted to visit the next day. I told her to come on Tuesday. I told her to look in the tourists' guidebook and choose some places of interest that we could visit.

She agreed and said she had a tourists' guidebook at home and would look for a few places of tourist interests. She wished me a good night and hung up her phone.

I called Clarissa next. As she was becoming happily accustomed to, she shouted my name in excitement. "Hey, Yolandi, my darling! How are you doing?" She asked. I replied to her that I was doing great by God's grace, mercy, and power. I asked her how she was doing. She said she was doing great, except that she missed me every day. I encouraged her to hold fast, and that in the not-too-distant future, we would see each other again.

I told her how happy I was to be in Casablanca, as it was the last but one city before I set foot on mainland Europe. I told her the last city was Tangier. She shared my happiness and wished me well on the last leg of my long road-journey to London.

I called Mum and Dad. As expected, they were very happy to have heard from me. Mum asked where I had reached; and sounding like a broken gramophone, I told her that I was in Casablanca, the commercial capital of Morocco. And that it was my last but one city before setting foot on mainland Europe. Mum was clearly happy for me. She passed the phone on to Dad. He had already overheard me telling Mum where I was.

He was happy that I was making some progress but lamented that air travel would have landed me in London a long time ago. I said to Dad that he was right; but I quickly interjected with the fact that I was learning a whole lot of life's lessons from my long travel to London by road and that I was glad I had travelled this way.

Dad agreed with me and said to me that I was a young man and full of energy, so he had all the confidence that I would accomplish the task I had set out for myself.

I spoke to my sister, Ameley, and had to repeat what I had earlier told Mum and Dad. She was happy and wished me a safe journey on the rest of my journey. I told her I still had a long way to go and that I would keep her abreast with my progress. I also spoke to Zutor and Fogar. They were so happy to have heard from me. They appreciated my courage in making the long journey to London by road.

I assured them that I was determined to see it to its successful end and would reach continental Europe within a week or two. I also spoke to Akogovi, my adopted brother. He was so happy to have spoken to me. He said he always remembered me and prayed for me too. He was happy on the progress I had made so far when I told him where I was; very close to mainland Europe. He also wished me a safe journey and God's guidance with the rest of my journey. I thanked him and wished him well.

My last call ended almost at midnight. I had nothing planned for the next day, Monday. So, I was relaxed and switched on the television to listen in and catch up with the current international news of the day. I tuned into CNN. I enjoyed listening to the various news items. I heard what was going on in the United States of America, the United Kingdom, the Middle East, Japan, and China. There was very little news on Africa, so I tuned into CGTN.

The programme running then was 'Africa Live', a one-hour newscast on how Africa was coping with itself, its neighbours, and the rest of the world. The newscaster was Hannah Viviers, a very beautiful young woman, who happened to be one of my favourite news anchors on CGTN. The news coverage was wide, detailed, and interesting. Hannah delivered it in a splendid alto voice. I switched off the television after half-an-hour. I had my bedtime prayers and went to bed.

Gameli joined me at the breakfast table the next morning. We decided to have a stroll through town. Gameli reminded me of the ordeal we went through when two security agents followed us to our guesthouse in Dakhla and took us to the police station to question us about talking politics in the Western Sahara. It was an incident that both of us could not easily forget.

However, now that we were Morocco proper, the same incident was much less likely to repeat itself. We left the guesthouse clutching our Casablanca guidebooks and maps and headed into town. We took a taxi and rode the rather short distance from the guesthouse to Central Casablanca. It took us just fifteen minutes to reach the town centre.

Casablanca was the largest city of Morocco. Located at the Central-Western part of Morocco bordering the Atlantic Ocean, it was the largest city in the Maghreb region and the eighth-largest in the Arab world. Casablanca was Morocco's chief port and one of the largest financial centres in Africa. According to the 2014 population estimate, the city had a population of about 3.35 million in the urban area and more than 4.27 million in the Greater Casablanca.

Casablanca was considered the economic and business centre of Morocco, although the national political capital was Rabat. The leading Moroccan companies and many international corporations doing business in the country had their headquarters and main industrial facilities in Casablanca. Recent industrial statistics show Casablanca held its recorded position as the primary industrial zone of the nation.

The Port of Casablanca was one of the largest artificial ports in the world, and the second largest port of North Africa, after Tangier-Med, a port about 40 kilometres east of Tangier. Casablanca also hosted the primary naval base for the Royal Moroccan Navy.

We wandered around Casablanca all day. We entered and window-shopped in most of the city's numerous shops and stores in the shopping malls all around the city. We did not buy anything but admired all and everything that we saw in the shops.

Casablanca seemed to have a comparatively higher female population than male. Women of all shapes, forms and sizes roamed around the shopping malls. They bought clothes and housewares as though Christmas was around the corner. Beautiful women too. They looked Caucasian by complexion, but as we later found out, they were Arab in origin and culture. We learnt that most of them practiced Islam and generally did not mingle with men who were not their relatives in public. That worried me a bit particularly when I remembered my newest friend, Miriam.

We were careful who we spoke to and what we said to them. In fact, I could not recollect talking to any woman around Casablanca. I remembered asking a man in the mall where the best restaurants were located when we wanted to have lunch. There were restaurants spread all around the city and most of them served Moroccan cuisine. I was not used to traditional Moroccan food, and for that reason, I always asked for plain rice and fish or meat stew anytime we went to eat at any of the restaurants. That afternoon, we dined at a Chinese restaurant. I had special fried rice with king prawns sautéed with salt and pepper. The meal was preceded by one of my favourite Chinese soups: wonton soup.

We walked a little more around Casablanca after lunch. I went with Gameli to the local turf club where horse racing took place. In fact, horse racing we learnt, took place every day of the week. Entry during weekdays was free. The weekends were heavily patronised, and the races attracted quite high entry fees.

On entry into the race course, Gameli almost made the same mistake I made, that had landed me in hospital. Instead of walking past the horses by the proper path, that passed in front of where the racehorses were tethered, Gameli wanted to use a short cut that would have made us walk on the hind side of the horses. I grabbed him and pulled him sharply back onto the foot path. My experience with the camels when I went out with Fatima in Laâyoune, was still fresh on my mind. We walked in front of the horses. A couple of them neighed loudly. That frightened Gameli who held on to my shoulder in fear. I calmed him down and explained to him that the animals were just neighing, which was like how we humans sneezed.

We walked to the stands where we took our seats. I told Gameli why I did not allow him to walk behind the horses I told him of my experience when I walked behind a camel. I told him that horses were twice as powerful as camels and were dangerous with their hind legs.

We watched five different horse races. Both young men and women placed bets on the horses. They shouted and urged on their chosen horses to run faster. And when a chosen horse won, the shouts got louder and very animated. The excitement was palpable in their voices, as they spoke so loudly and quickly in the Arabic language as though they were reciting some sort of incantation. And so, it continued throughout all the five horse races that we witnessed. Neither Gameli nor I was a gambler, so we placed no bets.

We enjoyed the afternoon just as spectators; and that was not only good, but highly fulfilling. The last of the five races we saw was quite dramatic. The race finished in what appeared like a tie; a beautiful iridescent white horse and a black stallion both finished at almost the same time. That caused a heated argument among the betters.

Those who supported the white house shouted and danced around their horse declaring it the winner. The backers of the black stallion were convinced their horse was the victorious one. The argument raged on and more and more people joined in. The judges came in, calmed everyone down and called for a complete silence.

Initially, they found it difficult to get the silence they called for. Eventually, there was silence. The judges replayed the race on a huge overhead screen. Everyone standing or sitting anywhere in the racecourse could see the screen clearly and closely. The race was played back. There was dead silence; one could hear a pin drop, all eyes were glued to the screens. The two horses came galloping across the finishing line at exactly the same time: 11: 07 seconds.

Consequently, neither the white horse nor the black stallion lost; they both won and the winnings were shared between them. That satisfied all concerned. We streamed out of the racecourse with the crowd, having enjoyed every bit of the day. We hired a taxi to our guesthouse. We reached the guesthouse after about a twenty-minute ride. It was almost seven o'clock and went directly to the dining hall for dinner. We had Moroccan food. I had couscous, with beef in a tagine with vegetables. Gameli had couscous with chicken in a tagine with vegetables.

The food was delicious. I ate to my fill and did not want any dessert. Gameli told me, he also had enjoyed his food very much. We spent some time chatting after dinner. As we made our way to our rooms, I informed Gameli I was expecting a guest for the whole of the next day, Tuesday, and would not be able to go to town with him. He wished me luck and we went to our rooms.

As soon as I opened the door to my room my phone rang; it was Miriam. She greeted me in Arabic and I responded to her in the little Arabic I knew. She expressed surprise as to how well I had said the *Alekum Salam* in response to her *A Salam Alekum*. I told her I could speak a little bit of the Hausa language of Northern West Africa, and the Hausa and Arabic languages had some similarities. She was pleasantly surprised and called me a man with many talents.

Miriam reminded me of her impending visit. I replied in the affirmative that I would be waiting for her. She said she had a surprise for me when she came. I asked her what the surprise was. She replied it would no longer be a surprise if she told me, and she would not let the cat out of the bag yet. I agreed with her and wished her a good evening. She asked me how my day had been and I spent another quarter of an hour telling her about our experiences in town earlier in the day.

I also told her of our previous window shopping at the malls. I even described the type of dressing that was prevalent in almost the whole of the city,; the Moroccan Kaftan. Almost every male we met in Casablanca wore one. Some people looked resplendent in new ones, while others looked ragged in old ones. I appreciated the beautiful ones. I also told her of how in a predominantly Muslim country, very few women wore Hijabs. Rather, as a sign of modesty many women and young girls covered their heads loosely with bright scarfs.

Miriam giggled at my surprise. She said that was Moroccan culture for me. She said even though Morrocco was Muslim, there were several departures in attitude and practice from other Islamic countries. This was due to the King and his Queen who were very modern in outlook.

Miriam arrived at the guesthouse a few minutes after breakfast. I met her at the reception and walked with her to my room. She was dressed in a Marrakshi Life Tuareg cotton-blend maxi dress with a mustard yellow shawl elegantly draped over her shoulders. Her slim wrists and elegant fingers peeked out of the dress's bell sleeves. The vertical stripes of the dress made her look taller than she really was, and the tunic neck allowed a peek at her long neck. She wore a pair of sandals woven from raffia and embellished with multicoloured beads. The outfit was fashionable and tasteful. I told her she looked magnificent and she beamed a smile at me.

She then sprang the surprise she spoke about at me; she opened her little bag and brought out a Moroccan Kaftan for me. She told me she wanted me to dress in a Moroccan outfit just like she did. I unfolded the dress and measured it with my height. It was perfect. The colour was a masculine blue and it had embroidery around the neck made with gold-coloured threads. It was really beautiful to look at.

I quickly changed into the Kaftan, wore an open pair of sandals, and we were ready to go. The excitement of the moment had altogether made me forget to ask Miriam where we were going to go to for the day. When I asked her, she pulled out her tourist guidebook and flipped through the pages. She spoke of a former orchard, quarry and landfill site reclaimed by nature and now managed in partnership with the Land Trust.

This once neglected area was a thriving oasis in Crayford boasting of several reptiles and various migratory birds. This sounded interesting. I was particularly attracted to the wildlife: reptiles and birds. But I waited to hear what Miriam preferred.

She also spoke of the King Hassan II Mosque. This was located on the coastline, just beyond the northern tip of Casablanca's Medina (old city). The King Hassan II Mosque dominated the entire city. Finished in 1993, it was the second largest mosque in the world, covering two hectares in size with the world's tallest minaret (200 metres high). The prayer hall could accommodate 25,000 worshippers, while the courtyard (which boasted of a retractable roof) could fit another 80,000. I was not quite interested in this and neither was Miriam; and so that was ruled out.

We also looked at the Place Mohammed V. The Place Mohamed V was the central plaza of Casablanca. It was home to many of the city's important official buildings, including the main post office, Palace of Justice, Prefecture, French Consulate, and the Bank of Morocco. The building facades were of the neo-Moorish style that French Resident-General Lyautey planned for the city as he set about modernising Casablanca in the early 20th century.

The square had a central fountain and well-tended gardens. During the evenings, it was a local favourite spot for promenading. The Place Mohammed V was attractive and interesting, but I think I was more interested in seeing the reptiles and the birds in their natural habitats and environment.

Miriam agreed to go the to the Crayford Oasis first, and the Mohammed V tourist site the next day. We set off in a taxi together. I was feeling so Moroccan and proud in my Kaftan. Miriam kept telling me that I looked good in my Kaftan. I thanked her for the compliments.

Soon we were at the mini-bus station where the mini-buses plied between Central Casablanca and the Oasis in Crayford. We took a 16-seater mini-bus. Miriam sat by the driver in the front seat and I sat next to her. The bus was full and all 16 of us, including the driver, sat quietly as we travelled on the beautifully tarred black asphalt road.

The time from Central Casablanca to the Oasis in Crayford was estimated at nearly an hour. We had hardly travelled the first quarter of an hour when a group of policemen, about five in number, fully dressed in uniform signalled our mini-bus to stop. When our mini-bus stopped, the sergeant among them came to the driver's window and spoke to him. I could not quite catch what he said to the driver as he spoke to him in Arabic and I could not ask Miriam to interpret what had been said, because I did not want to draw any attention to myself. Next, we were all asked to alight from the vehicle. Everyone in the bus apart from me and two Caucasian-looking couples, was Moroccan. I was the only black African among them. I stood close to Miriam and she held on to my hands. The Caucasian couples also stood next to each other, and the ladies held on to their partners' hands.

The police approached me and spoke to me in Arabic. I replied in English. He spoke back to me in broken English asking for my passport. I asked him whether this was an immigration border post. He looked at me and asked which country I was from. I told him I was an African, just like him. He insisted to know the country I was from. I told him I was from the Republic of Liberia in West Africa. He again asked for my passport.

I told him again that, since I knew, I was not going to a border post, I did not carry my passport with me. He asked me how long I was going to be in the country for. I told him one week. He then asked me whether I was a Muslim. I hesitated for a while and asked him why he wanted to know. He again said in broken English whether I was a Christian, Muslim, or Jewish.

I looked directly into his eyes and told him that my religion was sacred to me, and that I never discussed it. I then asked him whether Morocco did not practice freedom of religion.

At this stage, most of the other passengers started grumbling at the police. They spoke in Arabic ostensibly registering their disgust at how much time was being spent, and how their time was being wasted. I overheard one of the passengers asking in French whether the police picked on me because I was not Caucasian. The police looked in the direction of the one who shouted the question in French, looked down in embarrassment, and refocused his attention on a notebook he was holding.

The sergeant intervened and asked us to get back on the bus and continue with our journey. The policeman who asked me the questions did not look only powerless, but highly embarrassed.

We boarded the mini-bus and continued with our journey. Another forty-five minutes' drive brought us to the gates of the Oasis in Crayford. We alighted and walked towards the entrance of the centre. Miriam was firmly holding on to my left arm as we walked together to the main gate. We paid the gate fees and walked inside the park.

Initially, it looked like a safari park where animals were allowed to move around freely. However, a few metres' walk inside the park revealed several huts and enclosures built for the reptiles.

We walked past the first enclosure. We both stopped and looked inside the enclosure that was full of water. I could not see any animal. I asked Miriam whether she had seen anything in there. She replied in the negative. "Is this just an empty pond," she asked me in an apparent bewilderment. I replied it appeared so. But just as I was about to move on, Miriam held me back and shouted, "Look, look, crocodile!"

I turned, got nearer to the enclosure, and had a good look at the far-right corner of the pond. A huge crocodile of about twelve feet long lay motionless under the water. Suddenly, the reptile turned towards us and we both took a step or two backwards, although there was no way it could come near to us.

I took a good look at the reptile as came out of the pond and came closer to us. Soon a second crocodile came out of the pond and joined it. They both looked huge with their rugged backs, long snouts, and menacing claws. The first one had its mouth wide open. The second one did not open its mouth but had it closed, and had its eyes partially closed, as though it was sleeping. And then came along about a dozen baby crocodiles swimming in the water. It was charming and delightful to see because I had never seen a family of crocodiles, nor seen any crocodiles so close. Despite their clumsy looks, they had a certain beauty. Both Miriam and I took a series of pictures of them.

We moved on after spending about half an hour at the crocodile enclosure. There were so many other visitors to the park that day. The great majority of them came from Europe and the Americas. There were lots of kiosks around the park vending snacks and other take-away food items. We came to another enclosure just a few metres away from where we were at first.

As we approached the enclosure, we spotted what looked like a very large lizard clinging to the branch of a small tree inside the enclosure. I got closer and had a good look at the reptile. Miriam said it was a lizard. I said to her the reptile belonged to the lizard family but was not called lizard. I told her it was called an iguana. A further look around the enclosure located another three of the iguanas on the very low tree in the enclosure. I was excited at the sight, as this was my second time of seeing any.

We were still standing by the enclosure when one of the park keepers in charge of the iguanas opened the door of the enclosure and entered. We were now about 17 visitors standing by the enclosures. The park keeper picked up one of the iguanas, put the reptile on his shoulders and came out with it. A lot of the visitors around started taking photographs of the park keeper and the iguana. Miriam and I also took a few pictures.

Then came the moment of excitement. The keeper asked for volunteers to put the reptile on their shoulders. For the first five minutes, there was dead silence. One could hear a pin drop. Miriam held on fast to my left shoulder. I whispered in her ears the question whether she wanted to volunteer. That made her hold on even tighter to me.

"*Non*," she said to me in French.

"*D 'accord*," I replied to her in French too.

The park keeper explained the reptile was not dangerous and neither did it bite. It was safe to handle and pet. A woman raised up her hand and said, "I will try," with an American accent. Her husband looked into her face and smiled. The woman stepped forward and the reptile was handed over to her. She bravely held on to it for a couple of minutes and then put it on her shoulders. Scores of visitors rushed to take photos.

She handed the iguana back to the park keeper amidst of applause from the visitors assembled there. The park keeper then asked who would try next. I raised my hand. Miriam shouted no. I told to her to calm down.

I disentangled myself from her and walked forward. With the explanation from the park keeper that the reptile was not dangerous, I was not scared. I was confident I would show Miriam how brave I was.

The reptile was placed in my hands. I held it with both hands. I posed for pictures and so many of them were taken by the visitors around. Miriam took quite a few pictures with my phone and hers. I then placed the reptile on my right shoulder and gently rubbed its back. The paparazzi thronged forward and took lots of photographs again. The park keeper took the iguana back after fifteen minutes to a thunderous round of applause from the visitors. Miriam said well-done to me when I went back and held her hands.

We walked for a few metres and went to where another set of reptiles were; the snake enclosures. There were different types of snakes in the glass enclosure. In the far-right corner, I noticed the spitting cobra usually from Mozambique in the Southern part of Africa. There were lots of them also in the West African tropical rain forest. I could identify them because we had lots of them in the tropical rain forests of Liberia from where I came.

As we approached the case, the cobra reared up with the head pulled back and the neck hood flared. In this defensive position, it spat venom at us. Luckily, they were in a glass enclosure and the whitish venom landed harmlessly on the glass. I told Miriam and a couple of the visitors around the glass enclosure, stories about how dangerous both the bite and venom of the cobra were. I told them when it bit, it could cause severe tissue damage, swelling, and eventually death, unless the victim was rushed to the hospital quickly and an anti-snake serum injection administered to him or her. And should the venom from the cobra spray hit one's eyes, it could cause serious irritation unless it was immediately rinsed with water. Having divulged all that, I felt like I was an authority on African snakes.

There were other snakes on display. There were black mamba, puff adder, gaboon viper-also called the gaboon adder, the West African carpet viper, the ring-necked spitting cobra, and the boomslang, a type of snake species restricted to Sub-Saharan Africa and known as one of the most venomous snakes on the continent. The mix of the different snakes in the large glass enclosure painted a kaleidoscope of beautiful colours, that kept changing as the reptiles criss-crossed each other.

We stood and watched this beautiful sight for a few more minutes. Just as we were about to leave, another park keeper, this time in charge of the snakes' enclosure, came around holding a large snake. I recognised that type of snake. It was the African python with its distinguished grey and brown carpet prints all over its body. It looked beautiful. I knew that the African python did not bite. In the wild, it caught its prey by coiling around the prey, stretching and crushing it until the prey died, and then the python would swallow it whole at its leisure. It could be antelopes, lions, tigers and even humans. But it never bit as venomous snakes did.

We all stood and admired the park keeper's antics with the snake. First he coiled the reptile around his neck, undid it; then around his waist and undid it; and then around his torso and undid it. Anytime he undid the reptile, it easily disentangled itself from the body of the park keeper. Just like the case with the iguana, the park keeper invited the visitors to have a go at allowing the reptile to coil around the different parts of their bodies.

For about ten minutes, there was silence just as it was in the case with the iguana for five minutes. Again, one could hear a pin drop. I whispered to Miriam that I was going to try. Miriam did not reply. She did not even look me in the face. I raised my hand to volunteer anyway. The park keeper was excited. He invited me forward and had the reptile coil around my abdomen. I showed some bravery and kept on smiling as the reptile remained around my tummy.

The other visitors kept taking photographs with their mobile phones and their cameras. Miriam also took a couple of pictures using both phones. But just as I was expecting the reptile to start easing, and to be put around another part of my body, I could feel it moving the coil upwards towards my torso and tightening at the same time. I called out to the park keeper who did not realise what was going on at first. He tried to disengage the reptile from my body; but the more he pulled and tried to disentangle the reptile from my body, the tighter the reptile became on my body. The animal tightened its grip on me.

Fear had gripped me by now, although I was not panicking. The keeper grabbed the head of the reptile and tried to disentangle it from my body; but the more he pulled, the more the reptile increased its grip on my body. The park keeper momentarily looked confused and scared. He quickly called for help on his walkie-talkie radio. Quite a few of the other keepers rushed to the scene. I could see two ambulances also summoned to the place.

All sorts of thoughts raced through my mind. I thought of the remainder of my journey to London. I thought of my university, the London School of Economics; I thought of my parents in Monrovia; I thought of Clarissa, my love. I thought of my siblings and all the fine friends I had made on my journey so far. The coils of the snake became tighter, and I was beginning to have difficulty in breathing. I shouted out my concern to the ambulance staff and all the park rangers. The ambulance staff at the park laid me gently on the ground. Their panic was beginning to show; it looked like they had run out of options. I started crying out as the snake tightened itself around me more and more. It was then that the lead park keeper ordered for the snake to be tranquilised.

The ambulance men quickly injected a serum into several parts of the body of the snake; at least at five different places. Instantly, I felt the grip of the reptile begin to relax. It continued to ease and the park keepers quickly disentangled the reptile from my body. When it was completely removed around my body, it lay motionless on the ground. It was heavily sedated.

I was relieved that the reptile was not put down, but only sedated. I was also relieved that I had come out of the clutches of this huge African python without any injuries to my body. I attempted to rise from the ground where I lay, but the ambulance men asked me to remain lying down. They brought in a stretcher, placed me on it, and took me to the park hospital just nearby. Miriam rode along with me in the ambulance.

At the hospital, all my vital signs were checked; my temperature, blood pressure and my eyesight were all checked. Thankfully, there was no injury. I was discharged. The park keepers apologised profusely and thanked me for volunteering to take part in the eventful exercise.

It was late afternoon by now and we had not had lunch. I felt very hungry and suggested to Miriam we had lunch in the park restaurant, but she turned it down. She appeared more traumatised than me because of the incident. I calmed her down as we walked out of the park. She suggested we had lunch downtown Casablanca. We arrived in Central Casablanca just after an hour. Miriam suggested we headed towards the guesthouse and have lunch there instead.

I politely disagreed with her and she gave in and agreed to eat in town. We had lunch at the *Eldora* Restaurant in town after which we took a taxi and headed towards the guesthouse. Miriam went straight into the shower and washed down. She looked physically drained. I am sure she thought same of me too.

After the shower, we retired to bed for a siesta. After the scorching Mediterranean sun that afternoon, the cool air-conditioning lulled us to sleep in no time. We woke up around a quarter-past seven that evening. We had had a good rest. The guesthouse restaurant closed at eight o'clock so we hurried to the dining room before it would close. As we had dinner, I wondered where my friend and de facto travel companion, Gameli, had been all the while. I had it in mind that we would be both continuing our journeys towards Europe in a couple of days.

It was a Thursday, and what that meant was that I had just the Friday left in Casablanca. I had to continue my journey on Saturday evening. Gameli and I would be taking the coach from Casablanca to Tangier. That would be my last stop on the continent of Africa prior to entering Europe. I was not sure at this juncture whether I was excited or indifferent. There was nothing to feel nostalgic about, however, and so I experienced no sadness.

We sat down to a good meal. I had Lamb Niçoise with buttered rice and gravy. We added some Moroccan potato salad as a side dish. Miriam had the same. It was at the dinner table that I reminded Miriam of my imminent departure to Tangiers, my last stop in Africa. She told me she was aware of the dates.

She would have to catch a coach by midday that day to her family home a couple of a hundred kilometres outside Casablanca. That would take her about two hours on the State Intra City bus. My journey, on the other hand, would take at least, about six hours. I would have to travel from Casablanca, through the capital city Rabat, and then pass through Kenitra, Chechaouene and to Tangier, our final stop. The coach would make a couple of stops at Kenitra and Chechaouene.

We woke up Friday morning fresh and well rested. We were both full of vitality and an unexplained ebullience. No sooner had Miriam entered the bathroom than my cell phone rang. It was my friend and travel companion, Gameli. He told me he rang to remind me that our journey was scheduled for Saturday evening, that was just a day away. I told him I was fully aware and was just about to call him and remind him also.

He said to me he was on his way to breakfast and I told him Miriam and I would be joining him at the breakfast table soon. I had my shower quickly, got ready, and joined Gameli at the breakfast table. He was not alone. He had company. She was a beautiful Arab-looking young woman of about 25 to 28 years old.

She had typical curly black Arab hair that dazzled in the sunrays that occasionally penetrated the windows of the dining hall. She had a pert nose, luminous brown eyes, and a pretty round forehead. Her eyelashes were lush and long and she had a habit of fluttering to accentuate her points. Her name was Ameema. She was beautiful and charming.

Gameli introduced Ameema to us as soon as we took our seats.. She spoke good English and excellent Arabic. Miriam greeted her in Arabic; and for the next five minutes, they chatted as though Gameli and I did not exist. Suddenly, they realised they were being unhospitable and apologised and led the way to the breakfast buffet that was heaped with substantial quantities of different food items. There was fresh goat and cow milk, baguette freshly baked, cereals, omelettes, poached eggs, cheeses, fresh fruits, salads and stir-fried vegetables, and tea and coffee.

We ate a little of everything, and even went for seconds. We particularly enjoyed the pineapple juice; it was very fresh and sweet. We were so full we could not leave our table immediately. Indeed, we rested and chatted for a very long time.

It was then that Gameli informed Miriam and I, that Ameema was going to travel with him to Tangier. The idea was appealing to me, but I was not sure Miriam could do same. It would have been good company but we had not planned it. Besides, she had not informed her mum and dad. Neither had she informed her siblings. On my part, as I was getting nearer to Europe, I needed to begin to focus on my objective for this long road trip to London. I thought of the preparations that I had to put in place in Tangier before getting to Spain, my first European country on mainland Europe.

These thoughts quickly flashed through my mind as we continued to chat. Miriam and I congratulated them on travelling together and wished them real joy. We were so immersed in our conversation that we forgot it was time to clear and clean the dining room in preparation for lunch.

"Time to close the hall, please," came the sound from behind us in the dining hall. We all almost simultaneously looked back and saw this huge man wearing a chef's hat and apron walking towards us. He stood well above six feet and wore a long beard that appeared greyer as he advanced nearer to us. The long beard made him look like one of the swashbuckling soldiers who had just come back from the religious wars fought by Genghis Khan in the 13th century.

He greeted us politely and told us that the dining hall was being closed. He then reminded us that lunch was going to start at 12 midday prompt. We thanked him kindly and made our way out of the dining hall.

It was on our way to our respective rooms that Miriam suggested that we went to town together. I looked at Gameli and Ameema enquiringly, and even though they did not speak, they looked interested. I then capitalised on their apparent interest and asked whether anyone had a place in mind that he or she would want us to visit, without directing the question at anyone in particular. Miriam suggested we went on a submarine boat ride.

That suggestion was unanimously agreed upon and we all agreed to meet at the guesthouse reception at eleven o'clock that morning. We were all on time and we made our way out towards the city harbour some 15 kilometres away from central Casablanca.

This was not a military or naval submarine. It was a sailing ship redesigned in a special way. The usual sailing ship has three decks, going into the deep. However, with this vessel, the lowest deck of the ship; the orlop, was made of thick transparent plexiglass. All the sitting areas for tourists extended seven feet or more into the sea. This is why it was referred to as a submarine. Those sitting in the plexiglass orlop would be able to observe the wonderful marine world.

We got our tickets and waited to board the vessel. A bearded middle-aged man with receding grey hair came into the waiting area and drew everyone's attention. We were about 30 in number. He lectured us on the dos and don'ts while on board the ocean-going vessel. We were cautioned against moving from one seat to another, lest we interfered with the stability of the ship. We were also given lifejackets.

We put them on as the gentleman continued to instruct us on how they were to be worn. He demonstrated to us how to inflate the lifejackets in case of emergency. With the lectures over, we were asked to board the ship.

We walked the short distance to the ship in a queue. I held Miriam's right hand as we entered the ship. Gameli and Ameema too held hands. It was clear to me that all of us had bordered the ship in twos, and as couples. That reminded me of the story of Noah and the Ark as told in the bible; that all the animals entered the Ark in twos, male and female. I smiled wryly to myself at the idea.

We all took our seats. The ship sounded a sustained long blast which indicated that the vessel was leaving port. Just as the ship started to move, it sounded one short blast which indicated that the ship was leaving its neighbour which was berthed on its port side. On our way towards the breakwaters, the ship sounded another blast which indicated it was behind another boat going in the same direction.

And just when it was about to overtake the boat in front, it sounded another single blast indicating that it wanted to pass the boat in front of it on that boat's starboard side. That was on our ship's port side. We passed the breakwaters and entered the wide-open sea. The colour of the sea from below the deck, through the transparent orlop, was turquoise. No sooner had we gone about a kilometre than Miriam pulled on my shoulder and asked me to look in her direction.

There appeared a big white shark that swam close to the ship's side. The shark's snout touched the thick white glass that separated us from the huge fish. I took the opportunity to have a close-up look at the shark's fins. And when she opened her mouth, her serrated teeth all appeared, sharp, pointed and arranged in the form of a carpenter's saw. "What a creature," I sighed quietly.

Apparently, all the tourists in the section of the lower deck where I was seated were also attracted to the shark. I could hear lots of gasps, and other exclamations behind me. Gameli and Ameema, sitting right behind us, were quiet; but when I turned and looked at them, they had their mouths wide open, apparently in excitement. I could faintly hear Ameema whispering something into Gameli's ears.

We then saw a huge shoal of different kinds of fishes swimming past us. I was able to identify some of them. I vividly recalled seeing the blackfin tuna, the jumping mullet, the barracuda, mackerel, turtles, sea trout, halibut, and cod. I was surprised to see some of the fishes which normally stayed on the

seabed floating around and well. I saw the giant frog fish and the short-nose bat fish which normally would be looking for food on the seabed.

The fishes were brightly-coloured and of many hues. They ranged from the rainbow colours to any of the main primary colours in combination. I was able to identify the yellowtail fish with its tail a distinct yellow. And I said to myself quietly, "What a wonderful world; what a wonderful God of creation that we have!"

As we sailed further into the sea, and sitting about seven feet below sea level, the idea of seeing a mermaid flashed through my mind. No one I knew, had ever seen a mermaid. At least no one had ever told me he or she had seen one before. Just the mere fact that I was deep under sea water, and folk stories usually spoke of mermaids coming from the sea, made me think of seeing one by chance at the bottom of the sea. I turned gently and whispered my thoughts about mermaids to Miriam.

She smiled at me and told me in categorical terms no one had ever seen one that she knew of. She asserted that she did not believe they existed. We had been sailing for an hour and half, and it was time for lunch. We were told we were going to be served lunch on board the ship. However, we had to go to the galley and serve ourselves, as a buffet was laid out there for us to serve ourselves and come back to our seats to eat.

Every deck had a galley attached to it. There were three decks: upper, middle and the bottom decks. We were in the bottom deck.

We were to go in rows in a strict and orderly manner; four at a time. And this applied to all three decks. It started well. We went in fours to the galley walking and swaying slightly from side-to-side. As if by design, Miriam, Gameli, Ameema and I stood up at the time to go to the galley. We were the third group to make for the galley to dish our lunch.

Halfway to the galley, the ship began to roll from side to side. Soon, the rolling became severe as the ship's passengers began to fall on each other on both sides as and when the ship rolled. The rolling was quite severe. It was as if the ship was going to roll over on its side and sink. There was panic and pandemonium everywhere. I could clearly hear the ship's emergency alarm system going off. It sounded very loud.

I recognised it by the seven short rings of a bell followed by a long ring using the ship's horn signal of seven short blasts followed by one long blast. Miriam held on to me tightly. I held on to one of the hand rails along the inner walls of the ship. Food plates crashed onto the deck floor and there was a lot of shouting and screaming. The captain of the ship went to the bridge and announced that people on the upper deck had flocked rather too much to the starboard side of the ship. The ship had lost its balance.

The ship had listed towards its starboard side. He commanded all passengers on board the ship to resume their seats immediately. Even those in the galley, were to leave the galley immediately. As we turned and walked towards our seats, the ship took a massive dip onto its starboard side and scooped up a torrent of sea which water poured into the ship and drained down all the three decks, even to where we were located. This was greeted by loud screams and pandemonium amongst the passengers on all decks. From nowhere it seemed, a wave buffeted the ship on its starboard side, righting us. Everyone on board was in suspense, with bated breath, not knowing what would come next.

We were now nearly three hours at sea and were about 25 nautical miles from port. Just as the ship appeared to have stabilised, the captain made an announcement. He said the ship had to return to port immediately. He had just received the weather forecast which was not conducive for ships to remain at sea at that moment. A storm was expected any minute, from the north-eastern side of the Mediterranean towards us. The prediction was that it was it was going to be a tornado.

The captain of the ship had hardly completed his announcement than the ship started rolling from side to side again. Passengers were falling on each other. The huge tornado began to blow the ship in all directions. In addition to rolling, the ship began yawing, as if a mischievous child was holding it by a corner of the stern and moving it back and forth. The ship started taking in water.

We could hear the squeaking and groaning noises the ship was making from the buffeting of the severe wind, from where we were down at the bottom deck. The ship continued to list dangerously. Miriam, as usual, had her arms tightly hooked in mine. I tried to stabilise myself on my seat. I tried to stabilise Miriam too. I could not look back to see what was happening to Gameli and Ameema. They were as silent as frightened mice in the presence of a cat.

The ship had made a 360^0 turn and started making its way back to port. That was when the tornado was at its fiercest. At a point in time, it appeared to me the whole ship was lifted, tossed up into the air and dropped back on the surface of the ocean, like a toy. Again, there were shouts all over the three decks. Suddenly, the bottom deck, where we were, started flooding.

Sea water started pouring into in the ship in gallons. It happened any time the ship lifted and hit its bottom on the surface of the sea. I held on tight on to Miriam. She did the same. I started praying quietly to God to save us. I recited the twenty-third Psalm, *"The Lord is My Shepherd..."* many times over.

Soon we were ordered to vacate the third deck and climb on to the second deck. The sea water in the third deck was getting too much. We climbed in twos, just as we were doing for our lunch before the disaster struck, up the gangway. Our shoes and clothes were drenched. We stood by the rail, holding onto it fast. I thought of my home in Monrovia, Liberia. I thought of my parents, Clarissa, my siblings, and everyone I had left behind in Liberia.

I thought of the friends that I had made in Ouagadougou, Niamey, and the other cities that I had passed through to reach Casablanca. Then I thought of my university, The London School of Economics. All these thoughts flashed through my mind at the point of finishing reciting the twenty-third Psalm for about the tenth time in my head. The ship made another humongous and gargantuan list to the port side. I thought the ship had capsized.

It stayed on its portside for about five minutes at least, and then miraculously, in my opinion, it stabilised again. Neither Miriam nor Ameema said anything. I shouted to Gameli asking whether he was alright. He replied in a surprisingly confident voice that he and Ameema were alright and that all these misadventures would ease soon. "All shall pass," he quoted a famous African saying. I was surprised at his confidence, but I believed what he said. I continued reciting my favourite Psalm in my mind. To me, it was my only hope of surviving the ordeal.

The ship laboured toward port at the best speed it could muster, all the while rolling heavily, and intermittently heaving as well. The more the ship rolled, the more the women in particular screamed in fear. There were noises that indicated people were retching or were just about to retch on the ship's decks. In fact, looking around, many passengers on board the second deck had seriously soiled the floor of the deck with their vomit. The sense of fear was so strong people hardly noticed this.

The ship continued towards port. The furious wind, at this time, had started to calm down considerably. The lulls in the storm continued to grow. We were delighted to hear the captain announce from the bridge that we had only about half-an-hour's sailing time left to reach port. The relief was palpable. There were sighs of relief from all corners of the ship deck.

Some passengers resorted to clapping loudly and shouting with joy on hearing the captain's announcement. Some even burst into singing, although I could not decipher the language in which the songs were being sung. All I had on my mind was to reach port safely, go back to the guesthouse, have dinner, and have a good rest before the following day's long journey.

We reached port and were ushered out of the ship in twos. I looked around and saw the mess that the severe retching had caused on the deck floor. Holding on to Miriam's left hand, we climbed the gangway together. We reached the first deck and the situation there was no different from that of the second deck where we had left. In fact, it looked worse.

There was food scattered all over the floor. This was mixed in with vomit and was a horrible mess. I took my eyes off the scene and climbed up the next level. There we carefully walked to the jetty and disembarked from the ship. We all gathered in the waiting room. The captain of the ship, who stood just a few inches below six feet, addressed us. He first apologised to us for the ordeal that we had gone through. He did not blame himself for what had happened. Neither did he blame any one of the ship's company. He used a legal term usually used by Business Law Practitioners saying that the ordeal we had gone through would have been tantamount to *Force Majeure* if he had a contractual agreement with us. He said it was an extraordinary event or a circumstance beyond the company's control, and that it was the force of nature. In other words, the act of God. He congratulated us for staying strong and alert throughout the ordeal and wished us safe journey home.

It was now about five o'clock in the afternoon. The four of us took a taxi and headed towards our guesthouse. We reached the guesthouse after a thirty- minute drive. We were famished. Dinner was going to be served from six o'clock that evening. Gameli said he and Ameema would be joining Miriam and I at about half-past-six for dinner. I told him we would be there about a quarter of an hour earlier.

On reaching our room, as she was wont to, Miriam went straight into the bathroom. No sooner had she finished taking her bath than I entered the bathroom to washdown too. Soon, we were ready for the dining hall. We had had no lunch that day and we were really hungry. We reached the dining hall at about fifteen minutes past six as we had told Gameli and Ameema.

On reaching the dining hall however, Gameli and Ameema were already there waiting for us. They had told us they would be there at half-past-six, but they were thirty minutes early. "All the better," I said to myself quietly. It was our last dinner at the guesthouse and in the company of our friends in Casablanca. The next day would see us travelling in different directions to different countries. We ate well that evening. In fact, it was a combination of lunch and dinner. We had a variety of traditional Moroccan food mixed with Oriental and Western food.

We said our goodnights and retired to our various rooms. We checked our travel itineraries for the following day, had a little chat, and retired to bed because we were both very tired.

Miriam's coach was due to leave at midday the next day. She had already packed. We had breakfast with Gameli and Ameema and said our goodbyes. In fact, it was Miriam who said most of the goodbyes because I was going to travel with Gameli and Ameema on the same coach to Tangier. At half-past-ten that morning, I went to see Miriam off at the coach station.

She appeared not to like the idea that she was leaving me. I consoled her that I would see her again, this time in Europe, and that she should not worry. I also assured her that I was going to be in constant contact with her when I settled in London. She believed me and regained a more positive composure. Her coach left at midday.

She waved at me from seat number 53 on the starboard side of the coach at the window. And as I waved back at her, I got a bit emotional and my eyes began to well up with tears. Indeed, I would miss her too.

I got back to the guestroom and called my Dad, and Mum. I spoke to them at length and informed them that I was about to leave Casablanca for Tangier, the last city before I set foot on mainland Europe. Mum and Dad were ecstatic. They expressed their happiness volubly on the phone, particularly my Mum. I called Clarissa next.

"Clarissa, my darling," I said in a rather loud voice.

"Hey, Yolandi, my dear. I miss you so much," was the ecstatic response that came from the other side of the phone in an equally loud voice. In fact, Clarissa's voice was louder than mine. I responded by saying sweetly that I missed her too. We chatted for over thirty minutes during which we discussed many issues. She informed me that she was doing very well at work, got promoted and had saved a good amount of money. I spoke to all my other siblings. I also spoke to all the friends I had made from Ouagadougou, through Niamey to Casablanca. In the case of Casablanca, it was Miriam who had reached home safely and called to confirm her safe arrival at home.

Gameli, Ameema and I took the same taxi to the coach station. The estimated time of departure was ten o'clock that night. We had reached there about half an hour early. We got our tickets checked in and waited for the station master to board us. The coach, just like the one that brought us from Laâyoune, was another beautiful Chinese-made Yutong. The coach driver welcomed us on board. He started the coach, and off we were on our way to Tangie.

Chapter 12
Tangier

The distance between Casablanca and Tangier was 293 kilometres by road, and it took five hours forty-five minutes. The road was very good. It was an asphalted road all the way just like the ones from Nouakchott to Laâyoune, and from Laâyoune to Casablanca. There was no presence of the huge sand dunes through which the untarred road ran between Gao and Timbuctoo as I had witnessed on my earlier journey.

As usual, I managed to get a ticket for my preferred seat number 52. Gameli who had always preferred to sit at the front of the coach, immediately behind the coach driver, this time chose seats at the very back of the coach. He and Ameema sat on seats numbers 62 and 63 respectively. I could just see them over my left shoulder. Seeing them together made me think how nice it would have been if Miriam could have travelled with me too. However, that did not form part of my concentration at that moment.

It took us about half an hour to drive out of Casablanca Central on to the outskirts of the city. Another quarter of an hour's drive took us to the outskirts of a province called Benslimane. Benslimane was located on the Atlantic Coast. The N1 highway passed through the province and ran parallel to the beautiful seacoast. From my position on seat number 52 on the coach, I could see the beautiful turquoise waters of the Atlantic Ocean to my left.

I could clearly see the white spume of the ocean waves as they rose and raced towards the sandy beach, foam in brilliant snow-white hues as they rose and splashed and beat the sandy shores of the beach. Far off in the horizon, where the sky looked like dovetailing into the sea waters of the ocean were a few ocean-going vessels. They looked rather small in the distance, although these were gigantic ocean-going vessels carrying goods and logistics of all sorts from one country to the other. The seagulls flew in their numbers above the deep blue sea occasionally dipping into the sea water to catch fish that rose to the surface of the sea water.

I turned and looked to my right-hand side from the position where I sat. There again were the long arrays of the simple but nicely built seaside hotels and guesthouses. Several arrays of three to four storey buildings all painted in brilliant white colours adorned and lined the long stretch of the coastline. This stretch continued for about 2 kilometres, after which we had only the deep blue sea to our left, and the long arrays of date palm trees to our right.

The Benslimane coastline was not long. Thus, within the next few minutes, I began to read the road signs indicating that we were only about 5 kilometres away from Rabat. While Casablanca was the commercial capital of the country, Rabat was the political and administrative capital. Just a couple of kilometres to enter Rabat proper, the N1 highway veered and ran outside Rabat Central. I believed this was due to the rather heavy traffic that ran through central Rabat.

We could, however, see central Rabat from the distance. The tall buildings and the Atlas Mountain ranges in the background provided a beautiful kaleidoscope in broad strokes and thin spirals across the skyline even from where I was sitting in the coach. This reminded me of a similar scenario when I drove from Cape Town International Airport in South Africa towards central Cape Town with the Table mountains clearly visible to my left, and, to my right, the infamous Robben Island, where the former South African political prisoner and later President of the Republic, Mr. Nelson Mandela, was detained for twenty-seven years.

That memory of my visit to Cape Town, South Africa, flashed through my mind. I, however, concentrated on the beautiful Atlas Mountains of Morocco that were visible from the distance.

Soon, we had left Rabat behind us. We started reading road signs for the next province called Kénitra. We were to make our first rest-stop there. Kénitra was a city in Western Morocco, formerly known as Port Lyautey from 1932 to 1956. It was a port on the Sebou river, had a population in 2014 of 431,282, and was one of the three main cities of the Rabat-Salé-Kénitra region as well as the capital of the Kénitra Province. During the Cold War, Kénitra's U.S. Naval Air Facility served as a stopping point in North Africa.

The public address system on the coach was activated and the driver started to speak to us. He spoke in not quite fluent English. He also spoke in Arabic. He announced that we were going to take a half hour break at the Kénitra central bus station. It was now early dawn, and I could see most of the passengers yawning after having been woken up by the noise made by the loudspeaker during the driver's announcement. Soon, we were out of the coach.

I alighted ahead of Gameli and Ameema. We walked together towards one of the numerous coffee and tea shops around the bus stop, that served tea with bread that early morning. We ordered tea and drank it with Moroccan bread and scrambled eggs. I enjoyed the early morning breakfast because I did not have a good supper before we left Casablanca. We finished eating within fifteen minutes and used the remainder of the time we had, to walk around the Kénitra central bus station and its environs. Ameema held on possessively to Gameli's arm. This made me not only remember Miriam but miss her too.

Commercial activity early that morning at the Kénitra bus station was brisk. Local buses were leaving and arriving at the station every three minutes. We could hear the whistles of the nearby trains that ran within the city and had their main station not too far away. We also saw the hustle and bustle of pedestrians walking up and down the main streets that had dovetailed into the bus station.

Some carried luggage; others carried merchandise that they carefully balanced on their shoulders as they hawked their goods looking for customers that early morning. The main public address system at the main bus station called out for passengers travelling to Tangier to re-embark their coach. We all moved briskly towards the coach and took our seats. Ameema was still holding tight to Gameli's left hand as they walked past my seat to resume their own.

The driver entered the coach, had a headcount to make sure no passenger was left behind. When he was satisfied, he resumed his seat, started the engine and with a horseshoe turn, drove towards the N1 highway.

We left Kénitra at about six o'clock in the morning and headed towards Tangier. That was going to be about another two-hour drive. The next city indicated on the road signs was Tetouan. Tetouan was about forty five minutes' drive from Kénitra. Soon we passed by the outskirts of Tetouan and we could see the city in the distance to our right. Like the other cities before, the coastline was boarded by the deep blue sea of the Atlantic Ocean.

In Tetouan, we could clearly see fishing trawlers at sea hauling their nets with hundreds of seagulls in tow picking at their catch through the nets. These boats were not very far at sea and so we could see them as they hauled their catch through the nets. These boats were not very far at sea, and so we could see them as they hauled their catches on to their trawlers. We continued driving at full speed ahead. It appeared to me that the driver was making like 70 miles per hour, the standard international speed limit on most European motorways, although I believed I read from one of the pamphlets I picked up at the coach station, clearly stated that all the coaches had cruise controls pegged at 60 miles per hour.

I was enjoying the journey and did not pay particular attention to whatever speed the coach was driving at. Another few minutes of driving saw us approaching Tangier. We had left Tetouan well behind us and the road signs indicated we had 10 kilometres to arrive at Tangier. In a few more minutes, we started seeing buildings and seaside resorts that were located on both sides of the road. The hotels and guesthouses started showing up to the right side of the road. To the left, the spaces were full of tents, and what looked like private ski boats and surfing boards. I was excited we were getting into Tangier. I did not know and would not have known how my friend and de-facto travel companion, Gameli, felt. I was excited because, for me, Tangier was the last city on the African continent before I set foot on mainland Europe.

Suddenly, the reality of me entering Europe began to dawn on me. I remembered the promises I made to Clarissa, my parents, and my siblings about trying to enter the London School of Economics that year. I remembered the decision I made from Kasoa in Ghana not to fly from Accra to London directly, but to travel to London by road. I remember how thieves broke into my flat in Kasoa and stole all my money. I remembered the sterling job the Ghanaian police at Kasoa did to catch the thieves and retrieve some of the money for me.

I remembered my flight from Kotoka International Airport in Accra to the Thomas Sankara Airport in Ouagadougou. Then I also recalled in the quietude my shenanigans of all sorts on my travels through Ouagadougou, Niamey, Gao, Timbuctoo, Nouakchott, Dakhla, Laâyoune and, not too long ago, Casablanca. I heaved a huge internal sigh without making any audible noise. Soon, the driver of the coach announced that we were just a kilometre away from Tangier.

The driver reminded us to take all our belongings with us and be careful not to leave any personal items on the coach. He wished us a good stay in Tangier, and for those continuing the journey further, he wished us safe journeys. We alighted from the coach to a bright and fresh Tangierien morning. The morning dew was still falling and was pleasantly fresh. The sun had just started to climb the horizon and the little birds continued their delightful songs in the surrounding trees.

The sky was beautifully blue, and a fresh Mediterranean breeze blew through the atmosphere directing the morning dew towards the south-eastern direction from where we stood. That gave a clear indication to me that I was near the Mediterranean Sea. My dream of studying at the London School of Economics was becoming a reality. However, I still had a long way to go. I remembered that it was a long road to London, and I had to take things easy and pace myself and my activities.

We quickly looked for a taxi that would take us to our guesthouse. We had done the homework before leaving Casablanca. We decided to lodge at the *Riad Tingis*, a beautiful guesthouse located on top of a mountainside in Tangier. Some tour operators in the city referred to this guesthouse as a hotel. The taxi drove us straight to the guesthouse, and after checking in, we were ushered into our respective rooms. I was in room 112. Gameli and his girlfriend were a floor below me in room 102. The room was beautiful, clean and had an excellent ambience. A hibiscus flower-like scent pervaded the room. Breakfast was free. We quickly had our showers, had breakfast, and came back to catch up on the sleep we had lost during the long journey from Casablanca.

Tangier was a Moroccan port on the Strait of Gibraltar. It had been a strategic gateway between Africa and Europe since Phoenician times. Its whitewashed hillside, the Medina, was home to the *Dar el Makhzen*, a palace of the Sultans that became a museum of Moroccan artefacts. The *American Legation Museum*, also in the Medina, an 1821 Moorish-style former consulate, documented early diplomatic relations between the United States of America and Morocco.

Tangier had been the summer Moroccan royal residence since 1962. An important port and trade centre, the city had excellent road and rail connections with Fès, Meknès, Rabat, and Casablanca. It also had an international airport and regular shipping services to Europe.

Due to its geographic location, the coastal city of Tangier had received influence from the Spanish, British and French. Although, Morocco was a Muslim country, alcohol, night clubs and bars, were not illegal. It had an active nightlife and bar scene and there were lots of watering holes near the seafront. In truth, Tangier was a safe place to make my last stop on African soil before entering mainland Europe. There was only petty or no crime at all in the city except for the occasional scams and pickpockets, we were told.

We were also informed that we were unlikely to be assaulted or seriously hurt as tourists in the city. Tangier was branded as a super safe place for tourists. However, we were not tourists per se; we were just passing through and for me, it was a small but significant stop and a step for me on my long road to London. I woke up at about half-past twelve that afternoon. We were told lunch was between twelve midday and half-past-two in the afternoon. I decided to make a few telephone calls before going to have lunch in the dining hall. I called Clarissa, my love, first.

"Hi, Clarissa, my love," I shouted as soon as I heard her voice answering my phone-call at the other end.

"Hello, my babe," came the reply. I was so excited to have heard her voice. And from the squeaky-girlish voice that I could hear from her side on the phone, I concluded Clarissa was excited to have me on the phone. We talked at length. We talked about her job. I told her how excited I was that I was in the last African city to my first experience of setting foot on mainland Europe; Spain, to be precise.

She said she was delighted for me too. She asked me whether I had had lunch. I told her I would be on my way to the dining hall after I had finished talking with her. I spent about five more minutes telling her about Tangier. I promised her I would call again before going to bed that day. I then called my mum and dad and told them I was in Tangier. Mum, as usual, was very excited to talk to me.

Dad was equally happy. And as was characteristic of him as a caring but disciplined dad, he asked me to remind him of the date school was supposed to resume at the London School of Economics. I told him the university was going to resume on the 5th of September, and that I had more than five calendar months to reach there. He sounded satisfied but reminded me again, that I would have been in London months ago if I had flown from Robertsville International Airport in Monrovia direct to London. I had no intention of arguing with my dad, and so I agreed with him. He sounded satisfied as I conceded.

After calling and telling Miriam I had arrived safely in Tangier, I started getting ready for the dining hall. We did not talk for long. Miriam told me she was happy that I had arrived safely. She asked of Gameli and Ameema. I told her they also arrived safely and were in their room at the guesthouse. I did not call any of the friends I had made from Ouagadougou to Laâyoune this time. I would call them later in the evening.

I met Gameli and Ameema at the dining table. The sense of being alone dawned on me. I felt I had no company and was alone. And that was true because Miriam had gone to her family in a town in Casablanca. I told myself that was not a problem; and because I was going to stay in Tangier for only a week, I could manage that. Because Tangier was on the Mediterranean Sea that separated it from mainland Spain, there were lots of both Mediterranean and Spanish food on the table.

The Spanish dishes were referred to mainly as continental dishes. I had more of the continental food than the Mediterranean ones. One thing I could not resist, however, was the very sweet and delicious Tangerine fruit juice; it was so sweet that I drank lots and lots of it. We had a little chat during which I agreed with Gameli to spend only a week in Tangier before setting off to mainland Europe.

We briefly reminded ourselves where we were going. In other words, I told him I could not wait to get to London, England. He said he also could not wait to arrive in for Rome, Italy, the destination for his journey. We discussed the kinds of passports we had. We were both Africans and had no problems with our Liberian and Ghanaian passports respectively as we travelled across the borders on the continent of Africa. We, however, reminded ourselves that we had to show our visas for Europe, before boarding the ferry to Spain.

Gameli reminded me that he had a visa for Italy his final destination. And since both Italy and Spain were members of the Schengen Community of European States, he envisaged little or no trouble travelling through Spain. I reminded him that I had a United Kingdom of Great Britain and Northern Ireland visa. A UK visa for short. However, since the United Kingdom was not a member of the Schengen Community of European States, Gameli wondered if I was going to have any problems.

It was then that I explained to him that I had transit visas for Spain and France. I also told him that that since Gibraltar was a UK overseas territory, I would prefer to travel there as my first point of settlement when I arrived in Spain. Gameli agreed with me. He advised me and reiterated the point. He further opined that would make me acclimatise to a completely different environment where I would meet different kinds of people who lived and behaved in different ways.

I told him I would ponder over his suggestion and then make a final decision. He agreed with me and with that we rose and made our ways to our rooms. We agreed to meet at the dining room again in the evening for dinner. I entered my room and sat on the bed. I had reached for my phone to make a few calls when it rang. It was from Monrovia. It was not Dad; it was not Mum, or any of my siblings. It was from Clarissa. Clarissa, my love.

"Hello, Clarissa, my darling," I said loudly.

"Hey, Yolandi, my babe," came the reply from the other end.

"I have a surprise for you," she said without even exchanging greetings first. "What's that big surprise?" I joked back. She waited for about five seconds during which she giggled throughout and spoke again.

"I'm very happy you are in your last city on the African continent before leaving for mainland Europe; and I am coming there," she ended.

Totally surprised, I shouted back, "Where?" in a tone that was a mix of incredulity and excitement.

"Tangier," was the reply. "I'm coming to keep you company for the one week that you have in Tangier," came the response.

I hesitated for a couple of seconds and said in a cool and melodious deep voice, "Clarissa, my love, you are most welcome. That will make me so happy. I miss you so much."

Clarissa spoke to me on the phone for exactly forty-five more minutes that afternoon. I asked her during the conversation the mode of travel she would use. There were no direct trains from Monrovia to Tangier; in fact, there were no train travels between these African countries. And I knew she would not embark on another version of a Long Road to London; in which case, hers would be a very Long Road to Tangier. The only alternative would be by air.

There were several airlines that plied routes between the West African sub region and North Africa. We had the Royal Air Maroc (Moroccan airlines) that flew directly from Robertsville International Airport in Monrovia to Casablanca and Tangier. And so did airlines such as Air Egypt, Libyan Airlines, African Air, and a few others.

"I bought my air ticket a couple of months ago when you informed me that Tangier was going to be your last city on the African continent before entering mainland Europe," Clarissa said. She continued to tell me she kept it a secret from me, to surprise me. I told her it was a pleasant surprise and she was most welcome. We had arrived in Tangier on a Sunday morning. Clarissa was scheduled to arrive in Tangier the next day, Monday morning at 1100 hours GMT.

This was a pleasant surprise indeed. I spoke to my dad and mum and mentioned this new development to them. They confirmed the story and said they had agreed with Clarissa to keep it a secret from me. We laughed over it and I told them it was going to be a pleasant occasion indeed. They agreed and wished both of us well when she arrived.

I then spoke with my siblings, including my adopted brother, Akogovi. And the story was no different. They all knew about Clarissa's proposed visit but agreed with her to keep it under wraps until she broke the story to me herself.

After dinner that evening, I was torn between excitement and melancholy. Excitement because my fiancée, who I love so much, was visiting after so much had happened to me since I left Monrovia on this long road to London. Melancholy on the other hand because I would not have the freedom to make any new lady friends in Tangier. But that did not matter. As I lay on the bed, I thought of all the friends I had made from Ouagadougou to Casablanca.

I thought of Angelique in Ouagadougou; I thought of Fatima in Niamey; I thought of Ayeshetu in Timbuctoo and I thought of Miriam in Casablanca. I decided to make phone calls to all of them that evening. One reason was to check on them and see how they were doing. And the other reason was to pre-empt any of them springing a surprise visit on me in Tangier. My fiancée, the lovely Clarissa, would be flying in all the way from Monrovia and I did not want any distraction whatsoever.

I told each one of them I would not be keeping long in Tangier; and that I wanted to reach mainland Europe on time. When I spoke with Angelique, lo and behold! That was exactly what she said she had planned do if I were to be staying in Tangier for more than two weeks. I firmly dissuaded her from the idea. I told her because Tangier was my last African city before I reached Europe, I had a lot of immigration and administration protocols to sort out within the week before proceeding to Spain. The long and short of my message to her was that I would not have the time or space to host any visitor in Tangier. Angelique did not only understand me but empathised with me. She showed no sign of disappointment on the phone. I promised her I would get in touch with her when I reached Spain.

She sounded excited at this promise. She thanked me, wished me well and said to me in French, *"Rendez-vous, espérons-le, un jour plus tard; voyage sûr."* I replied to her in French saying, *"A bientôt. Ce ne sera pas long, Merci."* My short conversation with Angelique brought me memories of my sojourn in Ouagadougou. The teaching job I had; how I had to improve on my little French and use it for teaching; the dinners and outings with Angelique; and much more. All these raced through my memory as fast as they could.

Soon, I managed to speak to all the remaining three: Fatima, Ayeshetu and Miriam. It was excitement galore with each one of them. They all wished me well and promised to call me again before I left Tangier to cross the Mediterranean Sea.

My phone rang early Monday morning. It was half-past-nine. When I picked up the call it was my lovely Clarissa at the end of the call.

"Hi, Clarissa, my love," I said almost shouting into the phone. "Where are you?" I asked.

"I am at the Tangier airport," she said. And before I could ask whether her flight was not scheduled to arrive at eleven o'clock that morning, she cut in to explain to me that the flight was about an hour and a half ahead of schedule.

"I have passed through immigration and customs. I have retrieved my luggage and am sitting in the arrival's hall outside the immigration, baggage reclaims and customs areas," she concluded. I told her she had nothing to worry about. And that my taxi would take only half an hour to the airport. I joked with her that, what that meant was that I would be reaching her at our earlier arranged time of eleven o'clock, or just after. And that I was on time and she was ahead of time. She giggled loudly on the phone and said, "I cannot wait to see you, Yolandi, my love. I will sit here with the other arriving passengers calmly waiting for you, dear,"

My taxi arrived at the airport exactly at eleven minutes past eleven o'clock that morning. I paid the driver, and as he drove away, I looked up and read my way through the arrival's hall. Most of the signs and directions at the airport were written in Arabic, English and French. It did not take me long to arrive at where my lovely Clarissa was sitting. While I could spot her from about 50 metres sitting with her luggage by her side, she could not see me. She sat down calmly and all her concentration appeared to be focussed on her mobile phone upon which she gazed intently.

Then just about some five metres to reach her, she raised her head and saw me. She hesitated for a second or two. She appeared not quite sure whether it was me. And then when she heard me call her name, she left the luggage behind her, ran towards me, and literally flew into my open arms. We embraced each other for almost five minutes, and when she left my arms, she handed me a series of *bisous*, two on each cheek.

We intensely looked at each other's faces for another couple of minutes, kissed her on the lips, and we started walking towards her luggage. We did not create any scene. The whole arrival hall at the airport that morning was awash with lots of arriving passengers and families and friends meeting them hugging and kissing each other. We happened to be just a tiny bit of the action that morning.

We saw a man standing by Clarissa's suitcase with a small booklet in his hand in which he started writing. He was not wearing a police uniform and so we were convinced he was not one. He wore a pair of khaki trouser and a white shirt. He had a peeked cap on his head and looked to me as a security man.

"Excuse me," I said to him asking whether there was a problem.

"*C'est tes bagages?*" He asked us. I understood him clearly but decided to respond to him in English. Most Moroccans were bilingual.

"Yes, Sir, the luggage belongs to us," I replied in English.

"There was no one here and I thought the luggage was abandoned," he said in English. Before I could say anything else, I saw him cancel whatever he was writing in his notebook. Then with a very stern voice, he barked at us, "*Assurez-vous de toujours rester avec vos bagages à l'aéroport,*" he again said in French. This time I decided to respond to him in French.

"*Merci beaucoup pour votre comprehension,*" I said to him speaking good French. He turned his face towards me and looked at me with a friendly face.

He smiled and said, "Thank you," and walked away.

We hired a taxi from the airport and headed towards the guesthouse. We kept holding each other's hand and frequently looked into each other's face. It was as if we were rediscovering ourselves after just a few months of living so far apart from each other. We had missed breakfast altogether that morning and was at the guesthouse just in time for lunch. It was just past midday and lunch was ready at the dining hall.

I suggested we had lunch at one o'clock in the afternoon. In fact, Clarissa explained to me that she had breakfast on board the aircraft and was not immediately ready for lunch. She suggested we go to lunch at two o'clock that afternoon. She told me she was a bit tired and sleepy as she woke up at four o'clock at dawn to prepare and catch her flight at the Robertsville International Airport in Monrovia.

Consequently, she decided to have a nap for a couple of hours. Clarissa had a quick shower, changed into a gown, and went to bed that midday. She looked, as always, so gorgeous, even in a simple gown. Soon she fell asleep. She lay supine, facing the ceiling, with her eyes shut and enjoying one of nature's most important gifts. I took a good look at the Clarissa I left back in Monrovia just a few months before.

As she breathed in and out, I sat and gazed at the beauty that was lying down on the bed. The dimples on the cheeks could clearly be seen although she was not smiling. After looking at her innocent beautiful figure lying on the bed, I lay down beside her and soon fell asleep too.

Gameli rang me at half-past-one and alerted me about lunch. I told him we were scheduled to have lunch at two o'clock that afternoon. He said he and Ameema would join me at the lunch table at two. I quickly directed him to say, 'joining us at two', and not 'joining me'. He quickly asked who else would be joining us. I said to him I had a guest from Monrovia.

"Is it Clarissa, your love?" He asked with great anxiety. I had chatted with him about Clarissa at some point in time, in fact months ago, during our journey. "Yes, good guess," I replied. "I picked her up this morning from the airport," I concluded. Gameli congratulated me and sent welcome messages to Clarissa. We arrived at the dining hall to meet Gameli and Ameema at the dining table. It was exactly two o'clock in the afternoon. In fact, they were on time, and so were we. Both Gameli and Ameema stood up as we approached. He gently said welcome to Clarissa as he stretched his hand to shake her hand. Ameema walked towards Clarissa, placed both hands on her shoulders and gave her four *bisous*. She then welcomed Clarissa to Tangier as all of us sat down at the dining table.

"How was your flight?" Gameli asked looking into the direction of Clarissa with a pleasant smile.

"My flight was lovely," replied Clarissa with a smile that prominently displayed her beautiful dimples.

"Fabulous, welcome, welcome," he concluded with a brief look in my direction. I replied with a quiet smile. I then invited all at the table to approach the buffet table. We all stood up, almost simultaneously, and walked leisurely towards the table on which the food was laid.

The food that afternoon was brilliant. One could smell the sweet aroma of the dishes from where we sat. And as we approached the dishes, it became clear that, once again the food items comprised of more Spanish cuisine than traditional Moroccan. Spanish cuisine consisted of the cooking traditions and practices from Spain. Olive oil was heavily used in Spanish cuisine, and it was at the base of many vegetable sauces.

Hallmark herbs included parsley, oregano, rosemary, and thyme. The use of garlic had been noted as 'common to all Spanish cooking'. There was *Gazpacho*, made with the reddest, ripest tomatoes, olive oil, garlic, bread, pepper, and cucumber. They were blended until silky smooth, then chilled and poured into bowls or glasses to serve. So delicious, so refreshing. There was *Paella,* popular in the Valencia region. It was made of ingredients that included chicken or rabbit, saffron, runner beans and butter beans.

But the all-important element was the rice, ideally the *Bomba* or *Calasparra* varieties grown on Spain's east coast, which were particularly good for absorbing all the flavours.

Next was *tortilla Española.* This dish was made with eggs, potatoes, onions; that's it! Some purists even considered that adding onion was a gastronomic crime of the highest order. The Spanish omelette was so much more than the sum of its parts. The potatoes and onions were slowly fried in olive oil then mixed with the beaten eggs for the flavours to mix before cooking. Chorizo, ham, spinach, courgettes, or whatever was at hand, were added to make a tasty meal out of almost nothing.

However, we chose to have *la comida*, a large midday favourite meal in Spain. Lunch in Spain was a bit different from what we were used to in Africa, or Morocco, for that matter. The large midday meal, called *la* comida, had several courses, and usually included five to six choices in each. At home, Spaniards did not traditionally eat 'fancy' dishes daily, but still enjoyed a soup or pasta dish, salad, meat and or fish, and a dessert, such as fruit or cheese. We took full advantage of the six-course meal and dined to our fill much to everyone's satisfaction.

We remained at the dining table after a heavy lunch, as we were wont to, to plan the activities for the next day. Clarissa was new in town. In fact, all of us were new in town and needed to visit some tourist attractions. At that suggestion, Gameli reminded me, and quite rightly too, that since we were all new to the city of Tangier, it was better we spent the rest of the afternoon researching the tourist guidebook to find out the tourist places and locations in Tangier which could be of interest to us and discuss them at dinner time. I agreed with him. We rose together and soon were on our ways to our respective rooms.

Back in my room, I had long conversations with Clarissa. I told her how I missed her and thought of her each and every day of my long journey to London so far. She told me she missed me more, because I was the 'apple of her eyes'. I told her she was looking even more beautiful than when I left her in Monrovia. I held both of her hands and kissed them. She looked at me with admiring eyes and said thank you. With that, she reclined rather lazily on her back and started reading a magazine.

I picked up my tourist guidebook and started looking for tourist places of interest in Tangier. There was the *Hercules Cave.* An interesting historical site. Upon entering the cave, the first thing you would see was the breath-taking

opening to the sea. It was gorgeous in showing the silhouette of its contents through the opening. The cave had been used as a source for millstones, so one could see columns of rocks with circular shapes cut out of the stone; fascinating! The star of the show was obviously the cave's Africa-shaped window to the ocean, but it did not take long to also explore the various corners of the cave itself.

There was the *Medina of Tangier*. This was the beautiful site where tourists took strolls along a long array of landmarks. It was so nice to stroll through the *Medina*. There was so much to see there. You could see the restaurant from the Jason Bourne movie and also see the place where he jumped from one building to another building. A real beautiful area. The people instantly knew you were a stranger there, but they left you alone to do your own thing.

I also came across the *Family Morocco Tour* where there were excursions and routes from Marrakech, Fez, Rabat, Tangier and Casablanca. The organisers made the trip an unforgettable memory and guaranteed that our routes would not leave us indifferent. We would have tea with the organisers, travel in comfortable 4×4 vehicles, know first-hand the stories and legends of the country Morocco, sleep in the desert contemplating the stars and enjoy a camel ride. This was full of adventures and unforgettable experiences.

I then came across the *Cap Spartel*. This tour provided unique views and a very special opportunity to see first-hand the meeting point of the Mediterranean Sea and the Atlantic Ocean. This sounded great to me. I thought the tour provided an opportunity for a great experience, particularly the unique views and the very special chance to see the meeting point of the great and famous Mediterranean Sea and the gigantic Atlantic Ocean!

There was a caution that it could get very windy. That briefly took my mind back to the submarine sea trip that we took in Casablanca, that almost ended in disaster.

The last of the tourist attractions I came across was the *Corazon de Marruecos*. This was a two-day excursion into the Sahara Desert and which sounded like a truly amazing experience. 'Friendly and trustworthy' guides with Sports Utility Vehicles that was spacious and comfortable would be used for the trip. There would be regular stops for tea, coffee and sightseeing which promised to be awesome.

The whole two days would be efficiently organised allowing the perfect amount of time at each spot, ensuring we would not miss anything including sunset. We would lodge in a camp in the Sahara Desert which had breath-taking views. The food promised to be lovely and all staff were said to be kind and accommodatingly helpful. It allowed tourists to escape the hustle and bustle of Marrakech to see Morocco's fantastic natural environment.

I could not make up my mind instantly. More so, I had to discuss the options with Gameli, Ameema and Clarissa. Just as I put the tourist guidebook down, Clarissa woke up.

"Hello, my lovely Clarissa," I greeted her. She looked at me and smiled. The dimples came again; this time more pronounced than I had ever noticed.

"Hi, my darling," she said as I held her hand to assist her get out of bed. I asked her whether she had a good siesta. She said she did. It was there that I started to show her the various tourist attractions that I had looked up and found. Clarissa told me all of them sounded interesting.

I asked her which one among the lot attracted her most. She looked directly into my pupils, and with a smile, said, "Anyone; I hope to enjoy any one of them."

I was aware that I had only seven days to spend in Tangier before heading along towards mainland Europe. I made Clarissa aware of this. She advised me that we could do just a couple of the trips and then dedicate the rest of the free days to ourselves and catch up on many things. I agreed with her. It was almost dinner time and we started to get ready for dinner when my phone rang. I answered the call and it was Angelique.

I asked her how she was doing. I spoke in French. And I told her I was a bit busy and that I would call her back later. No sooner had I put the phone down than it rang again. I answered the call, and this time, it was Fatima. Like Angelique, she asked me how I was doing and I told her I was doing great. Again, like I did to Angelique, I spoke to Fatima in French.

I told her that I would call her back later. She blew me a *bisous* on the phone, and said, "*Au revoir.*"

All this time, my lovely Clarissa was busy looking through the tourist guidebook for Tangier. And as fate would have it, just as I asked her whether she was ready to proceed to the dining hall, my phone rang again. I hesitated. Then I thought it could be my parents from Monrovia. I looked at the number, said hello and the voice was that of Ayeshetu.

I asked myself what was happening to me that all these three women would be calling me right under the nose of my lovely fiancée, Clarissa. Thankfully, Clarissa did not even take notice of these happenings that evening. She was busy tidying up her makeup in the bathroom ready for dinner. I asked Ayeshetu how she was doing. She said she was doing great.

I complimented her, told her that I was busy and would call her back. She started to say things like I miss you. I said to her I would call her back and she would have plenty of time to express herself.

Clarissa was ready. We were on our way to the dining hall. I prayed to God quietly that another telephone call, this time possibly from Miriam, should not come through. Thankfully, no phone call rang through on our way to the dining room. I then put my phone on silent rather than switch it off just in case my parents or Clarissa's parents called.

As usual, Gameli and Ameema were at the dining table well before we arrived. They had not dished their food yet. It appeared they were waiting for us. Ameema and Clarissa again exchanged *bisous*. Both Gameli and I looked on admiringly. Again, we decided to go Spanish for dinner, this time, we chose to have *tortilla Española*, the dish, which was made with eggs, potatoes, and onions. The food aroma was strong. Clarissa held on to my left arm as we approached the food table. "This one has a very nice aroma," she said looking directly at the Spanish omelette.

"Yes, indeed my dear," I said with my full gaze on the Spanish omelette as well. I could hear Ameema whisper something into Gameli's ears but could not catch exactly what she said. My guess was she might have been echoing what I said to my lovely Clarissa.

We tucked into our dinners with full concentration. We asked for some red wine. The waiters brought us one of South Africa's very good red wines: *Nederburg*. None of us drank much, but we enjoyed the dinner very much with the red wine. We were not very good drinkers of alcohol;

however, by the time the evening's dinner was over, we realised we were left with a couple of empty red wine bottles. It was one of the best dinners I had had on my entire long road to London so far.

We rendezvoused to meet at the reception to go on our day trip after breakfast the next morning. It was then that Ameema reminded all of us that we had not decided on which of the trips to embark upon. I apologised for not letting them know earlier. I told them Clarissa and I thought a trip by boat to where the Mediterranean Sea met the Atlantic Ocean would be lovely. Gameli looked into Ameema's face for a couple of seconds and then nodded his head in agreement.

"Sounds wonderful," he said with a smile. "What do you think?" He asked his friend.

"Fantastic," replied Ameema. "That will take us really close to the coast of Spain," she remarked with a rather hoarse female voice.

"*Rendez-vous demain,*" I said to them in French.

"*À bientôt,*" replied Ameema in simple good French to my surprise.

We spent the evening chatting and remembering some of the good times that Clarissa and I had in Monrovia. We recalled the evening that I went to visit Clarissa at home for the first time and was met by the father sitting in front of the house. He asked me who I was and who I was after. It was my first ever visit to Clarissa's house, although we had been seeing each other in town six months' prior.

The question hit me hard, particularly as that was one of the reasons I felt reluctant to visit Clarissa at home. I summoned courage and told him that my name was Yolandi and that I was Clarissa's friend. He asked me what type of friend? I told him that the ordinary friendship that usually existed between young men and women. After receiving some convincing answers from me to his questions which centred on my family, work and religion, he nodded his head and called for Clarissa.

I stood quietly and full of fear that did not show. When Clarissa arrived, he asked her whether she knew me and was expecting me. And when Clarissa responded in the affirmative, he allowed me to enter the house and we walked into the house compound. Clarissa took me to greet the mother after which we walked into her self-contained one-bedroom apartment.

We laughed out loudly as we recollected similar events. I told Clarissa she looked beautiful. She looked into my face with a captivating smile that again prominently revealed the dimples on both sides of her cheeks. She told me I looked gorgeous. I told her she was beautiful. She held my left hand, threw her right arms around my neck, drew me closer to her and kissed me passionately.

I enjoyed the kiss, particularly as that was the first time I kissed my lovely Clarissa in several months. With that, we both bid each other goodnight and reclined to bed.

We met Gameli and Ameema at the breakfast table the next morning as had been the routine so far in Tangier. Breakfast was good. We finished early and as planned, we met at the reception exactly at ten o'clock that morning. We picked a taxicab and headed towards the Tangier port where different companies ran the boat-trips to where the Mediterranean Sea met the Atlantic Ocean to the Southwestern tip of Spain.

We were on operation *Cap Spartel*. The trip that would provide us with unique views and a very special opportunity to see first-hand the meeting point of the Mediterranean Sea and the deep blue Atlantic Ocean.

The taxi took about twenty-five minutes to reach the seaport. We had to quickly choose from over a dozen of the trip service providers most of whom had placed huge billboards by the roadside advertising their trips. There were a variety of them with interesting names. We saw the *Tiger Baby* Boat Trip, the *Auntie Dede* Boat Trip, the *Tangier Cruise* Boat Trip, the *Simbard de Sailor* Boat Trip and the *Alexander the Great* Boat Trip companies.

There were many more. The *Auntie Dede* Boat Trip company was leaving in half an hour. We decided to go with that company. We bought our tickets and waited in the boat company's waiting area. We were served with tea and biscuits.

Soon we were on board the *Auntie Dede* for our sea trip to the confluence of the great Mediterranean Sea and the huge Atlantic Ocean. The place was called *Cap Spartel*, where the north-western point of Africa, and the Atlantic Ocean met the Mediterranean Sea. As we left the breakwaters of the Tangier port, we were not disappointed. The picturesque views of Tangier were fascinating.

The buildings, landscape, occasional mountains, and hills all formed a classic kaleidoscope of natural geographical and human architectural beauty. The *Auntie Dede* moved full speed ahead. The boat was full. We were about 75 in number. It was a big boat. Even with the 75 of us on board, there were still many empty seats on both decks.

As we approached the *Cap Spartel*, we could spot in the distance the place where the sea, the ocean and the strait met. There were amazing panoramic views. The beautiful lighthouse stood on a hill right in the middle of the sea with its rays of bright light flashing from port to starboard. It was only about half-an- hour of sailing that brought us to *Cap Spartel*. Soon we entered the little port which had a capacity of berthing about fifteen boats at a time.

As we manoeuvred to enter port, the clear demarcation of the Mediterranean Sea and the Atlantic Ocean showed very prominently. We could see a clear straight line that divided two huge water bodies. One looked turquoise in colour, and the other a deep blue hue. It was a great spectacle to watch. We all focussed on this great feat of nature, particularly what looked like a long rope located in between the Atlantic Ocean and the Mediterranean Sea.

The boat successfully berthed. We started disembarking. Clarissa held on to my left hand. As we stepped out on dryland, not far away from the beautiful lighthouse, I noticed a huge billboard on which was written the words: 'Welcome to *Cap Spartel*-Tangier where the Mediterranean Sea kisses the Atlantic Ocean'. I drew Clarissa's attention to it. She read it and we both laughed and carried on towards the area where many hotels and restaurants were located.

One building caught my attention. It was a beautiful villa with sea views of the Spanish coast mountains of *Cap Spartel*. Built in 2007, it boasted of three bedrooms, and a living room for 10 people. It also provided large supplementary beds, two toilets, and one bathroom, arranged on two floors. It had heating, abasement, terrace, balcony, cellar, veranda, fireplace, outbuildings, and a very spacious kitchen.

It was wonderfully appointed with all the modern amenities one would want. It had a pool, air conditioning, sauna, smart TV with Netflix account, satellite, and internet access.

The description in the villa's brochure was very inviting. However, Clarissa and I were fully aware that we were on a day trip and would be going back to our guesthouse back in Tangiers in about three to four hours' time. I told Clarissa all that stuff was fanciful and that it was not carved for us. She agreed and we moved on.

We strolled through the township of *Cap Spartel*. All the boat passengers on our boat were told we were at liberty to roam around the town as we wished. We, however, had to be back in three hours, that would be four o'clock in the afternoon. Gameli and Ameema went in a different direction. We could not locate them since we disembarked from the boat. Clarissa and I stood on a small hill about ten feet away from the lighthouse to have yet a better view of the straight line that demarcated the two big water bodies.

The spot had three binoculars mounted on stands from where visitors could observe the meeting point of the two water bodies much further and clearer. What was even more spectacular was the stillness of the water. The deep blue waters of the Atlantic Ocean stood calm as she kissed the turquoise waters of the Mediterranean Sea.

The whole sight, as I watched it through the binoculars for about three minutes, reminded me of the greatness of God's creations. 'How grand are the works of His hands' I said to myself in quietude. I passed the binoculars over to Clarissa and watched her look through the instrument. She involuntarily started nodding her head in appreciation, as though she was responding to a question posed to her.

"Oh! my God!" I overheard Clarissa exclaim. "What's the matter?" I asked.

"Flying fish; flying fish; about a hundred of them," she said still looking into the pair of binoculars.

I looked in the direction far out at sea and caught the spectacular natural occurrence. A glide of flying fish simultaneously jumped out of the sea water to a height clearly over 6 metres and beautifully dipped back into the deep blue waters of the Atlantic Ocean. This was only about two feet away from the demarcation line that separated the two water bodies.

Five minutes later, the same spectacle occurred again and the crowd of about 30 visitors around shouted with joy. We then hung up the pair of binoculars for other visitors to use. We started walking back to town. It was now about half- past two in the afternoon. We needed to have lunch.

As we walked slowly towards the town centre looking for a restaurant, Clarissa, still holding on to my left hand, remarked that the glide of the flying fish that flew out of the Atlantic Ocean could have easily dipped across the demarcation line into the Mediterranean Sea. I told her it was a possibility, but schooled her that, nothing in the two huge water bodies ever got mixed up. Even the sea water from the Atlantic Ocean, and the Mediterranean Sea, although they met at the demarcation line on the surface of the water bodies, did not mix or cross over into each other.

So, the flying fishes, had they dipped into the Mediterranean Sea, would still have found their ways back into the Atlantic Ocean across the demarcation line. I further explained to her that it was the reason both water bodies kept different hues at the demarcation line. Clarissa inquisitively asked me why that was so. I told her that, it was one of the wonderful and miraculous works of nature.

She looked into my face, smiled and exclaimed, "What a Mighty God we serve!"

We checked into one of the local restaurants to have our lunch. It was now about three o'clock in the afternoon. Still, we had not seen Gameli and Ameema. We decided to leave them alone to enjoy each other's company on the beautiful *Cap Spartel*. We ordered for food. Again, it was a variety from both Spanish and Moroccan cuisines. Both Clarissa and I decided to go Spanish. We had grilled fish, braised rice, and French fries.

The meal was excellent. The fish tasted very nice. Both Clarissa and I enjoyed it very much. We had a glass each of French Red wine with our lunch. We spent over an hour and a half at the restaurant. By the time we left the restaurant, it was just ten minutes to four in the evening. It was then that it dawned on me that our boat was leaving port at four o'clock that afternoon.

It was a very long walk from the restaurant to the port. I told Clarissa we were late and that the boat was going to sail leaving us behind. Clarissa looked worried and suggested we took a taxi back to the port. Perhaps, we could reach there before four o'clock and hopefully catch the boat before it set sail.

The taxi we hired sped fast and we reached the port at about five minutes to four. We dashed to where our boat was berthed. It was too late. All the doors to the decks had been closed. The berthing hawsers—the two main breast ropes used to moor the boat to the jetty—had all been released and folded back into the boat. As we stood there, the boat started moving out of port. We heard her sound the three short blasts indicating they were getting out of the harbour.

Soon, the ship sailed past the breakwaters of the port. Clarissa and I could do nothing about the situation but could only stand and stare at our boat. I told her not to worry. Quietly in my mind, I put the incident to one of the numerous mishaps that had bedevilled my long road to London. I was not perturbed; I was not angry. Clarissa suggested we booked for another boat ride back to Tangier.

I suggested we go back to Tangier by road. There were lots of mini-buses that plied the route between Tangier city and *Cap Spartel*. It would take about an hour to reach Tangier city, and another fifteen to twenty minutes' drive would get us to our guesthouse. We got a taxi that took us to the mini-bus station where we boarded a 16-seater mini-bus and soon we were on our way to Tangier city by road. It was when we sat in the mini-bus that my phone rang.

I answered the call, and as I suspected, it was Gameli. He asked whether we were on board the boat. I told him that we had missed the boat and were in a minibus on our way to Tangier. Gameli asked me what time it was. I told him my watch read twenty-five minutes past four. It was then that Gameli asked again what time the boat was scheduled to set sail. I told him four o'clock and that we had missed it by just five minutes.

He screamed in what sounded to me like an embarrassment and said he had thought the departure time for the boat was five o'clock in the evening. He and Ameema had also missed the boat. I empathised with him and advised him to go to the mini-bus station and come to Tangier. He did. His mini-bus was the next one after ours. We arrived at Tangier Central station in an hour's time. We waited for Gameli and Ameema at the station. They arrived about half an hour after us.

We all took a taxi and headed towards our beautiful guesthouse located on the picturesque hills of Tangier.

At dinner that evening, we joked and made fun of each other on how we all got it wrong; how we missed our return on the *Auntie Dede*.

"How on earth did I think the boat's departure time was five o'clock," Gameli said with a loud laugh. "I just feel humiliated," he confessed.

I responded by saying, "We were well aware of the time of departure, but food and lengthy passionate conversations made the time beat us, and we got punished for it; we brought it upon ourselves," I concluded.

Ameema and Clarissa almost spoke at the same time. When they spoke, they both sounded the relief that missing the boat and coming to Tangier by road gave them all. They saw it as another opportunity for them to see the natural scenery of the Moroccan countryside from another angle. We all agreed; and with the ladies' comments, we approached the dinner table and started serving ourselves.

The food as usual was good. No one spoke as we ate. Not even a word between Clarissa and me. The same applied to Ameema and Gameli. It was a Tuesday. We were all scheduled to leave Tangier on Saturday. I would be heading to mainland Europe-Spain, Clarissa would be on the plane going back to Monrovia-Liberia, Gameli would be heading towards Rome-Italy via Spain and Ameema would be with him.

Thus, we had Wednesday, Thursday, and Friday ahead of us and available to use as we saw fit. Dinner was over. When I reminded them of our schedules by making my thoughts known to them, they all agreed and thanked me for reminding them. Clarissa, my lovely fiancée, suggested we all stayed home and play board or computer games on Wednesday and go out for another adventure on Thursday.

She suggested we all went to the cinema on Friday, and then we could say our *adieus* to each other on Saturday. Clarissa's suggestion appeared to have gone down well with everyone.

"Good idea," shouted Ameema from the corner of the dining table.

"I think I'll buy this idea," said Gameli. I nodded in agreement to all that was suggested. We then left the dining hall a few minutes after and headed towards our rooms.

It was early evening and Clarissa and I resumed our conversation from where we left off at the restaurant in *Cap Spartel*. We chatted and watched television at the same time. Most of the channels on Moroccan television presented their programmes in Arabic. Consequently, we tuned in and watched most of the television channels that spoke or presented their programmes in English. We watched news on CNN, CGTN. BBC World, Voice of Africa, and a few others.

We spoke of my university in London. Clarissa asked me to remind her of the name of the university I was going to study at. I reminded her that it was the London School of Economics. When she again enquired about the course I was going to study, I told her a Master of Business Administration. She nodded in appreciation with a lovely smile which again planted those lovely dimples on her cheeks. I looked directly into her face with so much delight on my own face.

I then held her left hand, threw my right arm around her neck and kissed her passionately. Clarissa enjoyed the kiss very much. When I let her go, she looked into my face again, held me closer to her body and kissed me in turn. I enjoyed this kiss more than the first one because it kept a bit longer than the first that was initiated by me. She went to the bathroom, had a shower and changed into her nighties.

I did same, and as we both laid down on the bed recollecting our lives back in Monrovia, we both drifted into deep sleep.

After breakfast on Wednesday, Ameema and Gameli came to our room with us. I brought out the game of Monopoly which I had brought with me all the way from Monrovia. I used to play this property game with Clarissa and our friends back in Monrovia. The board game looked new as I had hardly used or played it throughout my long road to London so far.

We all sat around the table and I unfolded the game on the table and distributed the start-up Monopoly banknotes to all the players. It was at this point that both Gameli and Ameema confessed they were not conversant with the game of Monopoly. However, they were both quick to express their sizzling desires to learn how the game was played. Clarissa and I volunteered to teach them as we played on.

Clarissa won the first game with lots of money in the bank, lots of houses and hotels at Mayfair and Park Lane. Ameema came second with houses at Regents Street, Coventry, and Piccadilly Circus. Both Gameli and I ran out of money and became bankrupt. Although, it was the first time that Ameema and Gameli ever played the game, they enjoyed it very much. Ameema remarked that the game increased a person's rate of thinking as well as skills in business management.

We played four more games after which we all walked to the dining hall for lunch. After lunch, we decided to have siesta in our own rooms. Gameli and Ameema took leave of us. We agreed to meet for dinner in the dining hall.

Clarissa suggested that we went out for dinner in a local restaurant for a change. I politely asked her to reserve that for when we went out on

Thursday. She understood me and agreed to stay in.

We came back from dinner to our room and turned on the television. We selected Channel 15 which showed movies. The movie, *Escape from Alcatraz,* was just about to be shown. It was a 1979 American prison action film directed by Don Siegel, which was an adaptation of the 1963 non-fiction book of the same written by J. Campbell and which dramatized the 1962 escape from the maximum-security prison on Alcatraz Island in San Francisco, California in the USA.

The main film star was Clint Eastwood and it featured other stars such as Patrick McGoohan, Fred Ward, Jack Thibeau and Larry Hankin. We both got glued to the television set as we watched this thrilling movie in excitement and suspense. At the end of it, there was a caption that reminded viewers that the film was based on a true story.

Clarissa remarked that the escapees performed a masterclass by successfully escaping from the jail. Watching the film brightened our evening. We were never bored. We chatted for about half an hour after which we said goodnight to each other and went to bed.

We woke up on Thursday morning hale and hearty. To my surprise, Clarissa requested that we have morning devotion. We, hitherto, had not had anything of such nature since her arrival. I did not disagree. I told her it was a brilliant idea. I reminded her that since we had more travelling to do in two days' time, it was perhaps appropriate to commit our dealings from today onwards, until we reached our next travel destinations, into the powerful and protective hands of God Almighty.

Clarissa looked excited. She produced her daily devotion prayer book and we opened to the devotion of the day. We read Psalm 91 in the bible and followed it with lots of individual prayers which covered our needs from God. We prayed for Ameema and Gameli. We prayed for our families and friends back home too.

After the morning devotion, we went to the dining hall for breakfast. After breakfast, Ameema reminded us that, although we agreed to go out on Thursday, we had not chosen where we were going. I asked Gameli whether he had any preference from the Tangier tourists' booklet.

He smiled and replied that he had seen something like a safari ride in the brochure but could not recollect the details. I reminded him of the details and everyone else listened in to what I said carefully. I told them the *Corazon de Marruecos* was a two-day excursion into the Sahara Desert with 'Friendly and trustworthy' guides by SUVs that were spacious and comfortable. There would be regular stops for tea, coffee, and sightseeing. The whole two days would be efficiently organised allowing the perfect amount of time at each spot, ensuring we would not miss anything including sunset. We would lodge in a luxurious camp in the Sahara Desert with breath-taking views.

The food promised to be lovely and all staff were said to be kind and accommodating. It allowed tourists to escape the hustle and bustle of cities, to see Morocco's fantastic Sahelian natural environment.

Gameli, Ameema and Clarissa were impressed with how I described the event into detail.

"That's the one," shouted Gameli from his seat as if he had a pre-knowledge of how the *Corazon de Marruecos* worked. Ameema kept looking at Gameli admiringly without saying a word. Clarissa who had a good read of how the trip worked was equally silent. She, however, reminded us that, if we were to go on that trip on the Thursday, we had to do two things immediately.

First, we needed to call the ticket reservation and buy our tickets before ten o'clock that morning. Second, since the trip was going to be a-two-day event, we had to cancel our scheduled cinema attendance for Friday. I there and then, without seeking a consensus, announced that the cinema was cancelled and we should leave the house at ten o'clock that morning for the tour take-off location. I rang the tour operators to book our places for the trip. They reminded me that the tour started at two o'clock in the afternoon that day and we needed to be at the starting location venue by one o'clock. I paid for the tickets with my credit card. Gameli asked how much it cost per couple. I told him. He dipped his hand into his shirt pocket and paid their share of the cost for the trip. I thanked him. We now knew we had to be there at one o'clock and I asked everyone to be ready by midday.

We all returned to our rooms, packed a few toiletries into our small bags, met at the foyer and walked out excitedly looking for a taxi. As usual, Clarissa was holding on firmly to my left hand. Ameema was doing same to Gameli. Soon a taxi pulled up, we were on our way to the *Corazon de Marruecos* station.

We reached the venue at a quarter to one o'clock that afternoon. The place was an open space with lots of small fast cars specially designed for desert travel parked in the distance. There were Sports Utility Vehicles too. We gathered in a large auditorium where we sat and listened to instructions regarding the *Corazon de Marruecos.* The cars carried only two participants at a time-usually man and woman-drop them at the sites about 15 kilometres from the station and would come back for them the next day about four o'clock in the afternoon.

The car would make a stop after every couple of kilometres to enable us to have tea and biscuits at specially designated stops along the way. There were no hotels where we could pass the night in the desert. We would sleep in small tents there till the next morning. The speaker warned, "sometimes (and not always he stressed) some reptiles wandered over the desert's sandy surfaces but would not be able to enter our tents. This was because the tents had high foundations and all their tops were fully and tightly covered."

He continued to say, occasionally desert antelopes, goats and even wildcats wandered in the desert at night; but was quick to add that they posed no danger to us since our tents were made of thick material and tightly sealed. On hearing these, Clarissa, still holding on to my left hand, squeezed my hand several times. I saw other participants looking into the faces of their partners without saying a word. Ameema did same. She looked into Gameli's face for a few seconds, then turned to look at us as if she had wanted to say something, and then refocussed her gaze on the speaker.

We set off at about ten minutes past two o'clock. Our driver introduced himself to us. He said his name was Khalid and was going to be our guide too for the next two days. We made several stops on the way for tea and coffee as was stated in the tourist's brochure. Altogether, there were about 25 cars that set off that day. We reached the desert campsite after about an hour and a half's journey and were shown where our tent was.

It was a fairly big tent, about six feet and six inches in length and four feet in width. The entrance into the tent had a gigantic zip that we had to open; and once you entered the tent, you could close it from inside. Inside, the tent was very well decorated. It had a comfortable mattress laid on the ground and covered with beautiful blankets, bed sheets, and pillows just like in most hotels.

"These look good and soft," remarked Clarissa.

"Yes, indeed," I said to her with a grin, although I had more questions than answers about what would happen during the night when one was fast asleep in the tents. Once inside the tent, the outside was visible but not clear. By this I meant standing outside the tent, you could not see the occupants of the tent; but once inside, you could see the silhouette of anything climbing on or moving past the tent. It was made with a sort of a translucent material.

We left our belongings in the tent and went for a walk in the desert sand. There were lots of attractions that were built in the desert. There was the oasis where little pools of waters like a river provided water for the workers and the people living there. There was a football pitch as well as a volleyball court in the sand.

There were vendors selling handicrafts and other paraphernalia around the campsite. In the middle of the encampment, just about 50 metres from our tent was a huge marquee. That was supposed to be our meeting place as well as the dining hall. We wandered around the desert for about an hour and a half. We started feeling hungry. Just then, a siren sounded meaning it was time for dinner. How timely!

We met Gameli and Ameema at the marquee coming in for dinner. Dinner was served and placed on the dinner table, but there were no dining chairs or tables. We had to sit down on Persian carpets laid on the floor in the marquee to eat our dinner. No one complained as dinner was perfectly served. The food, as expected, was predominantly Moroccan.

The four of us sat down with our legs crossed in typical Arabian or Yoga fashion and ate together. We ate with our bare hands. It was a buffet and one could go as many times as one wished. Once a course was finished, you could throw the plastic plates in the bin and serve your next meal in a fresh plastic plate. We enjoyed eating on the carpet as most Arabs and Muslims did. It was getting to six o'clock in the evening.

There was an announcement that there would be a movie after dinner. Clarissa said that our cinema scheduled for the next evening, which had been cancelled, had been virtually restored to us. We all smiled in affirmation and waited for the film to start. The film was *Sinbad the*

Sailor, a typical Arabian film.

It was about a fictional mariner and the hero of a story-cycle of Middle Eastern origin. Sinbad was described as hailing from Bagdad during the early Abbasid Caliphate. The film depicted the course of seven voyages through the seas East of Africa and South Asia where Sinbad, the hero, had fantastic adventures in magical realms, encountering monsters and witnessing supernatural phenomena. It was an action film through and through and kept us on the edge of our non-existent chairs. We all enjoyed every bit of it.

We arrived back at our tent almost at ten o'clock that night There were no electric lights in the tents. We only had two torchlights or flashlights provided by the organising company. The lights were bright. There was a second torchlight with a rather dim light. This was to prevent the tent from being pitch dark in the middle of the night. We changed into our night dresses, entered a special sleeping bag provided for us and slept on the mattress.

The mattress was soft and provided good comfort for sleeping. I said goodnight to Clarissa and then lulled myself into sleep with a myriad of thoughts. At about four o'clock in the morning, I felt Clarissa shaking with fear and drawing my attention to something on top of our tent. She held on closer to me and pointed to the top of the tent. Although, the texture of the tent was translucent, while we inside could see the silhouette of anything on top or by the side of the tent, nothing outside could see the inside of the tent.

I looked up and saw the silhouette of a reptile-like long creature creeping on top of the tent. I did not panic. I reached for my torchlight and beamed the bright light on the creature. It moved a bit and coiled up. It was a snake! Clarissa was still shaking with fear. I calmed her down and assured her that the snake would not be able to enter the tent. I kept the bright light on it for about ten minutes. It occasionally moved and then recoiled.

I told Clarissa to keep still. Summing up some courage, I used a stick that I had picked up on our walk and lay by our mattress to poke the spot where the reptile lay. I did that about four times while keeping the beam of the torchlight on it. I poked the same area where the snake lay a fifth time and it uncoiled and slowly moved away from the top of the tent.

"Thank you, Jesus," said Clarissa quietly as if she wanted the snake not to hear her voice.

"All is well," I encouraged her and asked her to go back to sleep. She told me she was still scared it might return. I assured her that, even if it returned, there was no way it could enter our tent. With that, we drifted back into sleep.

We woke up at about six o'clock in the morning. We were still on bed. We wanted to be out of bed around half-past-seven in the morning. All of a sudden, I noticed what looked like a desert goat standing by our tent. I was not sure what animal it was since I could only see the silhouette. Day was breaking, but it was still dark. I beamed the rays of my torchlight on it. The animal looked like a desert lion to me this time.

I said to myself, the Sahara had no lions. But then I remembered that there were mountain lions on the Atlas Mountains of Morocco. Again, I encouraged myself by saying, the Atlas Mountains were rather too far from where we were, and a lion, even a full grown one, could not have travelled all that distance through the desert to where our camp was. In my fright, I started going over the decision I made that had brought me to this pass.

I said to myself, this road to London was indeed a very long one. Would it not have been wise if I had gone to London by aeroplane? What if one of these desert animals attacked and caused us harm? All these thoughts raced through my mind. I said a little prayer in my mind and ended it with the twenty-third Psalm: *The Lord is my Shepherd*. I told myself nothing would happen to me or Clarissa. Not even an ant would bite us.

I pronounced the protection of God Jehovah on both of us. I did not tell Clarissa what I thought it was. I did not want her to panic. To her, a desert goat was passing by our tent. I was aware that animals such as the baboons, hyenas, gazelles, common jackals, sand foxes and some reptiles lived in the Sahara Desert, but not lions. Suddenly, I heard a bang. It sounded like a gun shot. Clarissa woke up. She held on to me asking what that was. I asked her to remain silent for a second. "Bang! Bang!" rang out two more volleys. This time, it was clear it was a gun. We waited calmly in our tent.

We saw someone walk past our tent. The silhouette clearly showed it was a human being. He stopped about six metres from our tent and stood by something on the floor. He was soon joined by another man. I wondered what was happening. It was nearly seven o'clock in the morning and the sun was just beginning to peep through the skies. I summoned courage. I woke up, sat on the bed, opened the zip across the top of our tent and peeped at the two men standing in the distance.

One was holding a gun and they both stood over an animal which appeared dead on the sand. I shouted out to them what the matter was. They spoke back saying they had killed a sand fox that was wandering in-between the tents laid out for us the guests. Clarissa listened intently. The sun was now halfway up from its hiding place. I summoned some more courage, came out of the tent, and walked towards the two gentlemen.

I saw the sand fox on the ground. I took a picture of it on the floor and came back to show it to Clarissa. When I told the guys, who I later got to know to be the security men guarding the tents, that a snake climbed unto our tent during the night, they told me it was normal. And that there was no way the snake could penetrate the tent, anyway. Clarissa got back her composure. We both came out of the tent and were directed to the communal washroom located near to the marquee where we had dinner.

I went to the gents and Clarissa went to the ladies. The bathroom was long and large. There were about 20 showers and 20 toilet-pots in the open for the use of the tourists. Not a lot of people were there when I arrived. I completed my *toilette* and waited outside for Clarissa. When she came out, we went back to the tent, packed our things, and headed towards the marquee for breakfast. We met Gameli and Ameema at breakfast.

We sat down on the Persian carpets and had breakfast. Gameli asked how our night was. I told him it had been fine. I did not want to tell him anything about our experiences at that point in time. I asked him how theirs had been. He told me it had been good, but they had a scare from what looked like a desert lion walking past their tent in the night. I still did not say anything. Neither did Clarissa.

We were to visit an oasis that morning before setting off back to Tangier. Clarissa asked me whether that was necessary. I told her that since we had paid for it and everyone else was going, we must as well go and enjoy the scenery as well as the experience. She agreed with me. We reached the oasis, after about a half-an-hour's walk through the desert sand. We had guards with us, armed with guns to protect us from any possible wild animal attack.

The oasis had a large stretch of water which looked like a river. It did not appear deep. We were, however, told that parts of it were deep and it harboured crocodiles. They told us the crocodiles were friendly and would not harm anyone, unless they felt threatened. We stood by the river and took pictures. We waded into the shallow part of the river. And so did other tourists. Suddenly, we heard a loud sound of a whistle followed by shouts of "Come out of the water, come out of the water."

We all dashed out of the water with great speed towards dry land. Exactly five minutes after leaving the waters of the river, two huge crocodiles walked majestically out of the water and came to lie down about ten feet away from the river. They looked beautiful. We were asked to go nearer and take pictures of the animals. In fact, we were even encouraged to stand astride the crocodiles and take the pictures so long as no one stepped on their tails.

No one responded to the second part of the advice. We all stood back and took pictures of the crocodiles from afar.

One brave man, who looked a Sub-Saharan African like me, walked towards one of the crocodiles. He approached the animal from the back. He walked over to the middle part of the crocodile astride, being careful not to step on its tail. The animal remained cool. Several tourists took pictures and the gentleman walked backwards as he left the animal. On his way, he was met with lots of applause.

His bravery reminded me of my own incident with the python at the Casablanca Zoo. How the reptile tightened itself around me and would not uncoil until it was sedated. Notwithstanding that episode, I told Clarissa I was going to take a chance. She did not respond. She was dead-still. It was obvious she was petrified. I handed over my phone to her and walked forward. I approached the reptile from the back. I stood astride over the crocodile just like the earlier tourist did.

Ameema, Clarissa, Gameli and many of the other tourists took pictures. Just as I was walking backwards away from the animal, someone from nowhere approached the reptile from its left side. The reptile felt threatened and snapped sharply at the person, ripping off most of the dress he was wearing. In taking that action, the reptile inadvertently slammed its rough and rugged tail against my right hand. I retreated fast and ran back to where Clarissa was standing.

The man who approached the reptile from the side sustained severe scratches to the thigh and leg. His dress was stained with blood. My hand also smarted from the slap of the tail. I remembered my misfortunes at the Casablanca Zoo. I asked myself whether this was a *déjà vu*. I had slight scratches to my hand which bled, but not much. The authorities were quick. The medical team came cleaned our wounds and bandaged them nicely.

It was now about eleven o'clock in the morning. It was time to go. All the 25 vehicles that brought us were on site. We left the desert one after the other. Another one-hour's drive took us back to Central Tangier. It was a memorable trip. The experiences were unique. Clarissa enjoyed every bit of the adventure notwithstanding any mishaps. To her, the positives she collected from the trip clearly exceeded the negatives.

I was glad she was happy. Both Gameli and Ameema expressed similar sentiments. And by the second hour of the noon, we were safely back in our rooms at the guesthouse.

"What an adventure!" I shouted as I threw my handbag on the floor.

It was our last night on African soil before my setting foot, for the first time ever, on European soil. I would be making the short journey from my guesthouse to the port on the Mediterranean Sea. Clarissa would be heading back to Monrovia. Her flight was at eleven o'clock in the morning the next day. Gameli and Ameema would be making their way towards the same place.

I would be taking the ferry bound for Spain. Gameli would be on the ferry towards Italy. We met for the last time as a group, for dinner that evening at the guesthouse dining hall. We were all in high spirits. That was evident to all the kitchen and dining hall staff who saw us. We dished Our foods while cracking jokes, giggles, and even loud laughter. I decided to eat Spanish, perhaps just as a dress rehearsal for the type of food I was going to be having from the next day forward when I reached Spain.

Clarissa also chose Spanish dishes. There were no Italian dishes, unfortunately, for Gameli to rehearse with. Both he and Ameema settled for Spanish food too. After we finished eating, we spent another half hour at the dining table chatting and exchanging telephone numbers and addresses. I gave them the address of the London School of Economics, the only address I had on my official documents. Gameli gave me an address in Rome which he had booked for while in Ghana. We agreed to meet for breakfast before eight o'clock the next morning.

It was a Saturday morning. We had finished breakfast together. We bade *adieu* to all those lovely kitchen and dining hall staff. One of them asked where we were going from there. I spoke on my own behalf and that of everyone. I told them I was going to Spain, the first leg of my European journey to my destination—London, England. I pointed to Gameli and said he was heading to Rome, Italy.

I put my hands around the shoulders of my lovely Clarissa and told them she was catching a plane back to Monrovia, Liberia. I concluded by saying Ameema was travelling to Italy with Gameli.

"Where is Monrovia, Liberia?" the elderly one asked with a smile, wearing a heavy grey moustache. His name was Moussa. "Liberia is a small country in West Africa, and its capital city is called Monrovia," I answered him. I continued to tell him that I also hailed from that country.

Moussa turned to Gameli and Ameema and said, "...and you; which country are you from?"

"I am from Ghana, also in West Africa and my lady friend, Ameema, comes from Casablanca here in Morocco." Moussa wanted to know whether Ameema was going to go back to Casablanca. Gameli replied with a single word, "No." He did not say anything further.

We bade farewell to the guesthouse staff at the reception. We hired one taxi that took all four of us to Tangier International Airport. We all alighted and walked my lovely Clarissa to the check-in desk. After check-in, I walked her to the departure gate as Gameli and Ameema waited for me. Clarissa waved goodbye to them from a distance. I gave Clarissa a long hug at the entrance of the departure gate.

When we separated, I noticed Clarissa's eyes had welled up with tears. She was filled with emotions. I pretended I did not notice it. I put my arms around her neck and gave her a passionate kiss.

"*Adieu,* safe journey; God go with you," I said to my lovely Clarissa. "Thank you and I will see you soon," she replied. She turned around and entered the departure hall.

Our taxi to the Mediterranean Sea port took just under an hour. We got our passports out and went to check in for our respective ferries. Gameli had a Ghanaian passport with an Italian Schengen visa in it. That meant he could travel to any of the European Schengen countries without hassle after first landing on Italian soil. Ameema interestingly had both Moroccan and French passports. Her French passport allowed her to travel to all Schengen and European Union countries as well as many other countries of the world that had visa-exempt travel agreements with the European Union in general, and France in particular.

I had both a United Kingdom non-Schengen visa and Spanish Schengen visa in my Liberian passport. We had finished checking in. Our ferries would be departing Tangier ports within a quarter of an hour of each other. Mine would be the first heading to Gibraltar in Spain. Gameli and Ameema would be heading to Rome in Italy. We took the opportunity to sit together for about half an hour. When the departure time was nigh, I hugged Gameli and Ameema and wished them safe journey.

"Bye, bye, safe journey," they both replied almost simultaneously. I turned around, waved back at them, and shouted, "Bye, bye."

The journey by ferry was smooth. The ferry carried well over 300 passengers and about 100 vehicles. The vehicles were parked on the lower and middle decks on board the ferry. Most of the passengers were travelling with their cars. They left their cars on the lower decks and joined us, the pedestrians, on the third and fourth decks of the ferry.

I took a seat in a comfortable corner of the deck where I could clearly watch the television set placed about five metres in front of me. There was a competitive football match being aired. The great Barcelona football club were playing their bitter rivals Real Madrid in Spain that afternoon. The match was being played at the Nou Camp stadium, home of the Barcelona football club. I got immersed in the football match. It ended in a goalless draw. Soon, I could see buildings in the far distance as we got nearer to Gibraltar.

The captain announced from the bridge of the ferry that we would be docking in port in about twenty minutes. I started getting my luggage in order. I checked that my passport was safe and secure in the right breast pocket of the jacket I was wearing. BefThe ferry carried well over 300 passengers and about 100 vehicles. The vehicles were parked on the lower and middle decks on board the ferry. Most of the passengers were travelling with their cars. They left their cars on the lower decks and joined us, the pedestrians, on the third and fourth decks of the ferry.

I took a seat in a comfortable corner of the deck where I could clearly watch the television set placed about five metres in front of me. There was a competitive football match being aired. The great Barcelona football club were playing their bitter rivals Real Madrid in Spain that afternoon. The match was being played at the Nou Camp stadium, home of the Barcelona football club. I got immersed in the football match. It ended in a goalless draw. Soon, I could see buildings in the far distance as we got nearer to Gibraltar.

The captain announced from the bridge of the ferry that we would be docking in port in about twenty minutes. I started getting my luggage in order. I checked that my passport was safe and secure in the right breast pocket of the jacket I was wearing. Before I could do anything else, my phone rang.

"Hello," I answered the call.

"Hello, dear," came the reply. It was Clarissa. She had called to inform me that she was at home.

"Great stuff! Thank the Living God!" I exclaimed.

"Yes, indeed, our God is good; He is a Living God indeed," she said back to me.

"Where have you reached now?" She asked curiously as her voice sounded.

"We are just five minutes from docking at the port of Gibraltar," I replied.

"Marvellous! Let me leave you to get ready to disembark. I love you," she said.

"Thank you, my love; and always remember that I love you too," I replied. Immigration processing at the port of Gibraltar was quite smooth.

It was not as cumbersome as I feared. In fact, it was much easier and smoother than some of the immigration posts that I went through in Africa on my long journey so far; far more civilised and decent. I was not asked any personal or intrusive questions. All that the immigration officer said to me was to enjoy my journey to London when I told him I was on my way to a university in London.

My passport was stamped with the number of years I was going to spend in the UK to do my course; and of course, plus a few months. In all, my passport was stamped with a two-year Tier 4 visa. I was pleased. I came out of the port and signalled to a taxi. I had not pre-arranged any accommodation in Gibraltar. The taxi driver spoke to me in Spanish.

"*A dônte te vas?*"

Although, I did not speak fluent Spanish, I guessed she was asking me for my destination. I had rehearsed a little Spanish exactly in preparation for this moment. I took out my small pocket diary and read out:

"*Por favor llévame a una Buena casa de huéspedes; no a un hotel.*"

The taxi driver, a beautiful Caucasian with long blonde hair, smiled and spoke back to me in English.

"How long are you staying in Gibraltar?"

"A couple of months, I am on my way to London, England, but I do not have to be there until September of this year," I said back to her in English. She told me that Gibraltar was bilingual. Both Spanish and English were spoken there, and I should feel free to ask anyone for anything I wanted in English. She told me she would take me to a good guesthouse, where there were some other Africans.

I thanked her. Soon we were in a beautiful guesthouse called *Villa Centralli.* I paid her twenty-five euros. She thanked me, gave me her business card, and told me to feel free to call her anytime I wanted a cab service. I checked in. All the guesthouse attendants spoke beautiful English. I was checked into room number 5225.

I opened the door to my room, put my luggage down, went on my knees and prayed to God:

"*Lord Jehovah God, you are the God of the rich and the God of the poor. Thank you for making me, a poor little boy from Africa, come so far on my journey to London. I thank you for your graciousness, provision, and care. Thank you, Father. And as I have set foot on mainland Europe, I commit myself fully to your service.*"

"*Watch over me, Lord, and take me safely to my final destination when the time is right. Your word tells me in the book of Isaiah Chapter 60 verse 22 that, '...when the time is right, I the Lord will make it happen'. Father, you have even made it happen for me already. When you give your children promises, you never renege on them. Thank you, faithful God. All these and other blessings I mercifully ask from you in the Mighty Name of our Lord and Saviour, Jesus*

Christ. Amen.”

With that short prayer, I went to the bathroom, had a shower after which I went straight to bed.

Chapter 13 Gibraltar

I woke up for the first time in my life on European soil. It was about five o'clock in the morning, Spanish time. We were an hour ahead of Greenwich Meantime in London. I heard a rhythmic cacophony of noises from the flowers, plants and trees that bordered my guesthouse. I drew my window curtains open and could see birds of different colours and breeds chirping and singing what sounded quite melodious to my ears.

I said to myself, these species of God's creations are praising their maker early this morning. It took my mind straight back to the tropical rain forest of rural Liberia where the same thing happens. In Liberia, this happens with louder and stronger noises made by the African birds. I sometimes referred to it as the African birds' early morning songs of praise.

I went back to sleep for a while. I woke up three hours later and I said another short prayer to God thanking Him for having brought me this far on my long journey to London. I had a shower and headed for breakfast in the guesthouse dining hall. I had become accustomed to breakfast in guesthouses having done same in all the guesthouses I had stayed at during my journey so far; all in Africa. But this time, the country was different. The continent was different. The dining room was different.

The dining room was much more beautiful and elegant than the ones I had seen and used so far on my journey. The room was neatly painted with a soft purple colour. There were beautiful oil paintings hanging in symmetry along the walls. Copies of paintings by renowned artists like Raphael and Michelangelo adorned parts of the walls of this magnificent hall. Beautiful chandeliers hung from the lofty ceilings of the room providing clear bright lights all around the hall.

The general ambience of the dining hall and its settings was superb. I said to myself, "Yes, this is Europe, and I am here; here in person." I looked up at the beautiful ceilings again and simply said, "Thank you, Lord."

I finished eating and headed back to my room. I sat at the writing desk provided by the guesthouse, pulled out my diary and started looking at the dates. I had three months more to complete my journey and be in London on time to start university. I had to be in London by the beginning of September. Student registration was to commence on 5 September. I had to be in London, latest by 3 September. I said to myself the planning started from then.

I looked through all the days of June, July, and August. I reminded myself that sightseeing, or better still tourism on my journey was to come to an end; or at least, be severely minimised. Although, I had paid all my university fees, I needed to do some serious work, at least for the three months, to get some European money into my bank account before I reached London. I decided to share my time of three months within three different countries, or at least I hoped to do so.

I would stay in Gibraltar for one month, then go to work in Barcelona for the following month and spend the last month working in Paris, France. I had a French visa. My UK visa was not Schengen; my Spanish visa was. These plans with their dates were tentative. I knew too well that things could change, and plans could shift, and that was why I earlier stated, at least I hoped so.

I had to look for work. I picked a free local newspaper that was pushed under my door. It had loads of local job advertisements in it. Just before I could flip the first page open, my phone rang. It was my dad.

"Hello, Dad," I said with much excitement in a loud voice. "Hello, my son. How are you?" The response came.

"I'm very well and excited, Dad. I have checked into a room in a guesthouse in Gibraltar and am beginning to settle down," I concluded.

"So good, my son. We are all so happy for you," replied my dad. "How is Mum and everyone?" I asked enquiringly.

"Everybody is fine. We are all here. Today is Sunday and we arranged to meet here and make a collective call so that everyone gets to talk to you on your first day in Europe," said my dad. "Your mum is here, and so are Clarissa, Ameley, Foga, Zutor and Akogovi; they are all here waiting to talk to you. Your nephews and nieces are also here," he concluded.

"Oh boy!" I exclaimed. For the next one hour, I spoke to Dad, Mum, and all my siblings. I spoke to Clarissa for twenty minutes. They were just as excited as I was talking with them. I spent over an hour on the phone with my family. I assured them that I was well and I looked forward to arriving in London in three months' time. They wished me God's blessings and I wished them same.

I spent the next half hour reading about Gibraltar in the visitors' handbook. It was quite informative. Gibraltar, a British overseas territory occupying a narrow peninsula of Spain's southern Mediterranean coast, just northeast of the Strait of Gibraltar, on the east side of the Bay of Gibraltar (Bay of *Algeciras*), and directly south of the Spanish city of La Línea. The territory, on Spain's south coast, was dominated by the Rock of Gibraltar, a 426m-high limestone ridge.

First settled by the Moors in the Middle Ages and later ruled by the Spanish, the outpost was ceded to the British in 1713. Layers of fortifications included the remains of a 14th century Moorish Castle and the 18th century Great Siege Tunnels, which were expanded in World War II. The sovereignty of Gibraltar has been a point of contention in Anglo-Spanish relations because Spain asserts a claim to the territory.

That was not of huge interest to me but it was worth noting. The guidebook also informed me of salaries and standards of living in Gibraltar. A person working in Gibraltar typically earned around 40,600 Gibraltar Pounds (GIP) per year. That is about 56,000 United States Dollars. I thought to myself that would be the salary for Gibraltar citizens occupying pretty good and high positions of employment in the territory. I would look for a quick and fast going job that could give me at least 200 GIP a week. I was sure I would get one.

I decided to go on a day's city ride on the buses. Tickets for the whole day, hop-on-hop-off red buses cost about just 10 GIP. I boarded the bus just in front of my guesthouse. There were 25 stops on the circular route before coming back to the stop where I boarded it. As the bus moved on, I took out my visitor's map of Gibraltar and started matching the landmarks as indicated on the map.

We drove through the busy streets of downtown Westside, the largest city in Gibraltar. We virtually crawled through the busiest and densest traffic as well as less busy ones. I sat at the very back of the bus, very relaxed and enjoying the scenery from the bus as it moved on. The mix of buildings, both tall and short, large and small, old and new were representative of the territory's history and excited me greatly.

I noticed that the inhabitants were predominantly white-skinned and Caucasian. I saw men and women, adults, and children, either riding in their beautiful cars, on the public buses, or walking along the pedestrian corridors of the beautifully clean streets entering and coming out of shops and office buildings. I took in every beautiful and exciting moment of the ride.

At bus-stop number 16 counting from my guesthouse, the bus made a stop. Suddenly, we were all ordered to disembark from the bus. It remained stationary for well over fifteen minutes. Some new passengers started to board the bus. The driver, this time, announced on the bus's internal public address system that all passengers, both new and old, should alight from the bus. He explained that the bus was terminating there and that we should board the bus parked just behind it and continue with our journeys.

I was so relieved because, initially I did not have a clue as to what was going on; particularly as I was just a newcomer to the city and the way things worked. We continued with our journey. At bus-stop number twenty-one, a short, smallish scruffy-looking man boarded the bus. The beard he wore made him look to me like a Mexican. He wore a bus conductor's uniform, red in colour with four yellow straps on the sleeves of the jacket mimicking those of a naval captain. He wore a crumpled white shirt with a red tie.

He wore a peaked cap with the word 'Inspector' written on it. He approached passengers on the bus individually and requested to see their tickets. I kept on watching him in amazement, entirely forgetting that it was going to be my turn soon. And soon it was my turn.

"*Boletos por favor,*" he said to me as I looked up straight into his face. I guessed what said.

"Sorry?" I replied to him in English.

He looked at me a little more carefully and said, "Your ticket please."

"Just a minute," I replied as I put my hand into the inner pockets of the jacket I was wearing. There was no ticket there. I knew I bought a ticket for the whole day. I looked in my breast pockets and did not find the ticket. I searched the side pockets of the pair of jeans I was wearing, still no ticket.

"I say ticket, please," he said again with a stronger voice that made almost every passenger in the bus turn to look at me. I read in the Gibraltar tourists' guidebook of how some people made it a habit to dodge bus fares in Gibraltar applying all sorts of tricks.

"Hold on, hold on," I said as I started to panic. Did I leave my tickets at the guesthouse? But then I stood up and dipped my right hand into the right back pocket of the jeans I was wearing, and lo and behold, the ticket was there.

"Here you are," I said as I handed over the ticket to him and at the same time wiped sweat from my forehead. He took it, looked at it carefully, punched holes into it and returned it to me saying, "*Gracias.*"

I replied him saying, "Thank you," in English.

As the journey continued, I realised I was still sweating all over. My shirt was wet and I kept mopping my forehead with my handkerchief. It had been a close call. I said to myself I had landed on European soil indeed, and I had to be more alert and smarter. I had to learn fast and imbibe many things in a very short period and on time.

I tried to remember how much money I had left in my bank account. I was imagining how all sorts of things could happen when I reached London. I thought of accommodation, I thought of the weather in September, I thought of university registration and I thought of university fees, although I had paid those in full. I thought of getting a job in the quickest possible time to boost my savings.

Before long, we reached another bus stop. When I raised my head to see which bus stop it was, the bus was at bus stop number 28.

"Ah, damn it," I shouted to everyone's hearing.

"I have passed bus stop 26," I said without realising it. I quickly alighted from the bus. I looked behind me and luckily the route was a straight one. The distance between the two bus stops was less than a kilometre. I said to myself, there was no need boarding another bus in the opposite direction. I started walking, and within a few minutes, I was safely back at my guesthouse. The time was far spent. It was evening and because I had not eaten any food for the last three hours that I spent on the bus ride, I was quite famished.

I looked at the time and it was a quarter-past six in the evening. Dinner would be served from half-past-six. I spent the fifteen minutes looking through the job adverts in the local papers. Some of them were in Spanish. However, the greater part of them were in English. I was still looking through the papers when my phone rang.

"Hello," I said, wondering who it was.

"Hi, this is Maria. The taxi driver who brought you to the guesthouse the other day," said the lovely girlish voice at the other end.

"O yes, I remember you. But I really do not need a cab service right now," I said to her.

"No, no, I'm not ringing you to find out if you need a cab. I was wondering if I could meet with you this evening at about eight o'clock. I have something to show you," she said.

"Oh really?" I asked rather absentmindedly. "*Si, Si,* yeah, yeah," came the reply.

"Oh ok, It's a deal. I will meet with you at eight o'clock in the guesthouse- lobby," I assured her.

"*Gracias,*" she said.

I said, "See you later."

I enjoyed my dinner that evening. I had Spaghetti Marinara with a bottle of Perrier water to wash the food down. I enjoyed the food very much, particularly as I was quite hungry. I walked smartly back to my room and had a shower. By the time I had finished everything and was ready for Maria's arrival, it was about fifteen minutes to eight o'clock.

I brushed my hair, sprayed a little of Ralph Lauren Polo perfume behind my ears, powdered my face and walked down to the lobby of the guesthouse. Maria arrived at exactly eight o'clock. She had parked her taxi just outside the gates of the guesthouse.

"Hello, my friend," she said struggling to remember my name. "Hi, hello, Maria, my name is Yolandi," I said.

"Aha, Yolandi, I remember," she said as she shook my hand.

We sat down in the lobby. People were coming in and going out of the guesthouse via the lobby. As the human traffic increased, so did the noise and commotion. Maria suggested we went to a less busy venue. I obliged. She drove straight to a café that was only about five minutes away. The café was almost empty. It was a nice café.

They served tea, coffee, biscuits, cakes, and many finger foods. Maria and I took the seat right at the back of the café. Soon, a young lady wearing a white apron and holding a little notebook and pen approached us. She was black and spoke English with an African accent.

"Can I take your order, please," she said in a pleasant voice. "Yes, of course," replied Maria.

"What would you like to eat, Yolandi?" Maria asked still looking at the menu right in front of her.

"Nothing," I said.

"Oh, don't be silly, Yolandi; come on, have something," she said with a smile. And when I started to explain to her that I had just had my dinner, she continued to press me to have tea and cake or something.

"Ok, hot chocolate and cake, please," I gave in to her persistent pressure. The waiter wrote it down in her notebook. She looked towards Maria without saying anything. She looked into Maria's face inquiringly.

"A portion of olives and hot chocolate," she said. The young lady scribbled the details on her notepad, thanked us, and walked towards the kitchen. I saw her drop the order sheet through a box into the kitchen while she squared herself up at the till to continue serving a waiting customer.

Maria started to talk to me. She welcomed me once again to Gibraltar. She told me since the day she dropped me off at the guesthouse, she had always thought of me. She had tried to come to see me the day after but was overwhelmed with her job. She told me she closed quite early on the day to meet with me. I thanked her profusely for the great kindness and hospitality she had shown me so far.

Just as she was about to tell me on what had brought her to see me, the young café attendant brought two steaming cups of hot chocolate to our table. She carefully put the tray down on the adjacent table, picked the items one after the other, set them before us, and then waved us bye. We thanked her and started drinking our beverages and eating the olives and the cake.

Maria turned to me after the first sip.

"How are you doing for a local job?" She asked with a great deal of passion and care written on her face.

"Yes, of course, I need a job. In fact, I was scanning through the local newspapers that carry local job advertisements just this afternoon. A nice little job that can pay me like GIP 200 a week would be great," I replied to her.

"Great," she replied. "What type of job would you prefer?" She asked further.

"Well, I do not have any particular job in mind," I replied to her.

I continued to explain to Maria that I would love to do any decent job that could give me a minimum of GIP 200 per week. I told her I had just three months left t o a r r i v e in London to commence my master's degree course in business administration. And that earning GIB 200 per week would be just nice. She looked at me again and smiled.

"Ok," she said. "I have an idea. I will call a friend right now and ask whether the vacancy he spoke to me about at the Grand Hotel of Gibraltar is still open." She called and spoke to her friend as I ate up the rest of the cake on my plate.

"Oh, really? Super!" She exclaimed as I watched her. She said thank you and put the phone down.

"Good news," she said looking at me. "Oh really," I asked. "What did he say?" I asked again.

"He said the vacancy of a porter at the hotel was still open," she replied. She continued to explain to me that the job was that of a front desk porter at the hotel and that they were paying GIP 250 before tax. I had wanted to ask what the net figure was but hesitated.

"What do you think?" She asked again.

"Not bad to start with," I replied smiling.

Maria informed me that the job was to commence the following Monday. It was a Saturday. Before I could ask the location of the hotel where I would soon be working, she volunteered that it was only 3 bus-stops from my guesthouse. That sounded good to me. I could even walk the distance on clear weather days, I kept saying to myself.

"But I will take you there today so you can meet the personnel manager who is also a friend of mine," she said as she dropped a couple of euro coins into the tray on the table, signalled the café attendant, stood up, picked up her car keys, and asked me to follow her. I followed her to her taxi and soon we were on our way to the Grand Hotel of Gibraltar. We entered the hotel reception and Maria spoke to the duty porter.

She asked of her friend and was told he was not at work that day. She was told her friend would be in the next day. She introduced me to the porter as a potential colleague. The porter greeted me warmly and asked Maria to let me come and see the manager the next day. She explained to her that she needed not come with me; and that I could come on my own at about ten o'clock in the morning.

Maria thanked her and we left. Maria dropped me off at the guesthouse and directed me on how to reach the hotel the next day. She told me to take bus number 133 from the bus-stop in front of my guesthouse and alight at the third bus stop, turn right and walk about 100 metres to the hotel. I thanked her and wished her a pleasant weekend.

As I lay on bed later in my room, I reflected on the brief engagement that I had with Maria. I asked myself whether it was God Jehovah who was answering my prayers as this new hospitality accorded me by Maria took me by surprise. I had no one in Gibraltar; I knew no one in the country; I had no relations or friends either. Surely, it must be the work of God.

I said to myself, "Indeed, God drives away flies from the back of a tailless animals." God is my Shepherd; He is my Rock and my Supreme Navigator and Carer on this my long road to London. That night, after dinner, I came back to my room and made a few telephone calls. I called Maria first to thank her for her hospitality on the day. I called Clarissa and narrated all the day's activities to her. She was delighted.

I called my parents too and told them of my impending hotel job. They were thrilled and advised me to remain focussed as I worked within the hospitality environment. I had my shower and went to bed early.

I arrived at the reception of the Grand Hotel of Gibraltar at about a quarter to ten on Sunday morning. I introduced myself to the duty porter who asked me to take a seat. He was serving a customer. No sooner had he finished serving the customer than he picked up the phone and made a call. My guess was he was calling the personnel manager who Maria's pal was.

He spoke for about a minute, dropped the phone, and asked me to follow him. We climbed to the first floor of the hotel. He knocked on a door and ushered me into the room.

"Hi, hello," said the gentleman at the desk as he pointed me to a seat. "Hello, Sir," I replied and sat down. The porter excused himself and left us. "What's your name?" He asked.

"Yolandi, Sir," I replied. "I mean your full name," he came back to me. "Yolandi Kolandi, Sir," I replied.

"And you are Maria's friend?" He quizzed.

"I met her last week for the first time when I hired her taxi," I said.

"And then you became friends?" He asked with a broad smile on his face this time.

"Yes, I must say a good friend who is very helpful," I said back to him.

"Good; very good. Maria is a wonderful colleague," he said as he handed over a form to me to read and sign.

I looked over the form. It had my full name on it. The term and conditions of the job of a hotel porter was on it; and I had to be on probation for three months. I did not inform him that I would be available for only three months. I signed the form and handed it over to him. He took the form, looked at it and placed it on a file. He then informed me that the position was temporary for only six months. It was a maternity cover for a female member of staff.

I told him I was fine with that. I still did not tell him I was going to be available for only three months. He asked me whether I would prefer a night shift, afternoon shift or a morning shift. I told him I was fine with any of the shifts. And when he insisted that I gave a preference, I told him I would like a night shift. That would be from ten o'clock at night to seven o'clock in the morning the following day. He confirmed the wages to me just as Maria had said.

"Do you have any questions for me, young man?" He asked. "No, Sir," I replied.

He told me I was free to go and he would see me the next day. I left and went back to the guesthouse. I went for lunch and had a good meal. Back in my room, I started to prepare myself mentally, academically, spiritually, psychologically, and physically towards my new job. Mentally by tasking myself to remain sharp and focussed.

Academically by learning and rehearsing some basic Spanish. Spiritually, by commending all and everything into God's hands. Psychologically by preparing for interaction with the types of colleagues and guests that I would be working with and physically to remain fit and strong. I was ready.

I topped all these up with the spiritual perspective by designing a new daily prayer rota for myself for the next three months. With these, I was ready for the job of a hotel porter at the Grand Hotel of Gibraltar.

I left home at about a quarter-past nine in the evening to work on Monday. I reached work at exactly half-past-nine. I introduced myself to the porter on duty who was just closing her shift and handing over to the night shift. I was glad I went early. I witnessed how the changing over was done. To my surprise, the personnel manager was still at work.

He came down and introduced me to both porters and instructed the night porter, whose name I got to know as Alindu, to look after me and teach me all that I needed to know about the job. I thanked him and he went back to his office. He left the hotel for home about fifteen minutes later waving us goodnight on his way out. It was now well past ten o'clock in the evening. The shift handover was complete.

The afternoon shift porter, Manuela, wished us goodnight and left. I was left with Alindu, my mentor for the night. Alindu originally hailed from Nigeria. He was quite tall, very light skinned, and was quite good looking. He wore a decent beard on his chin. He looked about 22 years of age and spoke good English, albeit with a heavy Nigerian accent.

He told me he was from the Igbo tribe of Nigeria and was studying Spanish at the University of Madrid. He took up the hotel porter job as a holiday job. I learnt a lot from Alindu that evening. He taught me so many things about the job from imputing and registering a guest to even accepting tips and gifts from appreciative guests. That evening, suddenly, just before the eleven o'clock, we had about twelve guests in a queue waiting to be registered and allocated rooms.

They appeared to have come on the same flight from the United States of America. Alindu allowed me to do the registration. I did all twelve without any mistakes, much to the admiration of Alindu. Soon, the reception was cleared of guests and Alindu and I got immersed in conversation. He asked me where I was from. I told him I was a Liberian who was on my way to London to study. He asked me which course I was going to do, and I told him.

He congratulated me and said Master of Business Administration was a good second degree. He then asked why I did not fly directly to London from Monrovia but decided to pass through Spain. I spent the next one hour telling him of all my experiences from Monrovia-Liberia, through Kasoa-Ghana through the Sahel region by road and now to Gibraltar. Alindu rested his chin in his palm and listened to me in amazement. He looked at me admiringly and told me I was quite an adventurous person.

I told him I threw a challenge to myself and learnt tremendously from all my experiences on this long road to London. He told me quite a bit about himself. He was sponsored by his Federal State in Nigeria to come and specialise in Spanish. He told me he liked languages and would like to pursue a master's degree in international relations after his first degree.

I told him that was a good second degree that would pave the way for him to join his country's foreign service on completion. He was pleased with my prediction and thanked me.

The hours rolled by and I started feeling sleepy at about three o'clock in the night. I dosed off a bit. Alindu was focussed on reading the newspaper. He advised me to have some black coffee to keep me awake. I did and kept awake till the shift was over. About three guests checked in around four o'clock in the morning. Again, Alindu allowed me to do the registration, which I had then become quite well-versed in.

The porter for the morning shift arrived at a quarter to seven in the morning. Her name was Cassandra. She was Caucasian and very pretty. She was tall and looked to be in her thirties. Alindu introduced me to her. We completed the shift change-over and left. That was the end of my first day on my new job at the Grant Hotel of Gibraltar. Or should I say my first night on the job.

I reached home, had a shower, and went straight to bed. I slept till the ringing of my phone woke me up around midday. I had had no breakfast and had caught up on the sleep I had lost at work during the night. When I picked up the phone, it was Maria. She asked me how the shift went and whether I liked the job.

I answered in the affirmative and told her how Alindu was of huge help to me throughout the night. I also told her of my joy in meeting with so many different people from so many different parts of the world who came to check in at the hotel. I told her of the twelve Americans who checked in at eleven o'clock the night before. She sounded happy for me. I thanked her all over again for this huge help she had accorded me. She told me I was always welcome.

Skipping breakfast that morning had made me very hungry. I looked at the time and it was half-past-twelve. I brushed my teeth, put on casual clothes, and went for lunch at the guesthouse dining hall. Being what I could conveniently term brunch, I enjoyed the food so much. I ate my fill and went back to my room to relax. I thought about the next three months of my journey before arriving in London.

I thought of Barcelona, I thought of Paris and of Amsterdam. But then, I reminded myself that I was not on holidays. I was going to university and it involved a lot of financial commitments. I needed to work and top up the money I had at the bank. I thought of discarding the idea of going to Paris and Amsterdam. Maybe I could visit Barcelona by train for a weekend and come back to Gibraltar to continue with my job.

Two weeks into my hotel porter job, I was paid. I was paid a week's wages in arrears. I was informed I would be paid the week's wages in arrears when leaving the job. I was fine with the arrangement. I took the opportunity to open a foreign bank account in Gibraltar. And because Gibraltar was a British overseas territory, the city was awash with British banks. There was Barclays Bank, National Westminster Bank (NATWEST), Lloyds Bank among others.

I decided to open my account with the NATWEST bank. I found this arrangement convenient as I was going to move to London in a matter of a few months. I had now become quite familiar with my job at the hotel. My wages were good. I paid reasonably small money on food. My rent was manageable and I was able to save good money every week. I had become friends with all my fellow porters. They were my colleagues and I regarded them as such.

Alindu and I were the only Africans among them. There were quite a lot of Asians who worked in the hotel. The Caucasians were just a few. Because I worked on the night shifts, I hardly met most of my colleagues who worked during the day. I enjoyed working with Alindu. Sometimes, however, when he was off duty, I worked with any of the other porters. The regulation was that the night shift was run by two porters.

At work I promised myself to be a respecter of all persons irrespective of colour, race, creed, or nationality. I always remembered part of that memorable speech made by Dr Martin Luther King while preaching in Montgomery, Alabama, USA, on the independence of Africa's first Sub-Saharan country to attain independence from British colonial rule. That was Ghana.

The speech partly said, "*...the Forces of the Universe are on the side of Justice. God has injected a principle in this Universe. God has said all men must respect the dignity and worth of all human personality. And if you don't do that,*

I will take charge."

I made these noble but strong words my principle wherever I found myself. It fitted quite well into my new job as a hotel porter where I had to interact with all sorts of people from different parts of the globe. The hotel staff- mix was highly cosmopolitan. The moral behind Dr King's speech kept me focussed and well controlled. I had no quarrel or problem with anyone.

The guests I served liked me so much for the way I served them and the respect that I accorded them. My personnel manager, Mr Desiree, always had good feedback about me. The guests wrote directly to him and expressed their appreciation for the services that I accorded them. On a couple of occasions, the manager called me and relayed these compliments and appreciations by the guests I served to me himself.

I was so pleased. All my colleagues appeared to be pleased with me too. Alindu, however, gave me a word of caution that I should not be carried away by these praises being showered on me, especially from the other porters. You can never be sure they all like you as much as they say he would caution. I told him I was focussed and would be vigilant. I found the night shift so convenient. I had the whole day, after the night shift to myself, and I was able to carry out personal chores and any other things I was interested in.

I made my phone calls to all my family in Liberia as well as the many friends I made during my travels through the Sahel. I called Angelique, Fatima, Miriam and Ayeshetu. They were all so happy to hear from me and how I was progressing nicely near to my destination, London.

Barely two months into my job at the hotel, I was summoned to the office of the manager one Monday morning. The manager told me he was interviewing all the twelve porters at the hotel, including those who wheeled guests' luggage into their rooms. The desk porters were six and those who did the room services were also six. The manager told me about an investigation that he was conducting into the missing luggage of one of the guests.

He was also investigating a fraudulent use of a guest's credit card that was used to pay at the hotel reception. The manager told me the credit card was cloned. He asked me whether I knew anything about this and I answered in the negative.

"Not even the foggiest idea," I said to him looking him straight in the eyes. "Very well, very well, young man," he said with an appreciating smile on his face. He told me he trusted me, and that he was going to interview all the remaining porters and get to the bottom of this case. He also told me he was going to report the case to the Gibraltar police. I encouraged him to do so, and with that, I bade him *adieu* and left his office. Days and weeks passed.

This issue had been the rumour and talk all over the Grand Hotel of Gibraltar. I spoke to no one about it; not even Alindu. I wanted him to tell me about it first, and not the other way round. On two separate occasions, I saw about four Gibraltar policemen in uniform visiting the personnel manager in his office. On the first occasion of their visit, I was again invited to the manager's office. The four police officers, three male and one female, all Caucasians interviewed me at length.

First, they asked me whether I knew anything at all, in any shape or form about the missing suitcase and the cloned credit card that was fraudulently used. I answered a firm no. I looked serious and I answered the questions with a straight face. They also asked me about the country of my origin, my educational background, my profession back in Liberia, what I was doing in Gibraltar and my mission in London.

I took my time and gave them comprehensive answers to each of their questions using very good King's English. At the end of the interview, they glanced at each other, arched their eyebrows with smiles on their faces, and asked me to go. I thanked them and left the manager's office.

I stayed on at the hotel that evening to start work on the late-night shift. Alindu came a bit early. We carried out the shift change-over earlier than usual, much to the appreciation of Philomena, the afternoon shift staff. Philomena was a beautiful young Polish lady and was an undergraduate in one of the Universities in Gibraltar. She said to us, she always came early to take over from Cassandra on the morning shift.

She chatted with us for about fifteen minutes. During the chat, she asked whether we were aware of the on-going investigations about the missing suitcase and the fraudulent use of a guest's credit card. Alindu looked at me, and we both nodded, signalling yes to her question. She again asked us whether we were interviewed by the manager and the police. We both answered in the affirmative.

Philomena continued talking to us. She spoke good English, albeit with an accent. She told us about how she was interviewed and the female policewoman was pressing her to mention anyone that she suspected to be the culprit. She told the officer she had not the foggiest idea of who might have been responsible and was not interested in knowing the person. She said she told them in strong language that her job was to come and serve guests as the concierge in the hotel; and that when her work was done, she was interested in nothing else but to leave and go home.

Speaking in a low tone, she warned us to be very careful. She told us of how she eavesdropped into a conversation by some of the other porters insinuating blame to either of us. She said she heard them speaking in broken Spanish that they suspected either Alindu or me. She did not name or point to who actually said that. She also hinted that we should be alert as they were planning to interview Alindu and me for the second time.

She further informed us that this second interview was going to be held at the nearest police station to the hotel. I told her not to worry as my conscience was very clear. I told her I had never taken anybody's property or money in my whole life and would not do it now. I told her I was self-sufficient and did not need any of those stolen items. Alindu was more vociferous and direct. He told Philomena that he did not have that habit in his DNA and would not develop it now.

He asked whether all the other staff were going to be interviewed at the police station. She told us she was not invited and was not sure whether anyone else was invited. She again advised us to stick to our grounds of innocence and not allow anyone to bully or browbeat us into false confessions. We assured her we would do. She gave each of us a hug, waved us goodbye, and left.

Alindu and I discussed how we were both interviewed by the manager during our shift. I told him how I told them the truth that I had no idea of what they were talking about. I told him of how they asked about my home country, my missions in Gibraltar and London as well as my educational and professional background. Alindu continued to nod his head in appreciation.

He told me how he was asked why he left Nigeria to come and study in Spain. He told me he answered their question with a question which asked whether Nigeria was a Spanish speaking country. He told me on giving that answer they looked at each other and laughed. Alindu continued that he reminded them that, the interview, and the issue under discussion, were not a laughing matter.

He said he urged and challenged them to conduct a thorough investigation to get the culprit and bring him or her to book. Soon, it was time to change shift and go home. Cassandra was early. No sooner had Alindu and I completed the shift change that morning than we were invited to the manager's office. We both went up, and to our surprise, the manager was already at post.

We were seated in the office where there were two gentlemen dressed in pairs of jeans, blue T-shirts, and blue jackets already in the office. The manager introduced them to us as police detectives from the local police station who wanted us to go with us to the local police station for further interviews. Armed with Philomena's warning, we were not overtaken by events. We were not surprised either. We told them to do as they wished.

Both detectives stood up and reaching into the pouches hooked to their belts, brought out manacles and asked us to stretch our hands. Almost simultaneously, Alindu and I shouted what those were for. One detective spoke in a calm voice and told us they just wanted to secure us until we reached the police station. I flared up immediately and exclaimed "over my dead body"! Alindu asked them whether they were mad.

He asked them what we were charged with that demanded them to putting manacles on our wrists. Alindu asked them in quality English whether they understood English Law or the Gibraltar criminal system. With that, I jumped in and told them not to think we were ignorant of the law. I reminded them that every individual was innocent until proven guilty in a credible court of law and not the other way round.

The two detectives were stunned and overwhelmed by our level of literacy and the knowledge of the English law we displayed. They immediately packed the handcuffs back into their cases. In yet another calm tone, one of the detectives asked us to come with them. We all left the office except the manager who looked worried and stunned at the resilience and brilliance of Alindu and I.

He knew we would be asking him questions when we came back to work. Questions such as why all the remaining ten staff were not invited to the police station. Questions as to why the detectives wanted to put manacles on our wrists when we were neither arrested nor charged with any offence. We sat in the unmarked police vehicle and drove the fifteen minutes to the local police station.

I managed to call Maria and briefed her on what had happened. She asked me which police station we were taken to and I told her. She promised to be there before long.

At the police station, we were put behind the counter. The police cells were behind us with some inmates chatting and making noise in there. It was now about nine o'clock in the morning. We had had no shower; neither had we had breakfast. We were offered tea and coffee, but we turned them down. Maria appeared at the counter looking as bright and gorgeous as ever.

She quickly spotted Alindu and I sitting behind the counter. I rose up and went to talk to her. I told her we were waiting to be interviewed. She asked whether we had eaten breakfast. When I answered in the negative, she offered to go and get us some food. I was delighted because I was getting hungry. Soon, Maria brought us some delicious club sandwiches and coffee. She gave Alindu his first, and then I got mine. We thanked her.

She left and asked me to call her after the interview. We wolfed down all the food. It looked like Alindu was just as hungry as me. We remained behind the police counter, with our cell phones in our hands for another couple of hours. Occasionally, we would turn and take a glance at the inmates in the cells behind us through the bars. Some of them winked at us; some just made victory signs towards us by raising their index and middle fingers to make a V shape sign.

We looked at them but did not react. Eventually, we were invited to the interview rooms. We were separated. Alindu went into interview room 1 and I walked into interview room 2. I was asked to sit down. I sat down and rested my chin in my palms. The two interviewers were busy filling in a long sheet of form. As I kept looking at them, my whole mind was on my family back home as well as my university, the London School of Economics.

I thought of my parents and siblings. I thought of what my lovely Clarissa would say when information on this matter reached her. I also thought of the London School of Economics where I had to be present for registration within the next fifty days or so. I thought of whether I could just have flown from Gibraltar to London to find a job before university started instead of staying in Gibraltar. What would the university officials think of me when these false allegations reached them?

My deep thoughts were interrupted when one of the detectives asked of my name. I gave him my name, age and nationality. But just before he could ask me the next question, the phone in the interview room rang and one of them picked it up. I thought I also heard the telephone ring earlier in interview room number 1. After speaking for about two seconds in Spanish, he put the phone down.

He stopped the questioning and told me the area superintendent in charge of the police station wanted to see me. They stood up almost simultaneously in a smart, uniform and military manner, took the lead and asked me to follow them. I met Alindu sitting on one on the chairs in the superintendent's office. The personnel manager of the Grand Hotel of Gibraltar was also seated in the office. The detectives were asked to leave the office and they did.

"Gentlemen," the superintendent started. "I am so sorry for this ordeal that you have been put through. You are completely innocent people, and I am again sorry that you have been brought here straight from your night shift. The culprit of the credit card fraud has been found out and arrested. The missing suitcase was actually checked out of the hotel and left at the Gibraltar airport by the guests involved," he said with contrition written all over his face.

"I'm deeply sorry, my very good friends," he said. He told us we would be comprehensively compensated for the gross inconvenience and defamation of character all these might have caused us. Both Alindu and I remained silent. And so did the hotel personnel manager, Mr. Desiree, who was so clearly embarrassed.

"Do you have anything to say to us, gentlemen?" The superintendent asked. Both Alindu and I hesitated for a moment. Mr. Desiree, the hotel personnel manager, kept looking at us with guilt written on his face. And then both Alindu and I spoke almost simultaneously saying the same words as we spoke:

"Why then were only the two of us brought to the police station for the interview?" We asked.

And before either of them could speak, I asked again, "Why did you not invite the other ten porters at the hotel to come to the police station, but only the two of us were singled out and invited to the police station?"

Superintendent Bowles looked in the direction of Mr. Desiree as if to say please answer the questions. Mr. Desiree was quiet and looked dumb. After a while, Mr. Desiree spoke and said, "All staff were questioned in my office." Quickly, both Alindu and I said the same words again almost simultaneously.

"But we were also interviewed in your office; right or wrong?" Mr. Desiree answered in the affirmative.

"Then why were we the only ones among the twelve to be invited to the police station and not the rest of the staff?" I quizzed. Mr. Desiree had egg on his face and appeared to have fallen dumb from the weight of his shame. Superintendent Bowles stood up, shook our hands and complimented us on how bright we were as students. He once again apologised on behalf of the Gibraltar police and asked us to come with him.

We descended the stairs from his office with him. He instructed his staff car driver to drop us off at our respective destinations. With that, we entered Mr. Bowles' official staff car and soon I was at the gates of my guesthouse.

Back in my room, I had a shower quickly and lay supine on my bed. I did not make any calls and neither did I receive any. All that occupied my mind that noontime was my university in London and the course that I had enrolled to undertake. The London School of Economics was an institution of very high reputation. Many African Heads of States, living and dead, had all attended and received their degrees from that institution.

The institution had a great range of distinguished alumni. It then dawned on me that I had to study hard and do well to make my mark as a reputable student while there. It was also my conviction that other students at the university would be children and wards of very rich and influential people from all over the world. They would have had their first degrees from very good universities and institutions around the world.

All that I had to do was to gird my loins, concentrate on my studies, and come out with flying colours with my Master of Business Administration degree. I also brooded on the rather unfair treatment that was accorded Alindu and I at the hotel. Why were the other ten porters not sent to the counter-back at the police station as we were made to do? Was it because we were the main suspects?

Did anyone harbour hatred and ill intentions towards Alindu and I at the workplace? Could we have been treated better? Was Mr. Desiree, the personnel manager, confused or biased against us? All these questions went through my mind as I lay on my bed. Still musing over the morning's events, tiredness took over, and I finally fell asleep.

I woke up close to half-past-six in the evening. I had a nightshift at the hotel that evening from ten o'clock. I quickly had my dinner at the dining hall and got ready for work. The 40 winks I had refreshed me so much that I was fit and ready for my shift later in the night. My phone rang. I picked it up and it was Maria. She said she was just passing by and was parked outside the guesthouse.

I invited her into my room, I told her if she was not in a hurry, she could come in for about thirty minutes. She obliged and came in. She sat at my writing desk. We chatted for some time on my experiences at the police station. I told her what happened from when they came for Alindu and I at the hotel. I told her how they wanted to put manacles on our writs and we both rebuked and told them off.

I told her about how only the two of us were taken to the police station leaving the other ten porters at the hotel. Finally, I told her of how, at the end of the day, the Superintendent of Police, Mr. Bowles, commended us and how Mr. Desiree, the hotel personnel manager, had egg all over his face. Maria empathised with me and encouraged me to be strong. She asked me to forgive them and concentrate on my work.

I reminded her that I had completed four weeks at the job already and had about eight weeks left for me to finish and proceed to London. She exclaimed and looked surprised at four weeks already gone from the day she picked me at the Gibraltar ferry port. I said yes and we both laughed. After a few more minutes, Maria asked permission to leave as she was going to continue working till late that evening.

She asked me when I was starting work and I said ten o'clock. We both stood up. She gave me a hug and waved me goodbye. She told me it was not necessary that I saw her off to the gates of the guesthouse. She said she was fine. With that, she smiled at me and left.

I reached work at about half-past-nine that evening. I was thirty minutes early for my shift. Alindu had not turned up. Philomena welcomed me and remarked that I was early. I told her I always liked showing up to work and other occasions early. It was not busy that evening. We chatted about a lot of things. She asked me how our arrest and visit to the police station went. I told her everything that transpired at the police station.

She listened to me with empathy and said sorry to me for all my troubles. Philomena was not happy with the police inviting only Alindu and me to the police station for interrogation. She asked why all the twelve porters were not invited to the police station. She advised me to be careful and that someone in the hotel might have made the two of us, Alindu and me, targets. A target to destroy our reputations.

I thanked her for her concern and advice. She asked me where I lived. I told her I lived at the guesthouse. She asked when I would be off so she could visit me. I asked her why and what the visit was about. She looked into my face admiringly, and with a smile said, "I want to take you out for dinner."

I smiled back. and said to her, "Oh, that would be nice."

Before long, Alindu arrived for work. He walked straight behind the counter and warmly greeted Philomena and me. It was almost ten o'clock and we had to change shifts. We quickly changed shifts. I continued chatting to Philomena while Alindu continued to update the computer with the latest inputs. I walked Philomena to the steps of the hotel on her way home.

She handed me a business card. The card bore her name, university, telephone number and e-mail address. She asked for my telephone number and I gave it to her. With that, she gave me a hug and stepped down the stairs on her way home. I re-joined Alindu at the reception. We discussed our ordeal extensively. Alindu appeared to be more hurt than me. I was also hurt but I took it in better stride than my colleague.

Suddenly, we were swamped with work. At about eleven o'clock, a Chinese delegation flooded into the hotel reception. They numbered about twenty-five. Alindu and I got busy checking them in. The bellboys wheeled their luggage into their respective rooms. Soon, it became quiet again. It was a few minutes past half-past-midnight. Alindu and I resumed our conversation. He told me he felt humiliated by the way we were treated.

He told me we were more qualified than any of the porters in the hotel and yet, see how we were treated. I calmed him down and uttered a few words of wisdom to him. I was virtually preaching God's word to him asking him to give it all to God to deal with. I also reminded him of the compensation that we were promised. He listened to me keenly and kept nodding his head. After a while, he heaved a huge sigh and said, "Whatever they do, I think I need to leave here and find another job."

I asked him, "Why?"

"You never know what they would accuse us of next," he said throwing both arms in the air despairingly.

"Don't worry, my good friend, God is on our side," I said to him. He nodded his head, and said, "Whatever the case is, I would leave."

On our next shift the following day, we went to work early on the orders of the personnel manager, Mr. Desiree. Alindu and I sat in his office. He offered us tea and coffee. I told him I was fine and did not want tea or coffee. Alindu told him the same thing. He then insisted we had soft drinks. We did. He also offered us biscuits and we did not reject them.

"Colleagues," he started. "I invited you here today, first to render sincere apologies to you for how you have been treated by the Grand Hotel of Gibraltar. In fact, we were wrong and I apologise on my own behalf and on behalf of the Grand Hotel of Gibraltar; we are really sorry," he concluded. Alindu and I briefly exchanged glances and refocussed our attention on Mr Desiree.

"I really can't fathom why you or the hotel management would pick on Alindu and I to be taken to the police station; why? Can you explain that to us?" I asked looking directly into his eyes.

Before Mr. Desiree could say anything, Alindu exclaimed, "Exactly! Can you explain that to us?"

Mr. Desiree looked down and up the ceiling, hesitated for a moment, and told us he had no explanation for that. He continued to say all the twelve porters at the Grand Hotel of Gibraltar should have been invited to the police station, and not only the two of us. He said the hotel management was wrong in doing that, and that on the instructions and advice of the Gibraltar police, the hotel management had decided to pay compensation to the two of us.

We were to receive 5,000 GIP each. On hearing that, we said nothing. Mr. Desiree added that, that amount would come as a separate cheque in our next pay packets. I showed no emotions. Neither did Alindu. We finished the rest of the soft drinks and biscuits and then left Mr. Desiree's office. The issue formed a major part of the conversation between Alindu and I throughout the rest of the night shift. We talked at length about the behaviour of both Mr Desiree and the Grand Hotel of Gibraltar.

I explained to Alindu that I was still on my long road to London and was just passing away time that I had on my hand to make some money before reaching London. I told Alindu that I had two more months before my university reopened and that I might want to move to another part of Europe for the two months before setting foot on English soil. I said to Alindu that I did not have any country in mind, but it would be a good idea to move on from these guys. I was sure I could get another job for a couple of months before leaving for London.

Alindu listened to me keenly with his chin resting in the palms of his both hands. He told me he could understand where I was coming from and bought into my idea. He said to me he was thinking on the same lines and that it would be good if both of us left at the same time. It was ten days to the end of the month. And we both encouraged each other to sleep over the matter, think deeply about it and come back with further ideas and suggestions as to how to execute our plans.

I reached home at about half-past-eight that morning. I went straight into the shower and had a good bath. I then went to the dining room and had breakfast. I was just about to retire to bed and catch some sleep when my phone rang. My first inkling was that it was an early morning call from my lovely Clarissa. I was wrong. The call was from Philomena.

"Hello, good morning, Yolandi," she said.

"Fine morning, Philomena, my friend. How are you doing?" I asked. "I'm doing good, and you?" she replied.

"Same here; I'm doing great," I responded.

Philomena asked whether she could come and visit me same day on her way to work. I told her I had just come back home from the night shift and was not sure what time of the day I would be available. She told me her shift started at two o'clock in the afternoon, and that she could come about one o'clock that afternoon. I told her that I was a bit fatigued that morning and wanted to have a good rest.

I told her she could come another day, or better still, we met on the day that both of us were off duty. She agreed and wished me a good rest. No sooner had I put the phone down than it rang again. I asked myself whether it was going to be a busy morning for me. I said hello and the voice from the other end was my lovely Clarissa.

"Hello, my love, Clarissa," I said. "Hi hello, my babe," she replied.

"Just to say a quick good morning on my way to work," she continued.

"Oh wow! That's lovely, my sweetheart; have a blessed day at work," I closed the conversation.

Thoughts of Clarissa's morning call and that of Philomena both raced through my mind as I lay on my bed. I said to myself, I was a hundred per cent sure of the relationship I had with Clarissa. What I was not too sure on, however, was the type of relationship that I would have with Philomena if we became closer. Would it be in the patterns of Angelique, Fatima, Ayeshetu, or Mariam? As I tried to find answers to these questions, I was gradually lulled into a mid-morning sleep.

I was off duty on the next weekend; Saturday and Sunday. Philomena was off on those two days too. I asked myself whether it was a coincidence or pre- planned by Philomena. And since Philomena had no control over the hotel porters' duty rota, I settled for the former rather than the latter. During a conversation that I had with Philomena on the coincidence of both of us having same days off, we agreed to meet and go out on the Saturday.

I was not sure where we were going, but as Philomena had been in Gibraltar longer than me and, therefore, knew the city considerably well and better than me. I left every decision regarding places to visit entirely to her.

We met on the stairs of my guesthouse that Saturday morning. Philomena wore a pair of deep sea-blue jeans and a white blouse with a light-blue jacket. She wore a pair of Nike sneakers and looked brilliantly beautiful. I wore a pair of beige khaki jeans with a beige jungle long-sleeved shirt on top. I also wore a pair of Nike sneakers, beige in colour with a khaki Nike baseball cap. I thought I looked elegantly presentable, at least for the occasion that we were about to embark upon.

On second thought, I thought I looked like someone on a safari on the *Masai Mara* in Kenya. In any case, I believed I was well dressed enough for the occasion. Philomena greeted me with *bisous* on both sides of my cheeks. I received them warmly and thanked her. I told her how beautiful she looked that morning. She thanked me and returned the compliments by telling me I looked handsome. I thanked her.

After a pretty short tête-à-tête, we decided to join the bus to Central Gibraltar. We stood at the bus stop for less than three minutes when one pulled up. We looked at the bus number and Philomena told me that was not the bus we needed to board. We waited for another five minutes and bus number 222 to Central Gibraltar pulled up. We boarded the bus and were on our way to Central Gibraltar. The journey took about half an hour.

During the bus ride, Philomena revisited the incident at the hotel concerning Alindu and I being invited to the police station with no other porter being treated the same. Before I could speak, she asked me whether I thought it was deliberate or it was just a kerfuffle. I told her I could not tell and that I had put that matter firmly behind me. I did not tell her of any compensation to be paid to Alindu and me. I also did not make it known to her at that stage that I was making up my mind to leave my job at the hotel. I thought of telling her at the most appropriate time. My answers to Philomena's questions made her refrain from talking about the incident anymore. She now shifted to and focussed on our day trip. She told me we were going on a Dolphin Safari. She explained it further that it was a dolphin watching trip and we had to go by boat. I nodded to indicate my consent.

She also said when we came back from the Dolphin Safari, there was a great movie showing that night. She said we would stay back and watch the movie before returning to Central Gibraltar on our way home. I smiled and nodded in consent. I asked her when the movie would end. She did not give me a direct answer but said, if the movie finished later than we expected, there were hotels around and we could stay the night in one of them. She added there were many hotels and that we did not need to book in advance; we could just walk in. Eventually, I spoke. I told Philomena what an interesting trip that would be.

The coach from Central Gibraltar took about an hour and a half to the seaside located on the north coast of Gibraltar. We reached the Dolphin

Safari site and there were so many boats available to choose from. We saw one that carried 25 tourists. We saw another that carried 125 passengers. While the smaller boats posed barriers to substantial walking space for us to move around and catch better glimpses of the dolphins and take pictures, the larger boats on the other hand provided plenty of space which was great; and since I wanted to see everything without others in my way, I was inclined towards a big boat. But then, Philomena thought otherwise. She thought the advantages of a smaller boat outweighed those of a larger boat. More so, we read from some of the Dolphin Safari brochures we picked up that, the smaller boats had the highest success rates for finding dolphins; about 99% success rate. I thought that was as encouraging as it was interesting. Some smaller boats also provided comfortable cushioned seating guaranteed for everyone. It was spacious enough so we could move around the boat to see the dolphins with ease.

Also, the expert crew provided personal attention to all passengers as the numbers were small. Consequently, we decided to go with a boat that carried 25 passengers. Actually, it was Philomena's decision and I agreed with it.

I remembered my experiences with boats during the earlier parts of my long journey to London where I encountered life-threatening incidents. I smiled over them. We got our tickets for the Dolphin Safari. Soon an alarm sounded, and we were called to board the *Santa Maria*, the boat we had chosen for the trip. We were professionally escorted into the boat by the crew. Every action of theirs from how they spoke to how they handled and ushered us onboard showed how professionally dexterous they were at their jobs.

Philomena held on to my left hand as we entered the boat. In a funny but quiet way, our entry into the boat again reminded me of the Noah's Ark story in the Christian Bible. But I quickly reminded myself that there were no floods around and we were on the great Atlantic Ocean.

Initially, I was a bit sceptical as to how many dolphins we would be able to see. Despite some of the brochures saying one could see as many as 500 dolphins at a time, I was still not convinced we could see any of them just so easily. However, as the boat sailed about 3 nautical kilometres away from the breakwater, we sailed into a shoal of them. So, my initial inkling was wrong; so wrong. First, we saw about 25 to 30 dolphins at a time jumping out of the water, chasing fish, playing and these were all within a metre of our boat.

The dolphins seemed to love the attention of humans so close to them. The crew on board were great, funny, and helpful. They told us all along what the dolphins would do after a jump and they were spot on. The dolphin jumped, went back into the water, did reverse jumps, and somersaulted in some cases. It was so delightful to watch. Philomena and I were so excited. She spent most of her time taking pictures while I focussed my attention entirely on the gymnastics being so skilfully displayed by these wonderfully-created amazing mammals.

We spent about two and a half hours watching the dolphins after which our boat sailed back to port. It was mid-afternoon and the clock had just struck two o'clock. We took a taxi to the *Yohan Plaza,* a huge shopping mall that accommodated a few cinema halls, lots of shops as well as quite a few hotels. The mall also had many restaurants which served food from almost every region of the globe.

There was Chinese, Japanese, Italian, Continental, Spanish, Arab and many other food categories. There were even traditional African food restaurants in the mall. I asked Philomena what type of food she would like. I expected her to say Polish. Surprisingly enough, she told me she would eat the type of food I would eat. I smiled and nodded. I told her I would like to have Italian food. She asked which type exactly and I said I wanted Spaghetti Marinara.

She looked up at me and said that was one of her favourite foods too. We agreed on Spaghetti Marinara and looked out for an Italian restaurant. It did not take us long to locate one. Philomena asked permission to visit the loo and I sat at the restaurant table alone. My phone rang and I checked who was calling me. It was Maria.

"Hi hello, Maria," I said.

"Hallo, Yolandi, came the reply."

"Where are you?" Maria asked and continued to say she went to look for me at the guesthouse but was told I had checked out.

"Yes, I am in North Gibraltar; I came here for a weekend break with one of my colleagues," I replied to her.

"Oh, that's nice. I was just checking on you. Have a nice time," she concluded.

"Thank you and I will see you when I return," I said to her.

Philomena came back and we ordered a couple of plates of Spaghetti Marinara. I ordered for a couple of glasses of South African red wine. *Nederburg* to be specific. Soon the food was served and both Philomena and I tucked into them. Both of us enjoyed the food very much. In fact, I wanted to request an encore but discarded the idea almost immediately it came to my mind.

I would not know what Philomena would think of my eating habits if I had gone ahead and ordered another plate. The red wine, as usual, tasted good and provided a delightful accompaniment to the dish. We finished lunch at about four o'clock in the evening. We left the restaurant and checked into the moderately-priced *Marengo* Hotel also situated within the shopping mall.

Philomena went online and booked two tickets for the movies that night. Altogether, the *Vue Cinema* was showing five different movies that evening. We had to choose from the five and both of us agreed on the film entitled *Around the World in Eighty Days*. This film was released in the year 1968. A little background reading on this film revealed that it was based on a novel authored by the French writer, Jules Verne, and was first published in French in 1872. We both dressed up in evening clothes and went to the *Vue Cinema* film house.

We went a bit early and had a light dinner. We bought some popcorn on our way to take our seats. The film started soon after we took our seats. The film was riveting. The main character, Phileas Fogg of London, and his newly appointed French valet, Passepartout, attempted to circumnavigate the world in eighty days on a £20,000 wager; approximately £2.3 million in today's value in the year 2023. Not surprisingly, by the time the film ended, we had emptied the whole bucketful of popcorn.

We retired into our beautiful hotel room. I told Philomena how good it felt for other hotel porters from another hotel to provide us with the same service that we, day-in-day-out, provided to others at our place of work at the Grand Hotel of Gibraltar. Philomena agreed with me and said it felt so fulfilling.

We chatted a lot throughout the night. It was there that Philomena told me of the plans she had made for the next day, Sunday. She said we would be visiting the Rock of Gibraltar for a complete day out. She said we would see Europa Point and visit the magical St Michaels Cave with wondrous stalactites and stalagmites with colourful lighting, no difficult climbing involved, and it would feel as if we were on a different planet as we walked through the vaulted high ceilings, and, of course, meet the famous Barbary apes with all their charm and mischief.

The next day Sunday, we set off after breakfast at the *Marengo* Hotel. We went in a tourists' open double-decker bus. The sun came out that morning brilliantly and the sea breeze from the Mediterranean blew to provide just the cooling we needed. It was a cool air that made us feel comfortable even though the sun was warm.

We first drove past the Barbery macaques. Our tour guide told us that Gibraltar was the only European destination where one could hang out with monkeys. The population of about 230 Barbery macaques that lived on the 400- metre-high plateau of the Rock are the only wild monkeys in Europe. It was one of Gibraltar's most iconic sights, especially when the monkeys perched on the cliff-edge munching on bananas.

The monkeys gave us a friendly welcome when we arrived at the top of the cliff. Remarkably, one monkey perched on my lap when we got out of the bus and sat down in one of the specially provided seats around the cliff-top. It was friendly. However, before I could realise, it dipped its hands into my breast pocket and snatched my mobile phone. The animal ran away with it while other tourists joined me in giving it a hot chase with shouts of 'drop it, drop it'.

The monkey got frightened and dropped the phone on the ground and quickly ran away. I got my phone back. We then climbed up to the top of the Rock of Gibraltar in cable cars. The views from the peak of the Rock of Gibraltar were astonishingly beautiful. It was worth a visit. From its 400-metre roof, we looked out over two continents: Africa lay just 13 miles across the Straits to our south, while Europe stretched out to our north with the sun-scorched mountains and plains of Andalusia.

The north coast of Africa was also visible from the Europa Point at the island's southernmost tip, from where we could see Morocco's *Jebel Musa* Mountain. According to legend, the *Musa* was one with the rocks before Hercules smashed through them, creating the two Pillars of Hercules. Amazing panoramic sights!

Philomena and I also enjoyed the huge blend of cultures that the trip provided. With me in particular, I thought I was getting a sense of how multi- culturalism would work when I ultimately reached London. I had read earlier on how London was branded the most cosmopolitan city in the world and I was just sensing a bit of that on this trip. My trip with Philomena, a Polish national, also gave me a feel of that multiculturalism.

From the top of the Rock, we had an incomparable position from which we surveyed the two countries of Morocco and Spain that had combined with British culture to give this territory its unique ambience. We also learnt that, centuries before the British claimed control of Gibraltar in 1704 during the war of Spanish Succession, long periods of Moorish and Spanish rule had combined to give this intriguing place a mixture of cuisines, architectural styles, and cultural mores that were added to by the arrival of northern Europeans.

Nowhere was this mixture more evident than in the old town, where British pubs sat next to Arabic restaurants and Andalusian-style townhouses. We also went to the border town and had a stroll across the border. No one asked us for passports as we went as a tourist group. It was one of the unique pleasures of visiting Gibraltar. We spent a few hours in mainland Spain by simply strolling across the border to the Andalusian town of *La Linea de la Concepcion*.

This was by far the most hassle-free way of changing countries and it afforded us the rare experience of standing with one foot in one country and the other in another. A great feeling. At that juncture, I took my phone out of the pocket to call my lovely Clarissa. I dialled her number a couple of times but had no response.

Due to how small Gibraltar was, we could walk from the centre of its old town to the centre of *La Linea* in under an hour and if we were worried about getting lost, all we needed to do was to follow the signs to Spain. Alternatively, if we were visiting from elsewhere in Andalusia, we could get the bus from Málaga to San Roque, from where it was a ten-minute taxi ride or car journey to *La Linea*. The whole touring party sat in the sun to enjoy an ale in the Mediterranean before leaving the place.

One thing the United Kingdom did extremely well was provide a decent pint of ale and one thing the Mediterranean did well was provide endless sun and spotless blue skies—yet rarely could the two be enjoyed together. Gibraltar's status as a British overseas territory and its position on the Iberian peninsula's most southerly tip, though, meant that these two great things were both in abundance there.

We took ourselves to one of the best British pubs called the *Horseshoe Inn* on the main street, ordered a pint of dark ale, and headed out to a sun-drenched terrace on Spanish soil to enjoy it. It was huge fun and a totally splendid outing for the day. I enjoyed it so much.

We arrived back at the hotel just before seven o'clock that evening. Since Philomena and I had late shifts at our places of work, we decided to spend another night at the hotel and leave early the next morning to Central Gibraltar. That way, Philomena could get to work at two o'clock in the afternoon and me later at ten o'clock in the evening. We chatted at length that evening as we whiled away the time. It was during that chat that I told Philomena of my impending departure from the job at the Grand Hotel of Gibraltar.

I explained to her that it was a decision taken by Alindu and I after long and careful thinking about the whole degrading incident in which the two of us were wrongly singled out and made scapegoats. I told her we were both so hurt that we did not find it difficult to make the decision to quit the job. Philomena listened to me in total silence with her chin resting in the palm of her left hand.

She occasionally nodded when I made certain points and explained some difficulties that both Alindu and I envisaged in the days ahead if we did not leave the job. Philomena asked me whether I was leaving straight for London from Gibraltar. I told her, I had just a week's more work at the Grand Hotel of Gibraltar. I would be leaving the job exactly at the end of the month. With that, I explained to her that I had two more months left before departing finally for my destination which was London to go to university.

After remaining silent for about three minutes, Philomena repeated the question on whether I was going to leave for London when I quit the job. I answered in the negative. Philomena asked me whether I would be looking for another job in Gibraltar. I told her I was not sure but had an idea of trying my luck in the north-eastern Spanish City of Barcelona. I further explained to her that if I got a good job in Gibraltar, I might consider it, but my focus and interest were both largely on Barcelona at that moment.

She nodded and heaved a huge sigh. She looked me in the face, held my hands, and gave me a hug that lasted for about five minutes. We continued to chat on other matters well into the night until we were both lulled to sleep by the pleasant and soft evening music played from the hotel's central music system that I had tuned into.

We woke up the next morning rather late. We quickly had our showers and breakfast, checked out from the hotel, and soon were on the coach heading towards Central Gibraltar. During the ride, I thanked Philomena sincerely for bringing me on this wonderful trip. I told her she was an excellent friend who I would cherish forever. She looked admiringly into my face, smiled mischievously, and refocussed her attention on the view of the scenery; landscapes and mountains and hills that we drove past.

I arrived at my guesthouse at about two o'clock in the afternoon. I decided to have lunch and then rush down to work early in order to meet with my manager to discuss my impending decision to quit the job. Thus, after lunch, I set off towards my place of work. I had arranged with Alindu to meet on the steps of the hotel, have a discussion, and then go to see the manager together.

We met Mr. Desiree at exactly five o'clock that afternoon in his office. He welcomed us politely and asked us to take our seats. He asked of our mission for meeting with him and we quickly informed him of the notice of leaving the job that we had for him. He told us it was within our rights to do so at any time. He asked us when our last day of work was and we told him just exactly a week from then.

Mr. Desiree looked worried and irritated and told us that he was sad we were leaving. He told us that we were his best porters and that he would find it very difficult to get replacements for us. To that, I said to him we were also equally sad we were leaving. I told him we did not feel safe or trustworthy enough to continue to work there. Alindu cut in and told him we were not sure what the next suspicion or accusation would be, and that it was better for the two of us to quit.

Mr. Desiree was silent for a couple of minutes and then spoke. He thanked us for our hard work and that he would see us again before we finally left. Alindu and I went to sit in the hotel's cafeteria to have some biscuits and soft drinks. When it was getting to nine o'clock in the evening, we went to the hotel concierge and did an earlier than usual shift-change with Philomena.

She appeared tired and left the hotel soon after the shift-change. I walked her down the stairs of the hotel to see her off at the bus stop. We chatted for a few minutes. I again thanked her for her huge hospitality and kindness accorded me over the weekend. The bus came and Philomena left. I waved her goodbye as the bus sped off.

Just as I was about to mount the steps and walk back to the hotel reception, my cell phone rang. As usual, my first thought went to my lovely Clarissa. No, I was wrong; the call was from Maria. She asked me whether I was at work. I answered in the affirmative. She told me she had just closed from work and was on her way home. I told her I was just beginning my night shift.

She wished me a good time at work and said she might pass by my guesthouse in the afternoon of the following day. I told her there was no problem and that I would be looking forward to seeing her.

The night shift went well. It was comparatively quiet. In fact, we were both catching up on some sleep when a delegation of about a dozen Japanese tourists came to check into the hotel at about five o'clock in the morning. We checked them in fairly quickly and efficiently. The room porters came for their luggage and shepherded them into their rooms.

Cassandra, the morning shift porter, was on time. She came in at about a quarter to seven o'clock in the morning. We had a smooth shift-change, wished Cassandra a good day, and Alindu and I left for our homes. My bus came early. I reached the guesthouse before eight o'clock that morning. I went for breakfast at about nine o'clock after which I came back to my room and hit the bed.

I was woken up by Maria's telephone call at about half-past-one in the afternoon. She said she was dropping off a passenger and would be with me within the next thirty minutes. I told her I would be looking forward to seeing her. Maria came in at exactly two o'clock that afternoon. I took her to the guesthouse dining hall and we had lunch together. She told me she enjoyed the food so much.

We came back to my room and started chatting. We talked about so many things including my impending quitting of the job in less than a week. Maria asked me what plan or plans I had after leaving the Grand Hotel of Gibraltar. I told her I would be looking for another job to do for a couple of months before I left Spain to my university in London. I also reminded her that I was fully aware that she helped me in finding my current job.

She smiled at me and said that was fine. As our conversation progressed, I told Maria that I would want to travel to Barcelona to try my luck there. I told her I did not know anyone there but would trust God and His providence to secure a job in Barcelona for a couple of months. Maria was silent for some time. And when she spoke, she told me I should not worry, and that she would see how she could help me by working something out for me.

I looked into her face and told her that would be marvellous if she could fix the Barcelona connection, as I termed it, for me. She smiled again and told me we should wait and see what God would do. Maria left exactly at half-past-three that afternoon. I decided to catch up on some sleep before setting out for work around nine o'clock in the evening.

I arrived at work at the Grand Hotel of Gibraltar a bit early. Philomena was busy checking in guests at the reception. It was my last day at work at the hotel. And so was it for Alindu. He also came in early and we both went to see Mr Desiree. We talked for some time. He told us that the two of us were his best and most hardworking porters at the hotel and that he would miss us a lot. We both said to him we would miss him too.

He handed over to each of us our Staff-Leaving-Employment papers to sign. We did. He also gave us our last pay-checks. Mr. Desiree introduced two young Caucasians to us that they would be taking our places at the hotel when we left. They were called Raphael and Gonzalez. He asked us to train them to the best of our abilities. That was our last shift at the hotel and the last for our jobs. We both promised to do so.

We left Mr. Desiree's office and went to join Philomena at the reception. The two new employees were also there. We went through the shift change with them. As I was wont to, I saw off Philomena at the bus stop. I told her she was always welcome to visit me at the guesthouse. I told her I would be leaving for Barcelona in exactly five days' time and I would love to see her at any time.

She nodded her head in consent rather unenthusiastically. She looked back and waved at me as her bus sped away.

Back at the reception, we continued our training of the new porters.

They looked bright and were quick to learn. We completed the nightshift with them and helped them with the shift change with Cassandra, the morning shift porter. Both Alindu and I bid farewell to Cassandra and left the hotel for the final time. I reached home that morning feeling a bit sleepy. I had a quick shower, went to have breakfast, and came back to my room.

I sat on my bed, put out a few calls to my family and my lovely Clarissa in Liberia. None of them answered the calls and I guessed it was due to the malfunctioning telephone network system in my country which happened occasionally. I tried one more time and when unsuccessful, I retired to bed and dosed off.

I woke up to the telephone call of my lovely Clarissa. She called at exactly half-past-two and told me she was on her lunch break at work. We exchanged pleasantries and continued to talk about many other things. I took the opportunity to run Clarissa through the rather lengthy itinerary that I had for the next five days.

"How are you travelling to Barcelona?" She asked. "By coach, my dear," I replied.

"How long will that take you?" She continued.

"By coach, it takes eleven hours fifty-four minutes along 1,105.7 kilometres of road on the Eastern Spanish coastline. By train, it takes nine hours seven minutes. But I prefer to go by coach just as I have done all through this long journey to London, starting from Ouagadougou."

"*Bon Voyage, mon cheri,*" she ended the conversation in French.

"*Merci, Beaucoup,*" I replied.

Immediately Clarissa and I ended our telephone conversation, the phone rang again. This time it was my dad. I greeted him respectfully in my native Creole English. We spoke for about a quarter of an hour. We discussed many issues. I took my time to explain to him my itinerary for the next five days just as I did to my lovely Clarissa.

He asked me whether I had secured accommodation in Barcelona. I told him I was going to lodge at a guesthouse and that there were plenty of them in the city of Barcelona. I further told my dad that I did not know which one I would get since I had not booked one.

My dad passed the phone over to my mum. Her first question to me centred on how many months I had left before reaching my university. I told her I had just two months more. I further explained to her that I would spend the two months working in Barcelona before leaving for London to start my university course in September. She asked me whether I had got the job already in Barcelona. I answered in the negative, but assured her that, with the providence of God on my side, I hoped to get one not long after arriving in Barcelona.

"Hmmm," said my mum in a low tone. "This journey of yours to London is really a long one indeed," she concluded.

"Yes, Mum," I replied. "I will put all my efforts together to reach there on time," I said to her.

"I agree with you, Son; when spiders come together, they can tie up a lion. I know you will put all your best efforts together and sail through," she encouraged me using an old African proverb.

"Yes, Mum; I've always been fascinated with challenges and the potential of sustained thinking and collaborative effort," I replied to her.

I spoke to all my siblings who were all aware of my impeding journey to Barcelona. They were all in good spirits and wished me well.

I got ready and was just about to go for lunch when I heard a knock on my door. It was about two o'clock. I knew it would not be Philomena because she started work at two o'clock that afternoon. Quickly my guess centred on the only remaining person I could think of: Maria. I opened the door and lo and behold, it was Maria.

"Hello, Maria, come on in," I welcomed her with a big smile on my face. "Thank you, Yolandi," she replied as she walked into my room.

We exchanged pleasantries after which I invited her to join me at lunch. She agreed and we walked leisurely towards the dining hall. Maria said she had not eaten all day because she had been fasting for the first half of the day. I told her that was good. I also asked her whether she had backed the fasting with prayers. She replied in the affirmative and explained to me that she had not done any work or driving during the fasting period.

I commended her and asked her to break her fast in a special way with me at our lunch. She thanked me and repeatedly said to me that she was grateful.

Lunch was excellent. The mouth-watering aroma was confirmed by the tastiness of the dishes. We remained at the dining hall for about thirty minutes chatting. I told Maria my plans regarding my impending journey to Barcelona. But as we continued our conversation, the dining hall staff informed us that lunch was over and that they needed to clean up the hall. They politely asked everyone who was not staff to leave the hall.

We obliged and walked down to my room. There, we continued with our conversation. I continued to brief Maria on my plans. Although, she did not appear enthused by my decision to leave Gibraltar for Barcelona, I nevertheless stuck to my plans. She kept nodding her head rather absentmindedly, and even though it appeared she was looking into my face, she was thinking of something else. I told her in some detail the questions my mum and dad asked me.

First, I told her about dad's question on whether I had already secured accommodation waiting in Barcelona. Maria just heaved a heavy sigh. She said nothing. I then followed up with the question my mum asked in respect of whether I had secured a job. She heaved another huge sigh. Maria finally spoke. She told me I should not worry about a job. She also said I need not worry about accommodation since there were so many guesthouses in Barcelona.

She paused for about a minute and told me she had contacted a friend in Barcelona about my impending visit. She said the friend, by name Anastasia, would meet me at the coach station when I reached Barcelona on the Friday. She would, on her instruction, take me to a pre- booked guesthouse.

She told me she had arranged a guesthouse for me because of conversations we had when I met her for the first time by hiring her taxi. She reminded me of me rejecting the suggestion of a hotel when she mentioned it and insisted that I wanted a guesthouse. I also clearly remembered that encounter. I immediately told her thank you.

Maria continued that Anastasia, her friend, would introduce me to a certain gentleman regarding securing a job for the two months I was scheduled to be in the city. She did not mention the name of the person to me but encouraged me to keep my fingers crossed and, with the providence of the true and living God, Anastasia would sort me out and all would be well. She asked me whether I had any questions to ask her.

I thanked Maria profusely and told her, in the most appreciative terms that I really appreciated her help since day one when I set foot on

European soil. I also told her, to her amazement, that she had virtually been my guardian angel since I set foot on Gibraltar soil. I thanked her again and told her that God Almighty, who could see in secret and could see in darkness, who knew all of her heart's desires would bless her and grant her all that she desired.

I finally told her that she would not only be a chapter in my life story but would be part of the story. On hearing my words, Maria got emotional. I had never seen her in that mood, for I knew how strong and fit she was. Tears freely flowed from her eyes and dropped on her chest. She stood up, wiped away those tears, gave me a hug which lasted for a long five minutes and informed me that she was about to leave.

Once again, I thanked Maria for her goodness towards me. I told her I would see her again before I finally left for London. And with that, I saw her off to her car which was parked in front of the guesthouse. I waved at Maria as she drove off. She waved back with tears still welling up in her eyes.

I came back to my room carrying some of Maria's emotions with me. It was almost five o'clock in the afternoon. I did not cry, although I was caught up in an unusual mood of melancholy. I knew I was stronger than sadness and so I tried to nip that situation in the bud. I succeeded. I regained my composure. I called Philomena at work and chatted with her for some time. She told me it was not busy in the hotel at that moment.

She told me she missed me. I told her I missed her too. She asked of the day of my departure and I said Friday. She said to me she would see me before I set off to Barcelona. Two days before I left for Barcelona, Philomena came to visit. She came in at about ten o'clock in the morning and told me she was off from work on the day. I welcomed her in and went to have a late breakfast with her. She told me she enjoyed the breakfast so much because, in her haste to reach me early, she skipped breakfast. We discussed lots of issues. Just like I told my parents, Clarissa, and Maria, I briefed her on the details on my itinerary relating to my impending journey. Philomena asked me whether I had my air ticket already. I told her I was going by Coach. And before she could ask me how long the journey would take, I replied it was going to take about eleven hours. She looked at me in wonderment and smiled.

Just as everyone who cared for me had asked of my accommodation and job arrangements when I got to Barcelona, Philomena also did. I explained the arrangements and the expectations that I had in mind to her. She nodded and told me that was fine. She sat on my bed and watched a bit of television. When it was lunch time we had lunch together at the guesthouse dining hall.

It was at the lunch table that Philomena surprised me with the information that she had secured a couple of tickets for us to go to the theatre to watch a show that evening. I quickly asked her what show it was. She looked into my face shyly and said in a rather sexy tone, *"The Lion King."* I said that was nice. But then, I also asked what time the show would end and what time she would reach home.

She told me that she was off the following day and would resume work on Thursday. And that she planned to stay with me at least for a whole day. I was mute for about a minute after which I raised my right thumb to her in agreement. Philomena and I left the guesthouse about six o'clock in the evening for the show. To some extent, I was fascinated, excited and anxious because, in Africa, I read and saw clips of *The Lion King* show. I had read and heard of Simba, Musafa and Nala. Others included Rafiki, Zazu, Scar and Pumbaa. I was thrilled but showed no emotions. Philomena brought an evening dress. It was a beautiful long flowing evening dress with embroidery around the collar.

I told her she looked stunning in her dress. I was dressed in an ocean blue suit with a white shirt. The neck of the shirt was open as I wore no tie. Philomena told me that I looked good. I thanked her and returned the compliment. The show was to start at eight o'clock that evening. We reached the theatre more than an hour early.

And because we had had no supper, we decided to have a light dinner. We entered a small restaurant within the theatre complex and had club sandwiches. The sandwiches were superb and we washed them down with soft drinks.

The show started exactly at eight o'clock that evening. Rafiki was the first character to appear on stage. His appearance was greeted with a huge roar of shouts and applause from the audience. He disappeared after making a brief comment. Other characters followed in succession and soon, the real show started in earnest. Philomena stayed hooked on the show as it went on while holding fast on to my left arm.

I refocussed my concentration on the show, although occasionally, thoughts of a new life in Barcelona flitted through my mind. I tried to keep these thoughts in check and concentrated on the show. The show also reminded me of my native Africa as some of the names resonated with some common names I was familiar with back home. The show ended after three and a half hours. It was almost midnight.

We took our time in getting out from the theatre as we were aware of the possibility of a stampede should people jostle to get out of the auditorium. It took us about thirty minutes of leisurely walking to get to the guesthouse. Philomena had a shower and went to bed early as she complained of tiredness. I stayed at the writing desk for about an hour on my laptop catching up on the day's local and international news.

When I had finished, I had a refreshing shower. I sat on the edge oy my bed, read a few verses from my bible, and said a short prayer. I switched off the light on the switch by my bedside and went to bed too.

I got up the next morning an hour ahead of Philomena. We had our showers and went over to the dining hall to have breakfast. All through my stay at different times in different countries' guesthouses on my long journey to London, I always preferred to have my meals at the resident guesthouse restaurants rather than eating outside. I remembered, though that I ate outside the guesthouse on a couple of occasions; but those occasions were really few. My strong preference was always the guesthouse dining.

Breakfast was so good that morning. Like the day before, Philomena told me she enjoyed it. I enjoyed it too. It was a Thursday and I was leaving the following day, Friday. Philomena suggested we go physically to buy my coach ticket at the coach station. I told her I was able to purchase the ticket on the internet via the website of the Coach Company. I also reminded her that she would be going to work at two o'clock that day.

She told me her next day of work would be Friday and that she took a couple of days off work. I told her that was fine. She continued to say, taking a bus to go and buy the coach ticket from the station would give us the opportunity to leave the guesthouse, stroll a bit and come back by lunch time. I agreed.

The bus to the coach station took about forty-five minutes. I did not have a lot to do as I had already packed my suitcase ready for the journey.

I was relaxed and kept watching and admiring the buildings and offices that lined the route. Philomena was busy on her cell phone. We arrived quite early since there was little traffic on that route. I enjoyed the ride.

I bought my ticket, paid for it with my debit card and got a receipt for it. Philomena suggested we went to downtown Gibraltar for window shopping, but I politely turned down her suggestion. I told her I needed time to rest and focus on my impending journey.

"Oh, so do you want me to go back to my house?" She asked.

"Oh, not at all!" I exclaimed. "I did not mean that, my dear; I just wanted to be home and your company is surely appreciated for as long as you want," I consoled her.

"Thank you, Yolandi," she said looking at me rather emotionally.

I calmed her down and told her everything would be fine. I assured her that I would be in touch with her anywhere that I found myself. Even in London. She heaved a sigh, hugged me for a few minutes, and we headed to the bus stop ready to board our local bus back to the guesthouse. We reached the guesthouse well in time for lunch. It was about one o'clock in the afternoon.

I safely tucked my coach ticket and my travel passport into my hand luggage. I was just about to suggest to Philomena to come along with me to have lunch when there was a gentle knock at the door. I hesitated for a minute wondering who it could be. I opened the door gently and there in front of me was Maria. I invited her in. She sat at my writing desk. I introduced the two ladies to each other.

I said to Philomena, "Please meet Maria, my friend." In the same way, I turned to Maria to meet my work colleague and friend, Philomena. They said hello to each other, although they did not know themselves. We all went to lunch together. Maria was happy to see me and openly talked with me about the following day's journey. I told her it was firmly on. I also told her I had bought my travel ticket and was packed and was looking forward to it.

She offered to come and give me a ride to the coach station and asked what my estimated time of departure (ETD) was. I told her my ETD and she said that was fine. The coach was scheduled to depart at 1100 hours GMT on the day. Maria reminded me of how coincidental it was that she, the taxi driver who led me into Gibraltar, was going to be the same taxi driver to lead me out of Gibraltar. We all laughed.

Lunch was over. On reaching the door of my room, Philomena went inside while Maria politely asked permission to go. She said she had a few jobs to complete that afternoon. I said to her permission was granted. I saw Maria off to her taxi parked just outside the guesthouse. She gave me a hug and assured me she would pick me up from the guesthouse at about ten o'clock in the morning the following day.

I thanked her for her kindness and told her that God would bless her. With that, she entered her vehicle and sped off. Back in my room, Philomena was busy watching a movie. It was an interesting movie that I once watched back in Liberia. It was Eddie Murphy's *Coming to America*. I joined her to watch the movie to the end.

She retired to bed to have a nap before dinner time. I utilised the time to put a few phones calls through. I did not call my family back in Liberia this time. Rather I called all the friends I had made on my travels to date. I called and spoke to Angelique, Fatima, and all the other ones in all the countries that I travelled through. They were happy to hear from me.

I told them I was travelling to the city of Barcelona for two months, before embarking on the final leg of my journey for London. They all wished me safe journey and asked me to keep safe. I thanked them and assured them that I had always been under the canopy and protection of God.

Philomena woke up early and left at about seven o'clock in the morning. She said she had a few things to do at home before going to work at two o'clock in the afternoon. She did not want to wait for breakfast. I saw her to the bus stop. She gave me a final hug and a quadruple *bisous* on my cheeks. The bus sped off. She turned and looked at me waving for a long time until the bus disappeared from sight.

I came back to my room, had my bath, went for breakfast, and checked out of the guesthouse. I thanked the staff at the reception for the excellent care they took of me. One of the staff asked me whether I was on my way back to Africa. I replied in the negative and told them I was on my way to Barcelona enroute to London.

"Oh, that's nice. Have a safe journey," they all said almost simultaneously. "Thank you very much," I said to them. "Take care of yourselves and stay blessed," I concluded.

I took my luggage out onto the stairs leading to the guesthouse and sat down waiting for Maria. It was almost ten o'clock in the morning. Maria was dead on time. She parked her taxi, and as she was about to climb the stairs, she spotted me sitting by my suitcase. She ran up to me and hugged me.

We descended and got into her car. We reached the coach station in about twenty minutes; twenty-five minutes earlier than when Philomena and I made the same journey by bus. That gave Maria the opportunity to reiterate some of the directives she gave me regarding who would be meeting me, accommodation and more. I thanked her profusely for her God-sent care and assistance that she had accorded me right from the first day I set foot on Gibraltar soil.

I came out of the car to remove my luggage. Maria came out too. She hugged me again and planted a couple of *bisous* on my cheeks and wished me a safe journey and God's protection. I thanked her too. Just as she was about to walk away, I jokingly asked her how much my bill for the taxi ride was. She looked at me with pretend seriousness and said sarcastically, "Don't be silly."

With that, she entered her taxi and drove off.

All passengers on the coach that Friday morning had checked in their luggage. The journey was called and we all entered the coach and took our seats. It brought back memories reminiscent of my numerous coach travels through West Africa's Sahel region on my long road to London. My seat number this time was 55. It was a window seat.

The driver entered the coach. He greeted all passengers, first in English and then in Spanish. He did a head count of the passengers and wrote something in a book which I guessed was his waybill. He reminded us again that the journey would take eleven hours and seven minutes. He wished us all a safe journey and took his seat. He spoke again, this time using the coach's internal public address system. Again, he spoke in both Spanish and English.

He asked us to wear the seatbelts attached to our seats. When he was sure we had complied, he released the handbrake and moved the coach gradually out of the station; and with a spectacular U-turn made by the vehicle at the first round-about, we were on our way to Barcelona. For me, I was on my way to the last city of my travels on my long road to London.

Chapter 14 Barcelona

We left Gibraltar at about eleven o'clock in the morning. The coach seats were very comfortable; in fact, more comfortable than all the coaches that I had boarded and travelled in at the different stages of my journey from Ouagadougou in Burkina Faso to Tangier in Morocco. So comfortable were the seats that it did not feel like we were travelling by road. For a second, I thought we were in an aeroplane.

However, the reality was that I was on a coach on my way to Barcelona in Spain, Europe. Most of my fellow passengers had their earpieces plugged into both ears. They were either listening to music or reading from their social media pages or playing video games on their cell phones. There was music in the coach too. The earpieces for the coach music were placed on each seat.

All the passenger had to do was to plug it into the socket located on the righthand side of our seats. Most people, however, ignored the coach music and used their own laptops and cell phones to do what they wanted. After driving for a kilometre or two, I spotted the signs for the city's motorways that the coach would use for our journey. That was after driving along the narrow lanes of roads that led from Central Gibraltar to the widening motorways. I saw motorways A-7 and AP-7. They were also known as the Mediterranean Motorway Málaga. This was because the same motorway passed through the Spanish city of Málaga.

Initially, I was not sure which one of these two motorways the coach driver would take. I brought out my road map, which I always carried along with me, and studied the roads. The A-7 motorway was a very busy highway with a high density of traffic, due to the fact that it was located directly on the coast and linked all coastal municipalities. Since in many sections the A-7 motorway was actually the old national road, there were many areas with just two lanes and narrow curves that forced vehicles to slow down to 80 km per hour.

Another major drawback was the quality of driving; there were numerous exits from housing developments with very short or no acceleration lanes, and often the driver on the right lane was forced to suddenly apply the vehicle's brakes due to the reckless entry of vehicles from these lanes. This applied especially to the section between Fuengirola and Marbella which was considered a particularly treacherous stretch to drive on. The section from Estepona to Guadiaro had a large number of roundabouts and also presented several sections with limitations in speed of 80 km per hour.

With the AP-7 motorway, obviously these disadvantages did not exist. The driver could enjoy a much more fluid and pleasant journey to the *Costa del Sol* municipalities. And the road continued after that all the way to Barcelona and beyond. It must be said, however, that both by distance and by travel time, there was no significant difference between the two motorways.

On the other hand, stress-free travel without congestions on the AP-7 had its price which varied considerably depending on the season and led many drivers to continue opting for the A-7, which especially in the summer, was completely saturated by a huge number of vehicles. The AP-7 charged two types of tolls: The normal rate was applied in the months of October to May, except Easter; the special rate was applied in the months of June, July, August and September and also at Easter.

I was travelling in June and I guessed the coach company might have paid the special rates. And so, AP-7 motorway it was.

It was now about an hour into the journey and we had left Gibraltar far behind us. We had already passed Estepona. Estepona was a small but beautiful resort town on the *Costa del Sol* in southern Spain. A palm-lined promenade, the *Paseo Marítimo*, ran next to the *Playa de la Rada* beach. Nearby were the restaurants and water sports facilities of *Puerto Deportivo*, plus a fishing port and the cove of *Playa del Cristo*.

The whitewashed old town centres on the flower-filled square of *Plaza de las Flores*, home to the eclectic artworks of the *Colección Garó* looked marvellous from the distance. We did not stop at Estepona but we watched the town's fishing ports from the distance. The town was one of the most popular destinations for both tourists and foreign residents alike on the *Costa del Sol*, yet even today it still manages to retain its old

Andalusian charm.

I realised from my pocket atlas that Estepona was located at the western end of the *Costa del Sol* at the foot of the *Sierra Bermeja* mountains. In fact, we could spot the *Sierra Bermeja* mountains far in the horizon forming a beautiful kaleidoscope of a mountain range on the other side of the road. It was a beautiful sight, even from the coach. Since the distance from downtown Gibraltar to Mijas was just 107.7 kilometres, and coaches took about an hour and twenty-five minutes to make that journey, our journey of just an hour plus had taken us quite near to Mijas.

In fact, we were almost entering Marbella by the time. We drove through Marbella, the last city before Mijas. Marbella was a city and resort area on southern Spain's *Costa del Sol*. It also formed part of the Andalusian region and the *Sierra Blanca* Mountains with the backdrop of 27 km of beautiful sandy Mediterranean beaches, villas, hotels, and golf courses.

To the west of Marbella town, the Golden Mile of prestigious nightclubs and coastal estates led to *Puerto Banús Marina*, filled with luxury yachts, and surrounded by upmarket boutiques and bars. Again, we did not stop at Marbella. We only saw the township from the distance in the comfort of our coach. We saw a line-up of whitewashed hotel buildings beautifully lining the Atlantic Sea coast, almost juxtaposed to the deep blue sea; beautiful!

I noticed on my road map that these hotels were known as the *Fuerte* Hotels. What added to this beauty was the range of the *Sierra Blanca* Mountains that appeared as a backdrop to these hotels located on the Marbella Sea coast.

It was not long and we started to notice the road signs that led into downtown Mijas. We did not stop at Mijas town. It was now exactly about one and a half hours' drive from Gibraltar. It was about half-past-twelve in the afternoon, I did not have breakfast and thought to myself that a stop in Mijas would have given me the opportunity to have one. That did not happen and it did not bother me so much since the town of Alfarnatejo, our first of the four rest stops on the journey was just about 83.68 kilometres away, and with light traffic, it could take about just another hour to reach there.

As it was with Estepona and Marbella, so it was that we viewed the township of Mijas from the distance from our coach seats. Málaga was the more dominant and bigger city within the municipalities in the region. However, we just saw the road signs showing the direction to Málaga, on the motorway, far to our east on our way to Alfarnatejo. Mijas was a municipality in the province of Málaga, in the autonomous community of Andalusia.

Located on the south-eastern coast of Spain, Mijas belongs to the region of *Costa del Sol Occidental.* Its centre was a typical Andalusian, white-washed village, Mijas Pueblo, located on a mountainside of about 430 metres or 1,476 feet above sea level, in the heart of the *Costa del Sol region*. We passed Mijas and were now firmly on our way to our first rest-stop, Alfarnatejo.

The coach pulled into the main coach station of the city and we alighted from the vehicle. Alfarnatejo was a town and municipality in the province of Málaga, part of the autonomous community of Andalusia in southern Spain. The municipality was situated approximately 50 km from the city of Málaga. It had a population of approximately 400 residents. The natives were called *Tejones* and the town's neighbours in Alfarnatejo were *Palancos.*

We were told before we alighted from the coach that, we had thirty minutes to spend at the rest stop. It was well past lunch time. I felt I had to eat something substantial before the journey resumed. I walked up and spotted a restaurant called *Restaurante Gerardo.* I entered and ordered some food for lunch. I asked for *Spaghetti Marinara.* This was a typical Italian cuisine very popular in the Spanish communities.

It was prepared using spaghetti with calamari, prawns, mussels and clams in garlic and fresh tomato sauce. It was a very typical local dish, very delicious and very reasonably priced. I enjoyed my lunch very much. I spotted a couple of fellow passengers who also had their lunch at the same restaurant. It took me about twenty minutes to finish eating my food. I had already paid as I had to pay for the meal upfront. That gave me ten more minutes before going back on board the coach.

I took the opportunity to do a brief window shopping around the numerous souvenir shops scattered in and around the bus terminal. Soon, time was up. I hurried back to the coach and took my seat. The driver entered the coach and conducted a headcount. He went back to his waybill, looked at it for a rather prolonged time, put it down and did a second headcount. It was there that he noticed that two passengers had not returned to their seats.

The couple on seat numbers 11 and 12 were not in their seats. The driver went back to the coach station office and placed an announcement on the station's public address system. They called out the names of the two passengers. For a few minutes, nothing happened. No one showed up. Another call was made after five minutes during which the names of the couple were mentioned again. This time the call made it clear to the missing passengers that the coach would leave them behind if they did not show up within the next five minutes.

Three minutes after the second callout saw an elderly man who looked to be in his late sixties, smartly dressed wearing a grey goatee emerge with a woman of a similar age walking briskly towards the coach. The man was of medium height while the lady stood well over six feet. They entered the coach, raised their hands apparently in apologies to their fellow passengers for the delay they had caused, and took their seats. The driver re-entered the coach, did yet another headcount and returned to his seat.

He did not address the two guilty passengers. He adjusted his seat, started the engine, released the handbrake and we were on the way continuing our journey to Barcelona.

No sooner had the coach moved and entered Motorway AP-7 than my cell phone rang. I struggled to pull it out of my handbag. I had put it there during my lunchtime and had since forgotten to take it out. It was at the bottom part of the bag. As I struggled to bring the phone out, thoughts of whom it might be raced through my mind.

I thought of my lovely Clarissa, my parents, my siblings and even Maria or Philomena. I managed to eventually pull it out. It kept ringing. I saw the caller identity and to my pleasant surprise, it was from Gameli.

"Hey, Yolandi. How are you doing, my friend," came his voice which sounded much enthusiastic and full of vim.

"Hello, Gameli," I replied. "I'm doing great by God's grace and power; and you?" I asked sounding equally enthusiastic but making sure I did not raise my voice to disturb my fellow passengers on the coach.

And before I could say anything, a clearly happy and elated Gameli briefed me on what had been happening since we parted company in

Tangiers. I headed for Gibraltar and he headed for Rome in the company of his dear Ameema. Gameli told me he had formally gotten married to Ameema and that they were expecting their first child in April the following year. He also said he was blessed to find a good and well-paid job in Rome.

He then asked me whether I was still in Gibraltar. I told him I had left Gibraltar that morning on my way to Barcelona. With that, he interjected and asked whether I was no longer going to university in London. He asked whether I had a change of mind. I told him my university place at the London School of Economics was as solid as a rock. I continued to tell him that I was going to be in Barcelona for the two months of July and August, after which the first week of September would see me in London ready to commence my Masters programme.

Gameli replied with compliments and wished me the best with all my plans. I told him I would call him when I reached Barcelona. I put my phone away and took out my pocket atlas. Just as I was about to open the atlas, the announcement came on the coach's internal public address system informing us that the next rest stop would be at Valencia. The driver told us that it was going to be a very long non-stop journey to get there.

He told us to break the tedium of the journey by enjoying the sceneries on both sides of the road. The distance between Alfarnatejo and Valencia was 578.6 kilometres and it was going to take over six hours to reach there. That meant we were going to reach Valencia at about eight o'clock in the night. We were all ready for any challenges that leg of the journey would throw at us.

We quickly passed Granada, the capital city of the province of Granada, also in the autonomous community of Andalusia. The township looked so beautiful from afar. We could see the beautiful *Sierra Nevada* mountains on whose foothills the city of Granada was located. We could also see the grand examples of medieval architecture dating to the Moorish occupation, especially the *Alhambra*. I looked at them and tried to spot them on my pocket atlas.

And when I spotted them, the thrill was indescribable. I was so elated and pleased that I had the opportunity to see these things in reality. As I kept admiring this beautiful scenario as the coach sped on, I read of the sprawling hilltop fortress complex which encompassed royal palaces, serene patios, and reflecting pools from the Nasrid dynasty, as well as the fountains and orchards of the *Generalife* gardens in my pocket atlas.

Our coach passed the next township of Lorca and was fast approaching the bigger city of Murcia. The city of Murcia also looked very beautiful from the distance. A quick look at my pocket atlas indicated to me the city of Murcia was a university city. It was also known for its architectural showpiece, where the ornate *Cathedral of Murcia,* with its mash-up of styles from Gothic to Baroque, and the colourful 18th century *Palacio Episcopal* which stood in striking contrast to the modern 1990s *Ayuntamiento* (city hall) annex which was designed by the architect Rafael Moneo.

I tried hard from my seat to spot some of these historic buildings in the distance. There were many buildings that lined the horizon. There was one which was the tallest of all and which I guessed was the magnificent 18th century *Palacio Episcopal.*

From Murcia, we passed the townships of Elche and Alicante, to our right along the Mediterranean Sea coast. From then on, the coach increased its speed and we were soon to arrive in Valencia. Seeing the name of the city of Valencia reminded me of the Spanish football team Valencia, just like Barcelona did. The road signs started to show signs leading to the city of Valencia.

Soon, we entered Valencia, and the coach made its way to the main coach terminal of the city. We were told we could rest for an hour before continuing with the final leg of the journey to Barcelona, which was about another 302 kilometres and could take another four hours.

A quick look at my pocket atlas confirmed to me that Valencia, was the capital of the autonomous community of Valencia and the third-largest city in Spain after Madrid and Barcelona. It was a seaport on Spain's south-eastern coast, where the *Turia* River met the Mediterranean Sea. It was known for its City of Arts and Sciences, with futuristic structures including a planetarium, an oceanarium and an interactive museum. The city also had several beaches, including some within nearby *Albufeira* Park, a wetlands reserve with a lake and walking trails.

It was now just a few minutes past eight o'clock in the evening. I got out from the coach and walked towards the area where there were many restaurants and open bars operating both inside and outside the coach terminal. As usual, I looked for a restaurant from where I could have dinner since it was about six hours ago that I had lunch. I saw one restaurant which bore an interestingly unique name. It was called *Restaurante Asador Argentino Gordon.*

I noticed another one with the name *Restaurante Navarro.* The first, by its name, sounded Argentinian to me. I had never eaten Argentine food. The second one sounded Spanish and I decided to settle for that one. I sat at one of the dining tables in the restaurant.

The waiter, a very thin Caucasian young lady, came to me and asked me what I would order. She spoke in Spanish and I replied in English. She smiled at me, took the order, and said thank you in English. It was getting to the latter part of the evening, and as such, I did not want to eat much. I ordered club sandwiches. I ate my sandwich which was delicious, paid for the food, and gave a tip of 10 euros to the waiter. She looked at the money, and smiled broadly, and said thank you to me in English. I bid the restaurant staff goodbye with a wave as I left the restaurant.

We all got back on board the coach. We were now on our last leg of our journey. The driver announced that Barcelona was going to be our next and final stop and that was going to be in an hour and a half. My cell phone rang. Who could be calling me so late in the night. I took out the phone and realised it was Maria. I spoke to her briefly. She told me Anastasia from Barcelona had called her earlier asking for our exact ETA. I told her we were scheduled to arrive at about half-past-midnight. She thanked me and said she was going to pass the information on to Anastasia. She also confirmed to me that Anastasia would be waiting to meet me at the coach station and would take care of me. I thanked her profusely and assured her I would call her on my arrival in Barcelona. If not immediately, perhaps when day broke.

One and a half hours quickly flew past. We started seeing road signs indicating to me that we were close to Barcelona. It was past midnight by then and so I could not see much of the scenery along the way. All that I could see were the beautiful streetlights that lit the roads brilliantly. I could feel the sea breeze that penetrated our coach as the road moved on tantalisingly close to the waters of the Atlantic Ocean that splashed and washed the seacoast.

The scenery in the direction of the Mediterranean Sea was dark. All that I could see were the lights of the ocean-going vessels including cruise ships that had anchored out at sea. The coach sounded three loud blasts as it negotiated the bends and curves that led to the main Barcelona coach station. Although, it was midnight, the station was brilliantly lit. There were streetlights and other lights all around the station.

I saw many people in the waiting area of the coach station waiting to meet some of the other passengers arriving in Barcelona by coach. There was a queue of the coaches waiting to enter the station that night. Our coach was number five in the queue. Other coaches from other parts of Europe and elsewhere stood in a long line waiting to enter the station when it was their turn. Our coach, eventually, entered the station and parked at its allocated bay. My focus was on the crowd of people waiting to meet passengers.

Some were carrying placards bearing the names of passengers they came to meet. Some were taxi drivers who were pre-booked by passengers to carry them to their hotels and other destinations. I looked for Anastasia, who I did not know. I did not see my name on any of the placards. However, no sooner did I alight from the coach and walk towards the waiting crowd than I heard someone call my name. I turned around and saw a young, but mature looking woman approach me.

"Hi, Yolandi, how are you?" She asked. "You must be Anastasia," I replied, her. "Yes, I am," she said.

"How did you recognise me?" I asked anxiously with a grin on both cheeks. "Ah, Maria gave me a vivid description of how you looked, so I can't miss

you," she said with a captivating smile.

"Good; very good," I said to her as if I was the naval captain of a ship at sea responding to my coxswain on the bridge of the ship.

We walked together out of the station. Anastasia took me to her car. She helped me pack my luggage into the boot of her car. And before long, we drove into the dark but very well-lit streets of Barcelona.

I slept soundly throughout the night as I was quite tired after the long journey from Gibraltar; some eleven hours or so. Anastasia and her partner comfortably lodged me in the self-contained basement of their house. It was a single room with a clean bathroom with a beautiful bath and toilet and kitchen. The room was well furnished with a comfortable soft bed with clean and nicely scented beddings,

It also had a television set on the wall directly facing my bed. I was comfortable. As was my habit, I stayed at my private and secure place in the basement and did not interfere with other people's business. It was midnight when I arrived and so did not bother my host with a hotel or guesthouse request. I had a shower in the morning, dressed casually, and joined Anastasia and her partner at the breakfast table.

He was called Stephan. We had breakfast together that morning. Maria briefed me on all the arrangements they had made for my stay in Barcelona, particularly in respect of a job and accommodation. I was thrilled when she mentioned accommodation because it gave me an indication that I would not be staying at the basement of their house for long.

We were to meet the chief personnel officer of the Barcelona football club's stadium, the *Nou Camp*, at two o'clock that same day. Anastasia told me Maria had called one Franco there that we were to meet with. He was to arrange a job for me. But where exactly, neither Anastasia nor I had any idea. It could be any job and I was ready for it.

She continued to tell me that she had also located a guesthouse that was not too far away from where they lived. And if I was interested, I could check in there on any day of my choosing. She also gave me the option of choosing any other guesthouse. I was thrilled, although I did not show it. Two of the most important things I needed with my move to Barcelona had been arranged for me, virtually on a silver platter.

Although, I had not yet started any job, nevertheless I was happy that the process of getting one or looking for one had been initiated. I was happy. Stephan got ready and left for work. Anastasia took two days off work to help me settle in. I told her I was grateful for her sacrifice. She went upstairs to her bedroom and I went downstairs back to my basement. I liked the basement but I knew I would not be there for long. I did not want to inconvenience anyone and would like to check in at a guesthouse as soon as I could.

We met Franco at exactly two o'clock in the afternoon. Franco interviewed me informally for about twenty minutes. When he asked me which languages I could speak and write, I told him English, French and a little Spanish. Without much ado, he led me to another office located above his on the third floor. There we met the director for human resources for the *Nou Camp*. He spoke to me in impeccable English. His name was William Coots.

His excellent English accent gave away his nationality. He was an Englishman who had been working in Spain for over fifteen years. Mr. Coots asked me a few questions. When he asked me for how long I was going to stay in Barcelona, I told him just a couple of months. When he further asked me why I was not staying longer, I explained to him that I had to commence a Master's degree programme at the London School of Economics in London in September.

On hearing that, he turned to and looked at Franco in anticipation of a comment from him. Franco told him that the scenario was perfect and I could fit into a job vacancy occasioned by a sick leave and which I could cover for the two months. Mr. Coots nodded in agreement and told Franco to carry on with the paperwork. He shook my hands and wished me well in my new job. I thanked him and wished God's blessings on him.

Back in Franco's office, I sat down without knowing the exact job that I was going to be given. Positions like security officer and office cleaner came to my mind. But then, my instinct instructed me to remain calm and wait for Franco to provide me with more details. It was not long before Franco gave me a twelve- page employment application form to fill in. He instructed me to write ticketing officer as the job title. I completed the form and handed it back to Franco. He looked through the form and gave it back to me to sign on the last of the twelve pages. I did.

Franco informed me that training for the job would be for two days and that would begin on Monday. It was a Saturday and that meant I had only the next day, Sunday, to prepare for training to commence. I told Anastasia that I would like to move and check into the guesthouse the next day. I further informed her that I had to start training on Monday, and that the guesthouse would be ideal. She nodded in agreement and promised to drop me off at the guesthouse the next day, which was a Sunday. She also gave me sufficient information on how to get to the *Nou Camp*, either by bus or train. She said I could also use a tram or go by Uber if I wanted.

We had dinner together that evening. Stephan chatted with me. He asked about my background and what I was doing in Spain. I told him about my long journey so far on my way to London. He appeared to be fascinated with my experiences right from Monrovia, through Ghana and the Sahel region of West Africa all the way to Gibraltar; and now in Barcelona. I asked him what he did for a living and he told me he was a banker. I told him about my impending course of study at the London School of Economics in London.

He spoke very well of the school and reminded me that many African Heads of States attended that university and also sent their children there to study. He told me he spent a gap year in London where he worked as a waiter at one of the top restaurants in the city many years ago. He assured me that I would enjoy my course as well as life in the city of London due to the cosmopolitan nature of the city. He told me the cultural diversity was brilliant.

I thanked him for the encouragement. We bade goodnight to each other; he climbed upstairs and I descended downstairs. Anastasia had long gone upstairs soon after dinner. Back in my basement, I packed my suitcase ready for departure to the guesthouse the next day. Just before midnight that day, I knelt by my bed, and in true Christian fashion, rendered one of the most powerful prayers of thanksgiving that I had ever prayed to God. I thanked Him for His protection for me throughout my long journey so far; I thanked Him for providing for me during the journey so far.

I thanked Him for giving me good friends on the journey, who did not only like me, but provided me with enormous help and tremendous encouragement; I thanked Him for my safe arrival in Barcelona; and finally, I thanked Him for my impending job that virtually came to me on a silver platter. I asked God to bless the house of Anastasia and Stephan for their astonishing benevolence and generosity, not forgetting Maria in Gibraltar, through whose endeavours and hard work I was being accorded this wonderful hospitality and a good job.

We had breakfast at the dining table on the Sunday morning. Stephan and Anastasia drove me to my guesthouse which was just about a twenty- minute drive from their house. They informed me that it would take about forty- five minutes by bus. The good thing, however, was that the guesthouse was nearer the *Nou Camp* than Anastasia and Stephan's house. Like Gibraltar, it was only about fifteen minutes ride by public transport, preferably the bus. I was grateful.

The guesthouse was called *Hostal en Barcelona*; translated into the English language, it meant Barcelona guesthouse. It looked so beautiful when I first set my sight on the building. Stephan remained in the car while Anastasia accompanied me with my luggage to the guesthouse reception. I was quickly checked in by the porter who handed me the key to my room.

I hugged Anastasia and said thank you to her. She encouraged me to call often and visit them at home anytime I was free and ready to come over. She bade me *adieu* and went to join Stephan in the car. I stood on the steps of the guesthouse and waved them goodbye as their black BMW X5 sped away.

I went back to my room, my first guestroom on Spanish soil, room number 025. "What a lovely number," I said to myself. I wished I could stay in the room for at least a year. But alas! I had to leave in just a couple of months' time and start my Masters programme at the London School of Economics. My bed was nicely made. The bath and toilets were spick and span. The towels were white and sparkling clean. The room smelt as though it was scented.

The ambience of my new guestroom in Barcelona was splendid. Like most of the guesthouses that I had stayed throughout my long journey to London so far, the *Hostal en Barcelona* had a beautiful dining room. It was quite spacious and had beautiful dining chairs and long tables made from the *Odum* species of wood. This type of wood was more common in the tropical rain forests of West Africa where most of it was imported from. The dining plates and cutlery were all made of stainless steel. The floor of the dining hall was a parquet of the mahogany wood species and was heavily polished. I finished having my dinner that evening and went to bed early. I had to wake up early, get ready and be at the *Nou Camp* by nine o'clock in the morning. Breakfast was served from seven o'clock in the morning at the guesthouse. I was pleased with that because it gave me the opportunity to have something to eat before caching the bus for work.

The bus took nearly half-an-hour to reach the *Nou Camp*. It was such a popular venue that not less than fifteen different buses, with different numbers, stopped at or passed by the *Nou Camp* from different parts of Barcelona. My bus number was 266; bus number 260 also plied the same route from my guesthouse. I boarded bus 266 and it took me to the gates of the *Nou Camp*. I was welcomed at the reception and directed to the training room. I walked into the main training room and saw just two people waiting in the room.

My first guess was that they were fellow trainees like me. Within the next five to ten minutes, 12 more trainees joined us in the waiting room. We were 15 in all. We began to chat freely amongst ourselves as if we had known each other before coming in for the training. At nine o'clock sharp, the main door to the training room opened.

In came a tall, middle-aged looking man, smartly dressed in a turquoise suit with white shirt and blue and yellow tie. He turned his attention to the laptop and projector that were on the table without saying a word to us. He then turned on the projector that beamed light on the white board hanging in on the wall in front of the class. There appeared just five words on the board: 'Welcome to the *Nou Camp*'.

He turned to face us with a smile.

"Good morning, class," he said in a loud husky voice which was just about audible enough for us to hear."

"Good morning, Sir," we all replied together. "Please don't call me sir; call me Mr. Gunther," he advised.

"Good morning, Mr. Gunther," we all said again in unison.

"That's better," he replied loudly, laughing this time as if he had known us, or at least a few of us before today. "I'm going to be your tutor for the next two days," he concluded.

He then went straight to business. He first asked each one of us to briefly tell him where we came from and what we were doing in Barcelona. About three quarters of us, the trainees, said they were British, they came from the United Kingdom and they were students on their gap years. Another fifteen percent said they were from the Asian continent; from countries like India, Bangladesh, Sri Lanka, and Malaysia.

They also claimed to be students studying Spanish in some of the local universities in Barcelona. Two of us were from Africa and the Caribbean: Liberia and Barbados to be specific. I told him about my impending studies in London and he appeared pleased. The rest of us were of Spanish origin; a very small number. I said to myself, "there we go, we had a miniature United Nations at this training session."

Mr. Gunther, Klaus Gunther as his full name was, told us that he was a German but had settled and been working in Spain for the past fifteen years. He told us that he was a retired footballer and used to play for Bayern Munich Football Club and the German national football team. He had tried football coaching for some time before taking up the job of one of the executive directors at the *Nou Camp*. He oversaw all training at the club.

The morning session was long and detailed. We studied how football ticketing and reservation were done, both manually and online. We learnt the theory of how the tickets for all football matches at the club were printed, checked, stored, and distributed. We also learnt about how early tickets had to be ready for a particular match. We were told not to print tickets too early or too late to avoid them getting into the wrong hands. Gunther informed us that ticketing fraud was very common at most football clubs, and that was a serious offence if one was caught in the act at the *Nou Camp*.

We broke for lunch at exactly two o'clock in the afternoon. We had lunch in one of the numerous cafeterias at the *Nou Camp*. Lunch was tasty and filling. We enjoyed the food and chatted with each other as we ate. We had some soft drinks and went back to the training room. The afternoon session started at half-past-three that afternoon. It was shorter than the morning session as the entire session was a practical one.

We went into the machine room. Mr. Gunther went with us but left us in the very capable hands of the machine operators in the ticketing rooms. We learnt how the tickets were printed. We took turns, under the supervision of the machine operators, to print a few sample tickets. We enjoyed other practical sessions that afternoon. We returned to the training room, and after feedback on our experiences in the machine room, we closed the training session for the day.

As I waited for my bus at the *Nou Camp* bus stop, I noticed one of my new course mates stood about a metre from me. It appeared she wanted to speak to me but held back for some reason. I noted that but did not talk.

The bus arrived and she entered the bus first. I followed soon after and took my seat next to her on a two-seater seat on the bus.

"How do you do?" I broke the ice.

"How do you do, Mr. Yolandi," she said with a broad smile. "Where in Barcelona do you reside?" She quickly asked as if she was afraid she could not and had to do so quickly before the thought escaped. I did not answer her question d i r e c t l y, but rather answered her question with my own question.

"How did you know my name?" I asked curiously.

"Oh, I wrote it down when we introduced ourselves," she said. She appeared curious and intelligent. I then turned to answer her question.

"I reside at the *Hostal en Barcelona,*" I said with a broad smile on my face. "Oh, that's brilliant," she exclaimed. "Your guesthouse is just next to mine.

Mine is called *Casa Con Estilo.* It's just about 50 metres away from yours," she concluded.

"Oh, really. That's good to know," I said to her.

She nodded gleefully, and with both her eyes admiringly fixed on me, she gave a chuckle.

"By the way, my name is Swapna, and I am originally from Sri Lanka," she revealed to me before I could even ask.

"Oh, how nice," I replied in a voice that sounded appreciative. We both suddenly realised that we were a couple of stops away from our bus stop. We shared the same destination bus stop as we were neighbours. We stopped talking for a while. In fact, we did not resume our conversation until we alighted from the bus. We walked together towards her guesthouse, the *Casa Con Estilo.*

We resumed our conversation as we walked. Anyone seeing us for the first time would have thought we had known each other for a while, or even had been buddies. We stood on the stairs of the *Casa Con Estilo* guesthouse and chatted for another thirty minutes. We exchanged phone numbers and wished each other a good evening. I told Swapna that, if possible, we could meet at the bus stop at half-past-eight in the morning and travel to our training together.

She appeared delighted with the idea and assured me she would do her best to meet me at the bus stop at the appointed time. I got home just fifteen minutes later after seeing Swapna off. It was about half-past-six in the evening. I planned to go to dinner at seven o'clock that evening and decided to use the half hour before supper make a few phone calls. Just as I pulled my cell phone out and wanted to make my first call, my phone rang.

I wondered who had beaten me to it? I quickly looked at the caller and it was Swapna.

"Hi, Yolandi," she started speaking. "I just called to inform you that I reached my room safely,"

"Oh great! That's perfect, Swapna,"

I then called my parents and spoke to them. First, my dad and then my mum. I told them briefly about my journey from Gibraltar to Barcelona. I particularly emphasised to them the tremendous amount of help that Maria, back in Gibraltar, had been to me, both in Gibraltar and Barcelona. I asked them to pray for God's rich blessings on Maria. My mum, in her typical devoted Christian fashion assured me she would put Maria, and indeed all those who had assisted me on my long journey to London, on her prayer list.

For some reason, I kept repeating to my mum to bless Maria. I also told them about my new job and the training I had that day. They were delighted. I called my lovely Clarissa and repeated the same information to her. She thanked God for His tremendous tender mercies on me and wished me well. I went through the same routine with all my siblings including Akogovi, our adopted brother. In fact, we never regarded him as an adopted brother but our own blood brother.

I still had about ten minutes left before going to the dining hall. I took the opportunity and called Maria, Philomena, and Anastasia. To Maria, I narrated how the journey went, as well as how I got the job at the *Nou Camp*. I told her of the huge and kind hospitality that I received from Anastasia and Stephan. I told her about the day's training after which I thanked her and wished her God's richest blessings. I spoke to Philomena too. Her voice sounded as if she was crestfallen. She told me she missed me. I said to her I missed her too. I told her about the journey from Gibraltar to Barcelona as well as my new job. She was delighted for me and promised visiting as soon as she could. I spoke to Anastasia and Stephan. I told her how easy my journey to the *Nou Camp* in the morning was. They were happy and wished me well.

After dinner that night, I watched television for some time. I tuned into CNN, Al Jazeera, the BBC and CGTN to catch up with what was going on around the world. I watched the BBC for a longer time as compared to the other TV channels as I was curious to see what was going on in my soon-to-be new country. I started noticing the black taxi cabs and red double-decker buses that no other country I knew of in Europe had.

I then said a little prayer and retired to bed. I slept well on my second night at the guesthouse. I woke up at six o'clock the next morning, quickly got ready, went for breakfast at half-past-seven and then headed out to the bus stop. Swapna was already waiting at the bus stop when I arrived. I asked her how long she had been waiting and she said just over five minutes. I then asked her whether she had had breakfast and she answered in the affirmative.

Bus 266 pulled up and we both boarded the bus. On the bus to work, I resumed my conversation with Swapna, who at that stage, appeared very happy in my company. I asked her whether she slept well the previous night and again she answered in the affirmative. She then joked that she had a dream about me. I laughed and said to her that all was well. I then asked what the dream was about. She laughed shyly and said she would tell me later. I nodded self-consciously.

We arrived at the training room at the *Nou Camp* at about a quarter to nine that morning. Training started at nine o'clock prompt and almost everyone was in class except one young man from Spain. Mr. Gunther showed us videos on how the whole process of ticket-processing for a football match was done. It was during this video that our latecomer colleague tip-toed into the room and quietly took a seat at the back of the class.

Mr. Gunther said nothing to him. The videos were very educational and showed us every process we had to observe as we managed ticket reservation and issued tickets for football matches. We did role plays, in one of which I played the role of a ticketing supervisor on a football match day. We had lunch at noon that day. The rest of the day that afternoon was devoted to the appointments that each one of us were given. In fact, all of us, but one, were all appointed as ticketing officers with our workstations based at the *Nou Camp.*

It was July and the schedules for the *La Liga* football matches for the season had been completed. The matches would resume in the first week of August. I was aware I had only two months at the job and would be leaving during the first week of September. I had to leave on either the 1st or 2nd of September as university resumed on 5th of September.

Although, the football matches of the *La Liga* had ended, the Barcelona football club played a couple of friendly matches during the break. It was at one of these matches that I had my first experience of working as a ticketing officer on the grounds. It was a friendly match between Barcelona FC and Atletico Madrid FC. Although, it was a friendly match, fans had to pay to attend the match.

The match started at four o'clock in the afternoon and I had to be at the *Nou Camp* by nine o'clock in the morning. We were paired for the job. Interestingly, I had Swapna as my partner and the two of us supervised both tickets already purchased online, and the ones purchased at the gates. The afternoon went well and both we and our managers were quite happy with the day's job.

I took the bus with Swapna to our bus stop. I saw her off to the steps of her guesthouse and I went home. Inasmuch as the work was interesting, it was tiring too. Thus, it did not take me too long to go to bed that evening.

The next morning was a Sunday. It was our day off. I took the opportunity to invite Swapna to dinner at my guesthouse. She came. We chatted for some time and walked to the dining hall together that evening. We enjoyed the food served that day. Swapna told me that although she was Sri Lankan, she did not always eat Sri Lanka food. She said she liked Spanish and Chinese cuisines. She spent the rest of the evening chatting with me and playing computer games, after which I saw her off to her guesthouse. I must say I enjoyed Swapna's company that evening.

The *La Liga* football season resumed in early August. My work had been going well. I was well paid; in fact, I was paid over and above what I expected initially. My take-home wages, after tax, were just a few euros shy of 500 euros weekly. I was happy. Added to the monies I saved during my last job in Gibraltar, including the compensation paid to Alindu and me by the Grand Hotel of Gibraltar, my bank account began to look very good indeed.

Just about the second week of August, we all went to work. Mr. Gunther summoned all ticketing officers and their supervisors to the training room for a meeting. Mr. Gunther announced to us that the *Nou Camp* intelligence network had detected a huge amount of fraud in the ticketing for matches at the *Nou Camp*. Someone, or group of people, working with the ticketing office had overprinted tickets and presumably got them into fraudulent hands to be sold on the unofficial market.

We all looked bewildered and started looking at each other's faces. I was worried. Was there going to be a *déjà vu*? I had a feeling this one would turn out just as it happened when working in the Grand Hotel of Gibraltar. I stopped worrying. I knew I was not the culprit. I was, however, wary of being made an innocent scapegoat as was the case at the Grand Hotel of Gibraltar. Mr. Gunther completed the meeting by informing us that Spanish detectives would be coming to interview all ticketing officers and their supervisors the next morning.

He even warned us they could be taking all of us to different police stations to conduct the interviews there if they wished. I asked myself whether lightning could be striking twice. Swapna was sitting not far from me. We exchanged looks. She appeared unperturbed. Just like me, she knew she was not the culprit and was relaxed.

In fact, she was more relaxed than me. I was worried only because, once bitten by a snake, one would always be wary of even a worm. I, however, raised my confidence level once I knew I was innocent.

I chatted with Swapna on the bus all the way home on this fraud issue. She told me in an assuring and confident manner that she knew it was not me and neither was it she. And as such, we should forget about it and concentrate on other things. I nodded and thanked her. I had wanted to tell her about my experience at the Grand Hotel of Gibraltar but hesitated. I stopped short of telling her.

And with hindsight, I thought I was right not to tell her anything about that experience. We arrived at the bus-stop, alighted from the bus and as I was wont to, I escorted Swapna to her guesthouse. This time, Swapna invited me in for dinner. I agreed and went in with her. We sat down in her room for about half an hour chatting. We did not chat about the *Nou Camp* ticketing fraud but other things.

Swapna, however, informed me that evening that when she briefly spoke to one of the porters at the reception that evening, she was told the Spanish police came to enquire whether any of the residents at the guesthouse sold, or offered to sell, football tickets in the guesthouse. She said she asked the porter why they came to ask and the porter's answer was as good as hers; he did not have a clue. We brushed that topic aside and walked together to the dining hall.

Dinner was served and the food was delicious. We came back to Swapna's room, sat, and chatted for another quarter of an hour before I left for my guesthouse. Swapna saw me off to the stairs of the guesthouse and wished me goodnight. In fact, before saying goodnight, she gave me a hug and told me not to think about the matter at the workplace. She told me to allow the police to do their work and that the culprit would be caught.

I reached home had a shower and went to bed. I totally ignored the ticketing matter at work once I knew I was innocent. However, I was still somehow wary due to how the police in Gibraltar behaved. Are they not all the same? When the rain beats the leopard, does it wash away its spots? Well, perhaps the Spanish police would be better than their colleagues in Gibraltar.

I did not want them to make me a scapegoat, then apologise to me later with a compensation package. I did not want any compensation. Let the truth be found out.

We all assembled in the training room the next day. Three Spanish police vehicles were parked at the training centre car park. Mr. Gunther came to speak to us. We were all escorted to the waiting police vehicles ready to be taken to the police headquarters for interrogation. It was a serious matter. I had seen it all before and was aware of how it could go badly wrong. Innocent people being wrongly tagged with wrongdoing. I had seen it all before.

The police vehicles moved in a convoy and headed towards the Barcelona police headquarters. We were all as silent as mice being taken for the slaughter. No one spoke. Swapna was not in my vehicle but I knew she was in one of the other vehicles. The three vehicles arrived and parked just in front of the main police headquarters buildings. We were instructed not to alight. We obeyed and did not alight from the vehicle.

I could see through the windows of the vehicle that my colleagues on the other vehicles did not alight either. The police officer at the steering wheel was on his walkie talkie for about twenty minutes. He turned to us and informed us that we were all going back to the *Nou Camp*. No one spoke. The silence in the vehicle was as deafening as thunderclap. Just as the police officer turned on the vehicle engine, I summoned the courage and asked him about the proposed interrogations at the police headquarters.

I asked him why we were going back. He turned back to look at me and said to me not to worry. He turned again and looked at all of us in the vehicle and said, "The culprits have been apprehended; they confessed to the crime and were already in police custody." His face did not look friendly.

All of us in the vehicle heaved huge sighs of relief as the vehicle drove back towards the *Nou Camp*. I quietly said to myself that another tragedy had been avoided on this my long journey to London.

"Thank you, Jesus," I said audibly without knowing. My colleagues turned to look at me appreciatingly as if to say 'well said' to me. A couple of them, however, said Amen.

Back at the *Nou Camp*, Mr. Gunther and six police officers addressed us at the training room. They said to us, none of us in this room had anything to do with the ticketing fraud. They said the culprits were all apprehended and they had confessed to the crime. They apologised to us profusely and thanked us for our cooperation during their investigations. We were dismissed and we all went home.

The next Saturday was a day off for me and all my colleagues too. No ticketing officer would be on duty at the *Nou Camp* because there was no football match on the day. Usually, even if there was no football match on a Saturday, some staff were requested to go to work. However, on that particular Saturday, all ticketing officers had a day off. Swapna and I took the opportunity and arranged a dinner outing.

She suggested we went to a musical and then have dinner in one of the best restaurants in Barcelona. I agreed. We met at the bus stop at about seven o'clock in the evening. The bus took about half-an-hour to arrive at the venue. Just like Gibraltar, the musical theatre was located within a complex of different buildings housing shops, restaurants of different nationalities, cinemas, theatres and other entertainment venues.

It was a huge complex of buildings neatly juxtaposed to each other. I said to myself I was in Europe. I was full of admiration for the very business-like manner with which the various businesses operated within the complex.

The musical we chose to watch was called *Joseph and the Amazing Technicolour Dreamcoat*. The theatre was well decorated. The stage was painted with multi colours that looked like a rainbow in on a rainy day. Soon the show started. There was dead silence within the four walls of the auditorium. The Joseph story, as it was told in the bible, was narrated entirely through song with the help of a narrator.

The show followed the story of Jacob's favourite son, Joseph, and his 11 brothers. After being sold into slavery by his brothers, Joseph ingratiated himself with the Egyptian noble Potiphar but ended up in jail after refusing the advances of Potiphar's wife. While imprisoned, Joseph discovered his ability to interpret dreams, and he soon found himself in front of the mighty but heavily troubled showman, Pharaoh the King. As Joseph explained the dreams that portended the imminent famine and told Pharaoh how to contend with the famine in Egypt, he became Pharaoh's right-hand man and eventually reunited with his family as prime minister.

Swapna enjoyed the musical as much as I did. In fact, it was the first time both of us were attending this particular musical. The only musical performance nearest to this that I had attended was *The Mikado*. It was an opera that I had the opportunity of attending back in Africa. Swapna told me she liked the musical so much and would love to see the show for a second time.

It was about eleven o'clock when the show finished that evening. I told Swapna I was hungry and she said she was too. Although, I never ate late, I was going to eat late that night. We entered an Italian restaurant which stayed open till the very early hours of the morning. In fact, almost all the restaurants and bars in the complex stayed open till late.

The restaurant was full of men and women of all ages, most of whom came for the musical and some of the other entertainments at other entertainment houses within the complex. Swapna and I took our seats at the table. The waitress, a beautiful young lady of mixed-race heritage, came to take our orders. I chose Spaghetti Marinara. Swapna preferred a deep-pan pizza with meat and vegetable toppings. We waited for another thirty minutes before the food was brought to our table.

The waitress apologised to us and attributed the delay to the congestion of customers at the restaurant that night. I told her not to worry. We shared each other's food and we enjoyed it.

We left the restaurant exactly at half-past midnight. We took the bus heading home. While on the bus, a tall man dressed as a policeman came on board and started checking passenger tickets. Swapna had hers in her bag. I did not know where mine was. The ticket controller stood over me for about five minutes while I searched all my pockets for the ticket. He then spoke to me in Spanish saying, if I had no ticket, he would take me to the police station that night. I said to myself, Police station again? *Tofiako! (Never!)*.

Just as he was about to speak to me again, I remembered that I had inserted the ticket in my wallet that was in the small bag I was holding. I took the ticket out and showed it to him. He glared at me, frowned and muttered: *"Eres muy afortunada,"* in Spanish, meaning I was very lucky. I heard him perfectly but decided not to say a word in reply to him. "Let him go with his trouble", I said quietly in my mind. I saw Swapna off to her guesthouse, bid her goodnight, and went home.

The days and weeks passed very fast. We were now in August and I had only a couple of weeks to leave Barcelona, and travel to my final destination, London. Meanwhile, my new university, The London School of Economics had sent me an email message. The message was reminding me of the days for registration, enrolment, choice of accommodation and commencement of lectures. I was excited.

I showed the email message to Swapna too and she was pleased for me. She told me she wished she could go with me to London and attend the same university as me. I told her she had ample time on her side for that to happen.

During my last week at the *Nou Camp*, Mr. Gunther called me to his office and reminded me that my employment was going to end in a week's time. I told him I was aware and that I was looking forward to it. He thanked me for my hard and dedicated work with the organisation during the rather short couple of months that I was in employment with them. I thanked him too for giving me the opportunity to work with him.

He informed me that the organisation had decided to give me a bonus of 2,000 euros as a goodwill gesture. I did not expect it. I thanked him profusely and asked God's blessings over him. Back on the bus that evening on my way home, I told Swapna what had happened in my meeting with Mr. Gunther. She was very happy for me.

Swapna and I had another weekend free. It was my last week at work before I left for to London. Swapna suggested we went out in the evening to a movie and then to dinner just as we did the other time. I did not hesitate in responding to her in the affirmative. She was delighted.

We went to one of the famous cinema theatres in Barcelona. These were located quite close to the seafront where there were many bars, restaurants, and entertainment centres. We decided to go early and have some drinks and dinner before proceeding to go to watch the movie. We sat in a bar cum restaurant called the *Rias Do Miño*. I ordered a bottle of red wine, preferably from South Africa. The waiter brought us a bottle of *Shiraz* wine from the *Nederburg* winery from South Africa.

She poured a bit in a wine glass for Swapna to taste. Swapna did and said it tasted good. I believed her because I knew the wineries of Stellenbosch, a university town located in the South Africa's Western Cape Province surrounded by the vineyards of the of the Cape Winelands and the mountainous nature reserves of Jonkershoek and Simonsberg, did indeed produce very good wines for export. The waiter filled our wine glasses and asked to take our food order.

I took a long sip of the red wine, which tasted really good before looking at the menu. I asked Swapna to make a choice. She said she felt like Spanish food that evening. I agreed. We had Spaghetti Casa. We were both cognisant of the fact that we had a movie to watch later and did not drink too much. The food was excellent and we both dined to our fill and satisfaction.

We settled our bill and started to make our way out of the restaurant when one of the security guards at the restaurant stopped us and asked whether we had paid our bill. With a stern face, I sarcastically asked him whether he wanted a tip from us. But just before I could say anything further, the restaurant manager, who was watching us, literally dashed to the scene and restricted the security man from saying anything further to us. He apologised to us and asked us to leave in peace. We said nothing further as Swapna and I left the *Rias Do Miño*.

We walked about five minutes and entered the *Filmoteca de Catalunya*.

This was the movie theatre where we had booked to watch the movie. It was a huge theatre with over a thousand seats. The movie hall was filled to capacity as the film commenced exactly at eight o'clock that evening. It was an American film. The title of the film was *An Officer and a Gentleman.*

The film featured a young man who had to complete his work at a Navy Officers' Academy as a cadet to become a Naval Aviator with the help of a tall and tough gunnery sergeant and his girlfriend. But the young man had a bad attitude. When he signed up for the Aviation Academy, he was met with the strict leadership of the gunnery sergeant who gave him a rude awakening in terms of relating to other people.

Through the sergeant's guidance, however, and an unexpected romance with his girlfriend—an outsider who hung around the naval base—the young man learnt tough lessons and discovered what he truly wanted out of life. Swapna's eyes were virtually glued to the cinema screen. She enjoyed every aspect of the film from the strict military disciplines, physical and fitness exercises, the romantic aspects of the film through to the graduation parade of all the newly commissioned naval officers. It was a fantastic film and I equally enjoyed every part of it. The film ended just after midnight and we walked to the bus stop to take our bus home.

Bus 266 arrived at the stop after waiting for it for less than five minutes. We jumped in and took our seats. Swapna asked me when I was leaving for London. I said to her in exactly a week's time. I would be leaving Barcelona the following Saturday. She nodded her head in acknowledgement.

The bus moved and stopped at the second stop from where we boarded it. And before we could alight, four individuals, three men and a woman, entered the bus. They were dressed casually. They started asking for passengers' Nationality Identification (ID) Cards. They started from the front and moved on towards us. All the people they asked produced the ID cards, plastics with names, addresses, and the holder's photographs embossed on them.

They approached us and requested for ours. Swapna showed hers. I told them I did not have an ID card because I was not Spanish. They then asked to see my passport or any documentation that made me a legal resident in Spain. I told them I did not have my passport on me and neither did I have any other ID on me. The other three colleagues joined the one talking to me.

They looked and behaved in an unfriendly manner. They kept asking for the passport and documentations, and failure to produce them would land me at an immigration jail. I summed up courage and asked them for their identities. They all pulled out their ID cards with 'Immigration Officer' boldly written on them. I did not panic. I told them I lived about another two stops from there and if they wanted, they could accompany me to the guesthouse and I would show them my passport.

Swapna looked terrified. I calmed her down and asked her to relax. The bus reached our bus stop and all four immigration officers followed me to my guesthouse. Swapna went with us. I pulled out my passport from my valise and showed it to them. The most unfriendly among them took it and spent about five minutes looking through it. He asked me when I was leaving Spain and I told him in a week's time. He gave me the passport and turned to leave.

But the lady among them stopped him and asked him to apologise to me for the inconvenience. He did and I accepted the apology. They bade us goodnight and left. I turned to Swapna, who by this time, had been sick with fear that I would be arrested and deported. I told her not to worry and that the incident was one of many that I had encountered during my long road to London.

I wanted to go and see her off to her guesthouse, but she told me it was too late in the night. The following day was a Sunday and we had nothing scheduled for the day. We both had our showers and retired to bed.

We woke up late on Sunday and had breakfast together. We came back to my room and my phone rang. It was Anastasia. She invited me to lunch with them at two o'clock that afternoon. I politely asked her whether I could come with a colleague from work who was visiting me. Anastasia had no objection to my request, so I went with Swapna had lunch with Anastasia and Stephan.

We stayed with them all afternoon and chatted at length. I also informed them of my impending departure to London the following Saturday. They were happy for me and asked if I had enjoyed my two-month stay in Barcelona. I told them my stay had been very enjoyable and I thanked them for the huge part they had played in it. Anastasia and Stephan saw us off at the bus stop where we caught our bus on our way home.

Swapna stayed with me all evening. We chatted, played video games, watched television, and had dinner together in the guesthouse dining hall. I saw Swapna back to her guesthouse. She had to get ready for work the next day and so did I. Back in my room, I continued with the gradual packing of my luggage in readiness for the London trip. I got ready for my last week at the *Nou Camp*. I then had a shower and went to bed.

Monday morning saw me at work at the *Nou Camp*. Word went around that I was leaving the job on Friday and that I was going to university in England. I confirmed that to any of my colleagues who asked me and they in turn congratulated me. On Friday, Mr. Gunther organised a small send-off party for me in the cafeteria. There was food in abundance just as there were drinks of all sorts. Colleagues joined in and enjoyed with me.

I received very encouraging goodbye messages and citations from my colleagues, which as a matter of fact, pleasantly surprised me. I thought of myself just as a simple temporary worker among colleagues who were permanent and were in higher positions within the organisation than I was. And for all these people to come to honour me on my leaving the organisation was something that made me very grateful indeed. I was also presented with mementos which I hoped to cherish for a very long time.

Swapna went home with me on the same bus as usual. I was packed ready to leave for London at eleven o'clock the next morning. I quietly relished the fact that, at long last, my long road to London would soon be a reality. I was quietly excited. And I put it all to the materialisation of my endurance genius; and of course, the Divine guidance of my Holy Father above.

Swapna stayed with me all night while I did the final packing of my luggage. She insisted on seeing me off at the central coach station in Barcelona. She asked me why I did not opt to fly to London by air. I told her inscrutably, that it was a long story that could not be easily explained. She looked bewildered but said nothing.

In a nutshell, I related to her how I started my long road to London by coach from Ouagadougou in Burkina Faso, all through the Sahel region of West Africa, from the deserts to the Mediterranean and would like to achieve that feat by reaching London in a coach, and not by an aeroplane.

She smiled and congratulated me for my determination, tenacity, and endurance.

We took an Uber together to the central coach station in Barcelona. We reached the station about an hour and a half early. I checked in and received my seat number on the coach. We took opportunity of the time we had on hand and went to have breakfast together. Swapna went back with me to the coach station. She hugged me and held on to me for about five minutes.

She told me that she would miss me and I told her that I would miss her too. Tears welled up in her eyes. I kissed her on the cheeks and said I would be in touch and would see her again soon. I told her not to be sad because I was sure we would meet up in London. With that, her face brightened with a big smile and she said just two words to me: "safe journey." I thanked her and went on to board the coach and took my seat.

I took my usual window seat and could clearly see Swapna from where I was seated. She could clearly see me too. The coach driver stood up from his seat and counted all passengers in the coach. When he was satisfied that we were all on board, he eased the coach out of the station. I looked in the direction of Swapna.

She waved at me and I waved back. We continued waving at each other as the coach negotiated a bend, then we were out of sight of each other; and with that, I knew I was on the last leg on my long road to London.

Chapter 15 London

Our coach was a huge one with the name *'Euro Lines'* boldly embossed on both sides. The make was a *Caetano Levante*, manufactured in Portugal and had a capacity of 55 passengers. The coach was full. We entered the A-75 motorway and headed north-east on *Carrer dela Canuda* towards *Avigunda dei Portal de I'Angel*. We drove for about 26 kilometres and the *Carrer dela Canuda* turned right and became *Avigunda dei Portal de I'Angel*.

After 64 kilometres, *Avigunda dei Portal de I'Angel* turned slightly right and became *Carrer de la Cucurulla*. After another 66 kilometres, the road continued and dovetailed into *Carrer de la Portafemissa*. This was to continue for about another 230 kilometres before entering the next set of roads, the *la Ramba* and then on to *Place de Catalunya*. I put away my pocket atlas from which I was able to follow the road network mentioned above.

I then took time to remind myself that I was well and truly on the road to London. The journey was 1,498 kilometres in distance and it was going to take 15 hours and 15 minutes via the A-75. We were to drive through the whole length of France passing through cities and villages within France and by-passing Belgium in the far north-east.

We had now left Spain behind as we passed the French city of Perpignan. The city was located near the Mediterranean coast and had a border with Spain. We drove by the coast and could clearly see the beautiful buildings in the city as we drove by. We did not stop but the views of the majestic buildings from my seat on board the coach were breath-taking.

The huge Gothic-and-Romanesque Palace of the Kings of Majorca had ramparts with views to the coast. That was my first ever glimpse of any city in the country of France. I was excited. We continued our journey and I continued to gaze out of my window with much enthusiasm and excitement. The road was lined with very large tracts of farmlands on both sides on which different kinds of edible crops were planted. There were buildings and sparse dwellings scattered along the farms as we drove on.

Soon, the coach driver informed us on the internal address system that our first rest-stop was going to be the next city and we would have an hour's stay. He did not mention the name of the city, but when I took out my pocket atlas and referred to it, I noticed the next city was Toulouse. I had never been to Toulouse. However, I learnt from school back in Monrovia that it was the French city in Europe where the Airbus aeroplanes were manufactured.

I said to myself I wished the coach could stay in Toulouse longer and we would be given a guided tour of the Airbus company and factories which manufactured aircrafts such as the Airbus A380. After another forty-five minutes' drive, we arrived in Toulouse.

Toulouse, capital of France's southern Occitanic region, was bisected by the *Garonne River* and sat near the Spanish border. It was known as *La Ville Rose* ('The Pink City') due to the terracotta bricks used in many of its buildings. Its 17th century *Canal du Midi* linked the Garonne to the Mediterranean Sea, and could be travelled by boat, bike or on foot. The city was a large modern city. While it was known for art, history, and culture, it was also the fourth largest city in France, partly because of its aerospace industry.

It was also the largest centre for aerospace in all of Europe as the home of the European Airbus headquarters and the French space agency.

The coach squeezed into one of the coach parking bays at the almost full main bus and coach station in Toulouse. The coach driver rose from his seat, stood in front us all and reminded us that we had an hour's break. And then he broke the news that surprised all of us. He said that Airbus welcomed all of us to Toulouse, and to make our transit memorable, the company had placed a coach at our disposal to give all interested people a thirty-minute drive-thru around the Airbus factory.

I asked myself whether this was a prayer answered or a dream come through. About three quarters of all the passengers accepted the offer and got on to the Airbus coach. It took us only ten minutes to reach the factory. Again, to my pleasant surprise, the drive-thru became a walk-thru. We were taken in batches through most of the accessible areas of aircraft manufacturing at the factory. The tour-guide was excellent.

He spoke fluent English and provided an in-depth description of how many of the manufacturing processes were executed each working day. I was very excited. The whole walk around the factory took about twenty minutes after which we were well fed at the factory's very large and posh cafeteria. Airbus gave us souvenirs which included a silver replica of the Airbus A380 aircraft.

The Airbus A380 was a wide-bodied aircraft manufactured by Airbus. It was the world's largest passenger airliner. I was so excited. At the end of the tour, and after a representative from Airbus thanked us for our visit, I took the opportunity and personal initiative to give a short speech in which I thanked the Airbus company for the hospitality that it had accorded us. Back on the Airbus coach on our way back to our London-bound coach, most of the passengers, none of whom I knew or was familiar with, took it in turns to thank me for the initiative I took to thank Airbus on our behalf.

Back on our London-bound coach, just as we were about to depart to continue with our journey, I noticed that my travel handbag was not with me. What had happened? Was it stolen? Did I leave it on the Airbus coach? Did I drop it anywhere? I remained calm and did not panic. The bag contained my cash wallet and an iPad which I always carried with me. I drew the driver's attention to this. He did not look amused. He shook his head disapprovingly. After a while, he spoke to me.

"Where do you think you left the bag," he asked in a neutral tone that depicted neither anger nor empathy.

"I'm not sure, you know," came my reply still looking around me. "Perhaps at the Airbus factory," I continued to say.

I could clearly see that neither the coach driver, nor the greater number of the passengers in the coach were happy with the situation. Clearly, I was delaying the journey. I was wasting their time and they were not amused. I suggested the driver drove our coach to the factory to ask before continuing our journey. To this suggestion came mixed and unclear sounds around the coach which contained no actual message; but their onomatopoeic sounds sent out not a single clue but mixed ones: some were amused and some were not.

On repeating my suggestion to the coach driver, the passengers made more audible noises, but still no one spoke or expressed anything. Thirty minutes had elapsed and still no one spoke. I expressed to everyone present how important that bag was to me. It contained my bank details and most of the information relating to the London School of Economics. Some passengers began to see reality in my predicament and began to show signs of sympathy.

Eventually, the coach driver reluctantly agreed to drive the coach to the Airbus factory to look for my lost handbag. But just as the driver was about to switch on the engine of the vehicle, there was a tap on his door. He looked through the window and saw a man, who appeared to have just dismounted from a motorcycle. He wore a helmet and dark glasses that covered his eyes.

"*Bonjour*," he said to the driver.

"Good afternoon," our driver replied in English. "What can I do for you?"

He turned, raised up a handbag, and asked the driver whether any of the passengers who toured the Airbus factory had left behind a handbag. He spoke in English this time.

"Yes, one of the passengers has been looking for his lost handbag," he said. "We were just about to come over to your factory to look for it," concluded the coach driver.

With that, the coach driver invited me forward to identify the bag. I shouted with relief that it was indeed my bag. The courier from the Airbus factory asked me to identify myself. He asked me for my name and I mentioned it to him.

"Do you have any ID on you?" He further asked.

I pulled out my Liberian National Identification Card which had a passport- sized picture on it from my pocket and gave it to him. He took a good look at it, looked into my face, looked at some paperwork that he was carrying. He appeared satisfied.

"*C'est* ça, *Vous voilà*," he said as he handed over the bag to me.

"*Merci, beaucoup, Très appréciée*," I responded in French with a little bow of my head in appreciation.

This saga had taken almost an hour. Relief was clearly written on the faces of almost all passengers, nevertheless. Like me, they were glad that all this hullabaloo was over. The engines were switched on and within seconds our coach pulled out of its parking bay and my long journey to

London, having suffered yet another setback, continued in earnest and unabated.

We hit the motorway and had about 886 kilometres more to cover in just over ten hours. We were well into a couple of hours since we left Toulouse. We had by-passed Bergerac to our east and continued towards our next major city, Bordeaux. Soon, we arrived in Bordeaux. The immediate thing that crept into my mind was that this was the city which made the fine Bordeaux red wines consumed and enjoyed by thousands of wine-drinkers around the globe. What a thrill!

I occasionally enjoyed some very good Bordeaux red wine and here I was in the city that produced them. I pulled out my little road atlas from my handbag and noted the following written information, among others:

"*Bordeaux* is located close to the European Atlantic coast, in the southwest of France and in the north of the Aquitaine region. The city is the hub of the famed wine-growing region and is a port city on the *Garonne River* in southwestern France. It's known for its Gothic Cathédrale Saint-André, 18th to 19th century mansions, and notable art museums such as the *Musée des Beaux- Arts de Bordeaux*."

"Public gardens line the curving river quays. The grand *Place de la Bourse*, centred on the Three Graces Fountain, overlooks the *Miroir d'Eau* reflecting pool."

We pulled up and pushed into the parking bay located at the main city centre. We were informed we had an hour's break. Would we be second-time lucky to be given a guided tour of one of the wineries in the city of Bordeaux? I was not sure. The driver stopped the engine and stood up to make an announcement. Was it going to be a guided tour of one of the wine producing factories that I thought of a moment ago? I doubted it.

"Good evening, ladies and gentlemen," he started. "Please note that we have just an hour for this comfort break in Bordeaux. The coach will depart exactly one hour from now. Enjoy your break," he concluded much to my personal disappointment.

We alighted, and because we had no invitation to any engagement in the city as had been the case in Toulouse, my body immediately reminded me that it needed food. I had to look for a good restaurant to have dinner. I took a stroll and walked down the *27 Rue Parlement Saint-Pierre* and there I spotted a brightly illuminated restaurant on the main road. It was just about five minutes' walk from the coach station where our coach was parked. It was called *Le Comptoir Fromager*.

A quick translation of the name of the restaurant read, 'The Cheese Counter.' I asked myself whether it was only cheese that was served in this restaurant. I wanted to have a square meal for my dinner, more especially as we would be travelling all night on the coach. I turned and looked at the opposite side of the road. And there I located another restaurant. This one was called *Le Bouchon Bordelais*, which when translated into the English language read 'The Bordeaux Cork'.

I asked myself what the word 'cork' in the name of the restaurant meant. Did this mean they only sold wine and beers at the restaurant? I did not think too deeply into this; more so as I had only a few minutes left to report back to my coach. I entered the restaurant and was pleasantly seated by one of the stewards. It was a very plush restaurant with an exquisite ambience.

The place was brightly lit and I wondered whether angels from God's heaven also came to dine there. Presently, the waiter placed a basket full of sliced French baguettes with butter and cheese in front of me. He then asked me in French what I would like to eat. I responded to him in English. I told him I wanted club sandwiches. He spoke back in English and asked whether I wanted the full house.

"What is full house?" I said to him enquiringly.

"Full house is with everything; half house is only cheese, bread and some sliced meat," he replied in good English.

"Full house, please," I said to conclude the order.

Soon I had a plate of very delicious French club sandwiches in front of me. I also asked for a glass of French Bordeaux, the red wine that was so popular in this city. I enjoyed my dinner, paid for it, and left the restaurant. I arrived at the coach station ten clear minutes before departure time. Soon we were on all on board our coach and ready to continue our journey to London.

As the coach sped off, the feeling of joy, at the thought that I would soon be setting foot in London, on English soil was huge. The idea of starting a Master's degree programme was also exciting. What was even more exhilarating was that at long last, my long road to London was becoming a reality. A spectacular reality as it had been accomplished by travelling by road all the way from Ouagadougou-Burkina Faso in Sub-Saharan West Africa.

As the excitement, tinged with a slight fear of the unknown, raced through my mind, I remembered all my family members back in Monrovia-Liberia. My pocket atlas indicated to me that we would be crossing the English Channel on a ferry at a French town called Calais. The crossing was to take approximately one hour, and I intended calling all my family members during the crossing.

A couple of hours' drive saw us far away from Bordeaux. We started seeing signposts for Paris. We were not to stop anywhere else until we arrived in the seaport of Calais. As we drove past the outskirts of Paris, I could see the famous Eiffel Tower, very tall and well-lit in the distance from my seat on the coach. Some of the skyscrapers and other buildings that made Paris look so beautiful were also visible from a distance.

After by-passing Paris and driving past the famous Charles de Gaulle airport on the outskirts of Paris, we joined a motorway with four lanes on each side of the road. It was a toll road and the driver had to pay for using it. It was wide and beautiful. We travelled on it for about an hour and we started spotting highway distance signs indicating Amiens, Lille, and Calais.

We did not pass through the Amiens town centre but by-passed it. I remembered the French football team, Lille, which played very well in the French first division football league and was located north-east of Amiens. We left Amiens township on the eastern side of the road and negotiated a long bend that set our coach directly towards Arques on the way to Calais. We by-passed the township of Arques to our east and the road changed to the one that faced Calais directly.

The highway distance signs started showing 22 kilometres to Calais. What that meant was that we would soon be arriving at Calais, and for that matter, Calais Port, within half-an-hour or so.

"England is beckoning," I quietly said to myself. A huge and quiet excitement dawned on me. Goose pimples appeared on both of my forearms. London, here I come! We started seeing the huge Atlantic Ocean as the coach negotiated a bend and entered the port of Calais. The coach driver stopped at the *Gendarmerie* post inside the port. The driver presented his documents to the *Gendarmes* on duty.

There were British Immigration Officers there too. With all documents inspected, we proceeded to the port-side. We waited until our bay for boarding the ferry was indicated by a green light. We were in a very long queue of about 200 vehicles, big, small, light and heavy. We did not alight from the coach. I saw with delight all sorts and sizes of vehicles entering the ferry in turns. All the small vehicles such as cars and small vans entered via a different lane to the middle deck of the ferry.

The coaches entered the ferry via another entry leading to the bottom deck of the ferry. We were still seated in our vehicle. Initially, I wondered how all these vehicles could enter the ferry. However, when we entered, I saw the magnificence that the ferry was. There were large spaces, almost the size of a football field on each deck of the ferry. I had never seen one so huge. I could then understand how all those vehicles could fit onto the ferry.

I was indeed in Europe, and very well on my long road to London. We were all asked to alight, leave our heavy things inside the coach, and carry only light and essential personal effects with us. I got out of the coach and climbed on to the first deck (first floor and then to the second). There I saw a shopping mall, bars, and restaurants on board the ferry. There was even a casino on board the ferry.

I looked through the windows from the seat where I sat and could see where the huge Atlantic Ocean met the huge English Channel. Snippets of my knowledge of history of the second world war raced through my mind. I remembered reading from my history books that it was the English Channel, backed by the supremacy of the British Navy that prevented the German soldiers, under the command of Adolf Hitler, from reaching the British Isles during World War II. Here I was, actually sailing on the waters of this great English Channel. How exciting!

Soon, I heard three short loud blasts. The ferry was leaving port. It went astern and then turned starboard and made a hundred- and eighty-degrees' turn. It started moving slowly but soon gathered momentum, and before long, it was full steam ahead. It reminded me of the sea trip I had during my travel through the Sahel region of West Africa. It also reminded me of my short ferry trip between Tangiers and Gibraltar.

The Tangier to Gibraltar ferry could not compare in size with the one I was sailing on. This was about three times the size of the Tangier to

Gibraltar ferry.

I enjoyed the trip, particularly watching very big ocean liners pass close by to our ferry. Not one or two but several of them sailing in tow with each other. It was so exhilarating to watch. I went into the restaurant to have some food as it was now mid-morning. I had some French baguettes with cheese and butter, scrambled eggs, baked beans, and a cup of coffee to go with it.

Suddenly, it dawned on me that I was being introduced to English food. The breakfast I had on board the ferry was mainly English breakfast. The thought of transferring from Mediterranean food to Spanish and French food, and now to English food went through my mind. I was truly on my way to fulfilling my dream of arriving in London by road from West Africa. Soon, I heard three short loud blasts, similar to the ones I heard as the ship departed port.

These blasts were to signal our ferry's arrival in port. From the window of my seat, I could see the words 'White Cliffs of Dover' clearly written on a billboard ashore. The captain of the ferry confirmed this when he shortly afterwards announced that we had reached the Port of Dover, and that we were entering port. When the ferry had berthed, there was another announcement on the ferry's public address system for all passengers to alight.

We were to alight in batches. Coach passengers were asked to go to the lower deck and board their coaches, followed by the owners of the smaller vehicles.

We all started descending the stairs to our vehicles. For some reason, I mistook the second deck on the ferry for the lower deck where our coach was. For nearly ten minutes, I was walking backwards and forwards looking for my coach without any success. I did not panic but dreaded the idea of delaying the coach from leaving the ferry.

I spent another five minutes on the second deck looking for my coach. I still did not find it. Soon, I heard the sounds of engines and the movement of the coaches out of the ferry. I started to panic at this stage. Why I did not go a deck lower to find my coach beat my imagination. Eventually, I found a staircase with the words 'lower stairs' written on them. I found the lower deck empty when I reached there. My coach had left.

They had to go out in turns and as directed by the ferrymen. I was left stranded. I stood for a minute looking on absentmindedly. How stupid could I have been? I summoned some courage and climbed back to the third deck and spoke to a ferryman. He asked me not to panic. He could clearly notice anxiety written on my face. He said to me the coach had left the ferry but there was 75% possibility it would wait for me at Dover Port.

He showed me the gangway from where pedestrians disembarked the ferry and asked me to go out and walk straight to where the coaches were parked in port. I began to sweat. I took out a handkerchief from my pocket and cleaned the sweat on my face. I walked the gangway out of the ferry and walked the short distance to where the cars and coaches were parked.

I realised that was the first time I had set foot on English soil, but that was not of essence to me at that time although it was significant; very significant. My luggage was on the coach. I had to look for my coach among hundreds of the vehicles parked at the Port of Dover.

I walked to and asked one of the officials dressed in a yellow reflective overcoat where I could find my coach. He told me there were thousands of coaches around and was not sure how he could help me locate my coach. I told him my story briefly and he calmed me down. He took out a gadget from his pocket and turned it on. It looked like a tablet. He asked me for the registration number of my coach. I did not know it.

He then asked me where I was travelling from and to where and I told him. He looked on his gadget, made one or two taps on it and then pointed me towards the north-eastern part of the port. He said to me my coach was parked about 100 metres away from where we were. I asked myself how he found out. That question was immaterial at that moment. I had to reach my coach as soon as possible, lest I was left behind at the Port of Dover.

I took his advice and walked in the direction he directed me. Halfway into my walk, I heard my name being called very loudly. I looked towards the direction from which the call sounded, and it was my coach driver. He waved and beckoned at me. I ran to him. He asked me to follow him and I did. I started to tell him what happened but he had no time to listen to me. He asked me to hurry up and that we were running late.

Soon, we were by the coach and I climbed on board and took my seat. No one spoke. My fellow passengers' body languages were not hostile either. Rather, most of them tried to suppress individual laughter. I took no notice of them. I guessed most of them would be thinking and saying 'not him again' quietly in their minds. I sat in my seat and said quietly to myself, "what a way to arrive on English soil."

The engines started and we were on our way to London. I was just 131 kilometres away from London. Despite everything, my long road to London was clearly becoming a reality. As the coach sped away, I saw the white cliffs of Dover to my left from where I was sitting on the coach. Soon we left them behind and got on to the A2 motorway that showed a sign clearly labelled London, with an arrow. I looked behind me and saw the huge English Channel and the huge channel-crossing ferries that we had left behind.

Just then, my cell phone rang. I was not so sure who was calling. I looked at the call and it showed a United Kingdom registered number. I answered the phone and said 'hello'.

"Am I talking with Yolandi Kolandi?" The caller enquired.

"Yes, I am Yolandi," I said firmly in anticipation of the caller identifying him or herself.

"My name is Heather, and I'm calling from the London School of Economics," said a lady with a beautiful voice.

Before she could continue, I cut in and said, "Yes, lovely."

"Our records show that you'll be arriving at the Victoria Coach Station in London later today. I just want to inform you that one of the LSE porters will meet you at the coach station and take you to your hostel," she concluded.

"Thank you so much. I'm most grateful," I said to her with a special excitement in my voice. "The long road to London is becoming a reality in a matter of hours," I soliloquised.

The journey on the A2 motorway in Kent dovetailed into the M2 motorway. What struck me first was the side of the road that the coach travelled as we set off from Dover. I was not all that surprised because I had read from a magazine back in Monrovia as a student that the United Kingdom was the only country in the whole of Europe that drove on the left side of the road. Be it a motorway, town, or country road all vehicles drove on the left side of the road in the United Kingdom.

Although, I had prior knowledge of this, it looked odd to me at first sight. As we moved along, because I was used to vehicles driving on the right-hand side of the road from where I was coming from, it felt as if our coach was driving on the wrong side of the road and was soon to crash into an on-oncoming vehicle. We drove past Ashford in Kent where I noticed the sign indicating in the distance a railway station where some of the Euro Star trains stopped on their way to Paris Nord station in France.

As if in confirmation, as I kept looking at the station in the distance from my seat on the coach, a Euro Star train pulled into the station. We continued our journey, and soon, the M2 motorway re-joined the A2 motorway. We drove past the huge farms and farmhouses of the Kent countryside. It reminded me of the farms that we drove past through some of the cities in France.

London was now only 18 kilometres from where we were. The excitement was growing. I called my parents and informed them that I was almost in London. I spoke to my dad first, then my mum, Clarissa, and then, the rest of the family members. They were just as excited as I was. I told them that a university porter would be at the coach station to take me to my hostel.

I could hear the buzz of excitement all around my family members on my cell phone. They expressed their gratitude to the Almighty God for having shepherded me safely so far. I said goodbye to them and refocussed my concentration on looking at the beautiful buildings that began to appear.

"We will be reaching London in ten minutes," the coach driver announced on the coach's public address to everyone's delight. We encountered heavy traffic. I started noticing red double-decker buses that transported people across the city and the black taxis with different and unique features from other taxis that I had seen in other cities. I saw the huge numbers of pedestrians trying to find their way as they went about their daily chores.

I saw British policemen in black and white uniforms and black helmets. Soon our coach turned into the Victoria Coach station and parked in one of the numerous parking bays. The coach driver thanked all passengers for their cooperation throughout the journey. I also stood and thanked all passengers for being so patient with me during my couple of mishaps during the journey. Everyone laughed. It was obvious they were happy the long journey had ended. We started to disembark the coach.

As I set foot on the ground, I knelt and kissed the ground, quite reminiscent of what some of the Catholic clergymen, especially the Pope, did on setting foot on foreign soil. I looked up and gestured gratitude to my God up there. I then went for my suitcase from the belly of the coach, got my hand luggage, and walked towards the passenger arrivals hall. Just as I reached the entrance of the arrival hall, a young man of Middle East appearance approached me and asked whether I was Yolandi.

When I answered in the affirmative, he assisted me with my luggage to a parked van just outside the arrival hall of the coach station. He welcomed me with a beaming smile, greeted me nicely and told me I must be tired. I answered in the affirmative. He told me I would have a comfortable bed to sleep on at my new place of abode and that I should relax. The driver, whose name I later got to know as Jamil, drove me through some of the busy streets of London.

My eyes, although tired from the long journey, were fixed on the many things of interest that lined up the streets of London. The shops, cars, taxis, pedestrians, overhead trains, underground stations, and many more. We reached my hostel after about half-an-hour's drive. Jamil kindly assisted me in carrying my luggage to my room. My room number was 25. I thanked Jamil profusely. He told me it was his pleasure to accord me such assistance.

Before he left, he gave me directions on how to reach the London School of Economics' administration block the next day. I was to go and register as soon as possible, especially as lectures were scheduled to commence the following week. He also showed me where the hostel cafeteria was, in case I wanted to get some food.

I closed the door behind Jamil, knelt by my bed, and gave thanks to God Almighty. I thanked Him for all the care He took of me right from the start of my journey from Monrovia-Liberia, through Accra-Ghana to Ouagadougou- Burkina Faso, through the Sahel countries of West Africa into Gibraltar-Europe and finally to my destination, London-England. With that done, I undressed, went into the bathroom to have a shower. I had a warm shower, my first in a London accommodation.

It was late afternoon but I did not feel hungry. I rather felt like going to bed for a well-deserved rest. And that was what I did. I went to bed and had a good deep sleep. I woke up at about midnight local time. I drank a small bottle of water and went to bed again until the morning.

The walk from my hostel to the London School of Economics campus took only about fifteen minutes. I was warmly welcomed by Heather, the lady who had earlier spoken to me on the telephone.

"How was your journey?" She asked politely.

"It was good, thank you," I replied in an equally polite manner. "Good, very good," she said.

Heather sat me down at a desk computer and helped me do my registration online there and then. She took photocopies of my passport, UK and Schengen Visas, and other relevant documents. I could see other new students also busy with their registration. Heather, after she was done with me, reminded me that lectures started on Monday. She also gave me my LSE students' identity card as well as a letter to the NATWEST bank to open an English bank account if I wanted.

I thanked her profusely and went back to my hostel. I met a few African newcomers like me at the hostel. And in no time, we became good friends and did many things together. Later that afternoon, I called my parents and spoke to them. I also spoke to my lovely Clarissa and all my siblings. I told them I was speaking from my hostel room in London. I told them I had completed my long road to London, and soon would consolidate it.

I did not explain to them what that consolidation would be, or the shape and form that consolidation was going to take. I went to the cafeteria to have something to eat. It was a well decorated hall. However, it did not look as posh as some of the guesthouse dining halls that I used on my travels through Europe. The food, however, was English and Malaysian and it tasted good. For me that was all that mattered.

Lectures started the next Monday. There were 75 of us students, male and female, of different nationalities across the globe in my class. We soon made friends and studied together and went out to eat together. I went with some of my mates to open a bank account at a NATWEST bank branch quite close to my hostel. The Master of Business Administration course had indeed commenced and I had to concentrate if I was to complete the course with flying colours.

Two weeks into our lectures, we were given a date for the traditional

Dean's welcome address. It was the day for new students and their families. It was going to happen in exactly in four weeks' time. I knew of this and had a plan to bring in all my family members from Monrovia-Liberia. I called my dad and informed him of the day of welcome by the Dean and wanted him, Mum, Clarissa and my siblings to come.

Almost everyone in my family was working and doing well. They could all afford visas and their air tickets to London. I would arrange a house for about a month where we could all reside once they were in London.

It took the whole family about three weeks to acquire their United Kingdom visas. Every one of them, including Akogovi, got their visas. The Dean's welcome address was going to take place on 7 October. My family flew into London on 4 October. I had arranged a six-bedroom house for all of us during their one month's stay in London. My mum, dad, Clarissa, Ameley and her kids, Zutor and Fogar as well as Akogovi were all so happy to see me. Happiness permeated every corner of our rented six-bedroom house. Mum nourished us with hearty Liberian food.

The Dean's welcome address was a colourful event. All lecturers and academic staff wore their academic gowns. The PhDs, with their distinctive black and round hats with dangling red strings, stood out among the procession as they walked majestically but slowly to take their seats. Those who held Masters Degrees, as well as undergraduates all wore their relevant academic gowns.

Families from all over the globe came to grace the occasion with their children and wards. The ceremony was just spectacularly elegant. There was a cocktail reception after the ceremony during which my family and I interacted with my friends' families, who had also travelled from their home countries. There was happiness everywhere as it was a realisation of many peoples' dreams to come to the LSE.

My parents followed me to see my hostel room after the ceremony. It was a small room but well equipped with everything needed by a student. We went home afterwards. At home, we had a celebratory dinner to mark my status as a full member of the LSE family. It was after dinner, in the full glare of all my family members, and to the total surprise of every one of them, that I called out Clarissa to stand in front of me. Everyone was baffled as no one knew what I was going to do.

Not even my lovely Clarissa. She obliged and came and stood right in front of me. I stood at a right angle to her. I dipped my hand into my pocket, produced a little box containing an engagement ring. I opened it, knelt before Clarissa, showed her the diamond studded ring, and asked her if she would marry me. She was stunned, and with an elated smile, she turned to look at all the family members around, still saying nothing.

"Would you marry me, my lovely Clarissa?" I repeated the question looking straight up into her face.

She heaved a heavy sigh, and with tears of joy in her eyes, said, "Yes, indeed, I will marry you, my dear Yolandi." I then slipped the engagement ring on her left ring finger. She helped me to stand up and we both got into a passionate embrace that lasted for about five minutes. I kissed her on her cheeks and said thank you to her.

I then joked with my family members saying, "That was just part one of the consolidation of my visit to London that I spoke to you about."

One week had already passed. My family had only three more weeks to stay in London. On one of the evenings, I called my dad aside to have a *tête-à-tête* with him. I told him I wanted to officially marry my childhood sweetheart, Clarissa. My dad responded positively to my idea and gave it all his blessings. That same evening, I called my mum aside and had the same conversation with her. Like Dad, Mum also responded positively and gave the idea all her blessings. I was delighted with their responses.

That night, I informed Clarissa about the idea I had floated to my parents. I told her we would be having a wedding in two weeks' time. I had already done the groundwork at a Baptist Church in South London where I had started worshipping on Sundays since I arrived in London. It was the Trinity Baptist Church in London. Although, taken by surprise and the short notice, Clarissa was all for it.

I told her that I had bought everything she needed for the wedding and the items were already awaiting her. She was thrilled. She asked about her wedding dress and I told her that too was ready. She then asked me how I managed to get her right size and colour. To that I reminded her of a conversation we had a few months ago during which I deliberately asked her of those details.

The wedding was planned for the 22nd of October. It was a Saturday. All invited guests to the wedding had received their invitations about two weeks before the big day. I spent most of the two weeks before the wedding attending lectures and attending to my special guests: my lovely family. On the days that I had no lectures, we all went out to the city to either dine, window-shop. or buy a few things.

We visited Marks and Spencer and Selfridges stores both located in Oxford Street. We shopped at Zara, Primark, John Lewis, and a few others too. My siblings all bought their clothing for the wedding during these visits to the shops. We visited tourist interests such as Madam Tussauds, Buckingham Palace, Trafalgar Square, the London Eye and the London Tower Bridge among others.

The clock struck five on the morning of 22 October. I woke up and started getting ready for the day's big event. The ceremony was to start at eleven o'clock in the morning. Clarissa was up and had gone to the home of the beautician who was to get her dressed and ready. This included the make-up; in fact, to get her generally and thoroughly ready to be driven to the Trinity Baptist Church in South London.

My mum and dad, and the rest of my family, got dressed up. Clarissa's dad, who flew into London for the wedding, was also ready in his Kentucky-cut three-piece turquoise suit. We all looked radiant. I wore a cream jacket, a white shirt and a bright yellow tie over a black pair of trousers. My dad and my brothers wore suits of differing colours. They all looked exquisite and radiant.

My sister, Ameley, wore a beautiful long purple dress that flowed along her body down to her toes. She looked stunning in her dress.

We arrived at the church at a quarter-past ten that morning. We were surprised to see almost all of our invited guests already seated. I sat in front of the church with Ben Machel, my best man, on my side. Ben was one of my university mates on the MBA programme at the LSE. He was from Mozambique and we had become very good friends since our arrival at the LSE. The church auditorium was silent. No one spoke.

Only the occasional cough and yawning could be heard and noticed among the guests. The officiating clergy, the Reverend Paul Yelsgnik, was already on the podium, dressed in his robes ready for the service to start. It was now approaching eleven o'clock in the morning. Actually, just ten minutes to the hour.

The organist, a fairly old man with a grey goatee, started playing snippets from George Frederick Handel's *Hallelujah Chorus* on the pipe organ. I thought to myself that sort of music would have come at the end of the ceremony. But it was a nice tune, nevertheless.

Just then, we heard a siren from outside the church building. We thought it was Clarissa that was being led to the church in a convoy. We were wrong. It was a police car that sped along the road nearby on an emergency. I smiled and refocussed my concentration on the upcoming event. No sooner had the police car passed with the noise of the siren than we started to hear the tolling of the church bells.

I stood up and looked back. I was right this time. Clarissa and the bridal party stood at the back of the church ready to be ushered into the church building. Clarissa's dad stood by her side. And soon the bridal march started with the church organist gracefully playing Mendelssohn's wedding march, to usher in the bride.

Rev Paul Yelsgnik signalled to all in the congregation to stand. We all stood. My lovely Clarissa, with her arm in her dad's, walked gracefully down the aisle. Soon she came to stand by my side. I whispered a welcome to her and told her she looked stunningly beautiful. She smiled her thank you to that. The wedding ceremony went very well. The wedding service took about an hour and a half. The sermon was short and straight to the point. In a nutshell, the preacher advised us to show love to each other and always remain faithful to each other. With Clarissa's right arm in my left arm, we danced towards the exit to the brilliant African tune called *Aseda,* which translated to mean "Thanks be to God" in English. Other members of the congregation danced to this lovely tune as we all exited the church auditorium.

We held our wedding reception at the prestigious London Festival Hall where the invited guests celebrated the occasion with us with food, drinks, good music, and dancing. We danced and made merry well into the night. We retired home in the early hours of Sunday feeling very tired but extremely happy. My parents, siblings and Clarissa's dad spent another week with us after which they flew back to Monrovia.

Clarissa stayed back with me throughout my studies. She supported me in everything I needed. She got a part-time job in London and was quite financially independent. I completed my studies with distinction. I had a couple of months left on my visa. Clarissa was expecting our baby that was due soon. Graduation was in a couple of weeks' time.

Clarissa, although heavily pregnant, accompanied me to the graduation ceremony which was held at the London Festival Hall, the same venue where we had our wedding reception. There was huge applause for me from all present when it was mentioned that I had attained a distinction on my MBA programme. I was elated. I felt very honoured and gave all the glory to God who, as far as I was concerned, had made all these possible for me, particularly the successful end of my long road journey to London.

Clarissa had a baby boy a week after the graduation ceremony. When the baby turned a month, we acquired travel documents for him. We decided to fly back home in a week's time. And after the week had passed, we arrived at London's Heathrow airport ready to board a plane back to my lovely Monrovia-Liberia.

I stood at London Heathrow airport's passengers' waiting corridor after I had checked-in and passed through security, watching aircrafts take off and land as we waited for our flight to be called. And as I stood and looked through the transparent glass, all that went through my mind was, indeed, my story had truly been that of a very Long Road to London.

The End

276